HORSE LATITUDES

HORSE LATITUDES

MORRIS COLLINS

DZANC
BOOKS

5220 Dexter Ann Arbor Rd.
Ann Arbor, MI 48103
www.dzancbooks.org

Library of Congress Cataloging-in-Publication Data

Names: Collins, Morris, author.
Title: Horse latitudes / by Morris Collins.
Description: Ann Arbor, MI : Dzanc Books, 2019.
Identifiers: LCCN 2018040061 | ISBN 9781945814761
Subjects: | GSAFD: Suspense fiction.
Classification: LCC PS3603.O454467 H67 2019 | DDC 813/.6--dc23
LC record available at https://lccn.loc.gov/2018040061

First Dzanc Edition: January 2019
Jacket design by Matthew Revert
Interior design by Michelle Dotter

Printed in the United States of America

10   9   8   7   6   5   4   3   2   1

"I did not go to join Kurtz there and then. I did not. I remained to dream the nightmare out to the end..."

Joseph Conrad, *Heart of Darkness*

"The photographs make a compassionate response feel irrelevant...The camera is a kind of passport that annihilates moral boundaries and social inhibitions, freeing the photographer from any responsibility toward the people photographed...The photographer is always trying to colonize new experiences..."

Susan Sontag, *On Photography*

"Without history and without destiny, the men throw themselves into a stillborn present that by dawn will become oblivion."

Cristina Pacheco, "La Ciudad del Placer"
(Translated by Connie Todd)

ETHAN CAUGHT THE FEVER in Mexico, rode it out for a few days at Yolanda's house, and let it break. But it flared again when he slept, woke him in his seat on the bus out of Nuevo Laredo and stayed with him. He felt it during the border crossing into Guatemala and he felt it now in the bar near the station. It came in waves, heat washing into sudden cold, the usual aches and pains, the short, bad dreams and free-fall dread.

He ordered a beer at the bar and took a table by the window. In this makeshift border outpost, most buildings were huts of palmwood and woven grass, or farther up the road, in the mountains, the way the bus had come, cardboard and plastic shacks with scrap-metal roofs. So the bar, with its concrete foundation and whitewashed stucco, seemed incongruous and blocky. A transplant from the cities. The one perma-nent thing built, he thought, for people like him, waiting for buses across the border. This was the fever throwing up errant symmetries. There were no people like him. The bus station consisted of a bench, a sign, a few street hawkers. These days no one crossed into Copal.

In the back, under a mosquito lamp, a drunk American was singing karaoke. He looked about fifty, with a close-cropped military haircut and wide, unblinking eyes. Probably a former Marine stationed down here in the eighties who transferred to the mercenary racket or just stayed on after his tour was up. Not that uncommon. Ethan knew the type from his previous trips to Copal. A shabby gringo pervert fleeing to Spanish-speaking countries without speaking a word of Spanish.

A few Indians and two off-duty border guards sat at the tables between them. They kept their backs to the American and stared out through the door and didn't speak. For a moment after the song ended the sounds of night swept into the bar: tree frogs and an owl screech, a distant radio, everything thickening into a warm tropical hush.

Ethan pressed his beer to his face. If his luck held, the Marine wouldn't come talk to him. He'd make it through the night here and catch the first bus in the morning. Maybe he'd find the girl before the others did. He couldn't imagine his luck stretching any further than that.

"Hey, partner," said the Marine, sitting opposite him suddenly. "You look like a friend of mine."

"I'm friendly," Ethan said. "But that's not quite the same thing."

The Marine ran his hand back and forth over his scalp with increasing urgency. He shook his head from side to side as he did it.

"I don't know about that attitude, brother. Down here, that is not a way to be."

"I'm just passing through," Ethan said.

"That's how it is. No one stays. It can get lonely if you're a civilized man."

"Are you?" Ethan asked.

"Let me tell you this," the Marine said. "I am the fucking foundation of the civilized world. Do you know why? I am a man in his natural habitat and I live accordingly."

His weepy, twitching eyes appeared bright and gelatinous. Like something you'd find at the bottom of the sea. Ethan raised and drank from his beer. He knew this kind of lucidity trembled on the other side of fever. The mind spiraling down into weird particulars.

Again he said, "I'm just passing through."

"Well this is as good a crossroads as any. Where you headed?"

"Copal."

"Shit," the Marine said. "Best wait until morning. And even then, vaya con Dios, brother."

About this the Marine was right: in every way the situation surpassed Ethan's capabilities, and he cherished it for that—a simple, terrifying truth against which the past, his whole life till now, lost dimension, warped away like an image reflected in a passing car window.

"Things are not good in Copal," the Marine said. "Then again, things are not top-notch here. Look at these losers—" He nodded at the guards who stood, slung their rifles over their shoulders, and headed away into the night. "—they're worthless. Children have been disappearing from the villages. Does anyone do anything? Does anyone investigate? Fuck no. They blame it on the Duende. That's right, you can't take a piss without showing some imbecile your papers, but children start going missing and they point their fingers at a freaking goblin."

He paused and shrugged and began to scratch his head again.

"My thoughts? My personal opinion? It's a load off. Who here can afford children? But people take it hard. My girl is upset. Her twenty-third cousin or some shit is missing."

Like all the gringo expats Ethan had ever met, the Marine wanted to wax poetic about the poor sixteen-year-old he was screwing.

"She cries all the time now, but she's a sweetheart. You have to understand that women down here respect something basic in you. They allow your manhood. They remain gracious to your nature."

Outside, a distant noise echoed down out of the mountains or shanties. Ethan closed his eyes and rested his head against the window, hoping that the glass, bordered as it was with the night, would be cool. An instinct from his previous life in the north. Of course the glass was warm.

Another flurry of noise, louder now, and closer, in the hills behind the bar. The shrill yapping of coyotes on the hunt. The Indians stood and crossed themselves.

"It's just coyotes," Ethan said.

The Marine looked bored or trashed, the bottom falling out on his drunk. He waved and knocked over Ethan's empty bottle. "Coyotes stick to the uplands. The scrub. They don't have them down here."

Ethan knew coyotes from his grandfather's farm in New Hampshire. They broke into the rabbit hutches the night he found his mother. No one went out to stop them.

"I'm listening to coyotes right now," he said.

The yapping came closer, hysterical, modulating, high-pitched as parrots. They were on the move and closing in and the Indians pressed themselves up against the back wall and began to pray. Ethan heard some other commotion in the street, a screaming woman, and then a new sound over the rest—the clear, high wail of a child.

The Indians crossed themselves again and sat. Ethan listened harder. The shrieking coyotes, the child, a crying woman and praying Indians, and the moment dropped into sudden focus: the child was screaming in pain. She was not just frightened audience to the coyote hunt; she was there with them. She was the prey.

He was at the door, standing. The Indians, rocking silently, did nothing to stop him when he reached down and grabbed one of their machetes. In every way the noise in the street was worse.

"Isn't anyone going to do anything?"

The Marine looked up from the table like Ethan hadn't heard him properly, like, as usual, he couldn't quite make himself understood. "I told you coyotes don't live this far south," he mumbled. "Maybe it's a flock of owls. It doesn't fucking matter. The town's on lockdown. They think it's the goddamn Duende."

When Ethan found them, three small and mangy coyotes, about fifty yards up the hill in a burnt-out clearing, they stopped and turned and faced him. The child on the ground was quieter, but still moaning and still moving. Beyond the clearing, a bamboo grove cluttered back into the mountain forest. If that's where the coyotes came from there could be more in there. Across the road, a few scrap huts stood crookedly on the sloping plane, but they stayed quiet and lightless and no one came out to help.

Ethan began to shout and wave and the coyotes stopped their attack and watched him, but did not move. He jumped, he shouted, and one of the coyotes jolted into motion and bit the girl on the ground. Then another one did and as the third one loped in toward her, Ethan started to run at them—swinging the machete, bellowing—and they bolted. They scrambled off, not like dogs, but faster, jerking away with the skittering motion of insects until they reached the bamboo canebreak where again they stopped and turned and stood waiting. He only had a few moments. For now, the coyotes were disturbed, but they wouldn't be for long.

The girl on the ground looked about seven or eight, big prey for such trashy coyotes, and she must have fought for a while—that was what he heard in the bar—but now she lay curled with her legs tucked against her chest, panting her way into shock. Standing in a wide flank at the canebreak, the coyotes watched curiously as Ethan dropped the machete and lifted the girl into his arms. He began to walk with her and the coyotes didn't follow. He asked her name and she wouldn't tell him, but he kept asking her. She was bleeding from her hands and arms, one of her legs, and a fleshy, tangled mess where her right ear was shredded. Slowly, people began to emerge from the huts. Somewhere behind him a woman cried out and he stood there in the street with the girl and waited.

Afterward, he hurried back to the bar and his bags which were, surprisingly, still there. The bartender was missing, probably off with the rest of the town looking after the girl, and the Marine was the only one inside. He raised his head from the table.

"Not an evil spirit after all?" he said. "You can see how the Spanish conquered this place with a fag on a horse."

Ethan picked up his bag and went out into the night. At the bus stop he changed his shirt and waited. Down the road, a red security light wavered from the Guatemalan border shack where maybe the guards were sleeping or drinking or playing cards. Beyond the frontier post, the road turned into the jungle, toward the Copal station. It was almost Madrugada, the blue hour before dawn. In his abandoned life, Ethan was a photographer, and the photographer in him should be drawn to this light, but here it made everything appear out of proportion, enlarged: the flowers and crescent leaves, the bare hills, the insects. Copal was the same way. It was a land out of another century or world, a dying, twilit country where you knew the night would be bad.

On his stunned walk back into town, he had seen a lake pooling out on the plateau behind the shanties. Under the slivered moonlight it hung flat and motionless and Ethan thought about what he would have to do in the coming days. Once when he went snorkeling off the north coast of Honduras he had watched pearl divers in boats out beyond the reef line grab weights and jump overboard. It was like that. Getting down there would be easy. You let yourself sink. Anyone could do it. But getting back without consequences, where the stakes rose with every moment, would be difficult.

The woman appeared out of the dark and stood before him. She was short and the gauzy border light dredged half her face from shadow. In one hand she held a woven sack, in the other a machete.

"I have something to show you," she said to him in English.

She held out the sack and he didn't know what else to do but take it.

"This is something you need. It is a relic. Taken from a conquistador. It is precious and magical and very old."

Ethan untied the sack and let it drop. He held the skeletal hand in his own hands. A man's hand probably, white bone bleached and broken at the wrist into jagged shards—a hand certainly severed.

"Please take it," she said and stepped closer to him, fully into the light. Hours ago, when his bus let out, she had been there, halving coconuts with clean, sure strikes of a machete and selling them to people to drink from as they got off the bus. He could imagine her severing this hand with the same skill.

"This is something you need." She touched his leg and her own hands were small and knobby, like strange windfall fruits. "This is something you need and it will not cost you much."

The fever seemed to sweep in from someplace outside of him, another bad feeling on the overly fragrant air. It blew through him, burned fast and then was gone, like a flare of marsh gas, and it emptied him out. He was shivering in the aftermath. Trembling as Samantha trembled, shuddering down through her medication into sleep. The woman reached out and placed her hand over his, so that together they both held the severed hand where a sliver of dried skin still stuck to the base of the thumb. Bones not long removed from their flesh.

"Please," she was saying, "it will not cost you much and is something you need. You are sick."

"I am sick," Ethan said.

"You are sick and this is a remedy."

He pulled away and left her holding the skeletal hand. Way up in the hills and in the forest across the street, birds whose cries he did not know began to announce what would have to pass for a new day. She said it again—"It is a remedy for those who are broken"—and it felt like the wrong way to start a journey, a curse or a bad omen, a reckoning, rigid and fair and as inalterable as the past.

On the last morning in New York before it happened, Ethan stood at the window and watched the sun breaking in slantwise shards off passing traffic. Down in the street, fifteen floors below, the noodle vendor assembled his cart. Behind Ethan, across the apartment, in the bathroom, the shower turned off, and he knew from when Samantha used to leave the door open that now she was pulling back the curtain, reaching for her towel, covering her face with it and not putting on the fan, never letting the fogged mirror uncloud before her. He thought to himself: if I crossed the apartment, if I opened the door.

Outside a car horn erupted.

Sometimes when he woke in the night he did not know her, her face ruptured out of dream, withered and shrunken, a face carved from tree bark, and later he will say to himself, this is how it happened. He will look for causes and impulses, but will find only a sequence, an unfurling of events.

A pair of pigeons flushed from the sill.

He turned from the window and went to the kitchenette. He cut up bananas and poured coffee.

To the closed door, he said, "It's going to snow. Don't forget your boots."

She sat across from him at the table with her lipstick already on and her contacts in and the untouched coffee going cold in her mug, and he did not know how to answer when she looked up and wiped some water from her throat and said, "Ethan, what are you thinking?"

Later, as she left, as she stood and turned and slammed the door behind her, he raised his camera from the table as if snapping a picture could halt the moment, unbuckle it from its consequences, but she was gone already and the digital display just showed the door about to close, a shadow outside it holding a woman's shape, leaving or coming in.

That night he met Mallory at a bar when Samantha did not come home and he could not simply sit and wait for some confirmation of his building certainty that whatever life he'd imagined when he married her was on the threshold of vanishing. The Azul was a two-story throwback Cuban lounge with high vaulted ceilings, slow-turning fans, and a forty-foot mahogany and marble bar smuggled into New York piece by piece from the Havana Nacional Hotel. They sat beside a picture window on the second floor indoor balcony. Below them, rows of candles guttered on the empty bar and flickered in wide, lengthening refractions against the top-shelf liquors. In the far corner, a spotlight cast a purple circle on the bare stage.

"I can't believe you called me," Mallory said. "Don't you have any other friends?"

She wasn't looking at him, but out through the window at the moving storm.

"I guess I felt some need of your company," Ethan said. "Your Midwestern optimism."

She didn't turn away from the window and he tried to stare at her, at the candle-glow on her round cheekbones, the gold flicker around her averted eyes. He tried to will her into meeting his gaze and she would not. Finally, he looked out, as she did, at the far horizon where thunderheads scudded in from the south like the lid of a tomb sliding shut. After the incident at the kitchen table Samantha left without her boots, and now the lights of the city pulsed and glowed on the clouds like heat lightning burnishing the edges of a building storm. It was a thing out of season, a typhoon dusk, a weird sky lit out of tropical latitudes of hurricane light.

"I've got no optimism these days," she said. "I'm all plague and woe. I'm rewriting my dissertation."

"I thought you were working on Chaucer? *The Book of the Duchess*? I thought you were writing about the white city on the hill?"

"It's taken a turn," Mallory said.

Still, she did not look away from the window. Outside, pigeons broke from the street and rose in cooing, hectic swirlings. They wheeled in the impossible light and Ethan felt the urge to raise his camera to the sky, to reach and lift it from where it hung around his neck, but of course it was not there.

"I think my wife is going to leave me," he said.

He saw Mallory blink once, very hard.

"Well, golly. You must feel pretty bad," she said.

Ethan realized that his glass was empty. He lifted it anyway.

"I feel like whatever I feel now is going to get worse."

She reached up with her right hand and touched one of her earrings. They were crystal baubles, Viking replicas, and were, as far as he knew, the only earrings she owned. They sold them uptown, at the Cloisters, the Medieval art museum where she worked and where she met Ethan when he came there to do a brochure shoot.

"You never told me her name," Mallory said. "Not once. And it's too bad because I like names."

"Samantha," he said, and tipped the ice from his glass into his mouth. It made a sound like teeth cracking as he bit it. Samantha. He tried to imagine her now. Samantha slinking through the city with her head down and her shoulders rounded, her arms crossed in front of her body, hugging her chest like a little girl walking home in the rain; or Samantha slouching over a bar, tossing her hair out of her face as she looked up toward the ceiling at the frail benediction of the lights there and smiled for a moment for nobody at all; Samantha stepping out of a cab and into some man's apartment building, winking at the doorman and disappearing behind a closing door of smoked glass. Samantha, after a year of marriage, a cipher still; Samantha whom he knew he could still love, but wouldn't; Samantha, now, certainly, inevitably, anything but alone.

The year's jealousy flared in his chest like a lit match. He wanted another drink but there was no server and he was sure that if he went downstairs to the bar Mallory would be gone by the time he came back. The curtain behind the stage slid open and a man in a tuxedo stepped into the spotlight. He was short, a dwarf, and perhaps because Ethan and Mallory were the only ones in the bar he angled his body out of the direct light and looked up toward their table. Under the slanting spot-glow, his black mustache seemed to droop away from his lip like paint smeared into an elongated frown. He began to sing.

"I tried to take her picture today," Ethan said. "As she left the apartment. I don't know why I did that."

Mallory turned, finally, from the window. He looked for disdain or anger in her eyes, but they simply seemed tired, unable to focus.

"You're a photographer, Ethan. Where's the fucking mystery?"

"It's just not something I do," he said.

And it wasn't. It was one of the myriad little weirdnesses in their relationship that suggested the larger dysfunction. He was a photographer and he photographed her so rarely—so rarely, anyway, did she allow candid shots. He could probably count them on one hand. There had been a few times during their courtship before he knew better, and once in Key West when he caught her by surprise. Early on, she let him bring his camera to bed as a sort of game, but he realized later that those moments were posed for him: Samantha from behind with her hand braced against the headboard and the flash shadowing the muscles in her arm, throwing the sweat between her arched shoulders into a rainbow of broken glass, or Samantha kneeling between his legs with her hair tied back and her eyes open and wide and staring straight up at the camera. A moment manufactured as carefully as the advertisements she developed. Nothing beyond her control.

"Do you think the monks drew grotesques and monsters into the margins of their Bibles to represent the terrors of the fallen world?" Mallory asked. "Or were they just mean and celibate and bored?"

Her eyes would not focus properly. There was something familiar about the dwarf's song, but the words were in Spanish and Ethan did not know any Spanish songs. The dwarf still faced their table, crooning up at them.

"Let me buy you another drink," Ethan said. "Tell me about the dissertation."

"Not likely. No one wants to talk about their dissertation. Not to you."

The dwarf's tone had changed. He was snarling the words, singing as if in a rage, and Ethan recognized the song now. It was "As Time Goes By" sung in Spanish. There was no piano. The dwarf sang and sang and stared up at them. The light leant his grimacing aspect the stilted, static look of a weeping clown mask. Ethan turned away. Outside, it had begun to rain in icy sheets, but still the red light hung over the city.

"What's with this light?" he said.

Mallory made a dismissive gesture in the air with her hands. She seemed barely able to lift them.

"The pigs are lurking about the crib," she said.

"Are you on drugs? Or is that Chaucer?"

"Ethan, are you relieved that your wife is leaving you?"

The song had not ended. Hail tapped at the window now. The dwarf barked the Spanish refrain over and over and the bartender made no move to stop him. Clearly, the singer was crying.

"It's a simple question, Ethan. It's not some trick. Are you relieved?"

The dwarf's expression was like something he woke to in the middle of the night, Samantha's face withered into dream. "Yes," Ethan said.

His cell phone began to ring and at first he didn't recognize the sound. It rang and rang on the table before them though he had no memory of putting it there and Mallory shook her head and looked out the window at the lit storm. She stood.

"I think you're in trouble, boy," she said. "I think you're about out of luck."

By the time Ethan got home the police were in the lobby. He saw them when he entered: two of them, in uniform, sitting on the green leather couches and talking to the doorman. One of them said something and the doorman laughed and shrugged and made a motion as if to spit on the floor. There was something sinister in the gesture, definitively cruel, and Ethan didn't like the way the police laughed along with him. He saw their heads turn as he entered, saw the doorman's smile harden into a toothy rictus; he saw the doorman nod toward him. He reached the open elevator, stepped inside, pressed the button and waited, facing outward, for the doors to close. The police, of course, were standing now, coming toward him, shoulder to shoulder with their wet galoshes squeaking in synchronized parody on the marble floor. They spoke his name, he looked away, and the doors slid silently closed. The elevator began to rise.

He wakes to this: Samantha woken, but not awake, in the dark. Samantha striking him, scratching. Almost no sound. Her breath comes fast and shallow. She moans as she struggles, like a sleepwalker—a guttural, grunting sound issuing from the other side of dream.

He knows by now how this will go. It's hard because he's holding her and in her dream she's fighting someone who's holding her, but if he didn't, he doesn't know what damage she might do. When she settles, when she wakes, when she says his name back to him, he lets her go. Then he's up and into the bathroom getting the warm washcloth and then sitting again in bed. He dabs her forehead, he kisses her, he turns on the bedside lamp. Its light is thin and white as watery milk. On the nightstand, under the bottle of vodka, there's thebooks he bought on trauma. She has never touched them. He places the vodka on the floor. He picks up the first book, opens it, closes it, puts it down.

"Samantha," he says.

He looks to where her nails draw blood on his arm.

"Samantha."

Her breath still comes fast and shallow, like a dog's after a long game of fetch. Sweat beads on her forehead as soon as he wipes it dry.

"Samantha. Sweetheart. Look at me."

She does. Eyes snap open, hard and sudden as a door slammed by wind. All pupil. By now he knows that this is just the flipside of catatonia. He needs to talk to her while he still can, as the flood of mania recedes, but before it is gone entirely.

"You see now that you are safe," he says. He's memorized this from the booklet, from the one workshop they attended together. "You are safe in your apartment, in your bed, in my arms."

He takes a breath, waits, speaks again.

"Say it," he tells her. "Say *I am safe*."

Her expression doesn't change. He can't meet her eyes anymore and he looks down, at anything else. The underside of her top lip is chewed raw. Red as a torn strawberry.

He knows she's supposed to say it, to repeat his words back into the world and let her speech repattern her fear responses. But he can't make her. It doesn't seem right to force her to do anything.

The therapist had said, *You seem to find two primary impulses: a dissociative state which serves as a protection mechanism, and a state of panic, flashback, induced repetition.*

He dabs her forehead again. Kisses her again. This next part is hard. Everyone, the therapist, the books, the trauma counselor tell him that she needs to address what happened, reconstruct the narrative, exert mastery over it, control.

"Samantha," he says, his voice as cool and level as he can make it. "Tell me what happened that night."

Her fingers loosen on his arm and instinctively, maybe, he pulls his arm away. He sees his blood already drying on the sheets. When she speaks, in the moment of her first syllable, the monotone dial-tone hum of it, the voice uttered out of a locked room, he knows this will be no different than any of the other times.

"There was a girl alone in the forest," she says.

"No, Samantha. That's not real. You know that's not real."

He's thinking: she stepped out of the shower, she sat at the table and then stood at the door. It closed.

He has said to her, a hundred times, a thousand: "This is not your fault, this is not your fault, this is not your fault."

He had stood at the window, he had sat at the table, he watched the door close.

Now it's too late. He knows she won't say anything, but he's talking just to talk, to hear her voice while he still can. "Tell me," he says. "I'm here. It's Ethan. I'm here."

He wants to hear her say his name. He wants to hear it on her lips. But the time for that, like everything else, is long past.

"There was a girl," she's saying, affect shutting down, hands unclenching. "There was a girl alone in the forest, and the forest was full of wolves."

LATER, IN THE SICK orange light of the motel room, Ethan examined Doyle's postcard. It was, he assumed, from somewhere in Central America. Copal, probably. The address was blacked out in heavy marker and he had no idea how Doyle had gotten it to him. The postcard was crazy in its way; it was thick and old, the photograph must have been taken with a Kodak 110 sometime in the eighties. It was an impossible postcard from an impossible source. Brendan Doyle had disappeared two years ago after rumors of a shootout with the Copalan police and Ethan did not expect to see him again. A fugitive gone native. Kurtz in the American tropics. Now, after everything, Ethan thought he could use Doyle's company very much. He put the postcard back in his suitcase.

Outside, something shattered and he peered through the window into the parking lot. Scraps of trash skittered on the wind like crabs out of a whale carcass, a junkyard hound dog roamed between cars, and prostitutes lounged at each end of the U-shaped curve of rooms and smoked crack. Ethan raised his camera to the window and snapped the shutter. He had traveled the world somewhat, he was not entirely cloistered from its realities, but he had never seen anyone smoking crack before. He zoomed in and held the prostitute in the shutter's eye. He snapped and snapped.

He stepped back into the middle of the room and photographed the window itself with its shade pulled open and the glass holding his blurred, unrecognizable image. He closed the shades, he turned to the room. He shot the bathtub he would never use, the shit-stained carpet and the semen-crusted bedcover. He shot the placard above the dresser that read in black stenciling ALAMO LODGE, SAN ANTONIO. He held the camera to the mirror and watched himself through its cropped eye. Through you, truth, he thought. Through you, the beefy decay of the recognizable world. He sat on the bed and wiped the memory card. Why would he want this truth? The filthy light of this room that recalled that other light to which he had abandoned Samantha. That other light and that other room. That other room with its white walls and its soft, rounded, padded furniture. The nausea of it, the orange and blue floral bedspread, the horrible neon light. The nurses with their Zoloft smiles and the feel of the chief resident's hand on his shoulder. The hill in the country and the grand, gabled estate—a place they should be picnicking, not a realm to which he should send her like a disgraced queen to a nunnery. The light of this room recalled all that. The drowsy reek of suppressed nightmare, the sopor that informed the place. He found himself wanting to scream. Now he wanted panic, chaos, the broken world boogieing in its own broken light. He picked up his camera and opened the door.

The junkyard dog, luckily, was nowhere to be seen, but Ethan heard, as he crossed the parking lot, a wild scrambling of rats in the strewn trash. The night overhead moved cloudlessly on and lights from cars on the overpass glanced off the windshields in the lot. It was not late and several miles away tourists probably walked under the shadow of the Alamo, strolled along the green lit waters of the San Antonio riverwalk. Ethan watched as a man wandered out from under the overpass and up to one of the prostitutes' rooms that bookended the motel. He saw her step off her stool in a cloud of rising crack smoke and strut inside. He saw the man follow her. He raised his camera and shot the empty stool, the cloud of hanging smoke. A dog barked, somewhere, at the flash.

"Hey, man," a voice called. "You trying to get yourself killed?"

He turned toward the voice. Beyond the chain-link fence separating the parking lot from the street, the motel swimming pool lay filthy and abandoned. A woman sat on the diving board. He could not see her face and body for the shadowings of the overpass, but the underwater lights marbled her legs with turquoise as she kicked them in the air. Ethan opened the gate and walked toward her. The pool squirmed with midges and other water bugs. A film of grease and oil rainbow-slicked its surface. Beneath it, the water was the impossible green of a tropical sea.

"This is a terrible pool," Ethan said.

"Hey, honey," the woman purred. "You get what you paid for, and you didn't pay for this."

Behind him he heard the gate clatter shut. He reached down to touch the pool and the water was soupy and warm beneath the layer of floating scum.

"You don't swim in here, do you?"

She kicked her legs. She had not stopped kicking them since she called out to him. In a new arrangement of water or wind the rocking turquoise illumination now played on the underside of her chin, the right side of her jaw. Her hair was braided into thick black coils. The weird waiting woman lurking between the ravage of the overpass and the trippy pool light aroused in him some feeling of the oracular. It was that kind of evening.

"You're not a cop," she said.

He shook his head.

"Then why you snooping around with that camera?"

"I wasn't snooping. I'm a photographer."

"Like for the papers?"

"Not really," he said. "Not at all."

"Then what for?"

He had no answer, not since he had quit his job. He felt perhaps that he should account for himself here. He could not.

"For myself, I guess. Like a journal or a travel log."

She laughed a smoker's laugh.

"Like an explorer," she said. "Like a man with a golden hat."

A current of sudden wind tunneled and gusted through the overpass. The pool light rocked on the fence like a disco ball.

"Like Columbus," she continued. "Like the man with a goat for a head."

Some tinny music started up far behind them in one of the motel rooms. A man began to scream. Ethan turned toward the noise and when he turned back she had pulled her legs up out of the light and into her body. She held her knees and rocked like she was about to roll off the diving board in a sad little cannonball.

"Where are you from?" she asked.

"New York."

She gave a squeal of delight.

"Oh, wow! I've always wanted to go to New York," she said like she was imagining Tahiti. "What did you do there?"

"I was married there."

"I've never been married," she said solemnly. "But I'm not really old enough."

She nodded her head toward the highway, toward the passing trucks and the rebounding blare of tinny music. He saw her braided hair flop out of her face, saw the thick curl of her mouth, some wet humor in her eyes. He wanted to photograph her.

"How old are you?"

She didn't pause. "Fourteen. I'm just a kid."

He fingered his camera. By any gracious measuring she was at least twice that, but he felt taken by the certainty in the statement. Like the one lucid moment when Samantha had insisted on her institutionalization and the dissolution of their marriage. *No, love,* he had said, *we can make it through this. I can help you.* He had said it and said it and been wrong.

He found himself raising his camera. He wanted to hold and frame her in his shutter's eye. He wanted to be able to gaze at this truth, too, and then erase it.

She covered her face with her hands.

"No," she said through her splayed fingers. "Don't bother with me. I won't show up on that thing."

The music from the motel was growing louder. It was some rap synched over an electronic Chopin sampling. His mother, in one of her episodes, once spent a month playing Chopin for eight hours a day. He remembered his relief when Samantha told him, their first night together, that she had quit piano lessons at twelve—as if that in itself served as some surety of sanity. He clicked the shutter again and again. The woman seemed to writhe under his flash.

"Why do you have to do that?" she moaned.

"It's not so bad. I'm not keeping them," he said and erased the pictures one by one.

She drew her hands away from her face.

"I'm sorry," he said. "I should have asked."

"Can I see one before you erase it?"

"You'll have to get off the diving board."

She shook her head with a child's vigor. For a moment he thought she might actually be fourteen. She opened her arms and began to kick her legs again.

"You should take your pictures and get out of here," she said. "You should maybe fuck off. Go to the Alamo. Go creep the green river."

Ethan backed away from the pool edge. Her voice had plummeted octaves into something hoarse and trembling, a voice wholly different from before, and he was certain, then, that this was her real voice uncovering itself against her will. It was a shift he recognized from his last months with Samantha and he had a feeling that she might begin to scream.

"Hey," he said. "I'm leaving. I'm leaving right now."

"Sure you are. Where do you think you can go?"

Her tone rose again into the teenager's bobbing lilt, but her eyes, what he could see of them, still blinked through trance. Across the parking lot, the john left the prostitute's room and began walking back, between cars, to the overpass. He stopped when he saw them and stood staring. Ethan looked away from him and turned to leave the pool.

"Where are you going?" she asked again. "Where do you think you can go?"

"South," Ethan said. "Mexico, maybe."

He knew it was true as he said it. Nuevo Laredo wasn't that far, and beyond it the continent fell away into limitless variations of forgetful possibility. There was Mexico and the realms farther south: the white beaches in Belize, Doyle, if he could find him, and the tropical shores of sea grapes and cane huts. Lotus flowers.

"Oh," she said. "Boystown. You're going to go to Boystown and take pictures of all the sad women."

"No, I'm not going to Boystown," Ethan said.

"Sure you will. If you come to San Antonio and hang here"—she waved toward the motel, the man still watching them from the street—"then you'll go to Mexico and hang out there. There are enough busted-up faces for your little camera."

She began to laugh.

"I'd come with you and show you around, but I'm not old enough."

———

Back in his room, with the shades pulled and the door barred, Ethan sat on the bed and considered Mexico. There were drawbacks: his Spanish was terrible and the border towns were dangerous, warzones, but get through them and into the interior and Samantha's money—he could not think of it as his—would go a lot farther. Direction was arbitrary, hardly a choice at all. He may as well head south.

He lay back on the filthy bed and listened to the music that had not abated, the same track looping over and over. The rap, the sampled Chopin. Again, he remembered, as he did frequently, his mother's swollen wrists, the blue ready pulse of her still knotted veins—often they were all that remained of her physical presence, the only thing that for him had not fled with time. He checked his watch. It was what Mallory called, in her playful butchery of the Book of Hours, Midnight Vespers. He imagined that now Samantha might sleep through the nights, or if she didn't, that her nights might be divided into their own allotted services of medication and dull sleep. She woke and slept and maybe would one day step back out into a world that he was sure must not contain him. He closed his eyes and let the music lull him where it would. At one point, still hearing it as he slept, it occurred to him that the past was the music of his dreams and it would never end.

HOURS BEFORE DAWN AND Ethan's driving south. There's the headlights on the open road and the exposed world fleeing before them: an armadillo scrabbling through the sudden brightness, the road itself, holding straight and long, unraveling like a skein of cloth rolling downhill. A future commencing just beyond possibility, something he must chase. In the last watches of the Texas night the horizon he drives toward is the cold blue of a vein pulsing under skin.

By dawn, clusters of thorned mesquite twisted with scrubby cactus line the road. The wind rises out of the south and waves of red dust lift and blow across the far plains. He rolls up the windows and swerves to avoid hitting a turtle, but hits it anyway. He sees its body spinning up into the air behind his car, sprinkling the road with slivers of shell. The sharp light of morning, the golden half-light, holds in the east, and for a moment Ethan feels entirely alien to himself. He's nothing but the present, a man heading south, untethered to anything but driving on the empty road toward the river and the signs for Laredo, where thin curls of smoke streak the air. It's a sweet dissociation. In the new light's false promise, it's a realm of perfect physicality. A static, concrete world of things and now.

He opens the windows again; he feels the too-warm wind. He knows how it is that you experience pleasure or pain in the moment, but you love and grieve in the future and the past. More than anything, loss is retrospective or projected. As it occurs, in the suddenness of the moment, you cannot tell, when you wake alone, whether your lover is in the shower or in another's bed. It's the photograph's trick: outside of time there is no haunting.

As he approaches the border he begins to feel vaguely afraid. It's a comforting feeling, warm and sure and realer than guilt or regret. He feels it and feels it and holds it close as he drives on over the flat reaches of the highway and into the coming day.

FIRST THERE WAS THE sea, moving in metallic sheets against the darkening horizon, then there was the shore, Playa Ratón, the beach of jagged coral, broken glass, and sand the soiled yellow of old bones. Beyond the shore, the wind-stunted thicket of sea grapes hung before the outdoor deck of the canopied bar. The air reeked of the rotting, windfall berries, and anyone taking in the view from the deck would have to do it through the perimeter of sea grapes. This time of night, this time of year, or century, there were only two men on the deck and they were not watching the sea.

Cunningham raised his glass, drained it, and wiped his forehead with the stained sleeve of his white linen jacket. Although little sun remained, he wore green mirrored aviator sunglasses and a yellow shirt that he kept unbuttoned halfway down his chest. It was the type of getup peculiar to Anglos in the tropics forty years earlier, and it seemed that he had been wearing it all that time.

"Really, General, are you sure your man Soto is coming?" he said. "I don't know how many of these daiquiris I can drink."

Guzmán shrugged and his oversized epaulets rose and settled like angel wings starting to open. It was, Cunningham thought, like all the uniforms down here, vaguely ridiculous. So much for meeting incognito.

Guzmán said, "Now, Barry, there was a time a man could be shot for insulting our national cocktail."

Cunningham held up his glass to the blue glow of the mosquito lamp. He turned it upside down. It was empty.

"A daiquiri? Daiquiris are Cuban. Named after Sir Francis Drake. There is no way they're your national cocktail."

Guzmán gulped from his glass and smiled. His teeth glinted bluely in the electric light.

"Ah, but Barry, you've been away too long. El Lobo has decreed it the national cocktail. It has been mandated, and history, as you know, is nothing before one of El Lobo's mandates."

"Maybe it's the nature of my work," Cunningham said, "but everywhere I go people are declaring that history is dead. Everybody is making mandates."

"And you have a problem with this?"

"It's just that I'm a man of principle. And principle is dependent on history."

The general had not stopped smiling.

Cunningham held his hand up to the light and snapped his fingers.

"Otro vez," he shouted when the bargirl looked his way.

He took off his sunglasses and blinked blearily at the lightened dark. He tried to smile but his mouth moved the wrong way, downward, like one about to be sick.

"What can I say? I'm easily convinced."

The bargirl who brought the drink could not have been more than eighteen. Her black hair sparkled under the mosquito glow; she smiled at him and then looked down when the general turned his gaze on her. Doleful, thought Cunningham. A village maiden. A treasure of Central America. The world, he thought, the slavering world is yet beyond her comprehension. Guzmán's buggy little eyes had assumed an aspect of kindling rage. It was boring to watch these petty violences play out, but it was always to be expected. Well then, darling, Cunningham thought, welcome to the new Copal.

Guzmán caught her wrist as she turned to leave. She stared down at the table, at Cunningham's drink. Cunningham tasted it and smiled but she did not notice.

"Excuse me," Guzmán said, "but can you tell our foreign friend here why the daiquiri is our national drink?"

"The daiquiri is rum and sugar and lime," she said. "And in Copal we have the purest rum and the sweetest sugar and the freshest limes. Copal is rich with treasures."

She spoke in nervous monotone. A schoolgirl reciting her lessons. There was nothing remotely sexy about it, but Guzmán bobbed his head with vigor. He was still smiling his big blue smile.

"That is very good," he said. "You are a pride to the nation. Do you have a boyfriend?"

Cunningham watched her face try to hold its smile and slowly collapse. There was no safe answer to that question.

Guzmán released her wrist and handed her a ten-dollar bill. Dollars were rare in Copal, and under the pulsating light, Cunningham could not tell for sure if her fingers trembled as she took it. She nodded and turned and left.

"I suppose you have her now," Cunningham said.

When Soto appeared, he came up from the shore, weaving through the windbreak as if he had been strolling along the beach and turned, like an insect, toward the light of the bar. He broke through the trees and loped up from the shadows and onto the deck. He stood for a moment away from the light with his head bowed. In the playing shadows of the new night Cunningham could not see his face. It seemed, almost, that he did not have one—there was the dark of the sky above him and the dark of his hat and the ribboned shadow about his features. The man himself, Cunningham thought. Of all the lunatics the world's warm shores flung at you, Soto was his own weird specimen. Cunningham drained his new daiquiri. A man in the service of righteousness keeps the worst company.

Guzmán was speaking.

"Soto, we thought you weren't going to make it. Barry thought you'd stood us up."

Guzmán sounded unsure of himself, Cunningham felt. His voice was suddenly hearty and jocular, a barman's convivial tone. The general was not convivial.

"Come have a drink," he said.

Soto did not move but stood and waited and whistled, a long, high, modulating whistle. A *Peter and the Wolf* whistle with more Wolf than Peter. It was singsong and flutey, something piped, and Cunningham did not like the sound of it. Then from beneath the trees crawled the child. He must have been crouched there, in the slight sandy incline before the deck. Mud streaked his face and his jeans were too long for his small legs, a sibling's pants perhaps. He wore no shirt and his skin held the fair coloring of the Spanish northerners. He approached Soto and Soto put his hand in his hair and then on his shoulder and led him over to the bar. The general, Cunningham saw, had begun to tap his gold ring on one of his medals.

"What's with the lad?" Cunningham asked.

"No se," Guzmán said. "But there are rumors."

It was fun to watch Guzmán churn. Perhaps tonight he would have trouble with the bargirl.

"I don't know what you expect," Cunningham said. "Deal with creeps and this is what you get."

When Soto returned to the table he brought the child with him. The boy carried a bowl of baby octopus.

Soto told him to sit and the boy sat with the men at the table. Like one with coattails Soto flipped out his jacket and swept off his hat as if preparing to bow before royalty. He sat.

"The boy has to eat somewhere else," Guzmán said.

"No he doesn't," said Soto. Cunningham had forgotten how strange his voice was. "Anyway, he doesn't speak English."

The boy looked down at the bowl and began to eat the octopus with his fingers. He didn't look back up.

"Our problem," said Guzmán, "is that the banana people have offered El Lobo twenty million dollars in cash if he ignores certain export taxes. The oil people have agreed to a similar figure. We would like to accept this deal."

Soto opened his arms in a wide show of beneficence.

"Do you know that I have crossed jungles to come here? The dart frogs are disappearing in the mountains and the Indians clamor for more guns."

"If the oil prospectors go into the interior, I'd like to guarantee them safe passage," Guzmán said. "But the guerrillas keep burning the banana groves. We cannot ensure the safety of the roads."

Soto shook his head violently, like a man trying to free himself from a cobweb. He looked to the eating child.

"This is so unbelievably petty," he said. "So they burn a field? So they arm some pitiful fucking inditos? That's it, no?"

"Forty million is not petty. And Barry thinks there will be a revolution."

"Barry always thinks there will be a revolution. Barry thinks it's still 1980," Soto said.

Cunningham reached across the table and snagged an octopus.

"Those are pretty good," he said.

"Why does the president need forty million dollars?"

"The Americans expect the roads they paid for. And their funds are long ago misplaced," Guzmán said.

"Is there no one else you can tax?"

"This year tax collection did not even cover government salaries," Guzmán said.

Soto turned his gaze to Cunningham.

"Tell me, Barry," he said. "Is it a revolution or a coup you're trying to prevent?"

"Hey now," Cunningham said as he reached across the table for another octopus, "we've got a plan."

After Soto and the boy left, Cunningham looked down the shore to where they had disappeared. He felt like a stage actor drafted into a sitcom. Here, in the shabby bar on the stricken beach, everything seemed to tremble at the edge of farce. The general licked his lips, straightened his epaulettes, and wiped his forehead with the silk ascot he usually wore about his throat. It was almost too boring. Wherever one went, Cunningham thought, one saw the same such figures strutting through the same postures: base greed and violence, silly uniforms, maniacal plans. Of course, the plan Guzmán had pitched to Soto was ludicrous.

Cunningham had known Soto in the States at Yale and he saw what happened to him in the jungles in the eighties. A colonial orphan blighted by the consequences of wars that had, even by Cunningham's standards, clambered into horror, Soto was not to be trusted. Such as they were, his methods were extreme, his principles devoid of clarity. As a contractor, he liked to think, of the oldest school, Cunningham had trudged all over the world. Everywhere was a pisshole and everywhere the bastions of order were crumbling. Usually, one found men like Guzmán, men who believed in nothing, who saw the chaos around them as a confirmation of that void, a blossoming of the nothing at the heart of their world. Such men were unfazed by the consequences of their actions, but their actions were easy to predict. Or there were those, like Cunningham himself, who believed strongly in their work, who felt ordained by duty. And then there was Soto. He believed in something for sure, he seethed with conviction and the rage of righteousness, but his reasons were forged in the reasonless crucible of a jungle war and could not be comprehended. Cunningham had heard rumors that the farmers at the edge of the cloud forest were now calling Soto *Duende*, after the folk-spirit who stole children in the night.

"This is ridiculous, General," Cunningham said. "Why send one maniac after a girl when you could send an army?"

"The world is watching us now. Their eyes are on Mexico and El Salvador. We must be discrete about how we handle our guerrillas. We would not want to make a mess for our American uncles."

The general's paranoia was also to be expected. It was another symptom of your typical banana republic war criminal. Their megalomania was such that they believed themselves beyond scrutiny, and were certain that they were always being scrutinized.

Cunningham nodded out at the dark moving water as if he had just noticed it.

"You can't blame the tourists for staying away," he said. "It's a filthy sort of sea. I wouldn't swim in it. Not if I were a shark."

Guzmán didn't seem to be listening. He was standing and raising his hand to the bargirl, and the bargirl was stepping out toward him onto the dark reaches of the deck.

"I think if you were a shark, you would like Copal very much," he said.

Axiom of the border: everything was for sale. Ethan came with one bag, a camera, his clothes, and knew that whatever he bought, he would leave with less. There was a time when the elderly would arrive by the busload from Texas, buy cheap medications that might kill them anyway, and then shuffle off again across the border. The markets were still filled with merchants and children and quack doctors hawking whatever wares they had to hawk, but now they were without customers. The merchants shouted and shouted, their cries rising like doves from a gonging church steeple, but there was nowhere for them to settle. It was all just noise. The disarray and panic of a Mexican market without any of the commerce. Ethan felt, as he found a cantina, ordered a beer, and sat on the outdoor patio, that he was listening to the death cries of a city at the end of its future. By night, cartels waged war on its streets; by day, bandits attacked even the most paltry of knick-knack shops with flurries of machine-gun fire. Now, even America's most desperate citizens did not risk the border towns. What does that make me? he thought.

He heard the boy before he saw him.

"Hey, señor, do you want some Xanax?"

Ethan looked up from his beer. The boy stood on the curb where the plaza met the street. He wiped his black hair out of his face with his wrist and held out his wooden medicine kit. On it there had once been a painted red cross. Now it was just the faintest, faded outline. Ethan knew he should have chosen an indoor cantina.

"It's cheap," the boy said. "It's almost free."

"No, thanks."

"It's safe. The doctor's my uncle."

Ethan picked his beer back up, drank from it, and found it empty.

"Can't you shine shoes or something?"

The boy dropped the medicine kit and whistled, whistled and waved as across the street, another boy leapt out from under the ripped awning of the farmacia and came hobbling toward them. Ethan saw by the way he dragged and stumbled and worked his crutch through the dirt that he was missing his right foot.

"I didn't mean it like that. I don't need a shoeshine," Ethan said.

A taxi lay on its horn as it swung off one of the side streets and into the boulevard. In Nuevo Laredo everyone blew their horns—to greet, to signal, to celebrate a soccer win or holiday—and the boy crossing the street didn't pay any attention. When he saw it finally, the taxi, he stumbled back, fell in the street and sat there as the swerving cab washed a cloud of red dust over him. Then he was pulling himself up, brushing dirt from his face, hobbling again, and standing before them on the curb.

"Shoeshine, señor?"

"I wasn't serious," Ethan said to the first boy.

The boy looked up at him, again wiped his hair from his face.

"He only has one foot," he said. "He lost it in an explosion where both his brothers were killed. Isn't that right, Juan?"

"That's right," said the boy with one foot.

"He lives with his grandmother because his mother ran off across the border to Laredo."

"Laredo's not that far," Ethan said.

"It's too far for a boy with one foot."

"It's too far for me, señor," Juan said.

"And his sister is a puta."

The boy spat on the cracked tiles by Ethan's feet.

"A King Kong puta," Juan said.

Ethan looked out at the street of red dust. There were no sidewalks and the gutters from the cantinas funneled into ditches that ran along the road. You could smell it always: urine and beer and the rot of heat. A shoeshine, he thought. Like everything else here, you could wreck it in under an hour.

"Okay, I'll have a shoeshine," Ethan said.

"Gracias, señor."

Juan dropped to his knees and began working on his shoes.

"How much?" Ethan asked as he buffed.

"Ten dollars."

"Fuck off."

He stopped a moment. "Five?"

"Three."

Ethan had never liked to haggle, but he didn't want to stick out and haggling was the norm here. A necessary part of the ceremony of the gringo in the border town.

Juan began to work again. The first boy pulled up a plastic chair, sat down next to Ethan. He picked up the beer bottle, shook it and looked disappointed. He pointed at his medicine box.

"Want some Viagra?"

"Do I look like I need Viagra to you?" Ethan asked.

He tipped Ethan's bottle over. It rolled off the table and broke on the tiles by his feet. Juan didn't flinch.

"You look like you need something, señor."

A wind came up. It was the worst here, Ethan thought, when the wind was up. The kicked dust rose and billowed, followed you like a tumbleweed. About a hundred yards off, near the border, the Mexican flag snapped in the new breeze. Ethan saw his ambered reflection in the fragments of bottle on the ground. The boy was right.

"Go away," Ethan said.

The boy did not go away. Instead he said, "Hey, señor, do you want to go to Boystown?"

A moment, then, when Ethan smelled the sewage from the Rio Grande wafting on the wind. A truck of teenagers in uniform pointing machine guns into the street, driving by in their pickup truck—policía or cartel men or some combination of the two. He knew that every so often you could make a choice that was worse than all the ones you'd made before. He dropped three dollars to the ground and stood up.

"Yeah," he said. "Let's go to Boystown."

Somehow the boy had found himself a donkey cart. They were walking together in the street, walking away from the cantina and the border and the hassle of shoeshine boys and drug hawkers when, as if the boy had conjured them out of air, an old man in a donkey cart appeared at the curb with his straw hat pulled down over his eyes.

"Here, señor," the boy said. "Get in the cart."

The old man seemed asleep. His face looked like a plum left out in the sun and the tips of his white mustache were stained yellow with tobacco.

"Is he awake?" asked Ethan.

"Of course he is awake. How else could he drive the cart?"

Ethan looked for a step up, couldn't find one, and pulled himself up and onto the wood plank seat.

The boy slapped one of the donkeys, shouted, "Wake up, Uncle," and jumped onto the seat beside Ethan.

The old man lifted his hat from his eyes, turned and looked back at Ethan.

"You want some Xanax?" he said.

"Christ," Ethan said.

"Viagra?"

"No, Uncle," said the boy. "Zona de Tolerencia."

"Okay, okay," he said and winked at Ethan. "Boystown."

He whistled and took up the reins but didn't crack them. The donkeys stomped and brayed and began to trot. Dust rose from the road and Ethan pulled his aviator sunglasses off his collar and put them on. The boy snickered.

"Look like a real gringo now, eh?" Ethan asked.

"Sure, sure," the boy said. "If you want more sunglasses, I can get them for you cheap."

Ethan nodded at the old man.

"I thought your uncle was a doctor?" he said.

"I have many uncles, señor."

Jeeps and taxis with blown-out windows passed them in the street; pickup trucks with machine guns mounted in the back rumbled slowly by. Ethan stared through his sunglasses at the teenagers who manned the guns. They were skinny and dust-covered and scared-looking. Three weeks earlier, in a saloon in Arizona, he had watched as a Navajo talked down a drunken trucker who had decided to pull a gun on him.

"You know, I'm half Indian myself," the trucker had said. "My mother was an Anasazi."

"No, she wasn't," the Navajo said.

When the driver pulled the gun, the Navajo laughed and bought him a beer, broke a bottle across his face and then bought him another beer. After the trucker left Ethan said, "Shit, man, what were you thinking?"

"I was thinking he didn't look too mad and he didn't look too scared," the Navajo said.

They passed a plaza with a fountain in the center and park benches under jacaranda trees where people sat and ate their lunches and read the papers and whistled at the police trucks that circled through the square. They went on and the donkeys brayed and snorted in the sun and to their left streets opened into strip malls: used cars, farmacias, Burger King, and yes, Ethan saw it and couldn't believe it—Taco Bell. They continued on to where the buildings became smaller: whitewashed Spanish bodegas, pawn shops, cantinas with sloping tin roofs slicing sun-glare off the splintered windshields of parked cars, and on into the maze of streets where thin and gangly dogs slunk between houses; on and on into the town and out of it again and through a new strip of bars and saloons, vanilla stands and knickknack shops. Ethan could see it, then, in the distance, Zona de Tolerencia, the walled city of the whores—Boystown.

"You excited?" the boy asked him.

"What?"

"Going to have some fun, eh?"

"Probably not," Ethan said.

"You don't like Mexican women, is that it?"

"No, that's not it."

"Don't worry, they are not Mexican."

"I wasn't worried," Ethan said.

"Migrants from Copal, Honduras, El Salvador, working their way across the border."

It was early enough that the streets weren't too congested. They turned right and began loping toward the walled city. Ethan took off his sunglasses and rubbed his face—they had been in the donkey cart over an hour.

He wondered what he'd do when he got there and then knew he didn't want to know. It was the middle of the afternoon and the sun bleached the sky into the pale brown of the desert. He'd go inside and find a cantina, he'd sit down. He'd start with a few drinks. What happened then—he was finding this more and more often—he couldn't predict.

IN THE DAYS FOLLOWING her release from the hospital, he used to watch Samantha sleep. At that point, still, he was spending his nights on the couch—she couldn't sleep yet, she said, with another person next to her.

"I wake up," she said, "and I think you're him."

Still, sometimes in the night, lying on the couch, he'd hear the sound of it from their room and he'd get up and walk to the door and watch her there with the covers tangled around her and her teeth grinding: molar on molar and jawbone suddenly tense, standing out. Then he'd go to her, sit slowly so as not to shake the bed, and put his hand on her brow. He'd touch her and say, "Easy, love. You're grinding your teeth again." He rubbed her brow and murmured and touched her hair and her jaw and then when she stopped, but stayed sleeping, he'd say, "We'll work it out, love, we'll get through this like everything else," and other times he just waited and said nothing because already she was turning in her sleep or his voice was broken and gone and now any sound could be too much.

ETHAN PAID THE BOY and his uncle at the gate and hopped off the cart.

"Good luck, señor," the boy said. And then, as if he were quoting a movie: "Don't do anything I wouldn't do."

Ethan laughed and felt for his wallet at the same time. It was still there.

"What could you do anyway, chico?" he said.

"There is nothing I cannot do. You should see me. I am the best dancer in the town. Isn't that right, Uncle?"

The old man touched the straw brim of his hat and lifted the reins again. The donkeys stamped their feet and began to walk.

"When I was your age," Ethan heard him say to the boy, "I was already a grandfather."

Ethan stood alone for a moment outside the main gate. Boystown. He'd heard about it for years—some sick city out of truckers' myth. Walled in with concrete and adobe and sealed with a Plexiglas roof, it was its own little village: six streets of bars and cantinas, back rooms and alleys, motels where no one spends the night. Zona de Tolerencia—an olive branch from the police to the cartels—here whatever you wanted was legal, and whatever was legal was cheap.

A car passing in the street honked its horn. He looked away from the walled compound. Gradually, the land rose and the city sprawled out into towns and villages, hills in the far distance of crooked pine and gray rock, highways turning south and into the interior, turning east and running to the Gulf. There was no reason anymore not to go inside and see this. If only to hold its damage up to his own.

He turned back to the walled city, its four street blocks of bare gray wall broken only by a walk-in police station, and alongside the station, a barred gate cut into the wall—the only way in or out of Boystown.

Once, before they married, in Boston in the winter, he'd wandered the streets with Samantha at four in the morning. They'd just left an after-hours bar and, starving for some food, they stumbled down Park Street through the snow blowing off the Public Garden, turned right into the dense twist of buildings and wandered through the crooked haze of a city in sleep. When they came to Tremont Street, they walked till again there were lights, the neon glow of a new city: Chinatown, with its teahouses and apothecaries, sex stores and peep theaters, their signs flickering out into the street, into the puddles and gutters and the alley sluice of slush and trash.

They found an all-night dim sum restaurant and sat by the window while men in the back, near the door to the kitchen, drank and played mahjong. Ethan poured Samantha tea and she poured it for him and sat with her right elbow on the table, her head resting in the brace of her hand, and smiled at him while he slid his fingers through her hair and talked and laughed and ate as the winter sun broke across the city. She took his hand and kissed his fingers—knuckle by knuckle, finger by finger—and then watched and pointed as the drunk white men stood from the mahjong table and hobbled out into morning, out and across the street to the peep houses and to the women already up, or not yet asleep, waiting in the cover of back alleys. "God," she said pointing at the men, at the girls sucking on diet sodas and shivering still in the rising blanket of kicked steam. "What do they want there? What's attractive about that?"

Now Ethan could tell her, if she were ever to ask again: they want to feel some hurt so much greater than their own. They want something different from their lives, something they can break, irreparably break, and then walk away from.

Ethan took off his sunglasses and shielded his eyes from the glare of sudden light. Then he went to the gate, nodded at the police guard, waited a moment on the threshold, and stepped into the dark city.

Inside, then, and the metal clang of the gate sliding shut. The sun came bleary and dull through the smoky gray Plexiglas ceiling and Ethan stood just beyond the threshold on the packed dirt road and waited a moment for his eyes to adjust to the dark of the compound. He began to walk. The road ran down and away into the gray distance;

it was lined with bars and Texas-style saloons with chili-shaped lights, dark cantinas with wood-plank floors and, he saw through the open doors, rows of square concrete tables, adobe walls, a bar with no visible bottles, no windows anywhere. And then also opening from the road, well-lit lounges as luxurious as hotel bars; he saw marble bartops and brass light fixtures, bartenders in tuxedos and women in cocktail dresses even the roughest cowboy wouldn't want to rip. Light cut off the bottles, gleamed off brass and chrome and polished marble and he kept walking though now he heard music rising from every doorway, jazz and big band and country and punta.

The road splayed side streets the way a river does tributaries. They twisted and curved into shadow and there he saw open doors, women sitting on stools outside in the road, alleys branching into alleys, and coming from them, the hoots and whistles and catcalls of women and men and men dressed as women. He stopped and looked up because he heard, or more sensed than heard, from far overhead the thumping of birds trapped inside the compound, flying against the Plexiglas roof. They rose and dropped and rose again—sparrows and crows, a red parrot and a canary—he watched them flutter from the roofs of saloons, flutter and bang against the glass and land only to flush again at the constant cacophony of music and laughter and everything else. He came to a raised boardwalk and walked under a saloon's green light. In the mud just off the planks, a rat gnawed a dead parrot under the neon pulse. Everywhere, he noticed now, there were dead birds.

Farther down the boardwalk, past the saloon, he found a lounge that opened off the street into a well-lit bar. He didn't want to go in but knew he didn't want to stay standing in the street. Inside, a man sat and played the piano. Ethan remembered a jazz club once, in New York, ice popping in a whiskied glass, the taste of bourbon on Samantha's lips. Again, now, he was sweating, and he felt it suddenly, the ache pulsing in the back of his throat. He stepped to the door and turned the brass knob. Birds startled behind him at the wave of music rushing outward.

He descended an ebony staircase and played his left hand over the brass banister as he went. For a moment, the strike of his ring against metal surprised him; it seemed something distant, an action and sound wholly external to him—a desk bell rung and rung somewhere upstairs in the hotel lobby that wasn't really there. And then he reached the floor and stepped into the lounge with the piano and the blue leather couches and the bar and the walls and the columns all sharp with light slicking on marble. Everything, the whole room, was empty but for him and a few others sitting on couches or at the bar, and the women whom he didn't see but knew must be there.

He went to the bar and ordered a scotch, which wasn't something you ordered in a Mexican border town, that much he knew, but still he ordered it here and the bartender who wore a tuxedo didn't scoff or anything worse but turned to the bar rack and pointed to where a full row of scotch glinted under the wide play of light from the hung chandeliers and the backlighting of the accent bar lights.

Ethan pointed, "Balvenie."

The bartender slipped a crystal glass from a rack beneath the bar, turned for the bottle.

"Rocks, sir?" he said.

"No, neat," Ethan said. A habit from another life it seemed: he always drank his scotch neat. And one of Doyle's lessons just remembered: never trust that the ice isn't made from tap water, never trust that the tap water won't wreck your bowels for a week.

The bartender poured, slid the glass across the bar.

"Would you like to pay now or put it on the entire tab?"

It took Ethan a moment to realize what he meant.

"No, I'll pay now," he said.

He sat there and continued to drink. Behind him at the piano, a new song starting up. In the back corner of the lounge a patron slowdanced with a woman in a red satin dress that seemed to shimmer and kick light like a cut ruby. The piano man began to sing and Ethan listened a moment and caught the tune. He couldn't remember the name but recognized it as Cole Porter. He put his glass down and swiveled on his leather bar stool. The place, he noticed again, was nearly empty.

"Say," he said to the bartender. "What sort usually come in here?"

"Sort, sir?"

Maybe it was just early, Ethan thought. Maybe that's why it was so empty.

"You know, who're your regulars? This place seems a little ritzy for a border town."

The bartender stopped wiping glasses and put his rag down slowly, put it down and folded it and looked back up at Ethan as if to say, look what you've made me do. Everywhere the crystal glasses sparkled and sharded light about the bar and Ethan knew that they were all perfectly clean, that this man stood here through every day and night and buffed his glasses past the point of any necessary polish. By now he knew enough about neuroses to recognize them pretty easily. Once you started looking closely enough, there were no sane people.

"Is this your first time in Boystown?" the bartender said.

Ethan nodded, sipped from his whisky and found that already it was gone. The bartender poured him another as he spoke.

"Boystown is not a border town, sir. It is its own city. What borders are there here? It is not Mexico. The laws here are not the laws of Mexico, they are not the laws of Texas. Here what you want you may have. And here, this lounge, it is for men whose position in some other world parches what thirsts must need slaking."

"What ho, Fortinbras," Ethan said.

"Excuse me?"

"This is a gay bar? That's what you're saying?"

"Sí."

Ethan turned again and looked at the dancing couple.

"And she?" he said.

The bartender unfolded his rag like there might be a present wrapped inside.

"Look," Ethan said. "I'm not a hick. I'm from New York. I've been to plenty of drag shows. I've been to burlesques."

"No doubt."

"I can even spell burlesque."

"Don't you think it's time to go?" the bartender said.

"B-U-R-L-E-S-Q-U-E," Ethan said.

Outside again, in the street, and the day fleeting now beyond the walls of the compound. A world, it seemed to Ethan, stricken by sudden carnival. Now the roads thronged with drunks, the stale air ripe with sweat and a steam of exhaled booze. Ethan stood in the street, looked up at the sky bleeding out above the Plexiglas and listened to the rising rush of it: laughter and shrieks, moans straining over music like voices

coming in fever, the flap and call of dying birds. He stood and wiped
sweat from his brow, stood and turned a dazed circle in the road, heard
then everything else beneath the general din: boots splashing through
mud, cash registers chiming open like typewriters finishing a line—
from a near window, flesh thwacking on flesh.

Ethan began to walk back the way he had come. He passed again
under the green light of the saloon, the dead parrot now just stripped
bones, feathers loamed in the marl of kicked mud. A woman called to
him from the alley. She sat on a stool under a slanted portico and her
face was inked by shadow, though the light from the saloon shone on
her wide right thigh, glinted on the open eyes of her children hunkered
just behind her.

Ethan resisted the urge to remove his camera from his bag. He
would not let himself frame and capture this. If he captured it he would
not feel it and the point was to feel it. He turned and went into the saloon, and as he did so he brushed against a cowboy, Mexican or Texan,
he couldn't tell, not with the way his hat tilted over his face—not that
he could tell the difference anyway.

"Watch it," the guy said without looking up.

"Sorry," Ethan said, still walking. "It's just that you're standing in
the doorway."

Inside, a short staircase opened into a room of concrete floors, a
row of wooden tables, a wood bar with no stools and no tap. Behind the
bar slouched a man who must have just lost about a hundred pounds—
loose skin wattled from his throat like an iguana's crest. Behind him
there was a refrigerator filled with beer. If there was anything else to
drink, Ethan did not see it. Men sat at tables and stood at the bar
with women who clung to their arms, laughed, drank their beer. In the
corner, toward the back wall, more women stood waiting against the
adobe.

Ethan moved to the bar.

"Dos cervezas, por favor."

"What you want? Bud Light, Miller Lite, Corona?"

Ethan wondered why he bothered with the Spanish at all.

"Corona," he said. "With limes."

The bartender stopped moving, seemed to blow air through his
wattle.

"Limes?"

"Yeah, limes. Limones verdes."

The bartender pointed at the empty expanse of the bar, the one refrigerator.

"No limes here, mister."

"That's too bad," Ethan said. "I like limes."

He took his beers and walked back toward an open table as far from the door as he could get. It was amazing, he thought, how this kept happening to him. How he was drunk before he knew it. He sat down, pulled from his beer. He did not like Corona. The day's first dawning at the cantina in the plaza seemed to be hours past. He drank again. It was just this sort of bullshit reasoning that he had to avoid. The day's first dawning *was* hours past, that's why it seemed that way. Also, he had just drunk fifty dollars' worth of scotch in a town where cash went a long way—that's why he was so drunk. *Always*, Samantha told him, *you make things more complicated than they are. You make choices*, she said as she stood at the door, as he raised his camera, *and then you account for them. The rest is pretty much bullshit*. In the dark, in the empty hours between when she'd pass out and when she'd stir again into morning, his guilt turned sometimes to rage, and later, when she thrashed through withdrawal or woke in the night clawing at him with nails already chewed to nubs, he would have liked to ask her, which choice, Samantha, are you accounting for now?

Still, sitting there in the back of the bar with the two beers sweating on the table and the night coming on with a traveling pageant of stumbling drunks, with fat men and men in cowboy shirts and mesh caps and men so gaunt they seemed skeletoned against their own ill-fitting clothes proceeding into the bar and claiming women whom they led by the arm or the hip or the ass up the stairs and into back rooms, it seemed to Ethan that the cause untethered, in the smoke of the room, from the effect. He lived in New York and afterward, when that life ended, he went to Arizona. He left Arizona, he left Texas. He sat here now and emptied the first Corona and reached, then, for the second, as she touched his hand and settled into the booth beside him.

"Not now," he said. "Not interested."

But then she touched his hand again and he turned and looked and saw that she was older than most of the others. Not old, not much

past thirty, but old enough here where youth might vanish in the space
of an hour. Her hair hung black and down and ovaled her face against
its frame. She did not smile at him, she did not reach up to touch his
chest or feel his biceps or mimic any of the other performances he saw
unfolding around the bar.

"I think I just came here to drink," Ethan said.

"Well," she said, and her voice was throatier than he'd imagined, a
hard, purred whisper, "I could use a drink as well."

"Right, sure." Ethan was standing now. "What do you want?"

"Manhattan up, orange twist, no cherry. Comprende?"

Ethan turned, stopped, looked back at her.

"You're fucking with me, right?"

"A Corona. Or maybe two."

At the bar and sliding money across the wet wood, grasping the Coronas
and turning to go when the man from the doorway, the cowboy with
the hat pulled low, put his hand on Ethan's shoulder.

"You bumped into me out there."

Ethan peeled the hand off his shoulder, palmed him five bucks.
He'd try the Navajo's tack.

"Buy yourself a few drinks on me."

He patted him on the arm, everything casual and cool, and went on.

Back at the table she touched his wrist, then with her other hand
reached for the beer, drank from it.

"You seem nervous," she said.

"What's your name?" Ethan asked.

She turned to look at him and cocked her head the way a parrot
might, but kept her body facing the bar, the door, the rest of whatever
this was.

"Yolanda."

"That's your real name?"

She put her beer down, he felt the weight of her fingers on his
wrist. Somewhere, outside, there was a scuffle in the street. Bottles
breaking, shouts and cheers like men at a cock fight.

"Why wouldn't it be my real name?"

"I don't know," Ethan said. "I just thought…"

"Yes?"

"I thought, that, well, you know."

"That whores are too ashamed to use their real names?"

Yes, thought Ethan. That's it exactly.

"No," he said. "But that you'd change your name to something exotic. That's how it is in the States, with strippers, anyway. Everyone is called Mystique or Kristal or Natalia."

"What's wrong with Yolanda?"

The conversation had turned strange and in that moment Ethan again felt himself reaching for his camera. Was she flirting with him or asking him a serious question? Her name was perfectly exotic and perfectly sexy, but it was also perfectly real. He had come here, he realized, to see some walking approximation of damage, a motif of ruined women. Perhaps he had not wanted real people.

"I'm sorry," Yolanda said. "I'm just trying to get a rise out of you."

Ethan drank from his second beer, found it, again, empty. Her skin looked dull and textureless under the smoky bar light.

"Was that a pun?" he asked.

"In Mexico, prostitutes never make puns," Yolanda said.

Outside, the police had arrived at the fight in the street. A voice echoed through a megaphone in faster Spanish than Ethan could understand. The blue throw of light from the revolving flashers strobed the inside of the bar. In the moments of illumination Yolanda's face looked hard and polished as stone.

"I'll go get us some more beers," Ethan said. His words came thick and slow now. He wondered if she even heard him.

Moving again through the press of bodies to the bar. What now, Ethan thought as he touched the cold glass of the bottle to his lips and returned to the table. Two Texans—truckers, Ethan assumed, by their mesh caps and the pocked scree of stubble on their cheeks, men who often shaved without mirrors—had removed the shirt of the girl at their table and took turns pouring and then licking beer off her breasts. There were men who did that sort of thing, and once you did it you were never anything else. Samantha had held her torn underwear up to the light of the streetlamps through the iced window.

He placed the beers on the table.

"So what happens now?" he said.

Yolanda brushed her hair out of her face with the back of her wrist. Her index and ring fingers were bubbled with burn scars.

"Any number of things can happen now," she said. "But I don't see why any of them should happen here."

"No," Ethan said, as another Texan peeled off his shirt and began dancing some awful boogie to music only he could hear. His boots kicked sawdust from the floor and his belly bounced over his belt. He gritted his teeth and closed his eyes and his hands balled into fists. If the girl who was at his table was twenty yet she didn't look it as she laughed and clapped and glanced down as if surprised by what her hands were doing.

"No," Ethan said again. "This is a terrible place. You're right, we should go, but I'd like to finish my beer first."

His beer, though, was already half gone, and maybe it wasn't such a good idea, finishing another beer. The noise of the bar and the street and the sound of trucks and dogs in the distance came together like the echo of a festival blown on a loud and strange southern wind. He found himself raising the beer again to his lips.

Yolanda stood and took his hand. She wore a dress of woven Indian silk and her hair reflected the strewn light of the bar and a raised scar twined from her collarbone down beyond where Ethan could see between her breasts. In the haze of drink and smoke he could not discern any expression in her eyes.

"Come," she said. "We can go upstairs. I have a room."

She took a step and Ethan followed. The sound everywhere of bottles set against wood. Lifted and set again.

"Wait," Ethan said. "I'm sorry. I don't want to."

She turned, stopped, curled a loose strand of hair behind her ear, braced her other hand on her hip.

"You don't want to?"

"I'm sorry if I've wasted your time. I'll pay for it."

She stepped forward, reached out to him. Just the tip of her right index finger against his stomach. A whisper of a touch.

"Of course you will pay for it. But what are you afraid of? Why are you here if not for this?"

The shirtless Texan passed behind her, dragging his prostitute by the wrist—leading, not following, her to the back door, through the hung curtain and up the dark twist of stairs. Clearly a way he'd walked many times before. Ethan watched Yolanda's face for judgment.

"It's that you seem nice," he said. "It's that I like you."

"All men like me and I am not nice. But neither matters."

Ethan's tongue felt thick against his teeth and from somewhere, suddenly, there came the distinct scent of urine. He looked down at her hand on his stomach from what seemed a great distance and pushed it away. When she didn't respond, he reached for his wallet, found it, and gave her what cash he had left.

"I've seen what I came here for," he said. "I don't do this. I'm not trying to be rude, but it's really awful here."

He turned and started to move away from her, toward the door. As if it could be that easy, to pay, and turn, and walk away. To escape without regret.

One, two, and then he was out through the door and back into the street, where again he met the man with the hat, the man who stepped in front of him and put his hand on his chest, his fingers pale, skeletal in the blue neon, and said, "You bought me a drink. Now it is my turn. It is only fair."

"Don't worry about it," Ethan said. "I'm on my way out."

The man did not move aside or lower his hand. Beyond him the twirl of flashers came no more; the police were gone and the street was almost empty. An old man sat in the mud and played the accordion. Somewhere, huddling nurses dulled Samantha into chemical sleep.

"I'm late," Ethan said. "I'm very late."

"No," the man said. "Excuse me, but this is unacceptable. You bought me a drink and then you sat with my girl. You sat with my girl and bought her at least two beers. I saw you do it."

"I'm sorry. I didn't mean to sit with anybody's girl."

"Please," the man said again. "My name is Javier. You bought me a drink and you sat with my girl and now it will be a great disrespect if you do not let me buy you a beer."

Ethan tried to smile. Not far off, a man was crowing like a rooster. Again the smell of urine, on the enclosed and fetid wind. The accordion player was on his feet now, wandering toward them, playing loud and off key, without harmony or melody.

"One for the road," Ethan said.

———

At a table in the back of the bar near the stairwell, Javier said, "Tonight you made me very sad."

He placed two glasses on the table, he produced a bottle of tequila, he took off his hat. Without it his face looked slack and loose, hung from his forehead like fruit gone rotten on the vine. His bottom lip fell away from his teeth and his gums were dry.

"Listen," he said. "Tonight you made me very sad. With the things you said about Mexico and with the way you treated my girl."

"I didn't say anything about Mexico."

"No, that's not true. I heard you say that this place was an awful place. Didn't I hear you say that?"

Ethan waved generally at the bar before them, the truckers and the prostitutes, the growing quiet and the door farther away than he'd like.

"I was referring to this cantina, not the country. We have bad bars in the U.S. as well."

Javier poured the tequila. There was something wrong with the worm at the bottom of the bottle. It was falling apart, flaking away, whirling and settling like sediment in a snow globe.

"Drink your tequila," Javier said.

Ethan did and Javier refilled his glass. Outside in the street, the man began crowing again. Javier reached down into his pants and pulled out a small tube of Vaseline. He placed it on the table, next to the bottle.

He said, "I do not understand why you came here? If you did not want to sleep with her? She is beautiful. Or anyway, she is not so bad. Not like some. And she is very kind."

"I didn't intend any disrespect."

"But you paid her! I saw you pay her. Everyone saw you pay her and then walk away. What are you saying, that she is the kind of girl you would pay not to fuck? Is that what you are saying? Drink your tequila."

By now the truckers and anyone else who had come down to party had gone away with their girls or gone home. What men were left in the cantina sat alone and without speaking, hunched and wasted, staring down into their drinks while the girls slouched quietly beside them and waited for what happened next. Ethan stood.

"I'm leaving," he said.

"Maybe you do not like women?" Javier said. "Is that it? I saw you leave the *Plátano Verde*."

"The what?"

"The fag bar."

"That was a pretty good bar," Ethan said.

Javier sprung up, stepped toward him and brandished the tube of Vaseline. He spread some right from the tube onto his lips. He smacked them together a few times.

"It is very dry here. The skin is always dying."

"Look," Ethan said. "I gave Yolanda all the money I had left. What do you want?"

"I want you to apologize to her. I want you to make amends."

"Okay, I'll apologize. Where is she? "

"In our room. In the back. It is not far."

"I'm not going into any back room," Ethan said.

They stood on the threshold of a bare room wavering under the candle flame: a couple of Coronas sweating on a square wooden table, an empty sugar cane chair, an elaborate papier-mâché nativity scene, and Yolanda sitting quietly in the corner.

"Please sit," Javier said, and Ethan did. Javier folded his knife and put it away. He stepped back from Ethan, circled the room and stood behind Yolanda. Somehow, in the moment between closing the blade and stepping again into view, he had pulled his hat back on. Yolanda did not turn around and he perched there behind her with his long hands draped loosely over her shoulders like epaulets.

"Well?" he said. "Apologize."

Ethan didn't think this was a shakedown, not anymore, but in the candle's shudder, he still couldn't read Yolanda's expression.

"I didn't mean any offense, Yolanda. You seem very nice."

Javier said, "Give me the bag, Yolanda."

She reached down and placed a blue Indian coffee bag on the table. Ethan could see by its shape that it did not contain coffee.

"A man's love is his pride," Javier said. "A man's love is his pride and you have spit on it. A man may do a million things. He may murder his brother, he may spend all night digging a hole in the dirt and into this hole he may put whatever he wants. Ten severed heads. Fifty severed

heads. A hundred heads! There is nothing to stop him. There is no order. Except love and commerce. In these things there are still laws, and
tonight you have disrespected both."

About this, Ethan could not argue. If there were rules of love or
order he had not abided by them. During the first of Samantha's three-
day detox holds, he had sat by her bed as if he had a right to be there,
hoping that somehow, by some alchemy, she would step back out of
this and into life and marriage with him. He stood. The tied bag, he
saw, was squirming on the table.

"I'm leaving," he said. "There's no reason not to let me go."

"You have apologized, but you have not made amends."

"Let him go," Yolanda said.

"I'm out of cash. What more can I do?" Ethan said.

Javier nodded down at the wriggling bag.

"Take it to the border. Cross over tonight."

Suddenly there was laughter on the other side of the door. Men
wandering in. More sirens in the road.

"No, I'm not going to do that," Ethan said.

"Let him go," Yolanda said again.

"But he hasn't even complimented my nativity scene," Javier said.

Ethan didn't know what to say. Was this a joke? Javier hadn't
moved, his hands were still draped over Yolanda's shoulders and his
long face hung heavily out of the shadow of his hat. He appeared in
aspect entirely without whimsy, some awful scarecrow come drifting
out of blighted fields, and behind him, in the nativity scene, there were
plastic dinosaurs—plastic dinosaurs and soldiers and real geckos with
red eyes slinking between the dinosaurs.

Ethan said, "I like the dinosaurs, but I'm not touching that bag."

Javier reached up and pinched his nose; he ran his index finger
along his open lips; he smiled.

"Where do you think you are?" he said. "What do you think this
is? Some Cadillac bar? Some Tijuana donkey show? Is that why you're
here? Did you come to see women get fucked by donkeys? Is that what
you think my girl should be doing?"

"Sure," Ethan said. "I came for all the shows. Donkey shows, iguana shows, chupacabra shows. Let every woman conjoin with every
beast. Present the virgins to the Minotaur."

Later, Ethan remembers it like this: Javier pushing Yolanda to the ground and flipping the table up into his face, so that the bottles, the bag, the weight of the wood itself struck him in the chest and he was stumbling back, already off balance, when Javier hit him with a tight hook to the cheekbone and it wasn't a great punch—not well aimed or well landed—but Ethan went down to his knees anyway from the shock of it, and then, when Javier's boot found his ribs, he was curled amidst the splintered ruins of an empty table and overturned chair on the damp concrete. He heard the knife open before he saw its blade flare in the candle's light and he knew he should say something but there was no time to say anything at all.

"Levántate," Javier hissed, and Ethan tried but he could not yet find purchase in the spinning haze of the room and his hands slid out from under him in the thrown wreckage of the table.

"Levántate," Javier said again. Ethan saw Yolanda step forward, step over him maybe, and take Javier's arm, the one holding the knife. She spoke to him in Spanish that Ethan could not follow and he shook his head and when he did the light from the cantina played quickly across his face and Ethan realized that the door must have been knocked open and whoever was still left in the bar was watching this happen, watching as Javier flung her off so hard that she fell back into the nativity scene while Ethan reached for a Corona and lurched and stood and shattered it across Javier's face as he loped toward him with the knife still at his side.

They stood there for a moment, Ethan and Yolanda and the patrons and prostitutes, in the stunned silence of the aftermath, as if everything that had just occurred was not possible, an action nightmared and then discarded in some other world—Ethan rising fast and swinging the bottle as his knees straightened, the shocking pop of glass and audible wet slitting of skin against bone and Javier reeling, already spraying blood like an Albert and Costello spit-take, dropping to the floor. Then Ethan just standing in the smoke and the bleeding bar lights, standing and panting and clenching the long jagged neck of the Corona.

Yolanda touched his shoulder, and then his arm, and then his hand. She wrapped her fingers in his, pulled him, and when he responded, when he turned and looked at her, she began to run.

The crowd parted for them, spread out for the whore and the gringo with the bottleneck trailing blood. Yolanda pulled him and he followed and they moved through the crowd, they stumbled and ran and broke out through the door as the bar again erupted into sound.

Outside, Ethan turned to run down the main street, down the street and to the gate, but Yolanda stopped and pulled him back into the dark cove of the cross alley.

"What are you doing?" he said.

"They will never let you through the gate," she said.

They stood in the corner where the alley met the main street. From inside the bar there were shouts and scuffling boots and men rushing out into the road. He stepped farther back into shadow and watched her as the humming neon sign slicked her hair green.

"I gave you all the money I have," Ethan said.

"Oh, shut up and come on," she said as she turned and stepped into the dark.

He followed her down the alley that at first seemed completely destitute of light—but not of sound. Women he could not see called to him from the doorways and high windows of whatever buildings framed the street. Salsa music and rap blared under the Plexiglas canopy and always about him he heard the feathered wing beat of rising birds. Once, they passed a man lying on his face in the street and Ethan sensed in the playing layers of shadowed dark the massing presence of waiting rats. A woman wept in some side grotto and another ran out suddenly into the road to beat on the hood of a car with a mangled toaster oven. Yolanda hurried before him and he stayed behind her, moving carefully. The dirt road was pitted and uneven and he stumbled through beer cans, broken glass, and strange deep puddles whose origins he did not wish to know.

She turned once.

"Come on," she said. "We do not have much time."

As they went on he began to perceive what little light there was: the blue glow of electric mosquito lamps popped in windows, weak neon light leaked from beneath uneven doorways, and like a photographic image slowly developing under the darkroom's red safety light, the alley unveiled itself to his inspection. Here stood no bars, but half-built buildings of crumbling concrete strangely latticed with iron-barred windows and sloping tin-shingled roofs. Now he could see the women he'd heard calling to him: they sat on stools under crooked porticos or watched him from high porches where, if one were to step through the empty doorways, some strange curl of darkened stairs must lead. They perched there and whistled and laughed. From a verandah above a woman wailed again and again, "Pero el llanto es un perro inmenso."

Ethan turned his gaze back to the road that wound past cars without wheels, turned and watched Yolanda walking quickly ahead of him. Above the music, he heard glass breaking and babies squealing and he looked up to the high porches and saw that where light shone the air shivered in a haze of swarming insects.

Then the road ended and Ethan was beside Yolanda, standing at the concrete perimeter wall. He turned and looked back the way they had come, but the street was dense with the new dark and he could not imagine treading that way again

"It's a dead end," he said, and knew then that she'd lured him down here.

She pointed to the base of the wall where the concrete met the street. "This is the only other way out."

He glanced down at the hole dug in the muddy earth. He glared at it a moment and then looked around to either shadowed side to see if he'd missed something.

"No fucking way," Ethan said.

"What? You are too good to crawl on your knees?"

The hole was no more than four feet wide and certainly less than three feet high. It was cut low and sickle-shaped and though the wall could not be very thick, the distance to crawl very far, Ethan could not see any light shining through. It was dark and sour-smelling and he felt the mud's wet slick with his boot's inspection.

"It's wet," he said.

"Of course it is wet. This is where the alley drains to. That is how the mud is soft enough to dig."

"And this leads outside?"

"Yes, it leads outside and into the street."

"Tell me again why I'm not just using the gate?"

"Because the man you hit is a traficante for the Juárez cartel, and in the Zone the police give free passage to the traficantes. You would be killed at the gate."

"None of that made any sense," Ethan said.

"Do you want to die? Or are you just an asshole?"

Ethan didn't see why it had to be one or the other. He peered down into the hole, where a spent condom floated on the mud like a jellyfish.

"I'd never fit."

"No," Yolanda said. "You are not as big as that. Now go. When you come through to the other side you will be on Calle Juárez. Walk two blocks to your right and turn left on Calle Jimenez and go to the twelfth house. When you get there knock and an old woman will answer the door. Tell her I sent you. Tell her you are here to help Mirabelle."

"Mirabelle?"

"Yes. Mirabelle. Are you too drunk to understand?"

"By half," Ethan said.

Yolanda touched his wrist. In the mist of bad light the scar on her collarbone looked like a raised seam of marble.

"Calle Juárez, Calle Jimenez, twelfth house, Mirabelle. I got it," Ethan said.

"Good. Now please go."

"Is there any chance that you'll be able to find my bag and camera?"

"Hurry," Yolanda said.

"You'll meet me there?"

"Yes, of course," said Yolanda already starting to turn back down into the alley. "Do not worry, this favor comes with a price."

On the last morning in New York before it happened, Ethan rose from the couch where he slept, stepped into their room and opened the window. He went over to the bed and sat down softly. "Samantha," he said. "I've made coffee."

She turned in her sleep, turned and covered her face with her hands and woke suddenly.

"It's cold," she said.

"The coffee's warm."

"Why's it so cold in here?"

"I thought I'd open the window."

"I hope you thought better of it."

"It's open.

"Ethan," she said, and looked at him for the first time and said it again, his name, like she was trying to fit it to what she saw, and could not.

"Yes?"

"It's the middle of December."

Ethan walked over to the bedside table and cleared it. He picked up the mug and the vermouth and held the vodka under his arm.

"We needed some fresh air."

"You're a sanctimonious prick, Ethan."

"I made you coffee," he said. "It's warm."

"Can you close the window?"

He closed it and pulled the shutters. Outside, the sun broke in slantwise shards off the windshields of passing traffic. He picked up the bottles again and walked to the door.

"Coffee's ready," he said.

"Don't pour those out," Samantha said as she pulled the covers over her face like a shroud.

Ethan sat at the kitchen table and waited. When he heard the shower come on, he began to sip his coffee; when he heard it turn off, he poured two bowls of cereal and cut up some bananas. He stood at the balcony window. Outside, blue clouds drifted across the sun. Down in the street, fifteen floors below, the noodle vendor assembled his cart.

"It's going to snow," Ethan said to the closed door. "Don't forget your boots."

When she came out she was dressed for work and her hair was up and he could see the warm water from her hair slicking on her neck like sweat. He touched her arm.

"How are you feeling?" he said.

They sat and ate and he stared at her across the table while cars revved and blew their horns and pigeons cooed and flushed and settled on the sill.

She looked up at him from her cereal. Already, even before breakfast, she was wearing lipstick.

"What?" she said. "What are you thinking now?"

He was thinking of how it used to be that she'd come out of the shower in the morning with her hair in a towel and glasses on because she hadn't put her contacts in yet. He remembered how he'd come up behind her, hand her her coffee, kiss her neck and her collarbone and her shoulders, how her skin would be beaded with water, how her hair where it escaped the towel would smell like lemon and mint. He was thinking that now she stepped out of a shower like that was all she needed to step out of, he was thinking that now her contacts were already in and she didn't smell like anything at all.

WHEN ETHAN BROKE THROUGH to the surface, he vomited and wiped his mouth and vomited again. He wiped the mud from his nose and wiped it from between his fingers and leaned back against the wall. There was something in his hair, a slick strand of plant or tendon that he jerked and cast from him as he would an insect that suddenly lighted there. He sat against the wall and gasped and tried to breathe through his mouth to avoid gagging again on the humid rot of the alley's reservoir, but when he did, he inhaled something like the skim off fouled milk and he was retching again on his knees in the street.

A block away, a fountain bubbled in one of the city's hundred deserted plazas. Ethan ran and threw himself into it. The water was oily and shallow. Drunks probably pissed there. It occurred to him that lying in the absurd fountain in the wasted plaza with the warm, likely infected water sloshing over him was the least stupid thing he had done all night.

Finally he stood, wrung out his shirt, and began to walk. The street was empty but for two lean and mangy dogs that limped the far sidewalk. The sound of Boystown's revelry wafted through the walled city in a static hum. Beyond that, there was little sound but the crunching of his feet on the street's pitted concrete, a car alarm sirening in the distance. The way was not lit and he knew that here, where mass murder was a daily occurrence, where cartels ravaged the streets with hyperbolic displays of violence, where shop owners pointed loaded shotguns at you as you entered their stores and nights quaked with the concussion of grenades—here a gringo did not walk alone after dark.

But he did and the night was empty and quiet and the air in the street was heavy with coming rain. He turned left on Calle Jimenez and walked a road slanting down into the far city where the houses stood crumbling and, like most that he had seen beyond the border, half built.

Three and a half walls were marred by gaping holes, the outlines of doors uncut and tiled roofs clearly unfinished, as if just after the town's conception the builders had fled some pestilence. He saw shadows move in the holes but could not discern their form. Now, in the near distance, he heard the soft gurgle and splash of another fountain. He counted the houses as he went and came to the twelfth one. He walked up and down the street and counted them again and arrived at the same house. It was no different than any of the others: whitewashed concrete, iron-barred windows and an iron-gated door, an eastern wall unfinished and boarded with plankwood and a Pepsi-Cola sign near its apex.

He sat on the curb. Certainly, it would be better to go back the way he had come and catch a cab near Boystown that would take him to the border, or to a hotel by the border. He could wake early and be gone, pay his twenty-five cents and slip through the turnstile and back into Texas where he'd left his car. He'd leave in the morning and drive; it might still be cool. He could find a beach at Brownsville or South Padre or farther north at Mustang Island, or he could go on to Louisiana. The future wavered before him with the nebulous possibility of a fever dream. He could imagine heat and bare shores, nights drinking cocktails that were too sweet and too cold on canopied decks surrounded by the sea. There was no reason to stay sitting here.

He stood and as he did so he knew he would not go back.

Once, he had watched the sunset with Samantha in Key West. They'd kayaked around the key and snorkeled with manatees in the cypress mangroves. They watched the sun fall and ate key lime pie so sweet that his teeth ached, and that night when he touched her, her skin was rough with blown salt. Ethan could feel it still, the salt on his tongue, and knew that he had stumbled beyond the borders of the real world, knew that there was that moment and all those that preceded it, and no imagined future could possibly unfold beyond it. He could not go back the way he had come. He could not walk these streets unmolested and—if Yolanda was telling the truth—unmurdered. And he could not believe the future he had imagined. Behind him, to the north, the named world, the world he knew, fell away into the jagged silhouettes of ruins.

He turned toward the door, walked up the cracked tile path. Nearby, a cock crowed in lightless confusion. Ethan looked down to his wrist but could not read his watch. He raised his hand and banged on the door and then banged again and again because he knew dawn was still a long way off. He banged and waited and listened until somewhere a light went on and he heard a slow scuffling from inside. The door opened to an old woman with a woven bonnet tied about her head. Ethan found suddenly that he could remember no Spanish.

"Yolanda," he was saying. "Mirabelle. I'm here to help."

The woman held up a paraffin lamp and peered closer, and he realized how absurd he must seem—some drunken gringo come wandering out of a brothel, standing in soiled clothes and a bloodied face, gesturing as to the deaf.

"Por favor," he said, and pointed inside. He heard windows opening, feet sounding in the street behind him, a dog barking and barking. He realized that he was leaning on the doorframe, supporting himself with one hand while the other still held the bottleneck. He dropped it and it broke by his feet. He looked down at the glass, where the glass must be, but could not see it. "Mirabelle," he said again. "Mirabelle." And then the old woman was turning and beginning to walk into the dark of the house, turning and looking back at him and nodding her head. In that moment, the night's thousand other possibilities fell away, and he followed her in through a hallway that smelled of vanilla and into a kitchen with a wooden chair and a table and a hung picture of the Virgin Mary listing on the wall toward a bead curtain and the rest of the house.

"Siéntate," the woman said, and he did, fell into the chair. She left the lamp on the table and stepped out of the room and turned off whatever other light she must have lit. For a moment he heard her footsteps passing through the house, heard the settle and rustle of her robes swish across the floor like fallen leaves swept against pavement, and then the steps stopped as suddenly as if she had just frozen there in place and stood standing and waiting somewhere in the dark of the house.

ON THEIR LAST NIGHT in Key West Samantha turned from the open window and let her robe fall from her shoulders. Outside, dusk bled the day's last light across the horizon and Samantha stepped out of her robe but put up her hair so that he could see her face, and walked to the bed where he sat as the purple light through the window spread across her left shoulder, her collarbone, her dark and salty hair. She did not close the shutters, but came to him on the bed and stood before him and took his head in her hands and pulled it to her belly. This is the memory's hinge, where he goes first, and where, always, it starts to bend. She pulled his face to her stomach and he kissed her skin, caked with the sea and her sweat, and the moment turned like a tide, became frantic, and they clawed at each other like drowning swimmers fighting to stay afloat—and then when they slowed and settled he turned her around so they both could look out at the sun on the water as sudden wind worried the curtains about the sill and the last purple light spread on her skin like a bruise.

IN AND OUT OF sleep and Ethan dreaming himself into the bar again, but this time sitting with Yolanda and saying, *where is the bathroom?* and her not understanding and him trying it again in Spanish, *dónde está el baño?* and her laughing and pointing and him waking, then, in the wooden chair, with the lamp's flame dwindling to darkness.

Revealed in its light: the room was empty but for the table, a sink, the hanging Virgin. Ethan had to piss very badly. He stood and the chair dragged against the floor and when he tried to steady it he heard his ring rapping on wood—he found his hands were shaking. His watch, he saw now, no longer ran—it had stopped at eleven thirty, though he had no idea how long ago that was. Very soon, he would have to find a bathroom.

Beyond the curtain the house was dark. Was there even a bathroom inside? Probably—but how to find it? No doubt the old woman was sleeping again, and perhaps there were others in the house as well. A husband? Siblings? Mirabelle—whoever she was? Outside, cocks began to crow.

Ethan sat and then stood, circled the room. He looked down at the floor. Cracks lined with uneven seams of sand and red dust ran through the concrete. Down the hall he had entered he could see that the front door hung unevenly against the first blue light of dawn. A breeze caught and soughed in the upper, unfinished rooms; the cocks kept screaming. Everywhere, now, he perceived the cloying smell of vanilla. In the street a car revved its engine, peeled out. Ethan made his way to the sink. It was empty but for two dry glasses. He rinsed them and put them on the table. What was left of the alley's slop had slimed into mud on his clothes, and he peeled off his shirt and scrubbed it under the faucet. He washed his face and his arms as thoroughly as he could; he put his wet shirt back on and waited a moment and listened.

Still, there was no sound of the old woman anywhere in the house. The street was quiet, his head ached from the scent of vanilla, he could not stand straight for the pressure on his bladder. He stopped waiting, unzipped his fly, and began to piss in the sink. He tried to hurry, but there was no hurrying it. Who are you, he thought, when you are doing this?

He never heard the front door open, but heard her footfall behind him, her voice.

"Please say the glasses are not still in the sink."

Still pissing, he looked over his left shoulder—there was no stopping now—and saw her, Yolanda, standing on the kitchen threshold, framed against the hallway in the day's first light.

Ethan tried to shrug.

"I didn't want to go creeping about the house."

She didn't say anything, just watched him for a moment until he turned away again, stared at the wall and listened to the sound of his urine on the metal sink basin, which seemed now as loud as a waterfall suddenly sprung up out of ether in the room.

"The glasses?" she said again.

He tilted his head back toward them. She sighed and stepped into the kitchen and set a bottle on the table.

"For when you are finished," she said.

He was finished. He zipped his pants, ran the sink for a moment, let it drain, and ran it again. Behind him, he knew she was watching as he stood there and refused to turn around. I'd be embarrassed, he thought, if I weren't so drunk. But he wasn't drunk, not anymore, and he realized that this was a sign of something else, some new collapse of character. A total lack of shame—another thing stripped from him before he realized it. He wondered how he looked to Yolanda, a stranger in her house pissing in her sink, and wondered more at how little he cared. Then he remembered to wash his hands and twisted on the faucet again, the third time now, rinsed his hands and faced her where she sat at the kitchen table. His hands were dripping on the floor and he dried them on his damp and muddy pants and held them up to the air, to her inspection.

"Manners," Ethan said.

She looked down at her feet as if she were embarrassed, though really, she could not be embarrassed. How could she be, this woman who must have seen far worse things that very night? She stared back up and past him at the far wall, the Virgin hanging there. He saw her play her thumb across a burn scar on her right index finger. For a moment the cocks stopped crowing and the room was warm and quiet in the slow, paling light.

"I've never seen a toilet with a faucet in it before," Ethan said finally.

She laughed, and as she laughed she reached up and forked her fallen hair out of her face with her fingers. A familiar gesture. Samantha, he thought, and then no, not her, he could never remember her doing that. It was the fingers in the hair that he remembered. His fingers holding her hair back, pulling it out of her face as she vomited.

In the time he stood at the sink the room had grown light. Outside, beyond their silence, the world was waking into screeching tires, occasional gunfire reporting on the wind. Ethan crossed the room and sat before her at the table. The bottle faced away from him and he couldn't read the label. He nodded at it.

"Am I supposed to hit someone with that, or drink it?"

She held the bottle out so that he could see it.

"Rum," she said. "From my hometown."

He lifted the bottle and read the label—Product of Copal—and didn't say anything. Doyle had told him how it was there, how girls would flee to the border; maybe they'd make it to Belize or Guatemala, or maybe they didn't even get that far before they met men, *coyotes*, who offered to ferry them into the United States. The women would join the men—often they had no other choice—and it wasn't until they were halfway there that the coyotes would raise the price. When the women couldn't pay they were beaten, sometimes raped, and then offered an option: rather than be turned over to the border guards, they could work off their debt. Two-thirds of the prostitutes from Mexico to Arizona were Central American migrants.

Ethan looked down at the table, then up and away at the Virgin Mary hung crookedly, as if she were about to fall, at the far threshold. He could smell Yolanda sitting across from him, could smell cloves and her sweat, cigarette smoke and rose hips rising above the vanilla scent in a steam of heat from her body. Her hair no longer framed her face in a tight black oval but was pulled into a ponytail so that he could see the whole of her jaw, her cheekbones higher and sharper than what was common here, and the start of her scar blooming in a wide crest above her collarbone before narrowing into a thin raised line across her throat and down into her breasts. He stared at it, and knew he was staring, but could not stop. He found that he wanted to reach out and touch the scar, to feel it under his fingers, and he knew she was watching him watch her, he knew she must see where he was looking and he turned his eyes back to hers, met her gaze and couldn't tell if the movement of pain he saw there like the ripple of wind across a lake's surface was a reflection of himself or something almost hidden, breaking through.

"Rum?" she said, and poured two glasses before he answered.

They lifted their glasses and touched them. It was a strange thing to do and he wondered who initiated it. Here the action was completely out of context, and his arm hung there, holding the glass in some perversion of an earlier toast, a moment jarred suddenly back to him: celebrating Samantha's promotion in her penthouse apartment, raising champagne flutes heavy with strawberries. The sound of crystal chiming on crystal. Wind and snow on glass. He drank and felt the kick of it in the back of his throat, the sudden pulsing in his lips, the capillaries opening in his face and the lightness of the empty glass in his hand. Yolanda smiled, poured them both some more. They drank in silence. Ethan had no idea why he was here beyond that, if he could imagine that every choice had led to this, for a year he'd wanted to see something he could not recognize, something as complete and incomprehensible as loss.

Now, though, he was sitting across the table from a woman who had a scar bubbled halfway across her body. He sat at her table and drank her rum and looked at her as if she were a painting, a model from his former life, someone to be photographed. If you tried hard enough you could render your life into a series of personal idioms—*incomprehensible, loss*—phrases that had no meaning beyond your own expression of self-pity. He thought again of his reaction to the way they touched glasses. When everything in the world is beacon to your own life, you are not living in the world anymore. He finished his rum. He wanted, suddenly, to leave.

"I don't know what to say to you," he said.

"You should start with *thank you*."

Ethan spun his glass around on the table. Spun it and clinked his ring against it and spun it again.

"I don't know what I should thank you for."

"I saved your life tonight."

"It's funny," he said. "But I don't feel saved."

Yolanda stared at him a moment and he was struck by the strange sound of his own voice, the bitterness in it. Away from Boystown's other whores, Yolanda looked young and tired. Her shoulders were bony under her shawl.

"How you feel and what you are can be two very different things," she said.

"It must be easy for you to say that."

"Because I'm a prostitute?"

Ethan didn't answer. His back itched, the air of the room felt heavy and warm, spinning and syrupy against his face. He looked at the bundle she had carried with her, swaddled in blankets like a baby.

"Is that my camera?"

She nodded.

"It wasn't easy to get back. Your clothes are gone."

"I guess I shouldn't have brought a camera into a brothel," he said. He watched her face as he said it, *brothel.* The word sounded obscene to him, soiled. He hadn't needed to use it, but had chosen to anyway. He did not want to know why.

"I thought maybe you were one of those men who likes to bring a camera to bed?" she said.

"I'm a photographer."

"Like for the newspapers?"

"No," Ethan said. "I took pictures of furniture mostly. Sometimes fingernails. For catalogs."

"In Boystown, we do not have any nice furniture," Yolanda said.

Ethan stood and moved to the sink. He washed his hands again and splashed water on his face. It was warm, brackish almost. It smelled gaseous, like an air pocket popping upward from a jungle river. He found himself scratching his jaw.

"I'm filthy," he said. In the moist heat of the room his shirt had not begun to dry. He stood before her, scratched his face—he could not stop scratching it—and watched her watch him. Now that the adrenaline of the night—the brothel and the bar fight and the flight through darkness—had diminished, his body felt simply swollen and empty, a clown balloon slowly deflating. He seemed to himself huge and gangly, everybody's lost gringo. He sat back down and poured another glass of rum.

In one continuity of motion, Yolanda pulled her shawl over her head, grasped its sides, shook it flat, dropped and caught one end and folded it all, gracefully, without putting it down. Ethan wondered at the simple dexterity of the action: it must be practiced, the balance of flourish and economy could not be haphazard. But why? In Copal, women line-dried their clothes and then folded indoors. He registered a pang that for a moment he could not place. Then, as it always was: Samantha. Samantha, for all her yankee breeding, could not fold her clothes. *What difference does it make?* she asked once and he answered— by this point sanctimonious and sure and feeling the first inklings of anger—*how can you expect order in your life when you don't maintain it*, and she'd just looked back at him sadly, her beautiful face not beautiful at all in the light of their room, but florid and splotchy, consumptive. She shook her head with a misery surpassing anything he'd seen before—his mother's futile bangings at Chopin, all of Samantha's little drunks up till now—a look forlorn past weeping and its attendant repair, a look that said, *even this is beyond me now, now to fold clothes is still too much.*

Here, that moment echoing in a perfect reverse. Yolanda placed her shawl in her lap. Her shoulders were surprisingly sun-darkened for a woman who worked by night.

"I once wanted to be a model," she said. "Two Dutchmen came to my island and offered to photograph me for a magazine. They said it could lead to much. They said maybe I could be in a calendar. They offered to bring me to Europe. They said that in Europe many were concerned by the plight of the former colonial subjects. But my father, he was Colombian and strict and he would not let me. He said, 'Yolanda, you do not know what such a deed might buy you.'"

She paused and waited, she seemed to want the line to set in. As if she were telling a parable, a story he was supposed to draw some lesson from, but it seemed simply leaden and false. If there were lessons to be learned, he would not learn them. He realized that he did not smell good. How's that for an epiphany?

"Well, now certainly you know what your actions buy you," he said.

"Tonight," she answered without inflection, a voice as cold as a mineral strain in fresh water, "tonight they bought you your life."

Another debt, Ethan thought, unpaid and unpayable.

"Who was that guy?" he said.

"He was a sort of pervert."

"What does that mean?"

"It doesn't matter."

"If you saved my life, I should know who you saved it from."

She reached out and touched his hand. Her fingers were rough, and whatever effect she had intended with her touch did not occur. He pulled his hand away.

"You must be very tired," she said.

He knew then that he was. The morning in the plaza came to him like splinters of remembered dream. She stood and took his hand again.

"Follow me," she said. "You should sleep. When you wake we will have breakfast."

He followed her through the curtain and heard the rattle and hiss of the beads behind them. She pulled him down a low hallway that opened into a doorless room. He saw a bed shadowed in the blue morning cool.

"Take off those clothes and lie down," she said.

He sat on the bed and pulled off his shoes without untying them and dropped them on the floor, where the caked mud of the alley crumbled to the rug. He stripped himself of his ruined clothes.

"I'm disgusting," he said.

She pushed him back on the bed and leaned over him and her scar looked like a purple vine twining down into her shirt.

"I'm sorry," Ethan said.

"For what?"

He closed his eyes.

"Are you going to tell me your name?" she asked.

"Ethan," he said, though he did not open his eyes. Already the room was spinning behind his eyelids in a sweeping drunken vertigo. First, Samantha would read in bed as he slept, then later, after it all, he'd sit and watch as she sweat and shivered into stupor.

Yolanda lay down beside him. He could feel the dent of her in the mattress, her breath on the back of his neck.

"Sleep, Ethan. We will speak in the morning."

"It's already morning," he said.

"Then we still have a long time until night."

Somewhere, the wind blew and strange noises carried on its gusts. He heard the fountain and a chattering as of frantic children. There seemed to be a hundred trees cracking in the gale. The wind blew. He turned, almost naked, in the bed. The rain he had smelled on his march toward the house did not come.

IN THE FIRST HOURS of the night, the woman set the bowl before Soto where he sat on the palm stump in the dust beyond her outdoor kitchen. She nodded at the soup.

"That was my last hen," she said. "The rest are roosters."

Soto looked up at her and smiled in such a way as men did not smile. His mouth turned upward and hung there, unmoving, affixed in a wide, rubbery caste. In the purple light that fell over the mountains, his golden eyes appeared wide and sorrowful so that he seemed for that long moment a carved specimen of anguish. Every few years, when the American priests came through the jungles on their missions to the Indians, they'd leave their extra picture books and pamphlets for her and her children. To her, Soto looked like the pictures of St. Sebastian, flayed and tortured, reveling in his torment. She stepped back toward the house and he stopped her with his voice.

"Are times as bad as that?" he said.

"I don't know," she said. "There are still plenty of lizards and I have eaten lizards before."

"So have I," Soto said. "When I worked on the railroad between the mines and the coast. Sometimes all I had to eat were these track iguanas. They were full of dirt and glass. They were disgusting."

He stopped and frowned and his frown seemed no different than his smile. A simple reversal of direction, but not of emotion.

"But when I was in America, you should have seen the things I ate. The great gluttony of it. Here, niños"—he held the bowl of soup out to the two children playing along the razor-wire ditch that bordered the road—"come have some delicious soup."

The children halted where they stood in the street and turned toward him. They did not move, each stood still on opposite sides of the wire-strung ditch. The pale northern boy Soto had brought with him sat separate from them under the last long shadows of the tin-roofed kitchen.

"Please," the woman said. "Eat the soup yourself. There is enough for them."

Soto seemed not to hear her. He threw back his head like a wolf about to howl and whistled his weird low whistle. When he looked back down the children were making their way over and around the razor wire, coming toward him.

"Have some soup," he said. "It is made of chickens."

The woman sat with him as the children ate. The sun was falling behind the mountains and the clay roads heading that way looked dark and blue, a vein of ice in a northern landscape. She touched his thigh.

"I was told that you were coming," she said. "And I was frightened."

"I heard about the bats," he said.

She gazed up at the empty sky, then looked back to Soto and then down. She left her hand on his leg.

"Ten people have died so far from the bites," she said. "All summer the bats come out of the jungle. At night it is not even safe to walk."

Soto nodded up at the looping twists of electric wires strung up against the darkening sky.

"Does your telephone work?" he said. When she nodded, he drew a handkerchief from his breast pocket and handed it to her. "There is a number written there. If you or anyone you know is bitten, you call that number. A man will come. He will give you the rabies shots."

She unfolded the handkerchief slowly and read the number and then once she had done that continued to stare into the cloth. The new night was silent but for the sound of her children playing. Lights flared, distant and wavering, in the high reaches of the far mountains.

"There are campfires in the jungle again," she said.

"It is the same everywhere," Soto said, and as he did so he reached out with both hands and touched the corners of her eyes. He trailed his fingers downward over her face and her tears followed his fingers. When he spoke to her his voice was like a sound out of the dark hollow of her dreams.

"People are ruined by the simplest things. The cattle die, so we are attacked by bats. The bats are not dangerous but we have no medicine.

There are many children and little food. We have obligations. There are strangers in the mountains in the night."

She watched the fires burn. She withdrew her hand from his thigh. She knew, she had always known, what price he would exact for his friendship. The distant flames wavered, almost green, not like fire at all. They seemed sure and peaceful, they glimmered with the constancy of stars. She told herself: if there are fires, there is food being cooked around them.

He nodded at the children where they laughed and ate.

"You carry a great burden, sister. I can help."

"I knew you would ask that."

He stood.

"Wait," she said as he turned, an action unstoppable, once it commenced. "Pablito," she said. "He is afraid of the Duende."

Soto was moving now, pulling his hat back down over his face, angling already toward the children and the silent pulse of the night beyond them.

"In this country," he said, "there is no Duende but me."

At dawn Soto broke through the undergrowth and came to the logging road. From there, still halfway up the slope, he could look down across the valley of green pine mountains pocked with intermittent hillsides logged bare. The roads out of the mountains ran down toward the village in winding red rivulets like the dry beds of rivers. From above, the village shimmered where the newly risen sun broke on the corrugated tin roofs of the shantytown. In the distance, the whitewashed colonial clock tower struck six times. Soto turned and began to walk again—behind him, the new train of children followed. Five boys and one girl, all filthy and limping in their ill-fitting shoes. They followed in silence as the road turned pitted and steep and distant coyotes called some confused howl, as if they had misunderstood dawn as the coming of a new dusk. Soto stopped once in the imperfect lee of crooked pines, where he passed around chunks of last night's meat to the children. He watched them eat it and then went on toward the town, where from his vantage he could see the glint of sun on machetes as people made their way to the purple cane fields that swayed under the wind of a coming storm.

ETHAN WAKES TO HEAT and the whisk of an overhead fan cutting air. For a moment the grace of waking without memory or knowledge of where he is—a warm room, the cut of the fan, white walls—and then realization, the drop in his stomach and sweat on his forehead and his thighs, the sheet sticking to his chest like a bandage to a gangrenous wound. Dread and morning and parching thirst. In the kitchen down the hall, the hiss and smell of frying oil. He sits up and peels off the sheet and lets the fan whisk air across his skin. It's little use, like diving into a heated pool on a summer day. Next to him, on the bed, are a pile of clean, folded clothes. A t-shirt, boxers, socks, blue jeans. He dresses, finds his shoes in the corner, puts them on and sees that the rug is crusted with mud where he dropped his old clothes. Few cocks still crow, though his watch reads eleven thirty. It's broken, he remembers, but it must be almost midday. He closes his eyes; he opens them; he walks down the hall to the kitchen.

"And you call Mexicans lazy?" Yolanda said as he ate. "I thought maybe you had died."

"If only," Ethan said. "And I never said anything about Mexicans one way or the other."

"Well, it's true. Mexican men are lazy. But so are all men. Everywhere."

Ethan reached for his glass from last night, filled it with water, drank it, and then poured another from the jug. Yolanda stood at the counter frying chicken and eggs on a hot plate. She had her back to him and wore a cream cotton dress with lavender embroidery along the straps and the bottom hem. The muscles strained in her right arm as she tossed the sizzling meat in the pan. Across the room his clothes hung on a makeshift line. Despite the fresh clothes, he must look terrible, though he hadn't looked in a mirror for at least a day, not since the previous morning in the motel in Texas when he stood and stared into the bathroom mirror as his complimentary coffee leeched the wax from the paper cup. He'd tossed the coffee down the sink, put on his sunglasses, and turned away from the mirror, grabbed one bag and left the others still packed on his bed. He'd walked out into the morning and toward the border where, between flashes of moving cars, the brackish river hung hot and yellow and motionless beneath the concrete border ditches.

Now, sitting at this strange woman's table, he thought that he must smell, but he couldn't smell himself. He felt liberated by his sudden lack of vanity. He reached down and took a bite of his food—chicken and egg and mealy avocado wrapped in a seared tortilla. His stomach roiled at the grease, at the fat of the chicken and the egg's gamy rubber, and he took another bite and then another. He watched her cook and watched the trembling of his own hands in the night's chemical aftermath. She wants me for something, he told himself. It wasn't money, that much seemed clear—she had seen him empty his wallet and she had no idea how much more he had access to.

He watched her cook. In the morning light, her hair that last night seemed black, unquestionably, tonelessly black, now glinted red and auburn and almost gold where the light touched it most directly. Beyond this, beyond some sense of her physical presence, her body, the way she smelled, the strange mix of mockery and tenderness in her voice, he knew nothing about her. With Samantha, always, he was too sensitive, too able to discern her moods. He viewed her, he realized, as a puzzle. He imagined that with intimacy and patience would come understanding, with understanding would come salvation. If he could understand why she did what she did, her drinking and infidelity and everything that followed, he could forgive it. But with his forgiveness flourished his contempt, and now he was struck, as he had been last night at the sink, by the strangeness of his detachment.

It's a question of debt, he thought. Of obligation and, as it always seemed with him—of guilt. Yolanda had saved him and now he would have to repay that debt. He knew with something like certainty that he could not help her. Whatever she needed, he would not be able to give. He felt, already, the melancholy of his eventual failure, of her disappointment and his guilt. Or no, perhaps it wasn't that. Perhaps she was simply scamming him, a gringo in a world in which he had no place.

He smelled coffee. She must have put it on without him noticing. He hoped the coffee was good; he hoped he was being used.

And then later—when she turned from the hotplate, handed him a teacup and poured him coffee that was so hot he could not taste it, and sat across from him with her own breakfast—he watched her eat as if in slow motion, her mouth opening around her food, closing; he watched the strange gentility with which she lifted her cup to her mouth by the saucer with her back straight and her eyes forward, watched as she tilted it toward her lips, as a cockroach skittered across the floor and the sound of trucks and music blared in the distance, watched as she lowered her cup and dabbed her lips with her woven napkin, and then as the idiotic discordance of the moment shattered with the cool lilt of her voice.

"I would like to tell you a story," she said. "But first we must decide whether or not you owe me."

"Yes, I owe you," Ethan answered.

"Good. Then the question is, what do you owe me?"

"My life, apparently. And breakfast."

She smiled and her voice changed, the accent thinning out. A voice devoid of coyness.

"The next thing to decide, then, is how to repay that debt."

"I'll make lunch," he said.

"First," she said, and smiled, and did not change her tone, "you will shut the fuck up and listen."

YOLANDA WAS BORN ON Santa Maria, an island off the Copalan coast in the Caribbean Sea. To the north there was nothing but the island-flecked ocean stretching on toward America, far beyond thought or comprehension; to the east lay more islands, Hispaniola, Cuba, the British and French territories; and to the west, past the wreck reefs and island cayes, hung the Copalan mainland, the mainland and her father's adopted country, a country to which he hoped never to return.

"Why wouldn't he go back?" Ethan asked.

Yolanda raised and lowered her glass, wiped her lips with her wrist, and again forked stray hair from her face. "Can't you just listen?"

Yolanda's father appeared on the island one day in a motorboat. He had no possessions and his shirt was shredded. When Marietta, her mother, saw him first—she was on her way to gather coconuts on the shore—she thought him some kind of wild man, a bootlegger, maybe, or smuggler. His hair flared out in a black mane, his beard was overgrown and tangled. He didn't anchor his boat. It washed toward the shallows, scraped over the reef, and when it was close enough to shore, past the coral shoal and the rock breaks, he dove overboard and swam to the beach.

She stood on the shore and watched him. Her mother had warned her about such men, had told her stories of pirates and guerrillas, mad men living in the mountains. The island was safe, her mother had always told her, but the mainland was different. On the mainland there was war and famine and pestilence. People were desperate. She watched him swim over the waves. At first he moved in a dark shadow through the water, like a shark. But he didn't swim as well as an islander, and he was gasping and churning up froth with his feet by the time he reached the shallows. The surface of the sea glinted under the hard afternoon light. There was no wind and the birds stopped their calling, it seemed, as he rose from the water. Yolanda's mother remembered this, this was how she always told it. The world went silent and still and he climbed up onto the beach and approached her. He approached her and she did not run. She was almost twenty; she held an armful of coconuts against her breasts; she stood staring. Several times before, when she was a little girl, her mother had brought her to the mainland, and she remembered parrots and old cars, loud music, the smell of food frying in outdoor kitchens. She did not remember dangerous men. He stumbled up the shore and stood before her. He ran his hand—this part Ethan thinks he might have imagined—though his drenched hair.

"Please, miss. May I have some water?"

She continued to stare. Oyster shells flecked like fragments of purple ceramics through his beard. On his right side his wasted shirt stuck slicked to his skin with blood.

Again, he asked for water.

She nodded down at her armful of coconuts.

"This is all I have with me."

"You must live near here. You could not walk so far with those cocos."

His voice came little louder than a whisper, raspy and dry like an old man's. Her machete lay sticky with coco juice at her feet and her arms were full, but he looked weak and tired. His side still seeped blood.

"You should not have swum leaking blood," she said. "The sea is full of sharks."

"We are not so afraid of sharks where I come from."

"The way you swim, you should be."

He laughed then, or smiled and opened his mouth and tried to laugh but could not for the dryness in his throat.

"If I carry those cocos for you, will that buy me some water?"

"We will see," she said, and let the coconuts fall to the sand and turned her back and put her hands on her cocked hips like the mothers in the market always did. "It depends on whether you can walk better than you can swim."

They were married two months later, Marietta and Camillo, two miles from the beach where they met. Her parents strung the breadfruit trees outside their house with lights and the town gathered in the old Spanish plaza. Camillo had no family on the island so he walked with her father and her father's brothers to the colonial chapel. He wore one of her father's white cotton Sunday suits, and as they went people cheered through open windows, whistled from the street corners and began to follow them. It was a mile and a half from her parents' house on the beach to the Spanish plaza, but they walked the whole way, and as they did more people joined and walked with them.

The Spanish, when they first came there, had laid the town center on a wide, flat plateau that the Indians had cleared for failed plantings. Eventually the rest of the town had been built on the mountainsides below the plaza, and the road from the beach was narrow and steep. What cars there were on the island back then could barely fit on both sides, and as they progressed, Camillo and her father's brothers, and then far behind them now, Marietta and her mother, the street filled with the crowd so that there was almost no space to move. People looking out their windows whistled and hissed and joined the procession. The road rose out of the low-lying tree break and into the cleared hills. It rose and rose and here the palm and clapboard pine homes gave way to pastel-painted stucco houses. For a while, still, the sea was visible; it flickered in coins of light through the spaces in the trees, and then it was gone—there was just the palm forest, the town, and beyond that the mountain jungle, dense and wetly green against the darkening horizon. Rain was coming, everyone could smell it. The heat was breaking fast and the sky darkened into a ripe, fish-gut purple. When the wind freshened, the fruiting vines that grew tangled about the town's few electric wires fluttered and dropped flowers over the gathering crowd.

The men reached the Spanish chapel. They closed the door and waited inside until Marietta appeared, wearing her mother's dress. Someone snapped a picture. Yolanda had seen it: her mother mounting the brick-cobbled stairs leading up to the chapel doors, wind held static in her hair and in her dress, and the air in the background going to lightning as a storm brewed, like the child she already carried, in the imminent distance.

Growing up, Yolanda knew little of her father's past. He was Colombian, originally, he told her, from Cartagena. In his youth he worked as a fish-

erman on the Caribbean coast just north of the Old City. Then he had
to leave. He fled north in a fishing skip with his brother. They reached
Copal on September fifteenth—Central American Independence Day,
a holiday fraught with wet season storms. It rained and rained. Water
poured down out of the mountains in makeshift rivers, waves rose and
broke over the seawall. The coconut carts and rum shacks that lined
the shore scuttled and drifted into the sea, the streets of the coastal city
were flooded. It was a strange first day in a new country, he told her.
As the rain bent the shade palms all along the waterfront almost to the
ground, they looked, Camillo thought, like frail field hands crippled
by toil. "I know it's strange," he said, "but that's what it seemed, that's
how I first saw that country, as a land of toil." And he turned out to
be correct.

Explosions sounded everywhere. Hundreds of them. Children
ran through the flooding streets holding bandoliers of fireworks and
matches above their heads. They couldn't find any dry ground to light
them on, so they set them off indoors on café tables, or scaled walls and
threw them from the tops of buildings. The wooden mansard roofs of
the summer houses and Victorian hotels caught fire and quickly went
out in the rain. The whole city burned and flooded and burned again.
Smoke drifted from the rooftops, clouds of hot steam hung above the
swamping streets. Everywhere the water continued to rise. A child
caked in mud wailed under a banyan tree as his friends scurried about,
trying to find the finger he'd blown into the water with fireworks.

They walked on, Camillo and his brother, and saw a horse, teth-
ered to an iron fence-post, floundering in the water. When they tried
to untie it someone shouted and pistol shots pocked the pooled water about their knees. They headed inland then, as fast as they could,
turned away from the coast and climbed the mountain roads, which in
the flood's wake were strewn with a drowned ocelot, a car door, uprooted scrub bushes and boulders washed free of the hills. Rivers of mud
swamped their path as the road rose and the ways grew lush and full
with mountain foliage. They walked all day while below them the city
burned and flooded; they dragged their bags through the mired lanes;
they wandered into the mountain's realms of solitude where children
with no shoes or shirts watched them from the cabins of burned-out
trucks and abandoned villages of stilt houses slid away, down the ra-

vines, in torrents of falling mud. In the far valleys, banana plantations wavered green and wet beneath the webbing of mist and Spanish moss on the higher hills. Here hung leaves as big as suitcases, flowers with petals as thick as a man's hand. That night they slept, covered by cut banana fronds, in the bed of a pickup truck. In the morning they crested the mountain and saw the sugar plantation spread into the distance against the thundercloud horizon, purple and still in the storm's windless aftermath.

"But why did you leave Cartagena in the first place?" Yolanda would ask. She had not yet looked for it on a map, but to her the name sounded majestic. Cartagena. The Old City. Cultured beyond her island imaginings.

"All the world is not as sweet as this island," he would say. "Now try your question in English."

Her father spoke English. When people asked him where he'd learned it, he'd say, "I don't know. Just something I picked up along the way." As if he were speaking of an old pair of shoes, the ability to wiggle your ears. *Along the way.* What way it was that forced him from Cartagena and then again from the plantation on the mainland he never told her. She knew just that one day he came to the island and met her mother on the shore.

"Darling," he'd say, "the mainland was no different than Colombia. There were the same injustices, the same sorrows. Never leave this island if you don't have to, and if you do, go far, far away."

On the island he worked, as he had in Colombia, as a fisherman. Before they were married, Marietta's father lent him money for a basic boat and gear, money that he paid back double within the first four months of marriage.

"I don't know, mon," he'd sometimes say in mock Cartagena Afro-English as he docked with his ridiculous haul. "Dese island fish be mighty trusting, dem."

He seemed touched by luck. Each day he'd haul like a man ladling from a cornucopia, as if the ocean were his own private bounty. He'd line bream and snapper, dive for conch and trap for crab and spiny lobster. Islanders begged to join him, to sign on as first mates or turtle spearers.

"No, no," he'd answer. "I'm not considering expanding. God hates pride and I've always loved turtles."

People began to talk in the village. Once another fisherman approached Marietta's father where he sat every evening at the coconut palm counter in the café.

"It's hard to imagine how a man as talented as that could become so destitute," he said. "Mother of God, he must have been in some trouble."

Marietta's father drank from his rum, forked a baby octopus from his plate, and said, "Did you know I'm expecting another grandchild?"

It was true. The family came quickly. A brother, Jose, followed Yolanda. They lived, all of them, on the shore not far from her grandparents' house. Yolanda learned to sail and swim and dive for conch with her brother. Some days after school, if her mother didn't need her about the house, she'd go down to the water and help her father unload his day's catch. There were no other girls at the docks. It was not a place most men would ever bring their daughters. But the fishermen respected Yolanda. She was Camillo's daughter, after all—Camillo, the man touched by the sea's bounty—and they could see in the way she dove for conch or swam with the boys in the lagoons on Sundays that she must carry in her blood some similar grace. Also, everyone soon agreed, she was a better cook than her mother. On holidays she served stews with octopus and garlic and fresh-caught crab in plantain flower bowls. Her early youth was as her father said it would be: sweet beyond most imaginings. Days passed in the coral wash of island sun, and at night, in the spring, when the currents moved in just beyond the windward passages, the forest canopy rustled under new wind and the air smelled like sea grapes and blossoming bougainvillea.

Her father began to catch less and less and then he was gone.

It started slowly: He'd go out on longer voyages, a day or sometimes two or three, longer anyway than seemed reasonable, and come back with half his usual fare. After a while the voyages grew even longer. He'd be gone a week at a time and come back with a necklace for Marietta from some distant port, someplace farther than you'd think his fishing boat could take him, books in English for Yolanda and Jose, but no fish at all. And then the typhoon struck while he was out at sea and they never saw him again.

Yolanda remembered rumors of squalls moving up the coast, small storms and flash floods, but nothing dire—just talk in the market and on the docks. No warnings came from the mainland and it was May anyway, too early for hurricanes. And then there was the day when the sky greened into oxidized copper and the temperature dropped and a thousand birds broke suddenly into the sky. Then it was just wind and the sound of wind, the world tearing itself apart as the lagoons emptied into the sea as if sucked through a straw, and the sea, then, rose up and lifted docked boats and dashed them against the boardwalk on waves dark with rent coral and river silt. The palm break on the windward shore uprooted to the air, the leaves of breadfruit trees screamed and tore against the wind, sand off the beach blew through the latticed windows of what few houses still stood.

Yolanda's grandparents did not survive the storm. The gale lifted and littered their house across the inland mangroves like the detritus of a shipwreck. In the days following the typhoon, Yolanda wandered the shore with her mother and her brother like travelers who find their destination sacked by barbarians. They walked and wandered, they wore no shoes and what clothes remained were tattered and muddy from digging for their grandparents' bodies in the flooded mangroves. They turned slow circles under the sad skeletons of still-standing trees. At night they burned bonfires on the shore, cooked what fish they could find. Every day they shoveled through the mangroves in the filthy marsh heat of the afternoon, where the dug clay writhed with the wattled iguanas that slunk out of the forest to scavenge the floating dead. Circling buzzards mottled the shore with their shadows and the town by the Spanish plaza lay deserted. Survivors swarmed to the jungle to collect windfall wood and fruit, and at night black howler monkeys no one had ever seen before clambered down to the shore and pillaged the beach camps. People spoke of aid missions that never came, or came to the other side of the island, or were seized by bandits. People spoke, for the first time, of guerrillas.

One afternoon Marietta found a canvas tarp for the children and they spent the rest of the day making camp, cutting and laying in stakes and digging a fire pit for the evening bonfire. They dug and cut, erected the tarp, and laid a circle wall of dried coral. When they were finished they were exhausted and hungry. They had no more drinkable water and the sky over the ocean had settled into a slow nectarine dusk. Everywhere fireflies flashed and the day's last light illuminated the distant whitecaps where the water broke on underwater shoals. Marietta and her children spent that night shivering into diarrhetic fever.

After three weeks, Yolanda said, two things happened on the same day: they gave up her father for lost, and Gabriel, one of his brothers whom they had never met before, arrived from the mainland. The official aid missions never made it to their side of the island, but Peace Corps volunteers had chartered a boat and filled it with clean water and what medical supplies they could find, and Gabriel came with them as a passenger. He appeared before them in the morning like a figure out of dream.

"You must accept it," Marietta had told the children while they cooked the last of their eggs on a wind-thrown scrap of tin. "Your father will not return."

For days they'd argued that perhaps he was safe but stranded at some mainland port, safe and waiting for a new boat or any other way to send word. But by then, by the third week and still no word, no sign of him or his boat, and her parents still not found, still lost in the mangroves, she said, "Children, my children, you must accept it, we must accept that he is gone."

And then there he was, this man who walked as Camillo walked, who loped and looked down at his feet and wore his beard short and close about his neck—a man coming to them through a shadebreak of sea grapes and broken palms, a man with the sun behind him, slicing the horizon into ribbons of wavering heat so that he seemed to tremble into form as he walked.

"Marietta," he said as he stepped into their camp through the smoke.

She looked up and did not speak and crossed herself as he stepped around the fire and put his hand on her shoulder and said it again, her name, and then told her his: "I am Gabriel, Camillo's older brother."

"Camillo is dead," Marietta said. Yolanda still, remembering it, this moment, does not know if she was asking or telling him.

"Yes, he is dead," Gabriel said. "In the typhoon."

"Are you sure? How do you know?" asked Jose.

"Yes, I am sure."

"But how do you know?"

He turned back to Marietta. Behind him the sky had settled into the dusty ochre of morning and the sea was the same color as the sky.

"You can come with me to Rio de Caña," he said. "You can find work there."

"How do you know my father is dead?" Jose said again.

"It is very easy to tell if a man is dead."

"I'm sorry," said Marietta, who had not been to the mainland since she was a little girl. "But this is my home. It is my children's home."

Gabriel waved his hand in the air. A general motion, a man passing benediction or condemnation.

"Look at this." He pointed now specifically—a monkey rooted through the shore's rubble, everywhere the smoke rose off scrub fires. "This is nobody's home anymore."

"No," Marietta said and turned her face that Ethan sees as Yolanda's away from the sun, away from Gabriel. "We will not go."

"Yes, you will. Of course you will. Please stop lying and start packing."

Jose, then, up and on his feet and raising their carved bamboo fish spear.

"My mother doesn't lie."

"Do not believe that. Even the best women lie. Especially when they don't know that you know what they know."

"And what is that?" said Marietta. A whisper now.

"There is no water or food here. And you are pregnant."

So they moved to mainland Copal, to Rio de Caña, the farming town in the basin between the mountains, the cane fields and the Rio Sulaco—the river that ran through the malarial jungle to the sea.

"You can imagine," Yolanda said to Ethan, "that my life had changed forever. I did not know it, but I had spent my life in paradise. And then came the hurricane and Gabriel and Rio de Caña, and nothing was the same again. After that it was toil in the fields from dawn to dusk. It was sunburn and starving nights. Look at my hands." She held them out to him. "It was calluses that will never heal."

"Are you sure your uncle was named Gabriel and not Michael?" Ethan asked.

Yolanda withdrew her hands from his sight.

"Your shame makes you very ugly," she said.

"I'm sorry," Ethan said and poured more rum. "It's just that I've heard this story before. It's just that something's wrong with me."

"And you think that means anything?" Yolanda said. "Step outside. Look around you. Everything is wrong with everybody here."

Her sister, Mirabelle, her missing father's last child, was born during their first spring in de Caña.

"My sister was different," Yolanda said. "She was special somehow. Our mother died giving birth, but Mirabelle never cried, and she did not stop growing even though she had little milk and less formula."

When they ran out of formula, they filled her bottle with Coca-Cola. As Mirabelle grew, several things became apparent: the first was that she did not have the constitution for field work, and the second was that she was exceedingly intelligent. Gifted, maybe. Gabriel taught her English, and she learned it quickly, far more quickly than either of her siblings.

"This girl is different," he said to Yolanda. "Maybe she is blessed. But I wish she would sleep through the night."

It was true. Mirabelle did not sleep. As a baby, even after her mother died and they had no milk to nurse her on, she slept fine, but as she grew so did her insomnia. Every night, in the hours past midnight, she'd wake sweating and crying, troubled by dreams and the memory of dreams. Yolanda held her, the shaken girl, as she rocked into waking. And when Mirabelle woke, the whole house woke with her. They lived in a former boathouse, a two-room, concrete-and-stucco rectangle perched on the bank of the Rio Sulaco. From the house to the cane fields it was a mile and a half, and work began at dawn. If you didn't report to the cane on time you lost the entire day's wages. There were not enough hours in the night as it was.

Finally, Gabriel reached the end of his tether. That was the expression Yolanda used, and when she did, Ethan stopped her, smiled and wiped his forehead, tried to appear something other than demented.

"Where did you learn that?" he asked. *The end of his tether*—it sounded so English, it sounded performed, and again he wondered how many people she had told this story.

She shrugged and said, "In a book, I guess, I don't know."

He watched her then, watched as something, worry or uncertainty, began forming in her expression. It came like a hardening, a contracting. Her cheeks drew in, tautened, her brow furrowed. Her eyes—he found, he could not meet her eyes.

"It is the right expression, this one, yes—the end of his tether?" she asked.

Ethan nodded. "Yeah. It's right on the money."

So Gabriel built them—Mirabelle, and by default Yolanda—a hovel of cratewood and galvanized tin down below the boathouse on the soft bank of the river. They lived there together through the heat of summer and the floods of autumn. Mirabelle woke every night, and every night Yolanda woke with her and held her and told her stories of the island where she was conceived and of their mother, Marietta, a woman Mirabelle had never known. Yolanda held her and told her how their mother met their father, how he once brought back a barrel of fifteen octopi from the reefs and filled their bed with them. She told her how their mother laughed, laughed a way Yolanda did not ever laugh, and screamed and chased him around the house swinging a still-squirming octopus like a weapon. They spent nights that passed like that into years: Yolanda returning home from the cane and waking when Mirabelle woke and telling her stories and rocking her through the winds and weird cries off the river.

And then Gabriel, who was nothing like their father, except that he walked as their father had and wore his beard as their father had, disappeared. In this way too he was like Camillo. One day he woke before the others and set out in the fleeing hours when the horizon wavered with the reflection of light on the other side of the mountains, light that had not yet risen but would rise soon. He set out in the hours where the dark clouds cracked like a black pot breaking into white ceramic shards, the same hours when Mirabelle was born and Marietta had died, in those hours of light announcing light, Gabriel, their father's brother, stepped out into the world, walked away from the river, toward the fields, and was gone.

Just the three of them remained: Yolanda and Mirabelle and Jose, fending for themselves in de Caña. Yolanda said it again: "My sister is different, she could not work the cane or the river, she did not have the constitution for it," and Ethan saw a child out of a Victorian novel, a frail willowy thing taking walks in the country with her governess, coughing into a bloodstained handkerchief, coughing and gagging as his hands held her hair back and the bottle of cough syrup clattered into the bathroom sink.

Yolanda left de Caña after Jose was macheted in the street. They killed him for no reason, or none that she could tell. As far as she knew, he stopped at the cantina after work and drank guaro with his friends. There was no fight or argument. No one was insulted. He was cut down in the street on his way home. She tried and tried but there was no way to reconcile herself to what had happened. Her father's death, her mother's, and now her brother's—a whole world of loss rupturing into her life. A freak storm strikes, a child of unusual difficulty is born into the septic tropical night, her brother's arms are hacked from his body—there was nowhere to place it, no way to conceive of a world of such violent possibility. There comes a point, she said to Ethan, when something happens and the world changes and then nothing will ever be the same. If I'd stayed I would have died. So I left. I left my sister to the care of the nuns at Qultepe and took a river boat inland to the Guatemalan border from where, I was sure, I would find my way to the States.

What she did find as she traveled north was far different. She reached the Suchiate river in northeastern Guatemala. To make it to the States, she first had to make it to Mexico; to make it to Mexico, she had to cross the river in the night and live till morning. Once across the river there were two routes to the border: the north route or the northeast route. If she chose the north route, she could follow the train tracks, hop on the back of the Transamerica Bullet and let it carry her into, and through, Mexico. The dangers here were clear: if one fell asleep, and many did, she would slip between the cars and onto the tracks, and even if she managed to stay awake, border guards and policía looking for bribes haunted the platforms where the train stopped. Still, for a woman traveling alone, this was the preferable route. The northeastern paths toward Hidalgo and Tabasco passed through the City of Martyrs, a makeshift border settlement where, while there was no train and few police, bandits patrolled the paths between the shore and the border.

Yolanda reached the bank of the Suchiate after a week-long trip north and east away from de Caña and the Caribbean coast, out of Copal and through Guatemala. It was dusk. She stripped and bathed in the river. She cleaned her clothes. Across the water, the rocky bank descended from a lush curtain of low jungle extending several miles into the fogbank that rolled down from the mountain horizon. Somewhere short of the mountains, invisible behind the fog and the jungle, lay the City of Martyrs, the migrant's port of call, where she could find fresh clothes, Mexican currency, and a safe bed to sleep in. It would not be easy to reach. The river was wide and fast-flowing after months of rain, and even if she could swim it, to do so would make her instantly recognizable as a migrant when she reached the far bank. Mexican bandits and ferryman and border guards looking for bribes or worse spotted migrants by the disrepair of their clothes.

So Yolanda wrapped herself in a blanket and waited in the shadow of the low gum leaves for her things to dry. After she dressed, she sprinkled her hair with rose water she had bought for Mirabelle several years earlier, applied what makeup she had, and put on a surgical mask and unworn platform shoes. She hoped that whoever waited on the other side—the ferryman, the guards, bandits and street hawkers—would take her for a Mexican woman running errands in Guatemala.

She set out for one of the many raft launches. The sun had fallen and the lights appeared on the far shore, blinking between the trees like the moving lanterns of phantom guides. In the stories she had been told as a child, to follow the lights through the jungles was to follow the Duende—the spirit that lured children into the forest. But she was not her little sister, she was not afraid of spirits and did not believe in stories, and she knew as she watched the lights flashing out of the crooked coves of shadowed trees that she was drawn to them, that she would cross the river and move toward the lights the way the fishermen on her island followed stars, or the way the fish themselves rose toward the lure of the reed lanterns rocking below waiting spears. So be it.

Yolanda forced herself to look away from the lights on the far bank. The water of the Suchiate, always murky and silt-brown by day, had settled into a hard, stony blue. A blue of quarried rock or a pigeon's breast—a blue so unlike the Caribbean waters of her youth that it seemed a different color altogether. In her days she had moved from the waters of paradise to life on a river, quite literally, of hardship. Now standing at this third water, she thought perhaps she was again entering a new life, heading into some new, charmed future.

The ferryman, when she reached him, was sniffing glue. He sat against the pylons to which his raft was moored and buried his face in a rag. He inhaled deeply, trembled and coughed and inhaled again. He let his hand fall to his side where it opened and closed about the rag like a weak pulsing heart. When she stepped into the clearing he raised his head vertebrae by vertebrae and glared at her through a web of fraught veins. His eyes lolled. He blinked and blinked and smiled.

"Good evening, miss. You are the most beautiful woman I've seen all day," he said.

She didn't doubt it. Water weeds strung his hair, a wet, red glue rash flowered around his mouth and nose, saliva seeped down his chin, and his clothes—a McDonald's shirt and a pair of jeans cuffed several times to reach above his ankles—were soiled with water and silt. It looked like he had spent most of his day huffing glue and falling into the river.

"Do you cross the river at night?" Yolanda asked him.

He shook his head and then began to nod.

"No. Never. Not even once. It is very dangerous. There are rocks and whirlpools and tree roots and crocodiles. It is the most dangerous river in the world."

She smiled, brushed a stray strand of hair behind her ear.

"Will you cross it for me? It is not quite dark."

"Of course I will," he said and tried to stand. "Get on."

Yolanda sat and held her bag in her lap as the ferryman punted. The raft was not large, a plank of cratewood tied to two connected inner tubes. It bobbed on the current and dipped under his weight as he worked his punting pole through the water. She wondered how he could stand in his state, and then thought that perhaps, through some strange symbiosis of man and current and glue, the waters braced the pole and the pole balanced the man and together they jerked on in oblique angles toward the distant shore.

"Did you know, miss, you look just like my daughter?" he said.

Yolanda shook her head. In the dark, with his back to her and the sound of the water breaking all around, he could not see or hear her reaction. It didn't matter.

"Yes," he went on, punting, leaning, punting again. "You could be my daughter. She was very beautiful. Chubby and short like her mother."

Yolanda tried to laugh. She was not chubby nor short and she thought, at first, that he was teasing her.

"Yes," he said again. "Beautiful. I miss my daughter very much."

He was not joking. Perhaps he had not seen her at all. Who knew what he could see through the glue haze and darkness and whatever else clouded his way over the river? Yolanda did not say anything. She watched the northern bank drift closer. There were more lights now between the trees, and sounds came, broken and distant, of cars and motored rickshaws. She would not ask him what happened to his daughter. He had his glue and his raft. She had the far bank, the Mexican border, and beyond. What should they do? Weep together? Tell each other sad stories? Huff aerosol vapors from a rag? The shore grew closer. The ferryman farted once and then laughed through tears. Yolanda touched her hair and then smelled the scent of rosewater and oil, her sister's smell, on her fingers. She touched and smelled and touched again and held her hands close about her face. The raft scuffed against the rocky shallows. A bird screamed from the wooded shore. She gathered her bag and began to stand. The raft rocked. The scraping pole. The waiting lights. The jungle.

She knew something was wrong when she broke into the clearing and saw the tree. At first she thought all the white pouches hanging from the branches were some form of chrysalis or cocoon, and then, when she drew closer, she felt relieved—it was nothing strange, just a tree where someone had hung her laundry, where many people had, a whole tree strung with laundry, a village's worth, puffing in the wind. It troubled her, though, it was wrong, everything leading to the grove—the mud path away from shore, the empty, silent jungle, and the cleared area where the tree stood heavy with laundry—it all seemed to condense into a new, sudden dread. Then she realized what had bothered her: it was all women's underwear and it was far from clean. The tree was a display, a trophy case. She turned to run but by then the circle had already formed.

This is where Ethan has trouble—where, on the bus ride away from Yolanda and out of Mexico, he finds himself running aground again and again. He can see the men's faces, all of them the same and Yolanda not Yolanda at all, but a shadow or less than that, a life disappearing around the edge of a closing door. What bothers him is that he does not feel outrage, he does not wonder at a world where women's panties are hung as trophies from a breadfruit tree. He sees it almost as something inevitable, the punch line to the world's worst joke. He thinks he should nod his head, mouth *of course*, and move on, away from it and back into a city where he will raise his camera, snap some picture, something easy and old, on black-and-white film, something that he will overexpose, bare to more and more light, until there are no shadows or lines—everything burning back to white.

Does it bother him that they did not rape her? Because in his mind they do, and he doesn't know what that means. It's the same every time, the sudden twitch toward violence and Yolanda, maybe, bent across a tree stump, its wood hardening to metal under her skin, the lantern light flickering into a neon exit sign and the huddled rats, surprised, spreading out like bubbles of mercury rebounding away from a shattered thermometer.

What he cannot imagine is what she told him actually happened: the three men, different men, stepping out of the brush, firing pistols into the gang, shouting and firing and filling the air with smoke that, when it clears, leaves Yolanda alone, but for them—saved. Ethan cannot imagine this at all. The sudden heroism, its perfect timing. The knights in the forest, the rescued maiden. It's unfair, impossible, and he cannot see it.

What he can see, though, is what happens next, the way they tell Yolanda who they are—coyotes—how they saw her cross the river and knew her for a migrant, how they followed her and saved her from certain rape and probable death, and now will be willing to escort her to the United States for the right price.

At this point, with the panic still pulsing beneath her skin and the metallic ghost of cordite and blood scenting the wind, she can do nothing but shake her head, *no*, and try to move on, but one of them, maybe the leader—Ethan imagines him as smaller, pocked face, a bandana, but he does not know—here Yolanda is brief, undetailed, cursory—blocks her way with his body, he smiles.

"Haven't you seen, miss, the dangers that lurk here? How will you cross the border? How will you make it to the States?"

There is, of course, a threat here. She is alone in the grove with three men. They have guns and they have used them. She looks back over her shoulder toward the road to the river, beyond it the river itself and all the paths that led her away from home to this clearing. The sounds of the border town grow louder with the approaching dawn. The hotels are not far, the plantain carts and cantinas, the electric rickshaws. It doesn't matter.

"How much?" she asks.

He names his price. It is expensive, but not prohibitive. She speaks English and there will be work in the States.

She nods. She goes with them.

Yolanda stopped there and refilled her glass and nodded at his. Ethan covered it with his hand.

"You should have known," he said. "It's the same scam every time."

He waited for anger to shoal in her eyes, for her to react the way Samantha would. Yolanda shrugged again, reached for the pitcher and poured some water into her rum.

"What choice did I have?" she said. "I went with them. At first it seemed like a good idea. They had already paid their bribes and we crossed into Mexico easily. We spent a week traveling east toward the sea. When we reached the coast there was a boat waiting, a cargo ship. They told me that it would ferry me to Miami."

Ethan watched Yolanda as she spoke, the way her mouth opened easily around her story, the flatness of her expression. He found himself thinking, if I were to photograph her, what would I see? There'd be so little there—drawn lips, eyes of cut marble. He'd need a catchlight flashing on her iris, sparkling in some lucent expression of pleasure— he'd have to fake the emotion. How different she must be now from the woman who followed coyotes onto a boat. He almost couldn't imagine it. But then, of course, he remembered the way that, after that night, Samantha's life seemed to slide from her like a snake from its skin. So no, it was not impossible—Yolanda's lack of expression or the way they

loaded her onto the boat and led her down into the cargo hold, unbolt-
ed the door, pushed her in and, of course, by that time, by the time she
could see all the other women huddled there in the hold, recoiling like
insects at the sudden light and then clamoring toward the open door,
the fresh air there and the chance, however vain, of escape—by that
time, it was all too late.

Five nights, then, spent in darkness. Perfect darkness. Darkness
darker than the developing room, darkness as a real thing, a solid, a
body bearing down on you, something you could cling to: the moaning of girls, some no older than twelve or thirteen, the mold smell and
urine smell and shit smell, the sloshing waste, the one small hole for air.

On the sixth day they opened the doors to the hold and one by one
led the women to the deck. At first, Yolanda said, she could not see.
The light flared on her eyes and blossomed, when she covered them, in
painful tracers. She could not open her eyes. The women around her
could not open theirs. The men seemed content to wait. This was a bad
sign. If they were docked in a U.S. port, they wouldn't let the women
writhe about there on the deck, wailing over their eyes. Yolanda knew
that she would not like what was waiting for her.

When her vision adjusted, she saw that they were still some distance out to sea, not docked after all, but floating two or three hundred
yards from a bare coastline of red crags and wispy shore grasses. The
earth between the rocks and the weeds was a dusty ochre, as was the sky
beyond it, stretching into the horizon. This was not Miami.

"Look there," one of the coyotes said, and pointed into the eastern
distance where, perched atop a cliff, an American flag flapped on an
isolated flagpole.

"See that flag?" he said. "Savor it, chicas. Because this is as close
as you are getting to the States until you pay off the rest of your debt."

"What debt?" one of the girls said. "We paid already."

Yolanda knew better than to argue. She'd been tricked and trapped
and there wasn't anything else to say. This wasn't a legitimate negotia-
tion, not a price you could barter down.

Still, the coyote affected the attitude of a legitimate businessman.

"You paid us for the bribes into Mexico, but what about food? And
petrol for this tanker? And bribes for the port guards? And the risk we
took? Those costs, too, must be covered."

Ethan stopped her there. He didn't need the rest. As he'd said before, it was a classic scam and he knew how it went. How they were
sold into prostitution for a certain amount of time, six months, say, to
pay off their debt, but at the end of that time they had, without knowing it, incurred new debts—housing or food or corner space, it didn't
matter. The cycle began again. So it was about money. The whole long,
sad story. She wanted him to buy her out of slavery. He felt a sudden
relief. It didn't even matter if her story were true. He could pay his way
out of debt and guilt. It was so American and it was the easiest thing
in the world.

"How much do they want?" he asked.

"No, you don't understand," Yolanda said. "I need a lot more than
your money."

Apparently, she had already bought her way out of slavery.

"I saved my money," she said. "I made some deals. I treated certain
people very well. I have paid more than they can ask, but it's not supposed to work that way and they don't want to let me go. It would—
what's the expression—it would set a very bad precedent. On the other
hand, they like to pretend that it is a business, that they are simply
trying to recover their debts. It's important for morale. So they have
threatened me. They have sent a man, a very bad man, a slave trafficker
of the worst kind, after my sister. He will find her in Copal and tell her
he is bringing her to me in America, and she will go with him because
she is young and does not know much about the world, and they will
hold her as my collateral."

Ethan did not know what to say. The situation was bloated with
damage. He had stood at the window as the noodle vendor assembled his
cart in the street. He had watched Samantha twitch through sleep and
tried to staunch her dreams with a wet rag. In the end it hadn't mattered,
and he could not imagine what Yolanda might want from him.

"Wait," he said. "You met these men in Guatemala. How can they
know where your sister lives?"

He didn't know why he asked the question, or why the answer
mattered to him. Her situation was not that unusual and he believed
her. But as with everything, he thought one more piece might somehow provide a new perspective, the one sure road to action.

He wasn't really listening. It was something about letters, how when they first brought her there, to Boystown, they offered to mail her letters home for her, to fake American postal codes to help the women protect their honor with their families.

He held up his hand. Something was wrong here, the whole thing was losing dimension, falling into static, useless detail, white noise.

"What am I supposed to do?" he asked.

"This man they've sent after my sister is very dangerous," she said. "He is called Soto, and he is a child trafficker and a killer. I can do nothing to warn her. I cannot leave here. I cannot send word. You must go to Copal and find my sister before he does. It will not be hard. He has other charges and responsibilities. Then you must bring her to my mother's island, to Santa Maria. There is an abandoned house there, and in that house there is a U.S. passport. After that it will be simple. You must escort her to the United States."

"And then what?"

"And then nothing. Debt repaid."

She held her hands out, palms up, empty. A woman displaying the sudden lightness of an unshouldered burden.

"You want me to go to Copal?" he said.

She nodded and he tried to imagine it: the nightmare cities, the jungles, the seething panic. A perfect row of fire ants marched along the far wall. From somewhere distant or near, he couldn't tell, came the incessant electric hum of a refrigerator knelling the empty hours of a summer night.

"Someone has made a pretty serious mistake," Ethan said.

THE FEVER HIT THAT afternoon, after Yolanda finished telling her story. Ethan had felt its first febrile pulsings earlier but in his paranoia he had taken them, the trembling and sudden sweat, as a new chemical thirst. He remembered Samantha's aborted attempts to dry out in their final months together. He remembered holding her as she shuddered into sleep and waking later to the slick of her sweat on his skin and the sound of her in the bathroom, rooting through the medicine cabinet. So he had thought it would only be fitting that now he should be going through the same thing—fitting that his compassion, as it always did, should take its own turn toward ruin.

But it wasn't that. He poured and poured the rum as Yolanda spoke and the trembling did not subside. The heat in his face thickened to a clammy sweat. He touched his skin, he wiped his brow. He sweat as he shivered and the Virgin Mary on the wall doubled itself and hung then at intersecting forty-five-degree angles that seemed to blur and squirm where they converged with a pulsing cloud of swarming ants. Hard as he tried, he could not tell the real picture from the imagined one.

"I'm sick," he said to Yolanda, but Yolanda was not there. The chair across from him was empty and her glass was gone. He thought for a moment that it was night, that he had fallen asleep and was waking to an empty house. But it was not night. The pale light of the Mexican afternoon still lit the room. Slowly, he recognized a discomfort that he been spreading in him as Yolanda spoke. His bones ached, his fingers throbbed, and where his hair stood on his arms his pores burned.

"I'm sick," he said again.

"You said that already," Yolanda answered as she placed a glass of water on the table. She was behind him then. She touched his forehead. "You have a fever."

She stood before him now and the room rocked away toward the bead curtain and the hall. He held the arms of the chair and raised himself slowly to avoid falling through the room's listing shadows. She must have drugged him. Kidnappings were rampant in Mexico. They were all over the news. He staggered back against the wall and again started to scratch at his neck. A radio went on somewhere and people began to laugh.

"Samantha, you have a fever," he said.

"Who is Samantha?" Yolanda asked him from the radio.

He turned toward the sink. What he needed was to wash his face. He knew that fever was not a symptom of being drugged. The room, for a moment, ceased its tilting. He stood shivering against the sink in the prostitute's kitchen. There was no way he could go to Copal.

"You see, I can't do anything," he said.

He spent the afternoon in bed and Yolanda sat by him. He twisted through the fever's haptic thrashings—he sweat and then shivered, he dreamt that he was a sailor lashed to his ship's mast. He passed through green waters bordered by dry red rock. In the far distance a volcano puffed smoke over a glinting white city. The high sun scorched his chafed flesh, his bare shoulders and upturned eyes, and he found himself awake and tearing the sheet from his skin. Yolanda lay a cold rag on his brow and held him as the tide turned, and he was again a sailor, mast-bound and freezing, while the night came on over the ocean. When he did not sleep, when he woke to Yolanda in the bed beside him, he was frightened by how good it felt, her skin against his, how something in his body, broken now and released in the fever's delirium of fleshlessness, rose and craved her touch. She held him as he shook, she held him as he had held Samantha into their final nights.

In the cool of the morning, with the fever broken, Ethan woke alone in the bed to the sound of Yolanda chasing chickens in the walled courtyard. The room did not spin when he stood and dressed. He walked to the doorless threshold, stood there where the chamber opened to the rest of the house, and waited. Somewhere in the back pavilion, beyond the hall and the bead curtain, he could hear Yolanda swearing at the chickens. He wiped his face and looked down at his wrist where his watch should have been.

He had not brought his cell phone with him from New York. In the days after Samantha was committed, in the days he had decided to flee the city, his apartment and his life there, everything that resonated with failure, he had not packed much. He tossed two duffel bags full of clothes into his car, brought one camera, but left his computer and phone and address books in the apartment. He would come back for them, or he wouldn't. In the moment it didn't seem to matter, and he was struck as he drove away from it, his home and his marriage, how few items of sentimental value he owned. It didn't seem possible, it should be harder to abandon one's life—there should be more to lose.

The money helped, of course. Without her money the escape would be impossible, but it wasn't just that. He had lost Samantha already, lost her in one moment at the kitchen table, or a long time before that even. He felt as he drove, as nothing appeared in his rearview mirror, that he was not fleeing a life at all—he was simply fleeing Samantha. Nothing rose from the road behind him. There were no roiling clouds or white birds flying in strange formation. By then he knew how it was, what Samantha had always known: you need no signs beyond your scars. Your loss serves as portent to your future.

Now, as the world slowly solidified in the fever's aftermath, the airy confusion gave way to aching joints and a fleshy, almost alien heaviness in his hands, as if his whole body had lost, and was now regaining, circulation. He grabbed his camera, he tapped his ring on the wall, he tried to cough. Yolanda, somewhere just beyond him, fussed with chickens and whispered *motherfucker* in the yard.

When he found Yolanda she was on all fours with a chicken pinned between her knees. Ethan raised his camera and framed her there: Yolanda wearing jeans and a faded black Voltron t-shirt with her hair tied back under a blue bandana, a chicken braced between her legs and a butcher knife slung pirate-style through her belt.

She looked up and put her hand over her face and turned her head as far from him as she could without releasing the chicken.

"It's not on," Ethan said.

Yolanda dropped her hand and pulled the knife from her belt and said, "Come here, Ethan."

He slung the camera around his neck and stepped out into the walled courtyard. Husks of corn and dried chicken shit littered the ground. He was not wearing shoes. She flipped the knife with the same easy grace as she had folded the shawl and held it out, handle first.

"I think you should cut this chicken's throat," she said.

As a child, Ethan had slaughtered chickens on his grandfather's farm in New Hampshire. He remembered not liking it, the crunch of severing vertebrae, the first splash of blood on the stump, although years later his mother insisted that he did it with glee. Begged to, even. It was one of the many stories of his childhood that his mother had liked to tell that seemed to be about someone else, someone he never knew. Here, there was no stump and no axe.

"Would you like me to slaughter your livestock before or after I go to the worst country in the Americas to save your sister from slave traders?" he asked.

She did not smile or lower the knife.

"Please," she said. "I do not like to do it."

Later, as they ate the soup she made and he recalled the moment following the slaughter—the way she plucked two feathers from the thrashing chicken's wings and formed a cross with them on its back, the way she held it as it quieted and bled out onto the ground—he knew that she had lied, that she could have slit the chicken's throat as easily as she'd handed him the knife. He ate and she stood at the sink and watched him. After all this, he wondered, what did she see? And what would she do if, after she finished appraising him, freezing him in this moment—what would she do if she found him, as she inevitably must, wanting, incapable of her purposes?

"Are you feeling better?" she asked.

"I don't have a fever. My ribs don't hurt too much. If that's what you mean."

"That's what I mean."

He still did not know what time it was, but he knew that soon she would ask him to leave. He worked the spoon through the last of the soup in his bowl but did not raise it. When the bottle broke across Javier's face Ethan had seen a flash of exposed bone, if that were possible.

"Why did you make me slaughter that chicken?" he asked. "You could have done it."

Yolanda did not move from the sink. She reached up to touch her hair and found her bandana. She flattened it against her head.

"You spent the night crying," she said. "The night before that you pissed in my sink and crawled through a sewer. Sometimes, I think it is good to let a man be a man."

Yolanda pulled off her bandana and put her hair up with a blue elastic. She was strikingly unadorned: wearing jeans and a twenty-year-old t-shirt, hair up, her face unmasked by makeup. It would have been easier to deny the alluring stranger who'd approached him in the brothel, but she had stripped that artifice from herself and stood before him now as a woman of his own age, tired, wracked by misfortunes of fate and class and geography. She wanted him to save an innocent girl from a similar fate. Such opportunities did not come often. The urge for redemption was not usually packaged with a chance to be satisfied. Many would call this a blessing.

"You are married?" she said.

"I was."

"You still wear the ring. I think when I met you I could tell you were a man of great devotion."

There was a sound coming from his mouth that might have been laughter. Outside of this house, another day turned toward noon, and he knew that in a moment he would be heading out into it, drawn by whatever gravity governed his journey south. Another decision made by circumstance, without his consent.

Yolanda touched his cheek and he could smell the dander of chicken feathers on her hands. She stood at the bead curtain and watched him.

"I hope your sister is a lot like you," he said.

"I don't," Yolanda said, and stepped into the hallway.

When she returned she was arrayed in the vestments of the night. Her hair was down and dark blue eyeliner shadowed her eyes into grottos. In this new garb she appraised him coolly, as a fury might, to see if he would be worthy of her efforts.

"I didn't intend any offense," he said. "It's just that I like you."

She went to the doorway and opened it, waited there. He realized that he was supposed to stand and follow her into the heat.

"That's nice," she said. "But it doesn't matter. You may not always like me, but you will always owe me."

"My camera is broken," he said.

"That's for the best. You will not want it where you are going."

"I need new clothes."

"Ethan," she said, "it's time to go. Are you coming?"

He looked out the door and considered Copal. He had been there several times to visit Doyle and had never liked it. The interior was a jungled basin of old volcanoes; the jungles gave way to dry forests, valleys, and rotten beaches. The cities were vast and sprawling and teeming with a growing presence of Mara Salvatrucha; the police were ridiculously uniformed, psychopathic survivors of the contras or Indian children drafted out of the mountains. It was a hot and weird country. Stripped of industry and infrastructure, its villages were shabby and collapsing, and it seemed a place without history, or a history only of dread. Unlike in Honduras, Guatemala, or Belize, here the Mayan temples in the forest were treated as if they were cursed. They crumbled into ransacked heaps in the jungle. Doyle had chosen it for his own private trip into ruin and Ethan had long decided that he never wanted to go there again.

Yolanda still stood at the door. There were children in the street. A light, opaque and milky as almond syrup, spread between the houses. Yolanda said his name and said it again. He reached out and lifted his broken camera, framed her there in the doorway. It would not focus. She was waiting for his answer.

Later, after the bus trip west out of town, a ferry ride and then another bus through the country and across the border; after the city's red roads opened to hills and shacks rigged of clapboard pine, cola signs, and leaning sheets of tin that trembled and twanged against the wind's gusts in some melancholy choir; after the descent through bare mountains where horses grazed on weeds by the side of the road and children from what few towns there were hawked their wares of warm coconut milk and bags of sweet water to the bus's diminishing silhouette; after the border crossing through ways suddenly lush and wild with shadow-dappled banana groves, warm wounds of blossoming bougainvillea, and the jagged towers of Mayan pyramids rising in the far distance above the jungle canopy; and then after that all gave way to the mountain city, damp and hot and trembling with music and the shouts of street hawkers and truck engines rumbling between gears and the air thick with diesel fumes and blown dust and insects and the briny smell off the tepid bay; after that and the next bus ride and the next border crossing and the first night in the colonial hotel and his call to Paolo, and everyone—Paolo, the hotel clerk, the detective who drove him through the dark—asked him the same question: *what are you doing here?*; after that and many nights more, Ethan remembered Yolanda's story, played it again and again in his head until it was like a mantra, a legend he could repeat to himself as if it were his own, as he headed out into ways unknown with something, for the first time in months, like purpose.

Ethan moved, those first days, with the pilgrim's steady somnambulism. His fever rose again during the trip out of Mexico, and his last night in Guatemala unfolded on its wavelength: the strung-out Marine and coyote attack, the coconut woman selling fake and gruesome relics. In the morning the fever broke and another bus came, and when he boarded it he was surprised to see that it was almost full.

The border crossing into Guatemala had been easy: there was no paperwork even if there should have been and it took less than an hour. The crossing into Copal, though, as always, was an exercise in chaos. For three hours the bus waited in a line no longer than fifty yards. Then, when it reached the border, soldiers poured into the cabin and ordered everybody out. Bags were grabbed and opened, clothes tossed in the road, a chicken escaped from its cage and began running for the border. A soldier chased it down and pounded it into the ground with the butt of his rifle. The rifle went off. People began to shout. The embarrassed soldier continued crushing the dead chicken for some time.

To cross the border, Ethan had to pass through a sort of airplane hangar where, while there were at least twenty officials milling about, listening to the radio or drinking coffee, there were only two active lines. Still, because there was no reason for anybody to go to Copal, the lines were short, and after thirty minutes Ethan reached the customs agent. The agent sat at a card table arrayed with five separate piles of papers, seven different stamps of official character, a pistol, and a bottle of Honduran beer. Sweat stains soiled his khaki uniform, but his brass buttons were polished. Behind him, out through the swinging metal doors, a clamor rose from the Copalan side of the border. Ethan wiped his face with his sleeve. He could not make himself understood. There were forms to fill out and the forms were incomprehensible. The guard peered at Ethan's handwriting. Dónde? he said again and again. Ethan invented an address for himself in the capital, the guard corrected his spelling and then stamped over the address with a red rubber stamp so that nothing could be read anyway.

The soldiers guarding the far door were still children, kids with bowl haircuts draped in uniforms that were far too big for them, that ballooned at the shoulders, reached past their fingers, covered up their shoddy boots. They showed Ethan their teeth as he passed. They all carried several guns. From somewhere overhead there was a snap and then a low, sighing buzz, like a passing flight of locusts, and the power in the hangar failed as Ethan reached the far exit. The guards threw open the gate to let light in and the throng of waiting Copalans on the other side rushed forward. The soldier-children began to shout and fire their guns into the roof and Ethan stepped out into it, the sudden clamor, the pandemonium of the street that disappeared immediately under the hundred hawkers' tables, the clouds of diesel smoke and hands grabbing at his arms, children selling melons and gum and cabbages, men shouting *taxi, taxi,* the migrants, surgical masks pressed to their faces, charging the border, falling and tangling themselves in the razor-wire security ditches, wrenching themselves free, and scrambling toward the airplane hangar, bleeding and shouting and holding their passports over their heads, giving their skin to flee the country Ethan now entered—Copal.

Somehow Ethan found the bus station, boarded another bus where everyone wore surgical masks—there were often rumors of some new flu—and waited as the bus turned away from the border and into the landscape suddenly green and silent, improbably flowered. As they crested hills or rode the mountain ridges, he stared down at the tips of Mayan pyramids above the jungle. He could imagine the wreckage of the bus moldering there at the base of those pyramids, unnoticed, scavenged by jaguars. The bus began to descend. They turned toward the sea and Mara de Leon.

His first night in Copal he spent in the heart of the city, just north of the docks, in the Port of the Duke Hotel. He arrived with one bag, with his clothes smelling of the bus, carrying no camera for the first time in years. He buzzed the outer door and waited for it to open, waited, and when it did, he stepped into the marble-floored lobby and then waited for the clerk to look back up from her ledger. He approached the desk but did not speak because he did not know what language to address her in. Here, on the northeast coast, they spoke Spanish and English, Indian and Creole—all, if he even recognized them, in dialects he could not follow. He waited and inspected the lobby so as to seem that he was not waiting—and then waited some more. Slowly, after a time, he placed his hands on the counter. The marble was wet with a warm film of condensation, but he did not draw his hands back, did not wipe them, as he wanted to, on his jeans. The room smelled like disinfectant and mold and fried fish. Above him an electric fan cut a slow circle in the stale air. In the corner, by the wide staircase, a potted palm tree drooped brown bug-eaten fronds toward the floor. Farther back, down the hall and across the terrace, he could hear the static burr of a radio from the hotel bar.

IN THE MORNING, ETHAN sits on the bed and looks out through the window's wooden louvers. There's nothing to see. Green ocean sloshing up against the shore, fishing boats in the far distance. Everywhere, even from within the hotel, cocks scream. Ethan stands and puts on his shoes and then realizes that he didn't remember to check them for insects. He waits a moment. If there'd been a scorpion he'd know it by now.

He pulls the fan chord but the fan doesn't do much. It spins and clatters and doesn't look like its bolts will hold and the room remains hot. He unlocks the slatted folding wooden doors and steps out onto the balcony. Now he can see the streets that lead down to the boardwalk, the red tile roofs, the sickly palms and the white haze on the western horizon. He smells coffee from downstairs, a bell rings in the maid's quarters. Yolanda had sat on the chair in her kitchen and put her hair down. Ethan remembers the way she watched him, her eyes suddenly wide like a child begging to be believed. He remembers the way she spoke: slowly, as you might, in a different world, tell a story around a campfire. Rehearsed and careful, whispered first to herself, voiced to the empty hours. *Please*, she'd said. *It is important that you understand how things were.*

The phrase echoed back from the last year of his life. Always, he'd begged Samantha to explain herself to him. To allow him to understand. As if once he comprehended all the pieces of their lives he could scoop them up and rematch and compile them, reframe them into whatever form they'd been lacking. Life reduced to an exercise in composition. So he'd say to her, *let me understand*. He'd say it when he'd find her alone at home, drinking and drawing the same pictures she always drew, the ones of the little girl lost among the wolves in the dark forest, the falling sun throwing the huntsman's shadow across the piney floor. Or, if he could, if he could say anything, he'd say it on the mornings following the nights when she didn't come home at all.

Samantha spent a day and a half in the hospital. When she came home she was wearing the clothes Ethan brought her—a blue button-up work shirt, cargo jeans—baggy clothes, her favorite clothes to wear around the house. She said, "I don't feel safe here anymore."

"Don't worry," Ethan said. "We have a doorman."

He was staring out the window, but he heard her walk into the kitchen, stop at the doorway.

"I'm just telling you how I feel," Samantha said. "Is there something wrong with that?"

He heard the freezer open, ice clink into a glass. The glug in the bottle of poured liquor like the sound of a car filling with water, the air pocket escaping.

That night when they went to bed he kissed her on the forehead and tucked the covers up tightly around her as he would a little child. He slept as far to the edge of the mattress as he could.

"I'm right here, Sam," he said.

She woke in the night, shaking. They had rolled closer to each other in their sleep. Her pillow was wet and her feet had pulled all the sheets from the corners of the bed.

"I wake up," she said, "and I think you're him."

"You think I'm him?" said Ethan.

"For a moment, when I wake up, I can't tell the difference."

Ethan tried not to wonder what difference she had seen in the bar.

"I'll sleep on the couch," he said.

"You don't mind?"

He pulled her hair back away from her face and kissed her forehead, her temple.

"I'll be right here if you need me."

That night, Ethan slept with the blinds to the balcony door wide open. He did not sleep for long. The lights of the city blurred through the glass in the smoky purple of an underground bar. He saw Samantha sitting at the table, the light, the frail, chemical light, bruising the Cosmo in her glass, and her fingers curled around the stem, lifting it to her mouth, her mouth barely opening and then in another second she's standing, touching the man's hand as she leaves, walking to the door the way she always walks—without looking back.

From the couch he heard her twitching into a dream from which he knew he could not wake her. He lay there and listened and stood and went to the threshold of their bedroom and watched her and closed his eyes and heard as if from a great distance, as if coming through a bad phone line, someone opening and closing doors, opening and closing them while Samantha shuddered in her sleep, shuddered and moaned as he stepped into the room and reached for her but stopped his hand short of her skin, stopped his hand and closed his eyes as her teeth chattered like something crackling on an empty line.

EVENING. ETHAN'S SECOND NIGHT in Mara de Leon. A breeze off the sea through his slatted windows. Gone now the continuous revving of trucks—just music starting up in the discos on the shore, and farther back, behind the hotel and the winding, rising streets of shotgun houses and plywood slums, the incessant insect drone of the jungle humming into night. Ethan watches the last reflected light recede over the water until it is just a thin line, a vein of sandstone, on the horizon. The sudden adrenaline of purpose is waning. He's lost here, in this country; he realizes this. It seems such a perfect, simple thing that he must do, but he's come to know the impotence of hopeless charity. *Samantha. Samantha.* He says her name until it means nothing, until its syllables echo hollowly about the small, warm room. Outside, past the descending rows of sloping red tile roofs, a lone tug chugs and glints on the metallic waves. The clock tower in the cathedral at the base of the mountains tolls the hour, but Ethan does not count the strikes. Still he has not bought a watch. There are some revels on the shore, laughter and shouting, the distant pulse of reggaeton, but otherwise the city seems remote and desolate in the tropical quiet.

Ethan walks across the room barefoot and picks up the phone. The line buzzes and clicks but does not ring. Then a voice on the line.

"Yes. Okay. What?"

The voice is heavily accented, Creole. The receptionist, maybe.

"I'd like to make an international call," Ethan says.

"Yes. Okay. Miami is ten dollars, American. By minute."

"No, I don't want to call Miami."

"What, buddy? Okay. Dallas is eight dollars."

"I want to call New York," Ethan says.

"New York?"

"Yes, New York."

The line cuts to static and a child's voice down the hall calls *Tuesday Tuesday*, or maybe it's not a child, but a parrot, and suddenly there's a car horn sounding in the street as a hundred dogs start to bark. And then Ethan standing barefoot in the darkening room, Ethan saying *hello, hello*, Ethan putting down the phone and picking it up again and nothing but electric sound, a hinge or a valve clicking on the broken line.

Ethan wanders into the streets of the mountain city. He's looking for a phone card. The heat slaps like a wet palm against his face and the mountains behind the hotel settle into a susurrant hush. He steps off the raised concrete sidewalk and into the ruined street; he walks the turning way to the sea. Nothing remains open around the hotel. The restaurants and cantinas are barred and dark, the pulperías only selling beer through cut wire windows. On the shore, a nearly empty disco blasts punta music into the coming night. Its open dance pavilion faces the water and several people, drunk already, stagger and dance and lean on the tables and never once look out to the sea. Under the vapor lamps, the palms around the disco glow purple and swarm with insects. Ethan continues down the boardwalk, past closed empanada stands and stores, long abandoned, that sold beach gear to tourists. He sees another open pulpería in the distance and he walks toward it. He steps over two drunk men as he goes, and women leaning against the seawall whistle and call, "hey, guapo," and he ignores them and walks on past the abandoned stores and desiccated coconut carts and everything here is salty and wet with heat, everything reeking of sudden loss: the wind-break palms twisted against the shore, the groveling men too stunned by drink to stand. Paradise just after the fall.

HE KNEW WHEN HE first met Samantha that his circumstances had changed beyond his control. The hopeless banality of meeting in a bar quickly gave way to something altogether different. At first basic city life: he was sitting in a terrible bar waiting for several terrible coworkers who always arrived late. He sat and drank and waited and didn't notice her at first. This was hard for him to believe later, when he looked back on that moment and tried to sever it from all its attendant mystery. How could he not have noticed her? She sat a foot away, perched on the barstool with her right leg curled under her, leaning onto the bar with one arm, letting her black hair fall forward over her shoulder and into the flat glow of dusty bar lights. He knows that now, remembers it now. Then, it was just the bartender reaching for his empty pint glass, reaching and asking him, *can I get you another?* And Ethan, not knowing how long he would have to wait, how much he'd need to drink, asking a question he never asked—"Do you have any specials?"

"Tequila mixers."

"It's a goddamn frat party," Ethan said. Then: "Sure, I'll have one."

The bartender grabbed a tumbler, a bottle of well tequila.

"And the mixer?"

"I don't know," Ethan said. "How about air?"

"Air?"

"Yeah."

"I don't think I can do that."

"How about ice? Ice and lime. Is that allowed?"

That's when she rocked her head back, tossed her hair out of her face, smiled at him.

"Did you just order tequila and air?"

"About now they're the two things I need most," he said.

"I know just how you feel."

Need. Like a sudden thirst. As a child Ethan had seen first-hand with his mother that what passed for passion was usually mania. Passion was isolated, its own storm, and in its eye there was no room for anyone else. But then there was Samantha. Samantha who seemed to reshape the world with the gravity of her desire. She stepped out of a room and the room seemed suddenly bereft, empty as a just-picked pocket. Ethan was used to city women who would banter with him, compete for power, allow him to limn the margins of their lives. Women who would give, but not give too much, who would be careful, also, what they took.

Not so with Samantha. She wanted him, it seemed, beyond any of his merits. She grabbed him once by his shirt while they were sitting in the park and said, "I could drink you like wine."

It was a ridiculous line. If someone else had used it, he would have laughed, asked her what type, asked her, perhaps, what she had planned for the cork.

But Samantha was serious. There was nothing about him that she didn't want, and at first Ethan said to himself, to his friends, *she's a perfect combination: always in need of satisfaction and so easy to satisfy.*

That first night, then, when he awoke in her apartment to an empty bed and stood there in the bare room wondering what to do—he could have left. Afterward, often, he'd wonder what might have happened if he had, if after he'd pulled on his pants and buttoned his shirt he had just crossed the empty living room, made it to the door, and if he could figure the locks—she had many—stepped out and away into the night. Perhaps, he thought at the time, that was what he was supposed to do, what she expected of him.

But he didn't leave. He stood at the door and watched the night moving beyond the far window. Outside, wind heaved—he could hear the dent of it on the glass. He stopped. Beyond the kitchen there was a door that he had taken originally, when they came in hours earlier, for a closet. Beneath it, leaked a thin, low line of light. Ethan was not impressed by wealth; it was commonplace in New York. It was the sort of thing that his mother had valued beyond measure and which he had found simply a pragmatic necessity. Without wealthy people or grants or ad agencies he would not have a job. Still, he wondered, how large is this apartment? He found himself feeling faintly ridiculous. He had woken alone in a stranger's bed wearing only his argyle socks. Fine, that was the state of things, the way the evening played out, but it was a hard state to ignore.

He could not leave. The night had presented itself to him as a sort of marvel: the perfect ease of their meeting and the more surprising ease of everything that followed. The way her fingers traced the rim of her glass, the way she told him that she quit piano at age twelve, the way she instructed him, finally, to wait, went into the bathroom, and stepped out of it wearing nothing. It was performed, yes, synchronized, but he didn't mind that. There was something to be said for perfect composition, after all.

So he knocked and turned the handle and crossed the threshold into the room hung with hundreds of drawings, pencil and charcoal, of a girl alone in a bare wood, tree trunks thin and long and leafless, a denuded forest or a forest of pine—he couldn't tell. In some, the girl stood, or walked, or hunted, it seemed, for berries through thickets of thorned brambles. In all, in the shaded distance, the diamond eyes of wolves gleamed above their snouts which, when he could see them, were low and slavering between the elongate trees. And she turned to him, Samantha, turned away from her easel where she sketched, and laughed when he said, for whatever reason, "I thought you were in advertising," and covered his mouth with her hand. She pushed him back, like that, with her palm over his mouth, walked him out of the room and into bed and said, finally, when she drew her hand away, "Let's get you out of those socks."

That night when she came to him, and pushed him back on the bed and covered his face and his shirt with charcoal streaks, she was strange and sweet and something to be reckoned with. She held him into morning and traced words onto the nape of his neck with her fingers—she wrote and wrote and he could not read the words. As the months followed, she seemed to ask nothing of him but that he slake some thirst he didn't mind slaking. She held a position at an advertising firm, she got him and his friends contracts, flushed him with work and love and it was easy to ignore the rest—the force of her affection whose other side he'd never seen, the nights where she'd retreat into her strange room, what she called *my tower*, to work on *Annie and the*

Wolves, the children's book she'd been writing and illustrating for ten years. She'd spend hours there, and when she'd leave she'd be numb and quiet and wouldn't speak, but beyond that their lives were easy. They lived well off her inheritance, and when she asked him to marry her—only seven months into their relationship—he could not imagine any way to deny her. So certain was her desire, so incommensurate with any of his merits, that it seemed she could not fail to charm his life. They married and he felt sure his future was not going to resemble his past.

For their honeymoon, because her firm was courting the Florida tourism bureau contract, they went to the Keys.

"Seriously," Samantha said. "Who goes to Key West anymore?"

They were sitting on the outdoor patio of a café that doubled as an art gallery. The tables were painted aqua green, teenagers played bongos on the curb, and across the street the sun set slowly, as it does in the tropics, over the gulf. It was their first night.

"We do, apparently," Ethan said.

"It's so 1927. We won't be able to tell any of our friends."

Ethan laughed and looked down at his plate. It was bright orange and clashed, he thought, with the creamy yellow of his key lime pie. He raised his fork.

"There's pie."

"There *is* pie."

On the far horizon the dusking wash of color began to congeal like a blood clot over the water. He raised his hand to get the waiter's attention.

"There's rum."

"Prove it," she said.

Later, as they drank, as the night came on, he snapped a photo of her.

"I didn't even see your camera."

"I wasn't going to leave it in the room."

"You know I don't like having my picture taken."

"We're on our honeymoon."

"I don't recognize myself in pictures," Samantha said. "I look smaller. I look like there's nothing there."

Ethan kept the picture. He didn't take many and he kept even fewer. In it, she's turning her head to the side to look not at him but at the sea, at the boats there, the darkening waves. She's saying something, though—her mouth is open and her lips drawn up in an expression of wonder. The day's last light tangles in her black hair. Condensation glints on the outside of her piña colada, but if you wanted you could say the blush in her skin is just sunlight, the glow in her eyes some kind of pleasure. Sometimes, when he looks at the picture, he knows it for what it is: a vanishing life tricked into permanence, the last perfect moment before the falling dark. Other times it's simply evidence and he tries to see her as she saw herself—diminished somehow. But for him it's just the opposite. If he could, he'd reduce the whole of their lives together to these photographs, moments outside of memory, stills that if you tried, could mean anything.

That night, that first night, Samantha can barely walk when they stagger up into the room at the Marlin Hotel. She's got her arm draped around his shoulder and he's holding her wrist with one hand and her shoes with his other. It's an old hotel—*Hemingway era,* says the plaque over the front desk. On the wall above the plaque hangs a dusty stuffed marlin. Its crest is beginning to crack and gray, beginning to look suspiciously like something pasted on.

"Caught by Papa himself," the proprietor said when they checked in.

There are no elevators and their room is on the third floor. The staircase starts in the lobby and leads outside, wraps around the perimeter of the hotel. It's covered, the staircase, but open to the wind. Their voices echo against the stucco ceiling. To their left rows of blinking lights lead down to the moving darkness of the water; to their right the concrete is stained by the mildew of blown rain.

"Christ, Ethan," Samantha says. "Why so many fucking stairs?"

"Because we decided to stay somewhere nice," he says. "Somewhere authentic. Would you prefer the Seashell Motel?"

Her head lolls against his shoulder and he can smell the raspberry and sweat of her hair. They still have a floor to go. She kisses his neck and her mouth is already dried out from drink. Her lips feel like rubber.

"Come on. We're almost there."

"Seashell Motel," she says. "Why does everything around here sound like it's about to go full-on porno?"

In the room with the sea breeze dancing the curtains through the balcony screen, Ethan pours her a glass of water and puts it by the bedside. He turns out the light, kisses her behind the ear.

"Goodnight," he says.

She tries to sit up on her elbows, doesn't quite make it.

"Excuse me, Ethan," she says. "But I think it's my honeymoon. I think you have obligations."

"Not to call on thousands of years of cretinous tradition," he says, "but I believe it's the other way around. The obligation is yours, and you are way too drunk."

"I'm never too drunk."

There's something about her insistence that he doesn't like. The indiscriminate want of it. They have all week and all the time beyond that. She turns her face into the pillow as if she's been struck and in the shadowy disarray of the bed her hair forms a noose about her neck. He rolls over, on top of her, pushes her hair away, kisses her throat, her collarbone, but she's impatient, and her hands are on his back, then on his hips, pulling off his underwear. He touches her and she's dry.

"You're too drunk, Sam. You won't feel anything."

"That doesn't matter," she says.

They passed the week in decadent routine. In the morning they'd ring the pull-bell ("So charming," Samantha said) for coffee. They heard it ring downstairs, and then there'd be the echo of the maid's feet on the steps, the clatter of vintage china. Once it came and the maid had left, Samantha would step out of the shower wearing a towel, or sometimes not even that. She'd affect Katharine Hepburn and say, "I'll take my coffee on the pavilion, m'dear." They'd sit on the balcony, drink coffee and eat breakfast and watch the sun climb over the Key. Afterward, they'd head down to the beach to walk or read. In the afternoons they kayaked among the mangroves or took glass-bottomed boats out to where the purple reefs glowed up through the perfect blue clarity of the sea. For lunch they drank piña coladas and ate fried conch or snapper. In the afternoon on the boats, Samantha filled Coke bottles with rum and drank them while Ethan snorkeled in the water lit by long columns of falling sunlight. The nights were not as bad as the first one; she wouldn't drink too much with dinner and she'd ride her afternoon buzz into evening. But still it was strange; he'd never seen her this way.

"I'm on vacation," she said. "It's my honeymoon, right?"

And then, later, when he pushed her further.

"Look, it's just sudden change. It freaks me out," she said.

They were sitting on the covered porch of a plantation restaurant with a gabled railing and square wooden columns, yellow trellised eaves. Below them, the lights of jeeps and motorcycles lit greenly in the fronds of the shade palms that lined the street.

"You sure you're okay?" Ethan said.

She reached across the table and took his hand, brought it to her lips. Her face and bare shoulders trembled under the guttering of table candles and the overhead mosquito lamp's flickering light. He realized, then, something he had known now for several days but did not understand. He preferred her like this. Wounded somehow. Drinking. Or no, that wasn't it. It wasn't that he liked her drinking, but that he felt comforted by some sign of vulnerability. He didn't want her hurt or frightened, certainly not that, but it was good to know that there was someone there beneath the unabashed confidence, the unremitting desire that felt, so often, like need. He'd noticed it most clearly during their wedding. The way she walked through the reception, the way the light seemed to cling to her, dazzle in her dress and on her skin, paint her black hair purple and gold and blue. She was a photographer's fantasy. She moved and smiled and seemed to absorb the guests' goodwill the way a plant does water. He watched her; he watched people watch her; he thought, who are you?

Now he could see her, maybe, as she saw herself: uncertain, stepping out into a new life like anyone else, someone for whom love was not a foregone conclusion. Because really, what did it mean if she did not notice that her life had changed, if she came to marriage as surely as she'd come to bed that first night? He looked across the table at her, the way she smiled, shrugged, the way some small sadness settled in her eyes. He was not frightened. He would not judge her weaknesses. He saw for the first time that she needed something that only he could give.

On their last day in Key West Samantha did not drink. They rose early
and rented kayaks on the western keys and took them into the mangrove islands where the water, so hard and blue in the open sea, turned
the swampy, mottled green of a turtle's back. The current died and
they cut slow circles through the narrow, cypress-shaded passages. He
let Samantha lead. He liked to stay behind her, to watch her paddle,
watch the muscles strain in her shoulders and upper back, see the sweat
dampen her tank top. Once he paddled alongside her, reached over and
pulled her kayak to his, kissed her. She laughed and touched his face,
splashed water on him.

"You'll capsize us both."

"You're getting sunburned," he said. "Put your hat on."

After following the mangrove waterways for an hour they came to
a beach of white sand hidden among the island thicket. They pulled
the kayaks to shore and ate a picnic lunch. For the first time that week
Samantha had not packed any booze.

"I want to snorkel," she said.

"There's probably alligators."

"It's salt water. Do alligators live in salt water?"

"I don't know," Ethan said. "I don't think so. But there might be
caimans."

"I don't even know what a caiman is."

"It's like an alligator. But smaller."

"I see," Samantha said. "So it's a smaller version of something that
isn't here?"

They snorkeled and manatees swam with them; they kissed while
treading water with their masks on. That evening they ate key lime pie
on the plantation porch. Afterward, Ethan said, "You want to go to the
Green Parrot and have a drink?"

It was not quite dark and the sun was beginning to shred the horizon over the gulf.

"No," Samantha said. "I want something else altogether."

On the plane trip back to New York he recalled that night, as he would
often in the following months, with some mix of wonder and building fear. He tried to remember it as he would a series of photographs.

Separate images, beautiful and untouched by consequence: his lips on her stomach, the sea's dried salt on her skin, her mouth opening as for air, the purple of the setting sun on her back and her ass. He tried not to remember how he felt—the building desperation between them, the sense that something depended on their lovemaking. He tried not to wonder what he'd never wondered before: what she was doing alone in that bar the night they first met.

The plane dipped and banked and turned toward land. They were almost home. Everything would be fine. It was documented fact, something to do with heat or magnetism: tourists turned strange in the tropics.

NIGHT IN MARA DE Leon. Insects trill in the banyan trees in the street. Ethan lies on his bed with the mosquito net pulled closed around him; the overhead fan creaks and wobbles and cuts the warm air. He has a phone card now, he knows he must call Paolo. In college, when they shared a house with their friend, the long-disappeared Brendan Doyle, Paolo studied Italian and spent every school break traveling to a different country. *I'm going to be a travel writer*, he said. *Because, you know, I just love culture.* Like most things Paolo said, Ethan wasn't sure how to interpret this comment. He didn't know whether it was affected sarcasm, Paolo's idea of a joke, or truly vapid. When pressed, Paolo said, *I'm just saying what someone else might say,* which didn't help.

After college Paolo got a degree in journalism and married a girl who, in the midst of her thousand insanities, decided for no discernible reason to start dressing like, as she put it, a Cherokee squaw. *It's all right,* Paolo claimed at first. *I just wish she wouldn't say 'squaw.'* In truth the costume wasn't much better: a buckskin jacket, chaps over leggings, incongruent white sneakers, and a construction-paper feather colored in with marker and glued to a paper headband. Ethan remembers a particularly uncomfortable Thanksgiving where she said nothing but "how" for the entire dinner. Paolo had just returned from visiting Doyle in Copal and was struggling with acute diarrhea—every five minutes he'd get up from the table and run to the bathroom. Ethan sat silently across the table from his wife.

"The turkey's delicious, Anne," he said.

She raised her hand, palm outward, then spread her fingers like a Vulcan.

"How," she said.

———

Paolo tried to remedy the relationship by taking her to Europe. New setting, he'd said, new air. He woke one morning in Belgium to find her gone, closets empty, the bill paid but beyond that no sign that she'd ever been there at all. When he came home he said, *you know, I'm totally over Europe,* and moved into an apartment in Spanish Harlem. For a year he didn't leave the city. When Ethan saw him last, it seemed he had acquired the stylistic ineptitude peculiar to young freelancers in New York. He fit a tight purple felt sports coat over an orange polo shirt. He wore aviator sunglasses and was eating a piece of pizza. It was eight in the morning.

"I thought we were supposed to get breakfast?"

"Hey, it's no problem," Paolo said. "We'll just call it brunch."

Over breakfast Ethan asked him, "I thought you wanted to be a travel writer?"

"I'm a travel blogger now," Paolo said. "I write for a web-based travel company. I write about trips you could take, if you wanted to."

"But you've never been to any of these places?"

"Well, you know, they only give me three hundred words per entry, and really I just link to other websites for most of my pivotal copy. You have to remember that it's a blog."

Ethan finished his coffee, looked down at his plate.

"Also, I don't think I ever want to go anywhere again," Paolo said.

Ethan pulls open the mosquito net, checks his shoes, and walks to the phone. He doesn't know if the phone will work or how long the phone card will last. A cockroach scrambles across the floor. Better than a scorpion, anyway. Ethan hopes that in all of Paolo's travels, in all the places he wandered through looking for something that could explain or prevent a life where your wife turns into a Spaghetti Western extra, where you wake to an empty bed and empty room, that he has been to Rio de Caña.

"*Nyet,*" said Paolo. "Never heard of it."

The connection crackled and hissed, bars of music and a man saying *good morning, ma'am* trembled on the line.

"Never?" said Ethan. "You don't know anything?"

"Nah—I'm doing a search now, and let me tell you, I'm pulling a donut here."

"That means you can't find anything?"

"*D'accord.*"

This was another thing Paolo did, slipped into other languages not quite accurately. Individually, he spoke each of them fluently, but like a purple sports coat pulled over an orange polo shirt, he could never quite integrate them into an organic whole.

"Where are you again?"

Ethan told him.

"I've been there. De Leon. That's a great city. There's this bar where you can get a Johnnie Walker Black for like, I don't know, ten lemps or quets or whatever the currency is. And I'm talking dobles here."

"Don't say dobles."

"Hey, sure. I hear you. That was totally gringo-landia of me. My bust."

Ethan looked out the window. The city hung dark and unlit. There was no nightlife and he could not see the ocean.

"Rio de Caña," Paolo said. "Why you going there anyway?"

Ethan told him, and beyond his usual inclinations Paolo was quiet for a moment. Ethan heard his keyboard stop clattering. Still in the background there were ringing phones. Burring voices. Music no one would ever want to hear.

"You know what you need to do," Paolo said.

"Maybe, Paolo. I don't know."

"You need to find Doyle."

"Don't you think if he turns up again, it'll be because he's dead?"

"Granted," Paolo said. "But that's why you called. You called so that I would tell you to go find Doyle."

"I don't think that's true."

"The two of you," Paolo said. "All of you"—it sounded on the line like he was turning his head to the side, about to spit—"can't just take anything in the gut. I mean, it's life. Fucking take it. But no, everybody has to freak out, everybody has to, I don't know, disappear."

The line buzzed. Outside, in the hills sloping down out of the mountains, birds called and paused and called again. A lonely, foreign sound, a call echoing, Ethan imagined, across the electronic distance. Paolo was right, but there was nothing Ethan could say to console him. He could not comprehend Paolo's choice to stay there, to stay banging away at his blogs through the night. When your life vanishes, how do you do anything but follow it? There had to be some kind of axiom there, some kind of deeper certainty. When you flay your life from you, what remains? Just the impulse to flay, the knife seeking new skin. The bird call came again and reminded Ethan that he should get back under the mosquito net.

"You know how to find him?" Paolo said.

"I think so. Maybe."

"Well, then. I got to head and file some copy. *Bonsoir*, Ethan."

And then the line was dead and there was Ethan standing there and replacing the phone and then turning and heading down into the hotel bar so that maybe tonight, all the spirits of the tropics willing, he could get some sleep.

In *ANNIE AND THE Wolves*, the small bit of it he read after Samantha committed herself, the huntsman's daughter flees his house at dusk. In this sense, it is different than most fairy tales. The child doesn't wander into the sunlit forest; she does not become carelessly lost. Instead, it opens at dinner, with her father, the huntsman, serving her a bowl of stew. The text is spare and summarizes only what is drawn above—it provides no insight or motivation. *The huntsman serves poor Annie stew.* Here we see him standing behind the hewn-wood table, his hands holding the bowl, at groin level, up to Annie's face, his fingers clawed around the wooden rim, tendons standing out in his wrist, and some mane of fur, or hair, Ethan could never tell, tangled up his arms. Steam rises from the stew, a sausage floats at the surface. There are potatoes maybe, root vegetables. Nothing about it, vaguely sketched as it is, appears disgusting, but in the background, in the space between the huntsman's forearm and the bowl, Annie's face crumples into a display of abject horror. Her mouth hangs open and slack long past some scream, her lips droop low, we see her gums. Next we see, from behind, the huntsman's hands on his hips, Annie's still-stricken face triangulated between forearm and bicep. *Annie, eat your stew!* Annie flees out into the forest. Her mother (we assume) sits at the door looking down, maybe sleeping, doing nothing to stop her. Annie flees. *Into the woods with the wolves.*

Ethan recalls it as she drew it—for each potential page Samantha had drafted dozens of illustrations. What bothers him is that from draft to draft nothing ever changed. She differed the medium (pencil to charcoal, the intensity of line and color) but made none of the artist's usual revisions: there was no change in composition or perspective or light source. The same furred arms and sleeping mother remained, the same static horror. Ethan thinks he knows what this means. In the false light of retrospect, it all makes sense: the way sex seemed unlinked to desire, the way she drank, how easily her reason abandoned her after that night, the way that night seemed not like a surprise, a sudden unexpected calamity, but a culmination, the final domino in a long chain.

He thinks he should have done more, but does not know what more he could do. Beyond certain facts (she grew up in Boston the only child of socialites, she went to Bryn Mawr, her parents died in a car accident), her past was unbreachable territory. She littered her depictions of it with small details: she told him the color of her childhood room, the name of her dentist, how she loved to sail and how she won the yacht club regatta at sixteen. He knew that as a teenager she wore her hair tied up under bandanas, always red or purple. He knew she named her first cat Doctor Theodore, and that her grandfather, when she helped him shovel snow at his house in Vermont, used to make her what he called a Black Strap, a mixture of boiling water, rum, molasses, and nutmeg. For him, her past was a tapestry of unlinked details, vignettes. Early in their relationship, the first night she stayed at his apartment, when he told her about his mother's death, she did not respond in kind—she did not try to hold her damage up to his own. He had assumed, always, that this was because of the way her parents died, the shock of it, their loss some terrain too painful to enter. Now he thinks he knows he was wrong.

And then there are other days where even that clarity deserts him. The past he imagines for her is simply that—imagined. Like a jigsaw piece, it fits the jagged hole of his need too neatly. If there was a history of abuse, if Samantha's life up until that night was a moving scar ready to be re-slit, then the fault was not entirely his own. He had waited at the table as morning assembled itself in the street. Her hair was up, he could not stop noticing that her makeup was already on. She said, *what are you thinking?* Ethan sees the moment as one of her illustrations: static, repetitive, the only thing that matters in the world, a moment outside of time. She asks, *what are you thinking*, he answers, the door closes and he raises his camera to capture her there at the threshold of something he cannot predict—but it's just a shadow, a woman slipping away, a darkness coming in.

ETHAN WOKE TO PRE-DAWN dark and the sounds he was beginning to know as those of morning: the first cocks crowing in the streets, fishing boats rumbling out into the bay. He got up, he checked his shoes for scorpions, he showered. The hot water was off, or maybe it had never been on. He shivered and washed his hair for the first time in three days and tried to remember not to swallow any of the water. Afterward, as he dressed, he considered making a list of things to do. He'd need more clothes—he'd bought two sets of new clothes by the bus stop in Mexico, but he couldn't travel all the way to Rio de Caña on two sets of clothes, not if he were going to convince Yolanda's sister to leave with him. The idea seemed idiotic enough as it was: a thing confused, something dreamed up as a joke and taken seriously.

"She'll never come with me," he had said to Yolanda. "Why would she?"

"You are such an American," she said. "You think you are the worst thing that could happen to a girl?"

He left the hotel to walk the waking city. The sun still low, rose over the water, and flooded inland against the moving line of mountain shadow in a wash of pink light. As it did, steam rose from the puddles in the pitted road. Ethan found a breakfast café and ate scrambled eggs and drank coffee as he watched farmers with straw hats pulled low and saddlebags full of beans and coffee and bushels of bananas ride in on mules out of the mountains. He reached into his wallet, unfolded Doyle's postcard, and stared at it in all its hopeless insanity.

The card had arrived, outside their door, over a year earlier.

"Did someone send you a postcard from 1980?" Samantha asked as she handed it to him.

Certainly it seemed that way: the paper was yellow and thick, the picture a blurry colonial cathedral set against an overexposed sky. The sender had blackened the town name out with a marker. There was no stamp, no postal code. On the back was a poem written also in marker, in Doyle's childish handwriting:

Fruit of memory,
you shall indeed be changed, Tommy, in the country
    of the dead,
with that echoing flower
in your little hand, the hand of a man chosen by destiny,
and those eyes beguiled by adventure.

The card haunted him like something dreamt into the world. A bouquet of flowers seen in sleep and then woken to, sitting on the nightstand dripping dew in a room smelling suddenly of mud and rain. It was a question of acceptance: he had not expected to ever hear from Doyle again. Doyle was dead or gone or missing—Doyle who had been disappearing for years, shadowing himself into the tropics like so many lost gringos; Doyle, once his best friend, now rotting in some heat-stricken prison or hiding, or just perhaps stepping one day into a jungle so wild with poisonous flowers and monkeys with men's eyes that there was no emerging from it. Until now—an enigmatic postcard appearing at his door, thick and heavy and smelling of coffee and dirt, a letter received, with all its impossible ciphers, from the dead.

The postcard demanded interpretation—but he could not interpret it. Was it a message, a riddle, a sign? Was he supposed to glean something from the poem? It was odd enough that Doyle, a man missing for over two years, would send a postcard at all, let alone a poem. Doyle did not write poetry. *Echoing flower, fruit of memory*—it sounded alien, more alien even than a poem appearing in your mailbox normally would. It sounded like something translated.

He tacked the card up to the bulletin board in his darkroom and stared at it in the low apocalyptic glow of the safety light. A cathedral, a poem, a hidden address. Like a row of ancient pictograms carved into a cave wall, he felt that read in the right order, they would explain where Doyle was, or what had really happened to him, or why, after so many years down there, he had finally gone, as they had always joked he might, full-tilt *Heart of Darkness*.

Ethan spent more and more time in the darkroom. Often, Samantha was out, and when she wasn't, when she came home for the night, she lolled on the couch, the room fruiting with the smell of spilled gin. In the darkroom, the old safety light buzzed and sizzled like a mosquito lamp popping through the tropic dark. The developing liquids, the stop-bath, reeked of Mexican vanilla. Ethan often thought that a life would be easy to fix in a world where everything was connected, where every action had a clear and certain consequence. Under the red light the cathedral wavered like a town about to fall to storm; he heard the front door open and then close. The postcard, he decided, did not mean anything.

Ethan finished his coffee and threw the last scrap of his eggs to a lurking dog. He did not like dogs, and here there was no escaping them. They skulked through the streets like jackals, wild and mangy and strange. Their fur, where they had it, was matted and rough. Alone they were pitiful, they howled and crept carefully around people, but at night, from his balcony, Ethan had seen packs of them loping the perimeter of the dark forest.

A pickup truck filled with plantains pulled up to the curb. The farmer hopped out and, on his way into the café, he kicked the dog so hard between the ribs that it lifted off the ground, twisted in the air like a cat falling out of a tree, and hit the ground running and yelping and dropping scrambled eggs from its mouth. The man nodded to Ethan.

"Buenos," he said, and stepped inside. Already, a pair of chickens pecked and tossed the egg scraps. Ethan stepped out and into the street and began to walk as an old man sitting on the corner grabbed his leg and said, "Look, look how it is here. Chickens eat their own eggs."

A doorbell chimed as Ethan entered the detective's office and a blue lizard scrambled across the concrete floor. The detective looked up but stayed sitting at his desk. He said, "Please do not worry, I'm sure she will be back by lunch."

"Excuse me?"

"Do not worry," the detective said again in English. "She will not run out on you for good."

"I'm not here about a missing woman," Ethan said.

As he stood, the detective put on a pair of pointed, wire-rimmed glasses. He ran his right hand quickly over his mustache, smoothing it down, and pulled up on his belt so that he sent a faint ripple through his belly, which rested now on his desk.

"Truly? There is no missing woman?"

"Afraid not. Is that okay?"

There was a noise then like a big dog barking, which Ethan realized was the detective laughing.

"Is that okay?" he said in between bursts of laughter. "Is that okay?"

He came around the desk faster than Ethan would have expected. He wore enormous white sneakers with little red lights that flashed as he walked. He pointed to a woven palm chair with the flourish of a maitre d' offering a VIP booth.

"Please sit down, sir," he said. "Not a missing woman? Not a cheating wife? If I were not such an ugly, disgusting man I would kiss you."

The night before, as he searched for a phone card, Ethan had noticed that while most of the stores on the boardwalk—the stores selling beach gear and clothing to tourists who no longer came—were closed and boarded, once he turned inland and walked past the markets, the winding reaches of the city held no shortage of paint shops or private detectives. For two whole blocks the shops alternated between stores selling tubs of pastel paint, and signs, each one more elaborate than the next, offering cheap detective work. On some signs, men hid in bushes and pointed telescopes at busty women with expressions that, depending on the sign, varied between lust and indigestion. On others, characters in wide fedoras peered out of cars or trees with telephoto lenses. And on one, a neon fresco of the last supper depicted Jesus peering over his black beard at Judas, as if to say, *I know what you're thinking because I've got the best private detective in town.* Parrots perched on all the apostles' shoulders while the apostles drank piña coladas. Certainly, Ethan thought, the detectives struck some deal with the painters.

"I am so grateful for this opportunity," the detective said as he examined the postcard. "This is excellent. This is very fantastic."

He walked around his desk, opened a drawer and removed a magnifying glass. Light through the window caught and refracted off it, glinted for a moment in the dusty room.

"You know," the detective said, "I can't tell you how nice it is to use this on something other than a photo of a naked woman. You have no idea how tiring that gets."

The blue lizard scurried up the wall behind him. The room was bare but for the desk, two chairs, and the low-hanging light bulb. Diesel fumes from the street puffed through the open window.

"Really," the detective said, "what is my responsibility? A man comes to me. He says, I think my wife is cheating on me with my cousin. He says, you must find out. I need to know. I need proof. So what can I do? It is my obligation. It is my profession. But say she is cheating on him—say every afternoon while her husband is at work, this cousin motherfucker takes her to his beach bungalow and fucks her so hard my camera nearly breaks. What then? Do I show the pictures to the husband? Do I say, yes, sir, you are a *cabrón*?"

"I guess so," Ethan said. "You want to get paid."

"It's not so simple as that," the detective said. He put the postcard and the magnifying glass down, rested his belly again on the tabletop. "You see, I get paid either way. But then, of course, it's a question of integrity, right? I mean I'm hired to tell him the truth. If I take his money and lie to him, it is like I am fucking him too. I am making him a *cabrón* all over again. So it is simple, right?"

"Sure."

"No. Again, it is not simple. Because what will happen when I show him the pictures? He will go home and sharpen his machete. Then he will go and cut up his wife for sure, and probably his cousin too. And then, maybe, the police will shoot him. But probably they won't. But maybe this cousin has a brother, another cousin. What is to say he won't decide to seek vengeance? Now it is the whole city chopping each other up while the mayor wonders why there are no more tourists and the guerrillas in the mountains wait for us to be so goddamn poor or dead or both that we need them. So you see? I have a disgusting profession."

"I didn't know there were still guerrillas," Ethan said.

"Guerrillas or maras or traficantes. I do not think even they can tell themselves apart anymore. But that is in the mountains. Here it is just people chopping each other up with machetes because they have nothing better to do. I wish the tourists would come back."

He pulled up his pants again and sent another ripple through his belly, peered over his wire-rimmed glasses at Ethan.

"Are you a tourist?"

"What else could I be?"

"Excuse me, sir," the detective said. "I do not mean to offend you, since I am honored that you chose me for this assignment. But that was a very stupid question. A gringo in this city? You could be an expatriate, which means that you could be a criminal or a pervert or both. Or you could be CIA. Or a Mormon. Are you a Mormon?"

"No, I'm not a Mormon."

"I did not think so. You are not clean enough. Why, if you don't mind me asking, sir, did you choose me, a disgusting little man, over all the other detectives?"

Outside, a truck backfired in the street. The room thickened with diesel fumes. Now the blue lizard was on the ceiling, its crest blossoming from its throat like a bright red flower.

"Your sign said you speak English and my Spanish es muy malo."

Ethan wished he hadn't inserted the Spanish phrase into his sentence. It was, as Paolo had put it, *totally gringo-landia*. The way the expats on the north coast spoke—an idiotic Anglo-Spanish patois. The detective smiled and reached into his pocket, pulled out a purple handkerchief and wiped his brow.

"Yes," he said. "I am the only one who does. I learned it in detective school."

"If they taught English in detective school, all the other detectives would know it, too," Ethan said.

The same strange barking sound, as if a dog could have a hairball. The detective laughing.

"Maybe you are a detective too? Where do you think I learned English if not in school?"

"You have idiom," Ethan said. "I'd say you did learn it in school. De las Americas. In the eighties. No?"

"Oh, very clever. Very clever. Definitely not a tourist. But I think you should never say something like that out loud around here."

He reached down and picked up the postcard again, smoothed down his mustache with his thumb and forefinger. In the street a cabbie began sounding his horn. The detective pushed his glasses back on his face and read the poem aloud.

"*The country of the dead*," he said. "That must be Copal, no? That is what Copal is for Latin America. A reminder of what can await you. From where you have come you may go again, no?"

"I don't know that it means anything," Ethan said.

"Still, it is a very beautiful poem, don't you think? I once wanted to be a poet."

The air in the room now almost unbreathable. The overhead fan spreading a layer of smog.

"What did he do," the detective asked, "this friend of yours, that he must hide?"

WHAT DOYLE DID WAS buy a bar. Or stay at his bar too late one night, or close too early—or more likely, it started far before that, Ethan often thought, when he thought about Doyle at all. In truth, beyond some arrangement of the facts as he knew them, Ethan found it dangerous to try to align Doyle's past with the catastrophe of his present. It was an impossible undertaking. There were too many poor choices to point at only one and say, there it is, the moment from which everything else erupted. Besides, it didn't seem to matter. Once someone is, by intention almost, a Central American fugitive sending out freaky postcards through avenues unknown, how do you separate the cause from the continual expression of the effect?

They met their freshmen year at Middlebury, where they were roommates in a leaky dorm that overlooked the playing fields. At first Doyle showed little sign of the man he was to become. He was a pale blond boy, soft-spoken and almost diffident—typically Southern, Ethan thought, in the cautious way he seemed to approach his Northern colleagues. He walked and sat with the rigid posture of a child born to a military family and he drank without peer. At the end of the first week of classes Ethan returned to their room to find Doyle waiting at their fold-up card table with two glasses and two bottles of whiskey—one of Irish, which he claimed for himself, the other of Scotch, which he presented to Ethan.

"It's the end of the day," he said, "and we need to take the edge off."

Ethan wanted to tell him that for the first time in his life he felt free from whatever neurotic discomforts, external or internal, honed themselves into an edge, but he imagined by the way Doyle arranged himself without smiling, in a perfect ninety-degree angle in his chair, that this was, for him, a serious affair. And it may have been, though later Ethan learned that these signs, a grimness of aspect and rigidity of posture, did not necessarily indicate Doyle's mood. Still, he did present the evening whiskey as a ritual of strange solemnity, and would barely tolerate a change in time or brand. Once, for his birthday, Ethan gave him a bottle of twelve-year-old Redbreast Irish Whiskey which he thought would be a welcome substitute for Doyle's regular thin and sweet Tullamore Dew. But he never drank it. *I'm a Tullamore man*, he said when Ethan pressed him. *I'm an undeviating line.*

Perhaps, Ethan thought, but whatever steadiness of purpose or personality Doyle imagined for himself was limited to the compulsions of ritual. Twice during that first year he dropped out of school and tried to join the Merchant Marines. Each time, somehow, his father caught him before he could enlist and drove him back hundreds of miles to Vermont. The second time came in early spring, and Ethan was there in their room, watching the walls of sleet blow down across the fields from Canada, when the Doyles arrived. Ethan watched the black Cadillac make its way in ponderous skids and jerks over the iced roads, he watched the falling sleet spark in the wide cast of its headlights. When the car stopped outside their dorm, Mr. Doyle stepped out into the storm, walked around the hood like a chauffeur, and opened the door for his son. Ethan remembers the moment, the old man—he was old then already, almost seventy—waiting for his troubled son to join him in the rain. Ethan remembers the gathering sheen of ice beading on his overcoat, and his bare, bald scalp. When Doyle finally slipped out—beside the old man's stiff authority he seemed effete and languid—he pulled off his woolen cap and offered it to his father. Mr. Doyle shook his head, touched Brendan's shoulder once, and walked back around the car.

After this, Doyle seemed to lose his desire to flee school. He became a Spanish language and literature major and met Paolo in a class on the revolutionary works of Alejo Carpentier. They moved in together, all three of them, in their junior year, and Doyle wrote a senior thesis on *El Cid*. After graduation, Paolo went to school for journalism, Ethan moved to New York to pursue photography, and Doyle, struck again by some wanderlust, joined the Peace Corps.

"I've heard," he said to Ethan one night just before he shipped off to Copal, "that down there a white man can fulfill every single sexual fantasy."

They were drinking in the White Horse Tavern in New York, the tavern where Dylan Thomas sat at the bar and completed, it seemed, his life's second ambition: he drank until he said, *I've had eighteen straight whiskies. I believe that is the record*, and then passed into a coma from which he would never awake. Now, the White Horse bustled with tourists without entirely losing what merits it must once have had—it was dark and wooden. They sat, Ethan and Doyle, under a bust of Dylan Thomas. They thought it fitting somehow. Winter was coming on, the sun was already a thin slit over the city, thin and thinning and growing dark. In the morning Doyle would be heading off for two years in the tropics, and until then they raged as best they could against the dying of the light.

"I'm talking everything," Doyle said. "The kinkiest power-of-Grey-skull orgasms you can imagine. A white man is a hot commodity down there."

"Sure," Ethan said. "Bring a horse and see if you can't get free hot chocolate for life."

They ordered another round of whiskey. Time and low light splintering through the ambered glass.

"Ten more to break the record," Doyle said.

"I don't think we'll make it. Do you?"

"What difference does it make? I'll die down there anyway."

Later, looking back on that moment, suspending it in time, it seemed portentous—a sign of dread already opening like a spider's egg in Doyle's mind.

"I don't want to become one of those guys," he said and finished his whiskey and nodded for Ethan to do the same. "There's nothing worse than a gringo who goes down to help and comes back with an eighteen-year-old wife. Or worse, stays down there while sixteen-year-olds fuck him for bean money."

Outside now, it was full dark.

"You're not one of those guys," Ethan said. "Still, try not to go full-tilt *Heart of Darkness* on us."

"The horror," Doyle said. "The horror."

Two years in, and two months before he was scheduled to come home, Doyle applied for an extension. After that expired he worked for a nonprofit AIDS education firm in the capital city. He taught prostitutes about condoms and went to the prisons to lecture members of Mara Salvatrucha about the dangers of needles and prison sex. Then, without providing any explanation, he picked up and moved south and started writing English ad copy for a rum distillery even though Copalan rum was rancid and not exported abroad. But the English on the bottle helped it sell in Copal, and many of Doyle's slogans were laughable: *Drink Me Now! The Best Rum for Powerful Taste! Start a Fire? Yes!*

Throughout this time Ethan and Paolo both stayed in contact with him: email, letters, the yearly visit. Still, as the political climate in Copal deteriorated, Doyle grew increasingly distant. He stopped writing emails, and his rare letters were fitful and fevered. He wrote once to Ethan on rum distillery stationary in sprawling, enormous handwriting:

Dear Ethan, I want to tell you what I know of the world. I have grown a beard and I have shaved a beard so I suppose you could say I'm burning the candle at both ends here, but there's an old Copalan saying that to get to the brothel you have to go there first. Make of that what you will. I've heard about Paolo's engagement and regret that I will not be able to attend. I no longer go to celebrations where the natives don't set the town on fire with their fireworks—I'm sure he'll understand. On that note (marriage), once one gets beyond the fawning pleasures of grinding to reggaeton in the local discothèque, one finds that even the most erudite of the colonial subjects is no more stimulating when it comes to conversation than your regular pueblo beauty. Several months back—you still have time up there, don't you?—I was at a prostitute's house, trying to educate her on the prophylactic wonders of your average Trojan when, mirabile dictu, her father blew off his own foot while trying to shoot a gecko through the webbing of the hammock in which he reclined. Sometimes I find insects in my stool. We really have fucked this place and fuck it still. Walking through the streets, a pleasant undertaking (ha ha), I experience certain lacrimations of shame.

I want you to know that the world is full of liars. We could fuck children if we wanted to. Believe me, I'd break my rum bottle, but then I'd have no rum.

Five years in, when he left the rum company, moved farther west to the Guatemalan border, and opened a bar, Ethan accepted, finally, that Doyle was not going to return.

It was not such a bad idea, really, buying a bar. It's what you did if you were an expat in the tropics and didn't need, or want, to keep a low profile. A whole community of expatriates had grown up along the north coast, and if you didn't speak much Spanish or mind a lack of culture—or violent crime, for that matter—if you were just there for the beach and the rum and the drawn-out days that settled into green and thrumming nights, if you didn't look anyone else in the eye to avoid seeing what miscalculation of purpose had led them there and didn't mind that the woman in your bed, whose beauty was incommensurate with any other thing in your life, was simply trying to survive, then it was fun and sun and paradise in the tropics.

But Doyle didn't build his bar on the coast. He didn't want the ex-Marines or CIA, the tired, wind-wrinkled fugitives or the men with knives in their boots and tropical shirts (in a country where no one actually sold tropical shirts), men who couldn't speak a word of Spanish, men who owned boats and hidden seaplanes—Jimmy Buffets with mean streaks. He wrote once to Ethan: *No one walks into my bar wearing a goddamn parrot.*

What he did want, Ethan could not tell. It became a haven, though, for locals—Doyle's. Men coming home after work in the cane or the mountains, or more often now, men starting their days after no work at all. For Doyle, each night settled into a comfortable routine. The night came on with bottles of beer and shots of rum or agauardiente handed round the bar. By midnight always, if not earlier, the men sang songs in Spanish and Indian dialects. No one spoke English except to sing, without knowing what the lyrics meant, the words to "Hotel California."

"I don't know what it is about that fucking song," Doyle said the first and only time Ethan visited the bar. "But people are batshit for the Eagles here."

Watching Doyle work behind the bar, watching him stand and pour drinks and laugh and shake hands and nod at his bouncers when arguments looked soon to be settled with machetes, Ethan thought, who does he think he is? Whatever it was he hated about himself, or found shameful—race or money or privilege—does he imagine that he can just shed it here, can turn and really become one of them? Does he think that they will ever see him as anything but a man, however kind, who has more than they can possibly imagine having? Or is it the opposite? Does he know that's not possible, will never be possible, and is it his difference, his privilege, ingrained and taken as almost inherent here, that makes him stay? Here, he will always be somebody.

And then there was the night when the fight broke out over the mermaid in the paper. In the past, Copalan newspapers had reported on government or trade or crime, but violent experience had long dissuaded most of them from this practice. It was easy enough to get killed in Copal. They didn't have to ask for it. Now they usually ran state-planted puff pieces, tourist information for imaginary tourists, or made-up tabloid nonsense—in this case, a photo of a dead mermaid who had supposedly washed up on the northern shore. The photo was distinctly fake, ridiculous, a ludicrous, ill-matching photoshop clusterfuck of woman and fish. The tail was purple, hugely scaled, and wider than the torso to which it was joined. She was posed face down, and on one shoulder a tan line was not quite erased. It became a national sensation.

That night at Doyle's, when the conversation turned, as it had many times recently, to the mermaid, one of the men sitting in the corner stood and said, "I'm sorry, but it is clear that this mermaid is not real."

"You'd think," Doyle had told Ethan years before, "that considering the state of this country there'd be an abridgement of national pride. But it seems to go the other way. The worse this place gets, the more people want to insist on how great it is."

And since the story had run, the mermaid had been adopted as a symbol of Copalan excellence. A sign that the nation was graced with wonders.

So for a moment the bar quieted. The men who'd been discussing the mermaid stopped and turned and put their drinks down.

One of them said, "There are fish with many heads in the rivers. No one denies this. There are jaguars with men's voices in the forest. And now there is this mermaid. Do they have mermaids in Honduras? In Guatemala? No. It is a sign of God's love for Copal."

"It is a toy made out of rubber," said the first man.

————

The ensuing fight had been bad. Machetes, bottles, even an old Navy cutlass drawn. The police were called and came quickly all things considered. Of Doyle's three bouncers, two had to be taken to the hospital.

After they cleared the bar, two of the police stayed and drank guaro. Doyle would have preferred they deplete his good rum stocks—it would bode better for the rest of the night. The guaro was cheap and rough, and it could make you weird. As it was, the captain was glazing out and it wasn't impossible that he'd taken something before the boozing started.

"They are stupid motherfuckers, these peasants," the captain said to Doyle in English.

Doyle didn't like it when people spoke English to him down there. It meant they were about to get chummy or mean. The captain was smiling, but that wasn't really a sign either way.

"You must think we are all stupid motherfuckers, eh?" He drank from his guaro and draped his arm around his deputy's shoulders. "Doyle thinks we are idiots and peasants. He laughs at us in the street."

His deputy clearly didn't speak English and the captain was no longer smiling. Whatever he was on had flared out and he was crashing fast with the guaro. His expression fell away and his face just hung fat and slackly, like all the flesh there had suddenly become too heavy to hold up.

"Maybe he is right," the captain said to the deputy. "Maybe you are an idiot." He pulled his pistol from his holster and put it on the bar.

"Closing time," Doyle said. "But take the bottle with you. On the house."

Everyone stood. It was just the four of them in the bar—the police, Doyle, and his one remaining bouncer. The police walked to the door. Two more steps and it was just another night where people lost hands to machetes. And then the captain turned and threw the bottle of guaro down hard at the ground. He had probably forgotten that it was plastic and wouldn't shatter.

"Don't you think I deserve another drink?" he said. He was still holding the pistol. "I think everyone agrees that I deserve another drink."

Doyle's bouncer stepped toward him with his hand outstretched, which he shouldn't have done, and the captain nodded and worked up some kind of smile and shot him in the leg. He might not have meant to fire, it might only have been a gesture, the pistol wave, but it didn't matter. The gun went off and the shot ruptured the bouncer's femoral artery and he collapsed, not even howling, just paling out and dead before Doyle could do anything.

At first the captain laughed when the man went down and then, when it was clear what was happening, he looked back up at Doyle and his expression wasn't right, his eyes hollow, dilated and bright against the droop of his wasted face.

Doyle had the sawed-off shotgun rigged under the counter, and he fired it from low, without raising it, and it blew out the palmwood front of the bar and splintered away the captain's right knee. The captain was on his back, flailing like a roach and screaming, emptying his pistol into the wall, the bottles over Doyle's head, and with his last bullet the face of his deputy, whose skull burst back through the bar's one window and into the trees outside.

Doyle ran upstairs, where he filled two duffel bags with his cash savings and several of his favorite books. He came back down and began breaking bottles, washing the floor and the walls with alcohol. The captain continued to bellow. Doyle grabbed a bottle of rum, put it in his bag, and went to the door; turned back, took another bottle, packed it too, and walked again to the door. He lit a match and stepped out into the dawn loud with the captain's wails, roosters and dogs woken by the gunfire, the whole town awake in the false and sudden light.

DRIVING THROUGH THE DARK in the night with the detective. He steered with one hand, pointed with the other out through the passenger-side window, past Ethan's face, into the hills. "Out there," he said, "there are bandits."

Ethan looked. The streets lay lightless, framed by banana plants and stands of bamboo; beyond that it was just the layered dark rising into black hills. The sky on the far horizon looked flat and cloud-streaked and empty. There were no stars.

The road bent and they took the turn quickly, crossing whatever lane might exist. Something darted from the street in the sudden wash of their headlights. A coyote, maybe. On their trip out of town, a dog pack chased the car as they passed beneath an overpass at the far end of the abandoned loading docks. Ethan was glad, watching the dogs snap in the growing distance, that he'd accepted the detective's offer of a ride. The dogs were a lot worse than the Guatemalan coyotes and he didn't want to wait at the bus station at dusk or take a bus along the coast road at night.

The forest gave way to fields of sugarcane, swaying under some breeze he couldn't feel. The road straightened and continued through the borders of cane, high and dense as English hedges, on into the night. The car sputtered and swerved over the narrow road. The detective was speaking.

"Here the Peace Corps volunteers were kidnapped," he was saying. "In the middle of the day. Not even at night and not even in a city and they took them into the fields. You can imagine what they did to them."

Ethan could imagine. Ever since Doyle first went missing, he'd scoured the internet for any mention of Copal, so he knew the story already: how the four volunteers, two women and two men, were dragged into the fields, what happened to the women there and then the men. It was the last straw before the Peace Corps withdrew from Copal. The detective kept talking, describing it anyway, not leaving anything to Ethan's imagination—how the men finally convinced their captors that they weren't CIA agents but aid workers trying to sanitize the local wells, how they let them go, how the four of them wandered down the lane too shocked to speak and boarded a bus, sat bleeding, the women half naked, and no one very surprised at all.

Ethan didn't want to hear this. He didn't want anyone else's nightmare stories. What he wanted was for the detective to stop talking. What he wanted was to reach across the cab and force his thumb into the detective's eye, to take his face and smash it against the side window. He could feel it in his right hand, the concussion of the detective's head against the glass, the give of his fat-slabbed cheekbones against Ethan's fist. He did not wonder at his rage. It was a new occurrence. He'd never been a violent person, but in Ethan's dreams of vengeance, he had done some terrible things. He thought of them, at first, as fantasies—the mind's way of coping with the violence that infected his life. But they were not like any fantasies he'd had before. They were not ethereal or contrived, he was not aware of constructing them. Instead, they came on as urges, diarrheal, palpable as pain, stark as a sudden thirst. He could actually feel the collapse of the detective's face against his hands—he could feel it and he wanted to consummate that feeling.

He watched the road turn again down out of the fields and toward the plane of lightlessness where the sea must be. On his trip through Boystown's night he had told himself that this was the reason he went there in the first place: to see a world scarred by trauma. Well, here, he had it. In Key West he had taken comfort in Samantha's signs of troubles until they erupted into his life, and now here he was again, heading through a landscape of damage. When he had first gone south, to Texas and then Mexico, he was only craving a geography uncluttered by memories of guilt, he was reaching for the purity of fear, the availability of grace in the presence of real suffering. He was not planning on coming again to Copal.

He rolled down the window. When he married he'd imagined his life spreading out before him like an undiscovered country seen from a ship's deck. His future rose, lush and mist-shrouded, full of possibility and still too distant to know the measures of. He figured that if he moved toward it, gave himself up to it, it could not fail to harden into form: a beach of white sand he could step onto. So he had sought it with abandon and it had turned out to be a mirage. The beaches he found were those he drove along now: hot and coral-sharded, bordered by cliffs of dry forest and cities long gone to rot—the old despair of the new world.

The detective had finished his story and was waiting for Ethan to respond. His sneakers flashed as he worked the pedals. He pushed his glasses back on his nose, coughed, and looked once at Ethan and then quickly back at the road. He seemed suddenly shy.

"Are there really guerrillas in the hills?" Ethan said.

The detective touched his glasses and then his mouth, and when he withdrew his finger, he did it with the deliberation of a man pulling a hair from his food.

"Guerrillas. I don't know what this word means anymore," he said. "Certainly there are paramilitaries, but Copal has not gone the way of its neighbors."

He gestured in the air like he was flicking something filthy from his fingers. He closed his eyes for longer than Ethan would have liked. The road rose into a sudden hill and the horizon of cane and jungle disappeared for a moment into a peak of sky.

"Copal has never undergone a Marxist revolution. When the rest of Central America burned, we endured coup after coup. Everyone was trained here. Everybody had a gringo uncle. You can blame whoever you want for that."

He turned as he spoke and peered at Ethan over the wire rims of what, Ethan realized, were his reading glasses. He glared a little, he furrowed his brow. Glancing down like that over his little spectacles he appeared like an enormous storybook owl.

"The interior is not like the coast," he said. "There have never been any incentives to make it so. Few mines remain because the railroad does not run and the roads are unsafe. Basically, we have farmers and then Indians and then, in the cloud forests, who knows?"

The detective stopped speaking, he left his hand outstretched and the gears unshifted, but the silence seemed temporary, a practiced pause. There was something performed about his speech. As if he'd been rehearsing this response for years. But of course Ethan had asked the same question when he first met him and received a different answer. The speech must be prepared for him.

"So are these men guerrillas? Certainly they are men whose interests are not El Lobo's. This country has no internal economy. We have CAFTA, we have our exports, our bananas and our coffee and our pitiful minerals. And now we have blight in the crops and a shrinking U.S. economy. This puts some pressure on El Lobo. So what do these men do? These guerrillas? They close the roads from the fields to the coasts, which makes things even harder for the exporters. When that is not possible, they burn the fields. Less and less cash comes in. At a certain point, El Lobo will be stripped bare."

"That doesn't help anybody," Ethan said, and immediately felt foolish. Again the detective was barking.

"I really do love Americans," he said. "I love you all so much. I have been married twice before, but now I think I am going to wait until the tourists return."

Ethan considered the moldy ruin of Mara de Leon and watched as the truck's lights swept on, and then over, a cluster of tin-roofed shanties set in the shadeless expanse of the cleared field. The tourists, he felt sure, were not coming back.

"Then I will marry some big American woman," the detective said. "A Miami Jewess, I think. They are not so different from Cubanas— and let me tell you, my friend, there is nothing better than a Cubana."

"I think you'd have to convert," Ethan said.

"So what? That should not stop a man from finding love. Besides, my grandmother's name was Perera. So I am probably a Sephard."

He let go of the wheel and held his hands up to the sides, splayed out through the driver's side window and in front of Ethan's face, as if he were indicating the size of a very large fish.

"This is what we are here—Spain's rejects!"

"And the Indians?"

The detective puckered his lips. For such a meaty face, his mouth was particularly thin.

"Maya's rejects," he said. "Same story, different empire."

He still had not taken the wheel again and Ethan had to ask, "Are you wearing your reading glasses?"

"Yes," the detective said. "For the signs."

For a time another truck trailed them. Ethan watched its headlights rise and fall on the undulations of the road behind. The detective was an unsteady driver, he slowed and accelerated as the mood took him, and the truck seemed to match their speed. It did not gain or fall back; its lights held their place as if constrained by rules of orbit.

"Have you heard of a man named Soto?" Ethan asked.

The detective checked the rearview mirror for the first time.

"No," he said.

He checked the mirror again, held his eyes there as if he were inspecting his own reflection.

"Never even heard the name?" Ethan said. "It's not that uncommon."

The detective accelerated. The lights stayed with them and then, after a time, disappeared so quickly that Ethan wondered if they had ever been there at all. The detective did not slow down.

"When I was a young man I wanted to be a poet," he said. "I lived in the capital back before the capital became what it is now. Many of my friends were literary types. They were saving money for the airfare to Buenos Aires because they intended to move there and become disciples of Borges. We were all very idealistic about things that did not exist. We were all little bitty Marxists. When things began to change, when the yanquis shut down their hotels and opened up training camps for Nicaraguans and Salvadorans, all my friends thought that it was their obligation to speak out. To write editorials so that people would know the truth. Do you understand?"

They continued on, after that, in silence. The road ran higher now. They'd gradually crested a plateau, and to his right, beyond the diminishing rows of cane, Ethan saw the flicker of fires in the valley. When he looked back to the road there was a man in it, walking far ahead in the middle of the lane. The detective slowed but did not stop.

"Hold on and get ready to duck," he said to Ethan. "You do not want to meet people in the road."

At first the man was in shadow, ambling ahead, stoop-backed and unturning, clothed it seemed in a dark cloak and carrying a staff or walking stick—a medieval friar or solitary penitent making his pilgrimage across barren lands. And then, as they approached and the glow of their headlights climbed over him and threw his shadow fifty feet down the road and into a wall of cane, he did not turn or step to the side or acknowledge the truck in any way. Ethan knew they should not stop, there was no good reason to stop, it was dangerous to help lone travelers on the roads at night. It was the oldest trap: pull over for a man in peril, get ambushed by a gang hiding in the cane. The detective, of course, was downshifting, then breaking. He was pulling over.

"Roll down your window," he said to Ethan, but Ethan's window was already down.

They puttered along next to the man. He was small and stood shorter still for his stoop; he wore a hood and worked his stick through the dust. He shuffled ponderously beside their truck and paid them no notice. He was saying something. Ethan saw his mouth move mutely, his lips widened and collapsed around his words. He was toothless.

"Father," the detective said, "do you need a ride?"

The man walked on and continued to speak to himself. He never turned his eyes from the empty way before him.

"Father, you should not walk in the middle of the road. There are cars and worse."

They waited there a moment. The night outside the truck was perfectly silent. No calls of birds or sounds of waves. Even the old man's stick, thrusting through the rubble of the road, was soundless. Ethan felt like one at the edge of dream, receding sense by sense into waking. He did not know what would meet him when he got there.

When Ethan came upon Doyle he was sitting in the ruined pavilion and talking to a stray dog. Flowering trees canopied the plaza, and he sat on a stone bench as wind off the water fluttered pink fallen petals about his feet and carried the briny smell of algae and dead fish through the town. He sat with his back to the sea and faced the narrow twist of winding cobbled streets that rose up into the hills. Directly across from him, stores on the shore sold fresh fish and empanadas. Behind him, fishing boats and charter vessels clunked up against the palmwood dock. Beyond the plaza, down along the malecón, lay rows of small concrete houses ornamented with iron-latticed windows and winding pastel-painted fretwork. Then the roads rose up again into hills and a larger, cobbled *plaza* surrounded by the town center, a mayor's office and police station and the cathedral clocktower: tall and brown and broken-looking. A gothic tower casting the days' first long shadows.

This was the route Ethan walked. The detective let him off at the outskirts of town at dawn, on a rocky, jungle-bordered road beyond which all he could see was the top of the cathedral cresting the trees. He walked and men on mules riding out of the mountains tipped their hats and passed him. Twice pickup trucks offered him a ride into town, but he nodded and smiled and waved them on.

The road turned and flattened and the jungle cleared. He came to the shantytown where stray dogs, or dogs so ill-fed they looked stray, slunk what thin tin-cast shadows they could find. Two children without shirts or shoes waited in the shade of a rusted-out oven by the side of the road. They ran to him shouting and holding up their pointer fingers like little prophets threatening vengeance from on high.

"Hey, gringo, gringo, one dollar. One dollar, gringo!"

"No, niños. No dollar," he said, and continued past the cathedral that he knew from the postcard. *Fruit of memory, the country of the dead*, a cathedral crumbling itself into the sky. Beyond the cathedral, the town opened into view. He had to trust the symmetry of moments like these. If Doyle sent the postcard it was because he was here, and if he were here, Ethan knew exactly where he'd be.

The two guards outside the discothèque slept slumped over their rifles. Ethan stood and watched them breathe. Each held a rifle clasped idly between his knees, and one had two revolvers, old and rusted, some banana man's six-shooters, slung crossbarreled, in his pants. They were children with guns and Ethan did not want to wake them. Their first reaction would be fear or shame and either one could lead to anger. He skirted them slowly and stood before the door of the club under the rising sun. From inside he could hear the electric thump of the reggaeton, and when he put his hand against the stuccoed concrete he felt it tremble to the beat of the music. A mangy goat regarded him from across the lot with an expression of discernible sorrow. It fixed its sad black eyes on him, and after a time returned to routing through the weedy trash. The disco was set against the water and Ethan could hear the dawn tide beginning to recede over the coral shoals. Whatever the club held, he'd have to go in after it. Ethan took off his sunglasses and opened the door.

Inside, the disco was divided into a bar area and a dance floor leading up to a low stage. The bar was empty, but on the dance floor there flourished a weird world of nocturnal revelry, where two dozen people jerked in some creepy approximation of a bump and grind. Mostly they were women. They shuffled and stepped, they sweat and closed their eyes, they bounced their hips in undulant humpings. In a lifetime disconnected, it seemed, to this moment, Mallory had read to Ethan a medieval description of Fairyland—and under the unceasing strobing of the neon lights the dancers here reminded him of the denizens of that realm: tranced and dazed and caught in a world of low light and sludging time. And over them all, Ethan saw now, reigned Doyle.

Doyle danced with a glee unshared by the crowd swaying about him. He wiggled and strut his way across the dance floor, he pulled women to him and pushed them away; his shirt was unbuttoned, and under the shuddering fluctuation of light his mad sneer appeared mirthless and rigid, a gargoyle's grin exposed by lightning.

Ethan stood and watched Doyle dance and felt the sudden free-
dom one feels when a menacing dream turns to nightmare. At least
now he knew what he was dealing with, and whatever it was, it was
another world altogether, a new wrinkle forever removed from any
choice made in any morning at any table in New York. Ethan felt
the urge to reach for a camera that was not there. He raised his hand
to Doyle but Doyle did not see him. Doyle had made his way to the
stage, where he frolicked with the club dancers, the women paid to
stay and dance as long as there were customers. He moved between
them, he bumped and bounced, he laughed over the hundred deci-
bels of reggaeton—he produced, in the blackened half-second between strobes, a dead chicken.

Even as Doyle plucked and threw its feathers from the stage, the
somnolent dancers did not notice the bird. Ethan alone was audience
to the spectacle of Doyle dancing with the chicken. He merengued and
waltzed to beats unheard and discordant. He twisted it by the wing,
held it before his groin, grinded with it almost down to the floor, and
when he rose he passed behind the dancing women and took turns
propping the half-plucked bird upon their bare shoulders where its
broken neck lolled and bopped in a florid parody of their dancing.

Ethan pushed into the dancing crowd. In their heavy, sluggish
thrustings they were hard to circumvent. Women with eyes half-lidded
clung to his arms and tried to pull him into their circles. On the stage,
Doyle Rockette-walked the chicken across a dancer's upheld arm.

He had almost reached the stage when Doyle disappeared. For a
moment he was gone—he had vanished in the space of a strobe—and
then Ethan saw him again, striding quickly away toward the fire exit,
like a man fleeing the scene of a crime. He neared the door. The music
throbbed, the lights pulsed, and Doyle was gone.

Approaching the desiccated plaza, Ethan saw Doyle from afar. He sat
there—strange and statuesque, totally still in some attitude of medita-
tion or penance as the trees dropped flowers about him and the moving
green and swampy sea glinted through the branches like a slithering
reptile. A miserable little dog stood at his feet with its head cocked, its
ears perked, and as he drew near, Ethan heard Doyle's voice addressing
it: "Have you killed a chicken? I think it's fair to say that we both like

chicken very much. But I couldn't kill one. Do you have blood on your mouth? Yes, you do. That's terrible."

Ethan passed the empanada store that puffed the smell of fry oil into the morning. He stepped into the pavilion with its cracked and mossy tiles, its heavy vines swollen with fleshy flowers hanging from trees and said, "Dr. Livingston, I presume." And Doyle, then, looking up, buttoning his shirt, standing beneath the canopy of blown blossoms, wiping his eyes, checking his watch. "Ethan," he said, as if he just saw him yesterday, as if whatever transpired in the club was simply mirage. "You must have taken a night bus. Not too smart. Not too smart at all."

SOTO'S THIRD DAWN ON the hillside. The last stars of morning hang and wheel on the bluing horizon. A thin slit of moon, pale and fragile as a child's femur, traces, in its quickening descent, the people's progress away from their homes and into the sugarcane fields. Soto has not eaten for two days and the children with him whimper in their makeshift cots of cut banana fronds. When they wake, they stare about with eyes wide and white against their dirty skin; when they stand, they stumble like fawns on legs still rickety and incomprehensible. They wake and stare and stand and do not speak. He paces to the top of the cleared mountain, watches the village and the folk there trudge into the fields. When he returns, the children are lined up single-file. He nods and they commence down the mountain and over the red, rocky scree of drawn and half-tilled earth. From afar, from the village looking back, as they crest the ridge, he wavers black and sun-stamped into the horizon and the children do not seem children at all but misshapen, palsied forms following in medieval procession. Then they turn and descend, drop back into the shadow of the yet-unlit reaches of the mountain, and come to the logging road that winds like a dry river into Rio de Caña.

This time of morning, after the cocks have been crowing for two hours and the men and women have clumped in silently in their flannel work shirts and their straw hats and carrying their cane-dulled machetes, the café is nearly empty. Mirabelle stands and scrubs at the wash basin. Her hair is tied back and her hands are already red from scrubbing. The predawn rush of coffee and eggs and baleadas for breakfast is over and the café is empty but for her. A gecko scurries across the concrete floor, up the pale blue wall. Through the open door, the street burns with dusty heat, but it is cool in the shaded blue of the concrete café and Mirabelle watches two men who lie on the raised sidewalk. Still, from last night, they are too drunk or sick on guaro to go to work. They will be lucky not to lose their jobs—or maybe they lost them already. Mirabelle turns from the door and begins to cut avocados.

She does not ever remember such constant heat. Rio de Caña sits low in the valley and the mountains to the north and the cane fields to the south and west form a basin that usually holds a cloud cover of cool air over the town. Now, though, the valley withers. The banks of the Rio Sulaco, the river that runs to the sea, hang low and muddy, balloon with swamp gas and bottle flies. The fruit trees in town have already fallen fallow, the fruit gone brown and knobby, and it must be the same in the forest, because people have seen howler monkeys prowling the outer villages. The Holy Mother in Her vestments of parrot feathers waits each night by Mirabelle's bed.

For months, She had been absent. Mirabelle had not seen Her since Rosa's death when She had appeared one morning under Rosa's bed and did not leave until after the girl died. Those days, during the illness, She had come small and horrible, with Her gallows noose cinched around Her neck and trailing between Her bare breasts. Her black hair dragged through the dust as She crawled on Her hands and knees about the floor. And then She disappeared. Mirabelle did not see Her in the mirror as she stepped out of the shower, she did not hear Her singing to her as she hung Mr. Bernal's laundry, or find notes from Her in her diary.

But now She had returned. Each night Mirabelle woke to Her, the Holy Mother, sitting by her bed, working Her red coral rosary. She did not speak. She bobbed and nodded in the sweating dark, She thumbed Her beads and wept to Herself. In the moonlight that attended Her, Her dress of parrot feathers glistened a moving blue and purple like the colors of the sea over the reef line at dusk. Her hair was hidden beneath Her macaw's crest, and though Mirabelle could sometimes smell the hot milk about Her bosom, she could no longer see Her breasts. Thankfully, the Holy Mother had abandoned the gallows weeds of Her double aspect—Ixtab, the suicide goddess. She had not begun speaking to her yet, but Mirabelle knew that soon She would. Sometimes at night, Mirabelle saw the Mother's blue parrot's tongue flick and wet Her beak. She had come as She always did, Mirabelle felt sure, to carry news or serve as portent and all one could do was wait.

During the day Her visitations seem frail and distant, a fragile skeleton of fever. But Mirabelle is not sick—she takes her temperature in the morning and knows now, after five years of this, that she must let her visions unfold as they will. Before she left for America, Yolanda spoke of the doctors there, how they had medicine that might improve her condition, make the visions vanish entirely. That was the only time Mirabelle saw the Holy Mother angry. Now, though, cutting avocados in the café, she feels as she usually does in the morning: a person apart from the girl who wakes each night to a goddess. For years the visions were enough to assuage her boredom, but now with Yolanda gone and Jose dead, and Rosa dead too, there is just Mr. Bernal and the café customers and the days feel real, certainly more real than the nights—they are long and dull and lonely. She is an object, she knows, of pity and fear. The townspeople feel toward her, she thinks, much as she does toward the Mother: some mix of love and constant dread.

The avocado meat piles on the cutting board. She scoops it up and fills the wooden bowl on the counter. The green meat is warm and fresh, thick against her fingers—she wipes them on her apron and begins to slice another avocado. She listens to the slick and cut of the knife across the board. The room smells of torn fruit, coffee, and eucalyptus. The men in town do not bother her the way they do other women. She has been old enough for years now, but they keep their distance. She heard their conversations in the street, even about Rosa, who was only thirteen. Last night Mr. Bernal touched her wrist and told her that she was beautiful. The Holy Mother's feathers smelled of mold and dander, jungle rot.

At first she does not look up when Soto enters the café. Everyone is at work in the fields and she assumes the footfall on the threshold belongs to one of the drunks. If she does not acknowledge him, he might leave soon. When she does glance up, finally, he is still standing there, Soto, with his ragged beard and dirty clothes and sheathed machete. Behind him, through the door, the street seems impossible with white heat, desert heat, a heat unknown to the jungle. When he speaks, his dry voice rasps like a snake uncoiling through dead leaves.

"Good morning," he says. "May I have some water?"

Mirabelle pours a glass from a clay pitcher and places it on the counter.

"Please sit down," she says.

He drinks and she refills his glass. He drinks again.

"Will you sit down with me?"

His voice, now that his throat is wet, sounds deeper—not a rasp at all, but a baritone. Echoing, performed, like a man calling from the bottom of a stone well. A clown's voice, or a fool's.

"No," she says. "I have to work. I may not sit."

He turns a slow circle in the room with his arms outstretched, gesturing at all the empty tables. When he faces her again he is smiling, and beneath the grime he has a pleasant smile.

"This is work? This is busy? But there's no one here. You are alone."

Mirabelle finds herself affecting the posture of the girls in the markets: hands on her hips and right hip cocked out, her scowl giving way to a smile. Now that their flirtation has ended, she expects him to turn away from her and sit down or go back into the street, but he stays standing. She begins again to cut avocados. She cuts them and he is silent, the knife clicks and clicks on the board, and still she does not hear his strange voice. She piles the cut fruit into a bowl, covers it, places it in the plastic ice cooler and begins to cut again. She does not look up and the world is now parched of any sound but her knife on the board, the meat of the avocado slitting and falling, her shallow, quickening breath. She reaches to the wooden fruit bowl for the next avocado and finds that there are none. When she raises her eyes he still stands there, haloed in the light through the door gilding the risen dust.

"Tell me," he says in his carnival voice, "tell me why you do not work in the cane."

"I don't know. I prefer this," Mirabelle says.

"That is not an answer. It is an inclination. Certainly, you would prefer to do nothing at all but drink wine and sit in your swimming pool and watch television. But you are here, right now, standing in this cool café instead of laboring in the fields. Why?"

"I don't have a swimming pool or a television," Mirabelle says.

He laughs and it is not an unpleasant laugh. She finds herself smiling too as if she'd said something very foolish, though she knows she did not. No one in town has a swimming pool. Even so, she smiles as if they have shared some joke and feels then, suddenly, that the Mother is at hand, or near. The Mother, as She always does during the daytime, feels like madness. Mirabelle looks past him about the room, and the room is empty but for them. Still, a madness trembles there, whether hers or his she does not know. Perhaps, as with her evenings with Mr. Bernal, as with everything maybe, she has misunderstood this moment.

The man steps forward and snatches a gecko off the counter. Its color changes from green to brown in his hand.

"Look at this petty evasion," Soto says.

He opens his hand and the gecko scurries up his arm and over his dirty shirt, down his black-and-gray camouflage pants to the floor.

"After a while, an unanswered question becomes a lie, don't you think?"

"Mr. Bernal," Mirabelle says. "The owner of this café. He wanted his daughter to learn English so that one day they could live in America. He hired me to teach her. After she died of cholera, he kept me on in her place."

Soto nods and blinks and for a moment she thinks he is holding back tears, though his eyes are dry.

"Cholera is a filthy disease," he says. "Disgusting and shameful. Shitting yourself until there is nothing left, until you are empty. I do not know what I find more frightening: to die that shamefully or to realize, once you are about to die, once you are empty, that all you have within you, all you ever had and were and imagined, was shit. And now that it is gone you are even less. Everything is shit and you are nothing without it."

No, Mirabelle thinks, you are wrong. I see through you now. The Mother has warned me of you. There is more in the world than that.

"There is Our Lady," she says. "She is the Lady of Our Lord and the Lady of the Gallows and She comes with mercy and splendor."

Mirabelle looks down sharply at the counter. She knows better than to speak of the Mother. She has seen her brother lying in the street with flies filling his mouth and she has held Rosa as she shivers and cracks her own bones into oblivion. She knows Her words, the Mother's words, peddle the world's madness, and their meaning for a man like him must long ago have fallen forfeit. He smiles his pretty smile and his scorpion eyes glint the color of golden rum. He reaches out to touch her, and, when she does not recoil, returns his hand to his side.

"Do not worry, darling. I too believe in mercy."

Mirabelle grasps for an avocado, but the bowl is empty.

"When I first saw you, I thought that you might be a missionary," she says and realizes as she says it that it's true. Beneath his smile and carnival voice he carries the Mother's terrible melancholy. He could hold her, she feels sure, and weep.

"I did not mean to be vulgar," he says. "Please do not think that I intend to offend you. It is just such a sad story you tell me. This country is ruined by all of the simplest things. Cholera. Malaria. Bad baby formula. Did you know in the States there is no cholera?"

She nods. Yolanda taught her English. She has heard all the stories of wonder. In Miami you will not die of fever, you will not be killed in the street by Mara Salvatrucha. There are no buzzards in the cane or fires on the roads. Then why hasn't Yolanda written in months? Why have the medical aid missions never reached Rio de Caña? The world is full of stories like market trash: you haggle them down to what you think they're worth, what you're willing to believe, and leave with less. The Mother has told her that she must not become a nun, but she has never felt this lonely before.

"I do not believe in America," Mirabelle says to the man standing before her. "And I do not believe the people who try to sell it to me."

"Tell me," Soto says. "Do you resemble Bernal's daughter?"

"She was only thirteen."

"Do you think that one person can ever replace another?"

"I don't know what you mean," Mirabelle says. His serious questions bounce on his lunatic cadences. She feels certain that he is luring her toward some inevitable conclusion, something out there in the heat, and with every answer she is going to it.

"It is a simple question," he says. "Can one person live for another? Do you have a sister?"

"Yes. In America."

"Your sister lives in America?"

"Yes. In Miami."

"And you, have you ever been to America?"

"No."

"So how do you know your sister lives there, if you yourself have not seen her?"

"She used to send money home."

"Of course," he says. "That is conclusive. Well, wouldn't you like to join her there?"

This time she laughs. His spell is broken. Who does he think she is? Does he think she's a child? It's true, in some things she feels a child, but she knows a coyote when she sees one.

"Go away. I have no need for coyotes. I am happy here." She tries to sound honest as she says it.

He steps back from her with his hands outstretched in some mock display of offense. His every move is unknowably strange.

"A coyote? Is that what you think I am? Mirabelle, you are unfair to me."

The Mother is suddenly near again. She feels Her sweating in the corner, smells the molting feathers and jungle rot. The Mother has prophesied: when he calls you, you must answer.

"How did you know my name?"

"Mirabelle," Soto says. "This is no accidental encounter. I have come all this way to find you. All the way from the Orphanage of Santa Qultepe of La Paz."

She does not say anything. This is wrong, certainly. He is madness, he speaks in a voice out of the grotto, he blinks the scorpion's eyes, but he has called her by name and the Mother is no use now. She has said, *you are an instrument to the suffering children.*

"Mirabelle," he says. "Come here, Mirabelle. I want to show you something."

He walks to the door, to the heat there, and she finds herself following. He steps into the street and she crosses the threshold and looks where he points and sees the six small children sitting on the ground against the concrete wall. They are dirty and sun-scorched. Their dry lips peel like garlic skin.

"Mirabelle, if you come with me," Soto says, "to the Orphanage of Miami, these will be some of your charges. Please now, they are very thirsty. Will you minister to them?"

ETHAN SAT ON DOYLE's verandah, looking out over the banana groves falling into green valleys still thick with morning mist. Doyle went inside, made coffee, and served it in clay Indian mugs. Grackles chattered and darted between the bananas.

"It's probably the only verandah within twenty miles of the coast that does not face the sea," Doyle said. Beyond the fogged descent of the hillside, the banana groves rose up the far wall of the valley in perfect ordered rows that fell away, finally, into untended jungle.

They sat without speaking on the tiled deck. Ethan put his feet up on the balcony railing and watched the risen sun illuminate distant groves of wild bamboo. He drank his coffee, which was good but not as good as the coffee in the local cafés. It was the type of thing that Doyle never took particular care with—or no, that wasn't it, Doyle took care in everything he did. In college he'd taught himself to walk with perfect and equal balance so that, in theory, he would never wear out another pair of shoes. It seemed a ridiculous idea, even after Doyle held up Ethan's sneakers which were worn down at the edges and said, *look, Ethan, you list.* So no, the coffee wasn't carelessness, but simply a detail unrealized, a lack of appreciation, maybe, or palate. Always, Doyle valued precision over subtlety.

Ethan said, "It looks like you've made a life here."

Doyle shrugged, nodded at the hemp-spun hammock hung from the corner of the verandah.

"I have a hammock, anyway."

"You do have a hammock."

"Do you know, Ethan, the singular pleasures of making love in a hammock?"

Ethan tried to imagine it and he imagined it like everything else: the rocking sides, the tangle, the impossibility of leverage.

"No," he said. "I definitely do not."

Inside, the house seemed smaller than Ethan would have thought from the size of the verandah. A bare foyer opened into a kitchen. Doyle's bedroom was large and empty but for a bed, several piles of books, and a radio. A bug-eaten potted palm wilted in the shadowed corner. The walls and ceilings were mirror-plated. Doyle pointed at their many reflections.

"Whoever used to own this place must have been a pretty good friend of Doctor Kinky," he said.

Ethan was sure that while Doyle had left the house empty, kept his clothes folded and packed and made no life there that could not be quickly gathered and hidden, he was the one who had installed the mirrors. Whatever urge Ethan had witnessed in the disco had subsided—Doyle seemed more or less as he had always known him to be—but Ethan had long assumed that there were impulses that had driven him down here in the first place. The letters had hinted at the simplicity of sexual conquest, unrelenting desire for something that never seemed fulfilled. Ethan remembered that evening ten years earlier in New York when Doyle had said, *down there a white man can fulfill every single sexual fantasy.* Maybe that was why he still had not fled Copal. Ethan stared at himself refracting away down a hallway of mirrors, Doyle at his side holding two Indian pottery mugs, the two of them doubling and doubling and doubling down into darkness.

The kitchen danced with geckos. They scurried up the walls, skittered between pots, hung along the edge of the faucet. When Ethan reached to pour from the jug of distilled water, a gecko started from the cap, and another clung to the rim of his glass and then darted off. For a moment as he stood there in the dark concrete kitchen, all of them, the thirty swarming lizards, froze where they clung, like a collection of grotesque ornaments. Then he set the glass down suddenly and again they were skittering toward whatever cover they could find.

"Doyle, your kitchen is full of reptiles," he said.

"They're anoles," Doyle said. "And they're excellent."

"They're everywhere."

"I know. I bring them in. I pay local kids to catch them. They eat cockroaches. This is the cleanest kitchen in Central America."

"Doyle, it's swarming with lizards."

"Have you ever seen a cockroach?" Doyle said. "Very disgusting."

It was ten in the morning. They sat and drank water and the lizards peered at them from behind glasses and stacked plates. After several years without seeing Doyle, Ethan had thought that it would be awkward to meet his friend again, this man who was now a fugitive, who lived some strange approximation of whatever life he had originally intended, who volitionally filled his kitchen with lizards. They sat and did not speak and it's fine thought Ethan, it's not awkward at all, this silence or anything else. He had imagined that Doyle would have changed irreparably, would be a man beyond recognition. He remembered, then, the incident at Yolanda's sink. I've got it wrong, he thought. It's not that I still recognize Doyle, it's that I don't recognize myself anymore. That last morning in New York when Samantha stood at the door, headed off to work and everything that followed, he said goodbye to someone who by then appeared as much a glyph as Doyle's postcard. It's that I don't recognize anyone anymore.

"Can we put on the fan?" Ethan said.

"I broke it."

"Why would you do that?"

"It was an accident. My machete was aflame."

"Your machete was aflame?"

"I was burning cockroaches."

In the low light of the kitchen, Doyle looked older than he had on the verandah. Already the first webs of sun wrinkles spread from his eyes, his pale blue eyes which seemed paler now, bluer as well, and hard, like bathroom tiles bleaching with age. In college there had been something restless about Doyle's gaze, something impatient. He'd look from thing to thing, person to person, his eyes moving around a room like he was constantly hoping that here, here would be whatever it was he wanted—and then moving on, always disappointed. Now, though, he stared at the table, his water glass, looked back up to Ethan, held his gaze there. His hair, which he kept short—cut himself, Ethan was sure—receded in a wide V. No doubt if he wore aviator sunglasses he'd look just like a mercenary, one of those gringos who always hid his eyes, even inside and in the dark, for fear that someone might see the heat-stunted synapses misfiring there.

"So you ended up with a villa in the hills after all," Ethan said.

Doyle nodded, played with the tassel of a sheathed machete.

"Of course, you're a fugitive."

"I am," Doyle said. "I am a fugitive."

"That must undermine the whole tropical paradise experience. Then again, this is hardly a paradise."

"But it is tropical."

"Sure," Ethan said. "Just look at all the lizards."

Afterward, Ethan told him why he was there and Doyle said, "That's the most idiotic story I've ever heard."

They were walking in the banana grove beneath his verandah. The trees grew in perfect symmetrical rows, and they wandered the shaded pathways between them down into the valley. Doyle, carrying his machete with him, chopped idly at banana fronds as they walked.

"I'm talking bar none, full throttle, the most idiotic story I've heard," he said.

"I admit, I could have done things differently," Ethan said.

"Here are some basic rules that are easy to observe. You never go back into the bar with weirdos. You never get sarcastic. Maybe you can get away with that in Mexico, but down here that's called machete death. Hack, hack, hack."

Doyle mimicked the action, hacked three times at the nearest bundle of bananas. He wiped his blade, splattered with unripe fruit, on his khaki pants.

"Are these your bananas?"

"No," he said. "But I'm paid to watch them. Make sure nobody steals."

They walked on into the valley and it grew hotter under the low-growing trees, where some mist still hung and the light came obliquely through the warm, wet air. It fell between the leaves like water over scaled steps and pooled where it could on the green-shadowed path.

"Why do you trust this woman?" Doyle said.

"Yolanda? She seemed desperate."

"Look around as we walk through town, Ethan. There's no shortage of desperation here."

A parrot screamed and flushed from the tree before them.

"Why would she lie?"

"I can think of a million reasons," Doyle said. "Maybe it's a drug scam? A prostitution ring?"

"No," Ethan said. "It's not like that. She saved my life."

"That doesn't sound likely."

They walked on, and they were low enough now that if he looked back over his shoulder Ethan could see Doyle's hill house painted yellow and green against the hazy, browning sky.

"Why do you say that? The guy had a switchblade. You said it yourself, I was fucked."

"Ethan," Doyle said. "Where is Samantha?"

"We're separated," Ethan said. And then: "She's committed herself."

Doyle turned and stopped and looked at him, but Ethan was wearing his sunglasses and he knew that Doyle wasn't able to see whatever he was looking for, that he saw himself, green and metallic and condensed in the mirrored glass. Probably, he wanted to tell Doyle everything about Samantha, as if Doyle's absolution, or Yolanda's, could equal her own. A tarantula dropped out of a tree, landed at their feet.

"Look," Doyle said. "A killer spider."

He nudged it with his machete and it scuttled back, yellow-spotted and hairy, a mammal almost, into the shade.

"Ethan," he said, "do you know how many times I have found a tarantula in my home?"

"No, I don't know that."

"Fifteen times. Fifteen uninvited tarantulas," Doyle said.

Inside again, and Doyle opening drawers, packing a duffel bag, pulling out maps and spreading them on the kitchen table.

"These maps are no good," he said. "They're too new."

Ethan walked to the table, looked over his shoulder.

"They're optimistic," Doyle said. "To say the least."

"Optimistic?"

Doyle turned away from the map and poured another glass of water. He had not stopped drinking water all morning.

"Yeah, optimistic," he said. "After he was elected, El Lobo ordered that all new maps match his intended—and totally unrealized—roads program."

Ethan looked down at the map, at the clear and perfect symmetry of highways, of towns linked by wide roads, of throughways traversing the un-travelable interior in straight and idiotic lines over the mountain peaks. He knew that in the mountains what roads existed were single-laned and unpaved, donkey trails that switchbacked like a frozen slinky in long loops down the mountainsides. He looked at it—the strange insanity of it, like his picture of Samantha in Key West, as if forcing it onto paper could conjure it into the world.

"How does anyone get anywhere?" Ethan said.

"A philosophical question, or a literal one?"

"Whichever you can answer."

"Where would they go?" Doyle said. "They use old maps, I guess. The new ones are for tourists, and in case you haven't noticed, the tourist trade is not exactly booming."

"Have they built any of these roads?"

"No. It's total fantasy. It's like with the hospitals. The Church will help subsidize them if El Lobo lets them set up missions among the Indians, which he never will since it's in everybody's best interest to keep foreigners way-the-fuck out of the interior."

"And the roads?"

"The roads are a moot point. Even if he had the machinery and the money and the labor, the guerrillas would never let him into the mountains."

"This is common knowledge?"

"This is the commonest of knowledge."

"Then why make the maps?"

"Probably to prove to the United States that their thirty million dollars in aid is going someplace other than the Caymans."

"And he thinks that will work?"

"Who knows?" said Doyle. "El Lobo is like everyone else in a uniform here. He is batshit to the extreme."

After he packed his bag, Doyle said, "I think we need to go to a bullfight."

Ethan was sitting at the kitchen table. Light through the skylight fell in a bending slash over the faucet and down to the floor. Outside, it was hot and growing hotter. The dawn breakfast was not sitting well in Ethan's stomach and all the lizards watched him with their glassy black eyes.

"Why do we need to go to a bullfight?"

"There's a guy there who might be able to give us some climate tips. See how things stand in Rio de Caña. And besides, bullfights are really excellent."

"I could use some new clothes," Ethan said.

"We can get you some clothes."

Ethan's stomach did not feel good. There was a heat and roil in his bowels. Something pulsed behind his eyes. His ring tapped, beyond his will, on the countertop. He would not think about it, becoming sick here. Doyle's bag was packed. He stood at the door.

"Doyle," Ethan asked. "I don't suppose you have a cocktail for the road?"

Doyle reached into his backpack and pulled out a plastic bottle of local, homemade guaro.

"Christ," Ethan said.

"Hey, it's noon somewhere."

Ethan had drunk enough guaro to know he didn't want to be drinking guaro. He had seen men lying dead in the street from too much of it, which really wasn't very much.

"Isn't the expression *it's five o'clock somewhere?*"

Doyle grinned and tossed the bottle to Ethan.

"Like, welcome to the tropics, amigo."

They passed the bottle of guaro back and forth as they walked. The path from Doyle's house led down out of the hills and into the arid lowlands near the beach. Below them, in the colonial pavilion, the clock struck, and faint electric music rose from the desiccated arcade on the shore. Once, as they walked, a pickup truck filled with girls in Catholic school uniforms drove by. The girls waved and whistled and the truck sped up into the hills faster than Ethan thought safe. Behind it, dust rose in a screen off the road. They walked and passed the bottle back and forth, and Ethan felt the heat in his face intensifying, growing tighter, as if he were hanging upside down and his head was filling with blood. A child climbed a ceiba tree by the road; the music from the arcade was tinny and false—carousel music from a different world. A beachfront in New England when he was a child. His mother standing and watching the carousel turn, the horses rising and falling through shadow. He felt dread opening in his mind, building beyond any comprehension. It's the guaro doing this, he thought and then no, it's not the guaro, but the path leading down into town, the arcade music, the tired Indians sleeping by the road, the thought, the idiotic, useless thought that he could help anybody. Where were they going now? To a bullfight? To Rio de Caña? He drank from the plastic bottle, but his tongue was numb to anything but the faintest taste of sweet smoke. His lips were dry and he licked them. *Throw it up,* he'd said to Samantha as she stood in the bathroom drinking cough syrup. *Throw it up or I'm calling an ambulance.* Just below them, scrub fires burned in the shantytown. A flight of blackbirds broke into the sky.

By the time they reached town, the colonial plaza was filled with beggars. Dirty children and old women, drunk men with no shoes—they were on them immediately. The children reached out and touched Ethan's hands, the old women mumbled and prayed; they made strange, wide crosses in the air; they cackled and parrots cackled too in the rows of planted fruit trees. The children pulled at his leg, touched his arm, called, "gringo, gringo, gringo;" the drunk men keeping a farther distance mumbled, "hello America, hello America;" the music on the shore blared with sudden static. The plaza smelled strongly of rotting fruit.

Once they were alone, they sat for a few minutes on a bench and finished the plastic flask of guaro. Ethan's head no longer felt heavy, but just the opposite now: light and airy, a balloon untethering from his body. Beyond the plaza—the cobbled circle, the spitting fountain, the ruined cathedral—the rest of the town sloped down the winding streets into a hazy shimmer. Ethan rubbed his eyes. They ached and he felt himself dry swallowing. He saw the bottle on the ground before them. Had they finished it? Had Doyle dropped it? The ludicrous red parrots scrambled and called in the trees above them. They nibbled at hanging fruit. Scraps of it fell about them on the bench.

"I like parrots," Ethan said. "Always have. But this is a bit much."

"Sure," Doyle said. "Parrot city."

"I mean, this is really pushing it. Don't you think they're pushing it with all these goddamn parrots?"

"Sure," Doyle said again. "Another of El Lobo's brilliant plans. When he took office he ordered a list of national treasures. Parrots were on it, right next to howler monkeys and crocodiles, I think. To attract tourists, he mandated that the plazas, our national historic sites, be filled with macaws. I suppose we should be happy he chose parrots over monkeys."

"Or crocodiles," Ethan said.

"The problem," Doyle said, "was that people started stealing the parrots and stuffing them into cages, suitcases, garbage bags, whatever. There's a huge European black market for parrots, apparently. So El Lobo demands that the fuckers are replaced. He fills the plazas with so many birds that even if you stole them hand-over-fist there'd still be enough for the tourists. And then he orders the police to shoot anyone they see fucking with the parrots. Of course people still steal them, but not as many. So voilà. Parrot city."

"And there are no tourists."

"It's like everything else here," said Doyle. "A decent idea in theory turns insane in practice. Seems to happen every time."

Doyle stumbled as they left the plaza. Ethan tried to forget the spectacle of Doyle at the nightclub. Very likely, it's the mad leading the mad here, he thought. Doyle stopped a moment and pointed at the cathedral, at its bone-colored plasterwork, its crumbling bell tower, its rounded arches.

"See that," he said. "It's the oldest clock in the Americas, one of the oldest in the world. It was a gift from the king of Spain. He was saying, *I'm keeping my eye on you.*"

"There's a lot of old clocks in Central America," said Ethan. "I used a detective to find you. He showed me a list."

"You shouldn't have done that. You shouldn't have used a detective."

"What did you expect me to do? Wander Copal looking at clock towers?"

"I thought you'd find a way. I thought you'd figure something out."

"That doesn't sound like me," Ethan said.

Against the dull brown of the clock tower, the perfect blue of the sky seemed hard and flat, dimensionless. A blue screen. Everything ends here.

After a moment Ethan said, "This guy had lights on his sneakers."

Grackles flew in and out of the belfry like wasps at a hive. They too wheeled flat against the eastern expanse of sky. Ethan turned and looked behind him, to the west. The rocky hills leading to groves of bananas and bamboo. The moving green of moss-webbed jungle rising into thicker mountains. You didn't want to go there. But what else could they do? They were at the end of the way here. There was nowhere to go but into the interior.

"What now?" Ethan asked.

"Now we get you some clothes, don't you think?"

Another drunk approached them as they walked at the edge of the plaza. His eyes were half closed. Saliva strung his beard. He stopped before them and held up his hands without speaking. A perverse magician preparing his trick. He dropped his hands, he smiled, he began to speak to them in fake English. Just noises, threads of syllables and nasal grunts that sounded, he must have imagined, like their language. They stepped around him and he followed, waving his hands and mumbling in nobody's English. He did not continue beyond the plaza, though. He waited at the periphery of banyan trees like a demented spirit that could not cross the threshold. He watched them as they walked away into the creeping decay of the village. He waved, he called in his tongues, he did not follow.

Full into day now and at the end of the mud street, just beyond a three-foot-high barrier of unlaid cement, the town market squirmed before them. Here the shouts of hawkers drowned out the arcade music. Before them the market seethed with movement. We're going there, thought Ethan. We're going there and I'm going to get some more clothes. Things will feel different with new clothes. Then we'll go to the bullfight. He liked the simple certainty in these thoughts—this itinerary that felt like purpose. It didn't matter that he was also certain that he would not like the bullfight. He would not like, he was even more sure, everything that followed it. He slowed his walk and Doyle went on a little ways ahead of him, immune to his building dread. Cars rushed down the street, beeped their horns and swerved around the cement pile, drove on impossibly into the market square.

Inside, the market trembled in its own insane carnival. People hawked their wares in rising sonorities from behind tables and market stalls. Indian women laid their goods out on green and red woven rugs. Children ran between them, Ethan and Doyle, selling packets of gum and mangos and heads of cabbage. They passed stalls of knickknacks— belt buckles and Zippo lighters, boot knives and woven machete sheaths—and went on into the stranger realms of the Indian market, where men pandered the bleached skulls of cows and horses, boots made of snakeskin, the bones of chickens tied up in leather pouches. They passed on out of the Indian quarter to where locals sold clothes out of the backs of pickup trucks or off flimsy card tables.

"Let's see what we can find," Doyle said.

Ethan selected a pair of khaki pants and two pairs of American jeans. He held them up to the light of the street.

The vendor named a price and Ethan paid it.

"You're supposed to haggle," Doyle said. "You know that."

"I don't feel like haggling."

"That's not the point. If you don't haggle you'll look like a mark. You'll look like some lost gringo. Anybody's punch."

"Sounds about right," Ethan said.

At the next stall, they bought Ethan a belt and some new mirrored sunglasses. They walked on and a teenager standing on the roof of a white van called to them on a megaphone.

"Welcome tourists, welcome tourists. Let's everyone welcome the brave American tourists."

"I see that kid every goddamn day," Doyle. "He knows I'm not a tourist."

They walked on, the kid called again from his drunken perch atop the broken-down van. A taxi cab honked and weaved and honked again through the crowded street.

"Yeah, you fit right in," Ethan said. Guaro-drunk and mean, he felt the ocean rot of the nearby pier in his mouth, the brackish salt smell of land's end.

"I'm not a mark," said Doyle. "I'm not an errand boy for a two-bit Mexican whore."

They went on, they came to a wide open array of stalls selling t-shirts and backpacks covered in all manner of English lettering.

"They receive boatloads of used American clothes," Doyle said. "Or they make them themselves. Check it out. The English doesn't make that much sense."

Ethan bought a black hooded sweatshirt. Printed on its back was a picture of a silver spaceship flying, it seemed, straight into a milky green sun. Below the picture IN TIMES OF NEED was written in blue and silver letters. Doyle handed him two tee-shirts and two polo shirts. They were each solid colors with stripes, like an admiral's epaulets, across the shoulders. Over the left breast of each was sewn a little black rubber insignia—TOM CRUISE ACTIONWEAR. Beneath it was a blue lightning bolt.

"You want to play hero," Doyle said. "These should do nicely."

"I've never known an eighteen-year-old girl to say no to Tom Cruise Actionwear," Ethan said.

Doyle turned away to face the raucous market, the screaming hawkers and revving cars, Indians carrying dead ocelots over their shoulders.

"The girl's going to be the least of your problems," he said.

Ethan haggled and bought the shirts and a black backpack for the equivalent of three dollars apiece, and as he stood in the thrumming market amidst the shouting in Spanish and Garifuna and Mestizo dialects, he felt he'd lost all hold on language. It seemed strange, a tenuous, fleeting thing: the beggar in the square mumbling in his own garbled tongues, whores calling to him from Boystown's shadowy corridors, the strange array of meaningless English emblazoned on all the clothes around him. He turned and for a moment he didn't see Doyle—Doyle was gone into the maelstrom of sound, and then, turning again, he saw him moving off, just ahead of him, toward the far end of the market. Ethan followed and wiped his brow and his skin felt wet, clammy. He remembered Samantha shivering into a hangover fever with the bed sheet pulled up around her chin, soaked through with sweat.

"You need to take some Tylenol, Sam," he'd said. "Look at you, you're burning up."

"My liver hates Tylenol," she said, and touched her fingers to her forehead. "Besides, I don't feel hot. I feel normal."

He crossed the room and sat down in the bed next to her, lay his lips against her skin, wiped her sweaty hair out of her face.

"You can't take your own temperature. You'll feel the same all over."

"Says you," Samantha said. "I never feel the same. Not anywhere."

Ethan went on to where Doyle waited for him beyond the market on the empty pier. As he walked, women took his picture with camera phones, called and whistled through their teeth. They smiled and stared at him and he could not hold their gaze. He felt for his wallet in his back pocket. It was still there. He put on his new sunglasses and looked up, away from the women, at the far horizon. The tide was all the way in. Past Doyle, he saw the sea hissing up against the coconut palm pylons, a lone cormorant flushing at one of a thousand noises, breaking into the dimensionless sky.

On Sunday mornings, before they were married, they'd wake in Samantha's apartment to bright sun through the skylight and the smell and hiss of coffee coming on in the kitchen. The first time this happened it surprised Ethan: he was drawn from a dream where someone played ugly music on a piano in his grandfather's barn. As he woke, the music thinned out into the regimented suck of water, the percolating drip and sizzle about the warming plate. He rolled over and pulled Samantha's hair out of her face. She was already awake.

"Why do you set it overnight?" he said. "You know I like to make coffee."

The sun through the skylight fell palely on her throat and her hair, her exposed face. Without makeup, lying on purple sheets under direct light, her skin looked soft and pink as undercooked chicken. He rolled away from her, onto his back.

"I like the coffee already made," she said. "This way I have coffee when I want it."

She shifted up against him and he turned and looked at her, her skin still strangely pink, her lips wide and dry. In that instant he did not recognize Samantha. Her hair was lighter, auburn or red, her mouth opened about saliva-strung teeth, her eyelids flickered as if she too had just been roused from nightmare. He reached and pulled her toward him, on top of him, out of the falling slash of sunlight. There it was. The light changed everything. He knew this, knew it beyond any other thing. He pulled her head down to his, buried his face in her hair that smelled of sweat and sleep. The coffee pot silent now, her t-shirt peeling off—both their hands working—over her head. Now, I could hold you through anything, he thought. Here in the silent shadow of morning where one right choice could serve as every remedy.

The week after they returned from Key West, they went to an after-hours function for Samantha's ad agency. The lounge they'd rented was lit with low purple neon lights. Under the lights, the row of black leather couches that hugged the far wall glinted as slick and wet as greased seals. Between the couches and the bar stood a series of round, dull metal cocktail tables filled with bowls of black olives and platters of meats and cheeses and cheeses wrapped in meats. The couches were empty and the food untouched; everybody stood around the open bar. It was a small crowd, not a great turnout, perhaps, or maybe, Ethan thought, intentionally small: an intimate gathering—staged, dark, and well lubricated. People stood in crowded circles and drank and, as they talked, waved their free hands at each other with the freneticism of a cuckoo bursting from a clock. Pretty soon, Ethan thought, a lot of people would start to spill.

"Ethan, you remember Jack," Samantha said.

"Sure." Ethan reached out, over several drinks, to shake his hand. "Good to see you again, Jack."

Jack was Samantha's boss and stood shorter than her by several inches. He kept his coal-gray hair in a military brush cut and he wore all his shirts at least a size too small to allow him the semblance of a larger man. His arms hung almost past his knees, a much bigger man's arms. The last time Ethan had met him he had tried to demonstrate wrestling moves.

"Hey, E," he said. His face was already sweating and there was an empty glass by his right arm on the bar. The ugly purple light muddied the vodka tonic in his hand. "How was the honeymoon?" he said. "Really appreciate you guys going to KW for us. Sam said she checked out the clientele."

"Sure," Ethan said. "It was nice. Got some sun."

"Well, we appreciate it. Not many people would want to go to KW for their honeymoon. Queer heaven, I hear."

Jack gave him a little fake punch in the arm, took a boxer's stance.

"Hope their vibes didn't mess up your game."

"No," Ethan said. "Thanks, Jack. We managed fine."

"Yeah," Samantha said, turning away from the bar with a Cosmo in her hand. "We managed sportingly."

"Great," Jack said. "Who wouldn't, right?"

Ethan wondered why Samantha hadn't ordered a drink for him. Right now, he thought, it was pretty clear that he could use a drink. Impossibly, Samantha's cocktail was already half empty. So it wasn't just Key West. She was laughing and touching Jack's arm. Under the lights her plum lipstick looked like drawn tar.

"Well, still," Jack was saying, "good of you guys to go down there. I mean, fuck, it was your honeymoon. You only get three or four of those, right?"

"Hey, man," Samantha said. "Lay off. I'm a newlywed. I'm all as-woon."

"You look it," Jack said.

What she looked, Ethan thought, was drunk. Her face was mottled with rising color, her hair was down—when had she taken it down?—and falling in light waves around her face. She licked her lips twice and her tongue twisted like an eel darting from amidst coral.

"Honey, could you get me another Cosmo?" she said.

Ethan stepped up to the bar. Jack still seemed to be talking about their honeymoon.

"Goddamn nice of you all," he said. "But hey, you know me. You know what I've always said. Two birds, one bone."

Ethan handed Samantha her Cosmo and waited on his martini.

"Hey," Jack shouted, "did I say bone? I mean did I say that?"

"Yeah, you sure did," Ethan said.

"Ha! Calling Dr. Freud. Gotta get my head out of the gutter. You know what they say about advertising. Sex sells."

"I've heard that," Ethan said.

Later, after Ethan wandered over to one of the empty cocktail tables and gathered a plate of food to slow Samantha down, they all stood in a circle by the bar. Rodney, a man from Samantha's office whom Ethan had never heard of before, had joined them. So had Paolo and his lunatic wife, Anne.

"I forgot you were going to be here," Ethan said to him.

"I've been filing copy for the firm," Paolo said. "Producing some text, you know?"

"Say, Ethan, can I get you a drink?" asked Rodney.

Ethan shook his head and popped an olive into his mouth.

"Drinks for everyone but Mr. No Fun?" Rodney said. "Does everyone else want some drinks?"

"Oh dear, honey," Samantha said. "It is very purple in here, isn't it?"

"Yeah. The light is something."

"Perhaps," Rodney said, "it just looks purple because you've been drinking Cosmos all night?"

"Cosmos are red," Anne said.

"That's a good one, Rod," Jack said. "Wonder if we could use that for our vodka account. Color Your Night."

"Paint Your Night," Rodney said.

"Drink Yourself to Death," Ethan said.

"Hey, this guy is Mr. Morbid."

"I thought he was Mr. No Fun?"

"Those olives look like a bowl of rabbit turds," Samantha said.

"Any news about Doyle?" Paolo asked.

"No. Nothing at all. Not a thing."

"This guy," Rodney said, pointing at Ethan. "This guy is an artist. I mean a real one. Not like us. He's a photographer. Am I right?"

Ethan placed his empty glass on the table.

"I do brochure shoots. Billboards. Catalogs."

Samantha's cheeks were flushed like a spreading bruise. She smiled at Rodney.

"It's mostly computers," she said.

Anne pointed at the empty leather couches.

"Don't those couches look just like reptiles?" she said. "Big slithering wetback reptiles."

"Like, fuck, Anne," Paolo said.

"Totally," Rodney said.

"Am I the only one here who realizes that this woman is totally fucking insane?" Ethan said.

Samantha wiped his lips like he had crumbs there.

"Don't swear, dear," she said. "You sound all faggoty when you swear."

"Not a swear man," Rodney said.

"Ethan thinks in pictures. He's made of light. Words aren't his thing."

"As usual, you're being a drunken bitch," Ethan said.

"It's true," Rodney said. "I find that there are men who can swear and men who cannot swear."

"I want another one of these children's drinks," Anne said.

"That is definitely not a children's drink," Paolo said. "It's a goddamn gimlet."

"It's another little baby drink. A Lime Rickey. All mashed up."

"Fashion photography," said Rodney, who was suddenly touching Samantha's arm to punctuate every sentence. "Must take quite a man to not be turned on by that. All those models."

"I've been doing hand shots recently," Ethan said. "Fingernails. Sometimes we don't even use real hands."

"If Anne gets another drink," Samantha said, "so do I."

"In case you haven't noticed, Anne is a human disaster. And besides, you still have half a drink."

Samantha tipped her glass back and emptied the Cosmo into her mouth. Ethan watched her eyes wince closed in something like pleasure. He felt suddenly like he wanted to sit down and cry.

"Hey, baby!" Jack said.

"Samantha," Ethan said.

"Mr. Judgmental," she said. "Mr. I'm-too-sober-to-fuck-my-wife."

"Hey now," Rodney said. "What ho?"

"Look," Ethan said. "I'm not jealous. I am not covetous. If you think it's okay to keep touching my wife's arm like that, just go ahead. It's not at all creepy."

"Hey, man, don't hoard. Don't covet. Don't snag what you don't want. That could be a slogan, right?"

"God," Ethan said. "Advertising people. This is the problem with failed writers. You're all such assholes."

"Shit," Rodney said.

"Admittedly," Paolo said, "I am not in advertising."

Ethan took Samantha's hand.

"Let's go, Sam."

"You can go, Ethan," she said. "I'm going to stay and eat olives."

The next morning he sat at the kitchen table and waited for Samantha to come home. He had stayed up the night before pacing the apartment in some mix of anger and growing fear. He had hurried back from the event, he checked his cell phone—perhaps she called while he was on the subway. He checked it again and again. He poured a drink, he sat down and turned on the television, and then he was standing again, this time at the balcony window. The noodle vendors were gone for the night and the bug-light glow of the shop signs flickered into empty streets. Samantha was out there somewhere: still drinking at the party, or in a bed with Rodney, or maybe, most likely, she had hailed a cab—she slouched in the green fake leather seats, her forehead rested against the cool window glass, she was coming home. He opened his phone and then closed it again. He would not call her. She had treated him, it seemed, with infinite derision. *Ethan is made of light, words aren't his thing. Ethan is too sober to fuck his wife.* As if he'd want to. Always now, her desire, which, when he first met her, seemed a grace he'd never deserve, appeared both indiscriminate and grotesque. She wanted and wanted and wanted but her need was beyond sounding.

And her mention of his work and Rodney's cruel reference to him as an artist—surely Rodney learned that from her. Yes, he capitulated to the world, to money and comfort and everything else. Who didn't? He was not Doyle, he did not want to let the world ruin him; and he wasn't Paolo, either. He was a working photographer, he lived well, he did not thrash through some parody of his desires. It was her own fear she scorned, and her fear was ugly. With her money she could do what she wanted, she could write and illustrate her children's books, she could spend her life drafting pictures of little girls being eaten by wolves—she didn't need to work. But she did work. She settled into a safety she begrudged more than anything else. He saw it now, standing at the window with the still night falling away into dawn and her out there somewhere, certainly not coming home, but moving, he felt sure, into some other damage. She hated the safety she'd built for herself and she would flay it from her life if she could. It was the most pitiful of self-destructive urges. At some point, to some degree, everyone abandoned their charmed life and lived as best they could in the world. What did it matter? There was purity in light but not in illumination. The light touched the world and the world appeared sullied. Get over it. We mold our own scars, we make our own mercy.

He turned away from the window, walked back into the kitchen, and poured three fingers of rye into his empty glass. He felt his heart coming hard in his chest, and when he raised the glass to his lips he saw that his hand was shaking. The drink wouldn't help; he was hours from sleep. How quickly certainty abandoned him. He had been married three weeks and he felt suddenly on the threshold of catastrophe. In Key West it had been different—there was drinking, certainly too much drinking, but also they had snorkeled under cypress mangroves, they had spent an afternoon sleeping beneath shade palms, holding each other through the green dapple of swaying tropical light. Tonight she had gazed at him first with a drowned girl's glazed eyes, and then, as he left, with something colder, a slithering anger, a reptile's uncomprehending obsidian stare.

He added some water to his whiskey to slow himself down, and immediately wished he hadn't. If there was a night for your own private bender, this was it. He stood at the counter, he stood again at the window, he put on Miles Davis's *Sketches of Spain* and stared out through the glass and watched the rain that was beginning to fleck at the outer window. He opened his phone and closed it again—the desire to call Paolo and see if he knew what had become of Samantha almost overwhelmed him. He saw her then in a room of dark leather furniture, twisting dull-metal floor lamps, slick, obscene light. He saw Rodney bending over her, moving his thick idiot lips across her body. How banal were his fantasies, how obvious. It was late. She was too drunk to come home. One should not resort to his simplest fears.

Perhaps Samantha's new coldness was a kind of punishment. In Key West he'd found succor in her drinking. For the first time in their relationship, he had felt powerful. She was broken and confused, clearly she was afraid—she needed him. He could give her pleasure or he could withhold it. He could grant her sympathy and understanding with a compassion greater than anything she'd ever be able to offer him. It was pathetic, he thought. You wanted her damaged? You wanted her vulnerable? Well now she is. Make it through to morning on your own.

Miles Davis was winding down. Samantha would never let him play this album.

"It's not *Kind of Blue*," she'd say.

Well, what was? he thought.

"Why settle for second best?" she'd said the one time they discussed it.

For a moment he was glad he didn't do gallery shows anymore. Not in years. He was glad he'd quit and he was glad she'd never seen them. Samantha was, he thought, with her childish and privileged sense of aesthetics, a total fucking philistine. The world was not divided between the perfect and the worthless. And if it were, where did she put their marriage?

Outside, there was still no sun, but the darkness on the eastern horizon was thinning into a lighter shade. He turned off the music, he sat on the stool at the kitchen counter. Whatever happened tonight, he would understand, he would love her better than he had. People were not infinite—whatever she was, he could touch and satisfy. He would lead her as in dance, he would fashion her need to his gifts. He poured another drink and heard her key in the door. He waited and raised the glass to his lips, his clarity must not desert him—but it was only a sound down the hall, someone else coming home. Light, then, through the window. Cars in the street. A mad woman, someone's cleaning lady, singing hymns. He waited and waited and slept.

When she came home he was making coffee.

"Where were you?" he said as she closed the door.

Samantha stopped in the foyer between the kitchenette and the living room. The angled light through the open windows smeared against her face and she stood as if frozen, slouch-shouldered, a clay statue roughly formed and unfired. He waited for her to speak but she did not. She seemed tranced somehow, she stood in the light and under it her features looked rounded and vague. He moved toward her, he tried to smell her, but the room smelled only of coffee.

"Where were you?"

She held up her hand to the glare.

"Can we talk in the morning? I need to sleep."

"It is morning," he said. "It's morning now. Look at all the sun."

"Ethan," Samantha said, "I need to sleep."

The apartment shivered with sun and the coffee pot began to hiss. She had not moved out of the foyer.

"I was worried," he said. "I made enough coffee for both of us."

She turned then, toward the kitchen, toward Ethan standing there at the threshold.

"Some coffee would be nice."

He took out two mugs and filled them with hot water to keep them warm.

"It'll just be a moment. Why don't you sit down?"

She did not sit. She crossed the kitchenette in two steps and stood before him. She touched his shoulder as if testing it, and then laid her head there.

"I'm sorry," she said. "I was a terrible bitch."

"I was frightened."

"You must have been frightened," she said in a dull tone into his shoulder.

He felt heat on his skin which he recognized, after a moment, as tears.

"It's okay," he said without knowing what he was referring to.

He stroked her hair and kissed the top of her head. She was just the right height for that. He felt his hurt at her cruelty dissipating, but it was not gone yet.

"Samantha, where did you spend the night?"

"I was ashamed when you left the party early. I was very ashamed."

The word seemed wrong to him. *Ashamed?* What did shame have to do with it? Already, we've gotten it confused, he thought.

"Did you stay with Rodney?"

Ethan had not wanted to ask that question. As if the asking could conjure the reality.

"I stayed with Rodney," Samantha said. "I was drunk and I needed someplace to sleep. I was very ashamed."

Ethan stepped away from her, heard but did not feel his back press up against the spatulas hanging on the wall.

"Nothing happened," she said. "Not with Rodney. He's barely a man. He's a room full of bad appliances. He's an ice crusher or a wine pump. He's a toaster oven. All chrome and good lines."

"Samantha," Ethan said slowly, "what are you saying?"

Now that he was standing away from her the sunlight was in her face again. Fresh rivulets of mascara flowed over old trails on her cheeks. She had been crying in the night.

"Nothing comes out the way you think it will," she said.

Ethan looked down at her hands grasping his sweater. They seemed small and pale, a child's hands making fists with the thumbs all wrong.

He twisted away from her and felt her fingers loosen, break from him like dry leaves from a bough. He poured the hot water from the mugs and filled them with coffee. Nothing she said made sense. The moment presented a choice and the choice was beyond reckoning. Still, he thought, if his choice was between loving or rejecting her, he would have to love her. Suspicion, he told himself, is a failure of compassion.

Pigeons fluttered about the window. Outside, the day turned toward noon. The city's haze of risen heat had already begun to cloud the far horizon.

"Here," Ethan said as he handed her the mug. "The coffee's good."

AT THE BUS STOP beyond the wharf, Ethan waited under a clapboard and tin lean-to while Doyle spoke to the drivers. A child with bare pustule-covered feet sat next to Ethan on the concrete and together they watched Doyle from the shade. Doyle kept pointing west, away from the ocean and the coast roads, into the interior. Each driver in turn, Ethan saw through the blur of the windshields, shook his head. Clearly, there were no buses into the mountains.

Ethan was drinking from a glass bottle of Coke. It was made with cane sugar and was sweeter than it was in the States. He didn't like soda very much, but the Coke was cold and the sugar helped draw out the dull guaro trance. The child was staring at the bottle.

"Hey, yanqui," the kid said. "Are you a gringo?"

Ethan nodded.

"I thought so."

Doyle continued to move between the coaches. An old woman selling sweet coconut water waved to him and pointed into the mountains. Ethan watched him turn, speak to her, and then follow her behind one of the buses.

"Do you have a dog?" the boy asked Ethan.

"No. I don't have a dog. I used to have—" The word wouldn't come to him and he motioned generally with his hand.

"Gato?" the boy asked. "A cat?"

"No," Ethan said, and then he had it. Tortuga. It was an island he'd been to once with Doyle, several years before.

"A turtle," he said.

"Could he do tricks?"

"No, he could not do tricks," Ethan said.

Doyle walked back around the side of the bus with the coconut woman and a younger man—an Indian in a straw hat with a machete looped through his belt. Afternoon was coming on and the grackles in the breadfruit trees had already started their crazy twittering. One of the sores on the boy's foot leaked puss and blood onto the dusty concrete.

"Can I have your Coke?" he asked.

"Sure," Ethan said as he stood and nodded at the boy, put his sunglasses back on, and stepped out into the road.

Ethan sat with Doyle in the pickup truck's rusted-out flatbed. The Indian, Johnny, drove and his cousin sat up front with him in the cabin. For some reason, Doyle had explained, none of the buses from town were running the western routes. It was strange. They weren't long routes, since the buses could only go so far west, into the lower hills—the middle mountains were barely traversable by car. Given time, horses or mules were a safer bet. The Indians were crossing the country, though, heading into Guatemala—they would take them as far as they wanted.

"Why aren't the buses running?" Ethan asked Doyle over the rev and jerk of the engine.

"All sorts of possible reasons. Road work, maybe. An accident. Flood warning."

Ethan took off his sunglasses. The sun settled a little lower in the cloudless sky, and to the east they could see it starting to reflect and move over the water. No roads ran directly between the town and the interior, and the pickup hugged the coastal highway for a while. To the right, the land lay barren and arid: yellow dust littered with rocks, trash, and chunks of ancient coral. The ground leading to the sea descended into a dry forest of withered brown cactus, flowering vines, and buttonwood trees stunted and twisted by wind into postures of agonized children. Ethan closed his eyes and then opened them again. The landscape had accrued some new menace. Jagged barrancas fell away toward the shore, sickly horses with distended, watery eyes and sharp ribs scavenged garbage by the side of the road, scrub fires burned in the distance.

They passed a schoolhouse and Johnny beeped the horn and waved at the girls sitting on the white coral perimeter wall. Were classes never in session? Ethan could not remember the last time he had passed a school in this country where the yard wasn't filled with students. The girls whistled and waved and Johhny slowed the truck but Doyle banged on the glass between the bed and the cabin and they drove on.

"We need to make it to Plaza del Porros by nightfall," he said.

The road turned and curved down to the shore. They passed a grove of shade palms and sea grapes, rotten picnic benches and half-spun hammocks—the last vestiges of the tourist resort at Playa Baranquilla. Here the sea looked hard and smooth as polished stone, it moved away from the shore in a layered spectrum of electric blue, aquamarine, and emerald. In the distance waves foamed softly on the risen reef.

"Good place for a cocktail," Ethan said and glanced to Doyle, but Doyle was not listening. He was looking to the west, the green pastures and grazing land there, the rising tropical plateau of cerros—low hills—and beyond it, the dark border of jungled mountains.

Finally, the road split and they made a left turn toward the interior, and Ethan felt it, the dread again, that this time he knew had nothing to do with guaro. From a closing distance, the mountains seemed bereft of grace or beauty. They were simply vast and overgrown; he could not see where the road entered them or where it went once the jungle closed over it. They drove toward the mountains and there was nothing beyond them. They loomed a hard dark mass, the sliver of sky above them as thin as the rim of the world seen from the inside of an urn.

Why were they going there if the buses weren't running? The idea seemed wrong to Ethan. Like when you're diving and you see a whole school of fish suddenly stop and tremble and turn suddenly—you flee with them.

Ethan nodded toward the mountains.

"You really believe they're doing road repair here? Two hundred miles south of the capital?"

"No," Doyle said. "I'd say that someone barricaded the road. Police or guerrillas or maras."

Ethan swatted a fly out of his face. Another landed in his ear. He'd felt this menace on the road for some time now.

"Which is worse?" he said.

"If it's police, they're probably just looking for drugs. Working a basic extortion angle. If it's the maras, it'll be robbery, and if there were women along, possibly rape. I can't imagine the guerrillas would be this far east. Not yet, anyway."

The road rose. They were climbing the cerros, entering the tropical plain. The sun, falling away to the west, lit now on the mountain peaks. A flock of white birds flushed silently from the road before them.

"Not to be pessimistic or anything," Ethan said. "But shouldn't we choose another route?"

"Do you want to go to Rio de Caña?" Doyle asked.

"I have to. I'm not sure what want has to do with it."

"You're set on that?"

"I am."

Behind them, far to the east now, the dry forest looked like a field of bones. Ethan felt some pleasure in the abridgement of possibility. There was the road into the jungle and the girl somewhere beyond it. You could abandon your vestments of the past here, because here what you did not abandon was stripped from you anyway.

"There are no other routes to Rio de Caña," Doyle said.

When they entered the jungle at the base of the mountains, the land immediately broke away on their right into a sharp muddy river gorge where a number of houses clung to the valley wall. They were built on stilts beneath the higher tree cover, but still it seemed that one good mudslide would wash them all into the lower canopy and hidden river below. To the left, the cut rock face, the exposed earth, giant roots of trees and groves of bamboo bound the road. The sun, so hard and bright outside, was diffuse here; it came in a spangle of green light, milky and moving. The jungle smelled of rain and flowers and no-where, even looking straight up from the bed of the pickup, could you see the sky. Ethan stared over the right edge of the road where the valley fell away hundreds of feet into groves of palm and wild bananas.

"We're probably safer back here than in the cabin," Doyle said. "At least we can always jump for it."

For the most part there were no more houses now. Just the rock-lined road, the jungle valley, the mist that shrouded the deepest descents. Far below, the sound of water. Above, around, everywhere it seemed, screaming birds. The road began to turn and level: they were approaching the first switchback.

"Now it gets fun," Doyle said.

Johnny took the switchbacks quickly—far more quickly than Ethan thought safe. He could feel the back tires spinning and kicking up stones on the full turns. Here, the road turned and turned and swiveled like a serpent winding into the mountains. Each switchback was nearly a hundred and eighty degrees—they seemed to be making little progress. The few times Ethan had driven in the mountains with Doyle and Paolo, they'd honked their horn on the switchbacks—you didn't want to meet another car coming around the bend. But Johnny whipped the turns wide and silently.

"Are they crazy?" Ethan asked. "Are they totally fucking crazy?"

He pondered the insanity of the road. Every hundred yards or so there was a stretch of guardrail, never much more than ten feet of it. Was this, he wondered, all that was left of a continuous guardrail, or had they just put up rail in places where cars were known to have crashed, as if it were the spot, not the road itself, that was dangerous. Occasionally, in the canopy far below, he saw the wrecked shell of a car or truck, rusted out and overgrown with flowering vines.

The road leveled and they passed a banana plantation where hundreds of rows of trees layered the mountainside down into mist and strange houses built from old truck cabins, tin sheets, and banana crates crested the lower foliage. A sign by the road informed them that the left lane was closed.

"What left lane?" Ethan said.

"Caution is not this country's strong suit," Doyle said. "They seem without the impulse."

There was a hint of sarcasm in his tone. A hidden judgment.

"Are you making an economic argument?" Ethan asked. "Pointing out some gross inequity?"

"You bet," Doyle said. "Most babies in my town are nursed on Coca-Cola instead of formula. There's already been a thousand murders in the capital this year."

"Doyle, is there some rule by which I'm supposed to feel inherently ashamed? I eat bananas, I used to drink fair-trade coffee, and in case you haven't noticed, I'm trying to save a girl from slave traffickers."

There was a scream in jungle just ahead of them. High-pitched and long. Ethan did not know if it was a monkey or a bird, a mating call or a death cry. The valley echoed with it and he saw Johnny's cousin in the passenger's seat cross himself. Doyle raised his eyebrows.

"Every spook or mercenary I ever met in this country told the same story," Doyle said. "They were doing something bigger than themselves, more important."

He wiped his face. Down here everybody was nervous and everybody had tics. Most Anglos had that one.

"For gringos," he continued, "revolutions and self-destruction are the same in that they are both forms of self-indulgence."

And what about you? Ethan wanted to ask. What is your life if not that? You came down here not out of compassion, but to cast aside some other guilt. You did AIDS work, you served some greater purpose, until what? Until that purpose became too small and you searched on? You became a fugitive, you danced into dawn with dead chickens, you stayed in this country where there can be nothing for you but torment and death when surely you could have fled. In college Doyle often made a show of reciting Yeats' "The Second Coming" in an absurd Irish brogue. Ethan recalled that now, Doyle standing on a barstool with a glass of Tullamore in his hand, trilling his r's scornfully around the edge of apocalypse.

Of course, Ethan wanted to say, *the best lack all conviction*—but then they heard the megaphone and the shouting and for a moment he didn't know what was happening. He saw the truck parked sideways in the road and the men on the ridge, and he knew then that they had turned right into the barricade. Whatever was going to happen on the road was happening now, and though he was afraid, had been for hours, Ethan felt some strange absence of terror: the moment unfolded clearly. Johnny slammed on the brakes and both of them put their hands up against the windshield. They'd done this before. Two men with rifles ran around the sides of the parked truck, yelling—though beyond their first calls of "Para! Para!" Ethan had no idea what they were saying, whether they were speaking in Spanish at all. The men on the ridge were pointing MP5s at them. They were police, then, or maras—if they were guerrillas the weapons might still be Russian. Here it comes, then, thought Ethan.

"Put your hands up and look down," Doyle said. "Don't make eye contact unless they force you to."

They were police, Ethan saw that out of his peripheral vision as they came closer. The khaki uniforms. The blue, white, and red of the national flag. The men on the ridge, though, were wearing ski masks. Probably they were local officers and, if they did seize any drugs, didn't want any gang retribution against their families. Still, the masks were ominous—Ethan had no idea what manner of men were pointing machine guns at him.

For a roadblock or a checkpoint, the police seemed undermanned. The three men on the ridge covered the two on the ground, but the ridge was overgrown and draped in greenery. They had the wrong weapons for their position and probably did not have any open shots. Clearly the officers in the road were nervous. One ordered Johnny out of the cab, the other, glancing over his shoulder every few seconds, held his gun on Ethan and Doyle.

The Indians walked to the side of the road and put their hands on their heads. They seemed nonplussed. Johnny took off his straw hat slowly and showed the officer that it was empty. He placed it on the ground by his boots. "No drugs," he said.

"Where are you going?" the officer asked.

"Zacapa," his cousin answered.

"Zacapa?"

"Guatemala," Johnny said.

"Ah, yes. Zacapa. Why?"

"My sister lives there."

"Why does your sister live in Guatemala?"

"Her husband is from Zacapa."

"They are all imperialists in Guatemala," the policeman said. "They'd claim us if they could."

Johnny shrugged.

"Don't move," said the policeman.

He checked the cabin. Looked through the dashboard and the glove box, peered under the wheels.

"Don't try to smuggle drugs out of Guatemala," he said.

Johnny picked up his hat, brushed it off, and put it back on his head.

"Okay," the second policeman said to Ethan and Doyle. "Get out of the truck."

Ethan hopped out of the bed and collapsed onto his face. His right leg was asleep.

The policeman jerked back as if he thought this were some kind of trick. "Stand up," he yelled. "Stand up!"

Ethan did, and slowly. The last time someone said that to him he had held a bottle in his hand.

"Sorry," he said. The Indians were laughing at him. How could they be so relaxed? The police had dropped hundreds of supposed Indian collaborators out of planes during the upheavals in the eighties. Now that they were standing next to each other, Ethan saw that the policeman who was speaking was older and higher-ranked—a captain. One of his front teeth was huge and jagged and his gums were bleeding. The younger officer had long black hair, longer surely than regulations allowed. He wore green American aviator sunglasses and kept smiling, licking his lips and smiling again. It was a look Ethan saw plenty of in Boystown. Either a psychopath or a half-wit.

"What are you doing here?" the captain asked.

Doyle kept his eyes down in deference. "I am from the HIV aid mission to Quiectepe," he said. "This is my friend from the United States. We were trying to find new locations for foreign aid allocation."

It was amazing how his arrogance, his bristling anger, disappeared. He seemed shy and uncertain. Just what they'd expect. An American idealist lost in a country he could not understand. Ethan thought that he too should try to affect such meekness, but realized that he'd already fallen out of the truck. His lip was bleeding, his hands were trembling and he was sure that if asked he would not be able to speak a word of Spanish. There was nothing to affect.

"Where do you live?"

Doyle gave an address in the capital. Two hundred miles away to the northeast, the police probably wouldn't know it. Doyle must be counting on their provincialism, their inherent respect for the capital, their fear of accidentally fucking up a chance to get additional aid. Still, if they brought him to the station and checked his passport, they'd find out who he was. Then, Ethan thought, had been thinking since they turned toward the jungle and the threat of a roadblock, there was a very good chance they'd be shot in the street.

"I do not understand," the captain said. He gestured slowly with his rifle at the surrounding jungle, the banana plantation behind them in the gathering mist. "There are no towns here."

The other one smiled and licked his lips, shifted his weight from foot to foot like he needed to piss. Ethan saw the reflection of a black-bird flutter in his mirrored sunglasses. It flashed, warped and distend-ed, across the glass. Not a blackbird at all, something bald and sickly. A vulture.

Doyle was smiling.

"No," he said. "Tonight we're going to Plaza del Porros. For the bullfight."

"There's a bullfight tonight in Plaza del Porros?"

"Yes," Doyle said. "A good one."

The captain nodded. He seemed interested.

"I am sorry," he said. "But the road is closed."

"But we have no drugs."

"The road is closed and dangerous."

The sun came slantwise now. They were still on the eastern side of the mountain and the light would disappear faster here. It gild-ed the edges of leaves and flowers so that the whole forest suddenly shimmered with strange parallel light. The world was sharp and lam-bent and the red petals of the blossoming bougainvillea, previously fleshy and sensual, now appeared hard and fragile, ceramic. A tree frog croaked nearby, and in the lingering light its call knelled another rare certainty. They didn't want to be on this road after dark.

"I see," Doyle said. "I understand, captain. Is it possible that we could pay a toll? For the effort of opening the road? Is that possible?"

He had delivered the line well. He didn't sound cynical, he had pro-tected the captain's pride. Another tree frog called, farther off now, to the west.

"Yes," the captain said. "That might be possible."

Driving again and the cool of the night coming on. Johnny taking the curves fast, even beeping now, racing the sun to Plaza del Porros. Ethan hugged his knees to his chest—he was still trembling in the barricade's aftermath, and separate from that, the night was getting cold. The road slipped into shadow. The gorge, to their left now, pulsed with green, wind-trembled leaves and webs of moving Spanish moss. Ethan could not see its bottom through the shade. It was his first cold night in the country.

"We're almost there," Doyle said. "You hungry?"

Ethan thought about it. He hadn't eaten since the morning. He must be hungry. The road ran straight and level. Up ahead, he saw the swaying glow of paper lanterns, the silhouettes of adobe huts hardening from diffuse shadows into form against the moving lantern light. Somewhere beneath the tree frogs' ubiquitous chorus and the freakish call of the night birds, music played and men laughed. Johnny rolled down the windows and honked the horn as they approached the cleared settlement. For the first time in hours, Ethan could see the sky: black in the upper reaches, settling into cobalt and a thin line of amethyst on the horizon. Against the wide view, the humps of mountains rolled on without end. The sea was invisible in the dark but Polaris had long risen and Venus, yellow as lantern flame, was in ascension.

According to legend, the Spanish established the bull ring at Plaza del Porros when they first landed on Copal's shores. Supposedly, the Maya or Lencas were so impressed by the Spaniards' bravery in fighting bulls that they granted them this area for what they thought were sacrifices. There was little to support the claim. The ring at Plaza del Porros was nothing more than a flat, cleared plateau surrounded by a low wooden fence and some palm and rattan-wood bleachers. On its left, the ring bordered the ravine—bulls had been known to horn-toss matadors into its depths. A row of concrete and soft-wood cantinas and cafés lined the northeast side of the ring, so you could watch the fight as you drank. Dirt roads entered the village of adobe and thatch huts and continued on, narrowing, into the jungle.

"It's ridiculous," Ethan said. "How did the Spaniards get the bulls up the mountain?"

"I don't know," Doyle said.

"And why would they have them in the first place? Who'd lug a bull across the ocean just to fight it?"

They were sitting in an open cantina sectioned between two stands of bleacher seats. Their table was pulled up against the ring fence and crested by a dry palm canopy. They were drinking Honduran beer.

Copal did not make its own beer and the Honduran imports, often smuggled, were the cheapest and most popular.

"It's just a story, Ethan. It's a mestizo fairy tale. Of course it's not true."

Ethan reached into his bag and pulled out his spaceship sweatshirt. He zipped it against the night's cold and read his beer bottle's label in the flickering lamp glow: *Salva Vida!* He drank from it, shook his head. Doubtful.

"There's no worse beer than this, is there?" he said.

Doyle grimaced, nodded, and signaled the waiter for two more.

"No, this is the worst beer in the Americas."

Their food came with the drinks. Doyle had ordered them a large plato tipico to split. Seared steak, fresh cheese, tortillas, and fried plantains. Ethan ate with little relish. He hadn't been hungry for days. The meat was well prepared, frighteningly fresh, bloody, but he had trouble swallowing. He chewed and chewed; his tongue felt slick with grease and his throat tight. From somewhere behind his eyes he felt another vestige of fever coming on. He slapped at a mosquito flickering at the edge of the lamplight. Dengue, in the jungle, would be a torment. He drank from his rancid beer and his bowels began to cramp.

They released the first bull into the ring. It trotted a fitful circle. It snorted and threw back its head and its breath plumed a red cloud in the night cool. Flying insects whirled and flashed in its rising vapor. No, thought Ethan, it's not cold enough for that. Across the ring, in the far corner near the drop-off, the matadors huddled just beyond the fence. They drank guaro and slapped each other on the back and they were not really matadors, but local cowboys who'd gotten drunk enough to give it a try. The first, as they cheered and helped him climb into the ring, could barely stand. His hat hung low and half askew over his eyes, he flailed wildly with a cutlass machete. He roared at the bull and the crowd roared with him.

Ethan did not want to watch. His beer was empty. The bull stamped and kicked at the mud, it turned another circle and bellowed and faced the cowboy. Ethan knew what would happen. The bull moved into and through the darkness. It blew its impossible red breath. There was no art to it now, no dance or bow. The bull trembled as the jungle trembled and the cowboy was not matador but rodeo clown. He lurched and swung and stabbed with the cutlass as the bull charged. Ethan looked away.

"God," he said over the groan of the crowd. "Do they all end like this?"

"Pretty much," Doyle said. "But, Ethan, can you do me a favor here, buddy? You think that guy is loco, huh? You think maybe he should have seen that coming?"

"Look at him," Ethan said and nodded out to the ring, where the audience distracted the bull by tossing beer bottles and fireworks at it while the other drunken cowboys dragged the mangled man out of the clearing and over the fence.

Doyle popped the last piece of meat into his mouth and wiped his lips with the back of his hand. A mosquito landed in the streak of steak blood on his chin. He did not wipe it away.

"What do you think is going to happen to you when you find this girl? If you do. What do you imagine?"

The night quavered with distant luminescence. Ethan saw it break-ing and flashing at the treeline, in the dark frond-grottos of the forest. The night birds called and called and their calls glowed in the trees. Ethan raised his hand and nodded for two more beers. Mosquitoes lit on his ankles, behind his ears, in his hair. He was aware that his hood was bobbing about his neck—he was shivering through his clothes.

"Ethan, what happened with Samantha?" Doyle asked.

Samantha. The name was jarring to hear on another's lips. A phan-tom bell ringing itself back into the world. He was certain that he would find recrimination in Doyle's tone.

"We've separated, Doyle. She was raped and she didn't recover. I basically abandoned her."

"And you feel responsible for this?"

Doyle had not paused before asking his question, he registered no shock, and Ethan realized that for him, a man who had killed a police officer and who lived his life devoid of intimacy, it might not seem such a big thing. Commonplace. Ten years in a world of con-stant catastrophe had ruined his perspective. Doyle still stared at him, waiting. Well, fuck him. What did he know? With his bloody mouth and his Peter Pan life. His freaky room of mirrors, and lizards, and dancing chickens.

"Hey, man," Ethan said. "I know it's not much to you. I mean, we all deserve what we get, right? With our money and privilege. There's got to be an accounting, right? Every action deserves its consequence?"

The bull ring now blurry with light and the plantains on the plate squirming in their own grease. Samantha had said, *what are you thinking?* and when she left, when the door closed behind her, he had no idea what he'd sent her into. At some point he'd set this calamity in motion and it still unfolded beyond his understanding. The action was done—his first mistake, his second—but the consequences were still coming. About this, Doyle was right. There was new damage brewing on the tropical horizon and he would go off into it.

A different cowboy stood in the ring now, swinging his machete. The bull reared and snorted and turned toward him and the cowboy fled, ran for the nearest wall, and dove into the bleachers. The bull followed him there, ran right into and then through the rotten fence and began thrashing about the stands as if it were trying to swim. People dove out of their seats, pistols fired, the bull bellowed and kicked and disappeared into the jungle.

"Another travesty," Doyle said.

Their beers arrived. Fallen lanterns ignited the trash in the ruined stands. The ground flamed suddenly like a conjurer's circle.

"Just tell me that you've considered the situation. Tell me you're not trying to kill yourself."

"I'm repaying a debt," Ethan said, and felt, for sure, that he was lying.

Afterward, they sat in the old man's living room and watched the bleachers burning in the distance. The fire caught and spread through the dry wood. Only what was already rotten would be spared. Outside, the old man cooked under a tin and cratewood lean-to while they waited inside, in the main room, on palm-tied sugar cane chairs. Through the small, barred window, Plaza del Porros burned. Something skittered above them in the cane roof. Ethan felt his fever still coming on. He sweat and trembled and sensed a heat and roil in his bowels. He might need a bathroom very soon.

"Doyle," he said, "there's no way in hell I can eat anything."

"You're going to have to, because Tireisias is making us dinner."

"It's impossible. I'm sick. I'll vomit. I'll shit myself. It will be disgusting."

"Ethan," Doyle said, "do you know how many times I've shat myself since I've been in Copal?"

"No," Ethan said. "I don't know that."

"Seventeen times. Seventeen times in ten years. It happens, and really, it's nothing to be ashamed of. You pissed in a whore's sink and now you'll shit yourself. Some would call that a trend."

He looked over his shoulder toward the sound of crackling oil.

"Tireisias is very poor and he's offering you his food. It's a magnanimous gesture and it will be a real insult if you don't eat it."

"And if I shit on his floor? Will that be a sign of my gratitude?"

Out through the dark of the doorway, the meat sizzled on the tin sheet while Tireisias hummed to himself. According to Doyle, at least thirty years earlier, a French missionary dubbed him Tireisias, and the name had stuck. "I won't lie to you," Doyle had said on their walk over the jungle road up to his house. "He's not even close to sane. But somehow he knows just about everything one could wish to know about Copal. Rumor is that he worked with the CIA in the eighties, but I'm not sure I believe that—and anyway, that's the rumor about everyone around here."

Tireisias was waiting for them, sitting in a plastic rocking chair, when they turned off the road and wandered up a machete-cut path through the jungle. He stood to embrace Doyle.

"I heard you coming," he said in English, and stepped into the mosquito lamp's green halo of watery light. He was wiry and tall for a Copalan, shirtless and impossibly thin, jackal thin—what little flesh he had sagged from his bony arms, his spine dented at his stomach. He embraced Doyle and then quickly released him. He was wearing, Ethan saw, a child's red plastic fireman's helmet and vest.

Doyle introduced Ethan and Tireisias smiled so broadly that the corners of his lips seemed to push almost beyond the borders of his face. A toothless smile jerking into realms of its own accord.

"Come in, come in," he said over the sudden call of a nightjar. "It's cold cold cold out here and you must be hungry."

The power went out as Tireisias placed their food before them. There was a sudden groan and hum and the whole house fell into immediate darkness. In the distance a few remaining fires still glowed, but Ethan could not see his plate. The food smelled strongly of fried grease and something else, something sharp and astringent, nearly rancid, and for a moment there was nothing in the new dark but the food smell, the clammy sweat of it, and then Tireisias's rustling footsteps, the hiss of a match and the room opening to the paraffin lamp's frail light.

Ethan looked down at the plate on his lap. Beans, rice, Wonderbread, and a ragged slice of fried pork, crusty with grit from the cooking tin. His stomach moved and churned and he reached for the bottle of rum that had appeared with the new light on the floor.

"Delicious," Doyle said. "Thank you."

Ethan nodded as well and tried to smile. He drank from the rum. He chewed and chewed. He did not want to vomit on the pine-needled floor. *Samantha*, he had said, holding the bottle of cough syrup to the broken mirror light. *Throw it up or I'm calling an ambulance.*

"So you are looking for a girl?" Tireisias said. His voice was high and scratchy, but his English was almost unaccented. Standing across the room, in the far corner watching them eat, he seemed as thin as the cane stalks in the wall behind him, a part of the house, an indoor scarecrow. "Well, I don't know any women in Rio de Caña."

Ethan waited and chewed and tried to swallow. Then why were they here? His pulse throbbed in his fingertips and his skin was improbably wet, lathered in sweat. It occurred to him that the world itself was sweating.

"But I do know the man she claims is hunting her sister," Tireisias said. "His name is Soto. Lieutenant Soto, I think they used to call him, but for no good reason. He's nobody's lieutenant."

Doyle put down his fork and reached for the rum.

"You've got to be kidding," he said. "*That* Soto?"

"There have been murmurs in the hills again," Tireisias said. "They say he's come out of the mountains, they say he's back in the villages and in the towns. He's buying children. He's passed this way."

The lantern fluttered and dimmed and went out. Tireisias stepped to the table and lit it again. Then he backed away, back into the shadowed corner. "Wait him out," Doyle had said on the walk up to the house. "He's mad, but he usually comes around to the truth."

"Soto was born in the ruins," Tireisias said. "In the places of bones and ill light. They say his mother was Colombian and his father

American. She had to flee Colombia and moved with his father to Copal, where he abandoned her. She lived with Mayans. She gave birth in the ruins and there was bone dust in his hair when he was born. He calls to children. He has the Duende's voice."

Something scrambled across the roof and Tireisias paused. Ethan found his throat working like a python's. He swallowed and swallowed but could not seem to get the pork down. He knew Doyle was watching him. He reached for the rum.

"Soto lures children from the street," Tireisias said. "When I saw him last we were in Managua. It was almost thirty years ago and he was playing the conquistador. We sat under a lime tree. Managua then was not as it is now. Things were happening there. It was changing. You knew you were at the threshold of a new world but you didn't know what kind of world it would be. He sat there with me and drank his aguardiente and smiled his scorpion's smile and I knew then how Managua would go. He glowed. He shone. He shackled himself to the conquistador's golden gifts. Anything you gave him there, in that city, he would bite."

Tireisias seemed to have paused. Against reason and possibility Ethan's plate was empty. The night was no longer cold and the bird calls that came now were not those of the night birds. New birds, new day. Some impossible dawn.

"And now?" Doyle said through a full mouth.

"He moves children."

"Sex trade?"

"Sex trade or slavery or who knows what? He doesn't use the usual routes. He's not your normal coyote. He collects the poorest of children. He leads them into the mountains. They disappear."

"Guerrillas, then?" Doyle asked.

"Maybe. He could be delivering them to the guerrillas. Enlisting them. Who can say? Why would he do that? He was never a reactionary or a communist. The opposite, really. He lived in the States. He went, I've heard, to Yale. Some say he sells them to the Indians. To fill the spaces of the children recruited by the guerrillas. There is no way to know. His motives are beyond reason. They are the motives of stones and old light. When I saw him last he wore a white suit and a Panama hat. He drank rum and smoked Havana cigars. His hair was almost blond and I saw him lead the gringos into Managua."

It all sounded too torrid to Ethan. A doubt that had seemed inconsequential in Mexico's chemical morning had been blossoming for days now. What did all this have to do with Yolanda or her sister? He considered the possibilities of coincidence, random convergence, but the center did not hold. Soto seemed a figure entirely out of proportion with the situation. Admit it, he said to himself. Doyle's right. That's why you like the idea. The impossible vastness of it. The terminal consequences.

"Why Yolanda's sister, then?" he asked. "She's not a little child. Why target her? Do you really think he's running extortion on Mexican whores?"

Tireisias shrugged, and when he did his plastic fireman's hat slid forward over his face. He pushed it back.

"Maybe he's not," he said. "I suppose it depends what the brothels are funding, but I've never known him to be involved with prostitution. Why believe this whore? Soto might just be a legend to her, someone else's bad dream. Maybe she was just trying to help her sister out, find her a compassionate gringo?"

"That doesn't sound right, does it?" Doyle said. "I mean, it's overly complex. It's unnecessary. Usually, things are what they are, or they're worse."

Outside, in the jungle, a monkey howled.

"Do you have a bathroom?" Ethan said.

"I do not like to give advice," Tireisias said and Ethan thought he saw Doyle smile. "But Soto is the bastard child of colonial rot. He thinks Copal owes him something. You are an American, a gringo. Here there is probably nothing that you cannot take. But if Soto covets this girl, you should not try to steal her from him."

He nodded at the door leading to the outdoor kitchen.

"The bathroom's back there. Past the cook stone. Check for snakes before you use it."

Ethan ran out into the night. The wheeling stars and jungle pulse and throb in his bowels. Another day coming on in the south.

"Rosa," Mr. Bernal called from the back patio, "will you bring me some mangoes?"

Mirabelle waited a moment in the kitchen to see if he'd correct himself, say the name again. But he did not. He had only been on the patio for half an hour, but he must already be drunk. Or very tired. Drunk would be better for him. He would not realize his mistake, the shock of it, like waking from a dream where the dead speak to you. In Mirabelle's dreams the dead often spoke.

"One moment," she called.

She took a mango out of the refrigerator and washed it in purified water. Mr. Bernal would have chastised her if he'd seen. He always claimed that it was unnecessary, that tap water would be fine. "Did you know," he said the last time he saw her washing food with jug water, "that the average person eats two rats a year without realizing it?"

But after Rosa and the cholera, it seemed a sensible precaution to Mirabelle. She wondered if he too hoped to get cholera, to join his daughter that way. But then, how could you? It was devastating and disgusting—he had been unable or unwilling to approach Rosa's sick room. He didn't even burn her clothes himself. He had sat on the patio, as he did now, and prayed as Rosa shat into a bucket through a hole they cut in her mattress. When she was dead she weighed no more than sixty pounds and it was Mirabelle who washed and dressed the body. Since then, more cases had been reported in the far villages, by the river. As always, people were beginning to suspect the Mormons.

Mirabelle cut up the mango and placed it on a plate. She trimmed the skin and poured a glass of water. Mr. Bernal would probably need it. Outside, through the kitchen window, the light over the bare mountains settled into a shifting, aqueous blue—a strange, undersea fish tank light. She turned away from the window but did not go yet out onto the patio where she knew Mr. Bernal would be sitting with a glass of rum, a cigar, maybe—though she did not smell it yet—and his feet on the card table. Dogs barked in the street, and the kitchen dimmed into a blue dusk. She stood and waited, even hoped this time, for the Mother to appear, but she was alone in the room and she did not know what to tell Bernal about Soto's visit.

Tonight Soto was escorting the children to the river, where a boatman would ferry them seaward. There, he'd said, they'd change boats, head into Belize, and fly to Miami. It seemed an impossible distance to her, too far for the six kids, but Soto had assured her. He had said, "I am a professional and my associates are very careful. Tomorrow afternoon," he'd said, "I will return from the river. I will, by then, expect your answer." He had bowed to her slightly, an action genteel and archaic and as strange as if he'd kissed her hand. He had bowed and turned and walked away, and without speaking the children had followed.

"But why me?" she had asked just before then. "Why not hire an American girl? Why have you chosen me for the orphans?"

"You were revealed to me, Mirabelle. Of you, I had already heard. Your kindness, your patient ministerings to Bernal's daughter, those deeds were not overlooked."

Overlooked by whom, she wondered? He spoke with the authority of an attending angel. Someone who could bestow grace or judgment. Again, she remembered the Mother's words. *When he calls you, you must answer.* But who was it that called to her? And why did she wish to go with him? The Lord called to Abraham and Abraham said, *here I am*, and to say that, to say that to anyone—herself or Mr. Bernal, Rosa or Jose—the dead who took no notice and passed, she hoped, no judgment—to say that, *here I am*, to make such a rigorous accounting, seemed a task beyond possibility. Where was she that the Lord would call to her, or that the Mother would approach in anything but Her veils of sorrow and dust? Rio de Caña? This arid, heat-blighted town with its fields of dead cane, its tepid, cholerous river, and the sad old man on the patio who loved her, loved her dearly—but as what, she did not know. Daughter or wife? His love, she felt sure, was both sad and sinful, and it terrified her that she could not tell the difference.

But how could she answer his call? In this town, where most families had worked the cane for two centuries, she was a stranger. A girl without mother, woman without prospects, child on the brink, she knew always, of sanity. And what use were her visions now? She was not special or beautiful or ordained for any duty. She was caretaker to a ruined man, seeress of Ixtab the suicide queen and her Motherly double, Our Lady of Sorrow. Or she was worse than that. She was a mad girl living in what she knew must be sin.

"Mangoes, eh? Where are the mangoes?" she heard Mr. Bernal cry from the patio.

She carried the plate across the house. If she went with Soto to America, whose call was she answering, whose desire did she fulfill? She thought of his festival voice and his scorpion eyes. He was terrifying—a spirit come courting from the hills—but also he was beautiful. She felt his need for her like a firm hand pressed over her mouth.

She opened the screen door and stepped out onto the walled patio where Mr. Bernal sat under the canopy of a mango tree. The yard was dark, and for a moment its objects—Mr. Bernal, the table and trees and bottle of rum—were invisible to her beyond their blurring silhouettes. They seemed an underwater shoal seen at night by a lampless diver—outcroppings of darkness gathering in the bluedark, jagged trembling shapes diffuse and wavering. She waited a moment on the threshold and looked past the lime tree, over the wall at the far horizon: a paler blue, smooth and welcoming, the star-flecked sky over the river and the sea. When she looked back down, the patio had settled again into form. She crossed the tiles and placed the plate of mangoes on the table before Mr. Bernal.

"Thank you, Mirabelle," he said in a voice wet with drink or grief. A liquid chortle, the consumptive's slow drown. "It took you a while. I could have plucked and peeled one with my fingernails."

"Tsk tsk," she mouthed, more an action, a shaking of her head than a sound, and she wondered if he heard her at all. "Not after you've been drinking rum you couldn't."

She reached for it, the rum, the smooth brown of its glass reflecting for a moment, as she lifted it, one lone star directly overhead.

"Do you want me to take the bottle?" she asked.

"No, I do not want you to take the bottle."

He tapped his glass and raised his unlit cigar.

"Then I would have no rum to go with my cigar."

She put the bottle back on the table.

"Sit down," he said.

She did. She couldn't see much but she could see that his eyes were wet and staring up into the spindle of mango branches. How was it, she wondered, that she saw him at all? By what light was the night unveiled? Did it radiate from far-off towns, or from insects flashing in the forest, white orchids opening in the dark, red gecko throats rupturing into call, or did it rise from all the wet and broken eyes staring up into the night? Mirabelle reached across the table, lifted the bottle of rum and drank from it. She knew these thoughts, knew that their strange, vagrant luster preceded the appearance of the Mother. Please, not now, she thought. Or not yet.

She put the bottle back on the table. Mr. Bernal still stared into the trees. Mirabelle felt the heat of Her, the gathering presence. She closed her eyes and breathed as slowly as she could. There came the chirp of insects, the slight whisk of wind through the mango and citrus trees. The night ripened with smell: eucalyptus and lime, hard, dry dust, heat and frogspawn off the river and the fruity caramel of the open rum, the last departing vestiges of the good earth.

Mr. Bernal spoke out of the quiet. "When I bought this house, that lime tree was barely a sapling. I grafted it myself. I shaped it myself. It is my fruit. Do you know what I mean?"

Mirabelle nodded. It was as much a truth as a lie. Everything, she felt sure, meant something, and none of it had ever been revealed to her.

"Rum and cigars," he said. "They are like women and children. They are meant for each other. Can you have a cigar without rum? Ridiculous! Of course you cannot. I cannot even imagine it. Of course, the world is full of things I cannot imagine."

He drank from his rum and held up his cigar, put it in his mouth and then took it back out. It remained unlit.

"Or maybe they are men and women, eh? They are meant to go together or they are meant for nothing."

He looked down, finally, from the tree canopy and stared at her through the night's new sick fragrance. Venus in slow ascent.

"Come closer," he said.

When she did, he put his cigar down slowly on the table and reached up and opened his wide and trembling hand and patted her head. He patted it and then stopped, held his hand there and traced it slowly again, down the length of her ponytail. Beneath the heat of the night she could feel the heat of his hands through her hair.

He drank again. "Do you remember your first haircut?" he said.

She did not remember anything from her youth. She had never been to her mother's island.

"No," she said.

"It's too bad. A girl's first haircut is a beautiful thing."

When he pulled her head to his she closed her eyes. She felt the open wet of his mouth on her throat and the teary wet of his mustache on her face. When she stood he was already staring again into the trees.

"I'm leaving," she said.

"Be a good girl."

"No," she said. "I'm leaving."

"In my day," Mr. Bernal said, "we would have killed all these Mormons."

SOTO STANDS ON THE riverbank and flashes the lantern three times out over the dark, moving water. The children huddle, not far from him, behind a brake of wild bamboo. He waits and smells the air; the water level is low and the bank reeks of the flowers that have blossomed from the drying river clay. Fish bones and crusty webbings of frog bodies clutter the bank's lower reaches. He flashes the light again and this time the signal returns, three quick blinks from within the mangroves, and then the soft swish of paddles against the water, parting downcurrent, for the approaching canoe.

Soto whistles a low tune, a nursery whistle, a dreamsong that, like the sudden palpable change of light or location, announces nightmare.

"Come now, children," he says, and whistles again as they shuffle around the bamboo and stand before him, small, shivering, smeared with the blue mud of the riverbank and the dirt of the road. Now the boat, first a sound, then a shadow, sharpens into form. A long Indian canoe with two rowers fore and aft slicing it toward them, downstream. It cuts and turns against the current as it reaches them, the rower in the back puts down a paddle and pushes it onto the bank. The lead rower waits for Soto to help, to reach down and pull the nose onto shore, but he does not. The Indian jumps out, grabs the canoe and nestles it onto the riverbank. He nods at the children.

"These are all of them?"

Soto spreads his hands, shrugs, and opens his eyes in a wide clown's pantomime.

"We were expecting more," the Indian says. "Last time there were more."

"And when did anyone ever promise you that the future would resemble the past?" Soto says.

"Hey, friend," says the Indian in the back, starting to stand and then thinking better of it. "What are you saying?"

"I'm saying that here are six children. I have suffered them into my care. I've scarred my mark onto these hills. If youth were so abundant you would not need these, would you?"

The Indian on the shore puts a cigarette into his mouth, lights it, lets it glow a moment in the dark and then realizes his mistake, thinks better of it. He drops the cigarette into the river.

"This should be symmetry enough," Soto says. "Where I come from, your people are the keepers of bones and pitiful crops. I was born, you know, into your ruins. Is that what you'd like?"

"What are you, anyway?" the first Indian says. "You an Anglo?"

Soto smiles and nods to the children. He whistles and birds in the trees wake to his whistle and call back to him. Something rustles and barks on the far bank. One by one, with the Indian gently helping, the children step into the canoe. Once they push off, the lead rower says, "Next time, there will be more, understand?"

Soto shrugs again and waves vaguely toward the children. The canoe banks and turns and heads out into the deeper moving waters with the dip and splash of paddles, one of the children coughing then ceasing then coughing again, and all of them disappearing downriver in the phosphorescent glow of their silent, diminishing wake.

IN THE MORNING MIRABELLE served the workers before they headed out again into drying cane. There was less and less of it, it seemed. The men talked of blight, the foreman insisted on drought, but with cholera at the river, disease in the cane, rumors again of guerrillas in the mountains and roadblocks on the eastern roads—the men grumbled increasingly about the Mormons.

Mirabelle looked on all of them, as she worked, with a cold pity. Last night on the patio, she had made her decision. She packed her one small bag in the last watches before dawn. She did not have many clothes and she took even fewer. She would find clothes enough in America; she would find Yolanda. Into her bag she placed her Indian rosary, her English Bible and journal, a photograph of Jose posing with several of his friends in the cane, and a green beaded brooch that had belonged to her mother. She did not take any of Yolanda's remaining possessions. Yolanda must have everything now that she could want—and Mirabelle did not need any mementos to remember her sister. Besides, she would be seeing her soon.

So, for the last time, she cooked for the men and smiled and watched them eat and talk and drink coffee before stepping out through the open door, out into the heat and empty streets, the drying cane and their own waning lives, of which Mirabelle had never had a part and now would flee for good.

Let them live here, she thought, and God grant them grace. Let them continue to work and live, let the Lord find them temperance and peace, and Lord, let me leave. She imagined Soto, his terrifying strangeness, his alien beauty, and then—guiltily, because it came second—the orphans she would serve, the life she would live as if it had always been calling her, sounding from across the sea or someplace closer still, Soto coming down over the mountains with her miserable charges, calling her from before her birth, from her conception on the island, a life waiting like the Mother in the shadows, the revelation in the portent—a world forming just beyond her perception.

Unlike Rosa, who had enjoyed serving the men and talking and bussing plates, Mirabelle took some pleasure in the cooking.

"Do you remember my mother's hands?" Rosa had said. "Swollen and rough as starfish. Do I want that? What man would want that?"

But the men had seemed perfectly interested in Rosa. Mirabelle heard two of them speaking about her once in the street.

"I know she's only twelve," one said. "But I don't know how much longer I can control myself."

Control yourself? thought Mirabelle. Of course you cannot. One had no control. The world acted through you and all you could do was obey. When he calls, you must answer. Perhaps this was blasphemy, certainly it was, but what had she ever chosen? Her mother chose to leave; maybe Yolanda did too. She had no idea what choice Jose made to get himself killed and no one would tell her. Always, men whispered around her, but they did not change their conversations. She felt a sick jealousy when she heard them speak like that of Rosa, and now that Rosa was dead, her jealousy had not abated. It still rose in her like bile when Mr. Bernal wept against her neck, her bare collarbone. At night she seethed and turned and watched as the Mother thumbed Her rosary and nodded Her blue feathers and did not speak.

After the men left she washed the plates and made more coffee. Soon Mr. Bernal would wake and wander down to the café. He would stand in the street a moment as he always did, like a stunned thing. He would turn a circle in the dust and stare at the sun—a man looking for a sign, a flock of birds, a star in impossible diurnal ascent, some sad and soothing augury. When he didn't find it he would look down and blow his nose in the street, he would cough and step inside. He would say *good morning, Mirabelle*. He would never inquire about business. And today, when he turned his gaze from the sun and stepped forward into a moment for him whose curse would be that it was like all those that preceded it, he would enter the café to a new loss. But at least, she thought, she could leave him clean dishes and fresh coffee.

Mirabelle picked up her bag from behind the counter. She could hear the coffee brewing and the sun, now breaking over the red pine scrub mountains in the east, came hot and slanted into the café. Already, she was sweating. She wiped her face, she checked her hair in the side mirror. She was not vain. Nor, she thought, was she pretty. But still, Soto would be here soon, and she'd have to do. Whatever that meant. She tied her hair up with a red cloth. Hopefully she did not appear wanton. When the two gringos entered she turned away from the mirror and toward the door.

They stepped inside and stood uncertainly on the threshold, spread-legged and sweat-smelling, purposeful as the angels in the cathedral glass at Qultepe, ones perhaps attended by trumpets, messengers like Soto, come for her. The one who entered first, a step ahead of the other, looked as many gringos did in Copal: his face boiled into a dark leathery red, a Marine's buzzed hair, bright blue eyes. And the other, thin and sweating, fair also and darkly tanned, but still unburnt. He wore a sweatshirt tied like a belt around his waist, sunglasses too big for his head—so many, it seemed, wore sunglasses—and a black t-shirt with odd golden epaulets. They both were ridiculous.

"Good morning," the first one said. "Is this the only café in de Caña?"

She nodded, still holding the bag.

"We're closing," she said in English.

They looked at each other as she spoke and then down at the bag. They did not seem surprised by her English.

"Well, we're hungry," said the first one, the one who looked like an American Marine from the old airbase. "We've been traveling since before dawn. Over the mountains in a pickup truck. All we want are some baleadas and coffee."

"Some coffee would be really good," the other one said.

When she didn't move, when she stood there, he looked again at her bag. The sunlight fell like a sash across his absurd golden epaulets, his black shirt. He still wore his sunglasses.

"Permisso," he said. "I mean, excuse me. But are you going somewhere?"

She didn't answer.

"Where did you learn English?" he asked.

"My sister taught me. She lives in America."

"Of course she does," he said, and took off his sunglasses, opened his eyes wide to the sudden change of light. They were also blue and bleary and bloodshot. He was probably drunk.

"Look, Mirabelle," he said. "I've seen your sister. I mean, I know her. I'm telling you because, really, that's why we're here. Yolanda sent us. I'm supposed to bring you to her because, Mirabelle, you are in a lot of danger."

Ethan watched her face as he spoke Yolanda's name. If there was a lie, if there was some trick afoot, she'd betray it here and now. He was looking for wonder and surprise and he got them both: wide eyes, open mouth, a word caught there, unvoiced. Slowly, with a sadness inappropriate to the action, she placed the bag back on the floor, and he knew then that she was packed to leave, that they'd almost missed her, that Soto had been here and would return.

"Has a man come to see you?" he said. "Has he asked you to go with him?"

She nodded and Doyle shifted behind him, looked out through the open door to the empty street.

"You have met Yolanda?" Mirabelle said. "You know her from Miami?"

So that was what she believed, Ethan thought. That her sister had made it to America, to Miami. They had planned to take it slower, feel her out—but till this point he had botched every part of his delivery. Maybe he would not to wreck this.

"Not Miami," he said. "Texas."

It was a small lie, barely a lie at all. Hopefully she was not testing him.

"Oh," the girl said. "I did not know. Maybe that is why I have not heard from her?"

Doyle stood and walked to the door. He looked outside. Ethan did not like his nervousness. Doyle had passed through the roadblock with ease, but the packed bag on the floor haunted the room like a genie's lamp. Ethan considered the situation again and again and he could only reach one conclusion. For whatever reason, they had converged here—he and Doyle, Mirabelle and Soto. There was no other way to see it. About this one thing Yolanda must not have been lying: Soto was coming.

"This guy," he said. "This man who's coming for you. You cannot go with him. That's why Yolanda sent me."

"He's going to take me to America," she said. "To minister to the orphans. He has a place for me and he has called me by my name."

Yolanda had said, *my sister is different. She's gifted somehow. Or blessed.* Now, though, Ethan saw this blessing for what it was: the hard, cold line of it, the small twitching thing at the edge of the void. He knew it as he knew the perfect photo on a page of similar takes, as he knew Samantha's infidelity: a combination of elements shuddering into form. The dull tone of Mirabelle's voice, its lack of affect that had nothing to do with the fever in her eyes. The meaning she placed in a meaningless gesture: *he has called me by name.* He had seen this look hundreds of times on the demented passengers of New York's subways and recognized it now for what it was—the certainty of the mad.

The expression dissipated, a passing fit. Again she looked like an eighteen-year-old girl, confused, as she should be, beyond measure.

"Mirabelle," Ethan said. "Mirabelle, I promise you that whatever he's coming for it will not be that. There will be no orphans. There will be no America. It doesn't work that way. It's simply not legal. Besides, you don't have a passport, do you?"

He watched her face and saw that she did not need convincing. She looked down at the floor, at the bag there, her booted feet. She sighed. So she's not an idiot, anyway, he thought.

"How far is the river?" Doyle asked from the doorway.

"About two miles. Downhill."

"Okay," he said, still staring at the horizon, the empty hills there and the roads leading to the jungle, the jungle that gave way to Rio Sulaco. "Let's get walking."

"So, what?" Mirabelle said. "I am supposed to go with you? With two Anglo men? This one"—she nodded at Ethan—"is drunk."

Doyle turned away from the door. He had produced an open flask of guaro.

"Chica," he said, "we're both drunk, and not as drunk as we should be. Personally, I don't care what you do. Who wouldn't want to stay here? This place looks great. Driving in, I saw a horse that was almost alive."

This was a strange side of Doyle. A change from the self-righteous exaltation of Copal's devastation. It's good to know, thought Ethan, that fear makes us all nasty.

"That wasn't a horse," Mirabelle said. "That was a donkey."

"Are you telling me I don't know a dying horse when I see one? Are you saying that maybe I can't tell a donkey from a horse? Because if anyone's confused here, it's you."

"I feel confused," Mirabelle said. "I feel very confused."

Ethan saw Samantha standing in the doorway, under the hard sunlight. *I felt ashamed,* she said. *I felt very ashamed.* He put his sunglasses back on and picked up Mirabelle's bag.

"I promised Yolanda," he said. "I promised your sister that I would bring you to her and bring you to America."

He placed his hand on her shoulder and felt her shudder and move against his touch. Really, she was just a girl, and Soto was out there somewhere, on the road.

"Was it a vow?" she asked. "Did you take a vow?"

"Yeah, it was kind of like a vow," Ethan said.

Mirabelle took a step toward the door, and when it came easily, she took another. Ethan let her shoulder trail away from his outstretched fingers, out toward it, the impossible future.

She stopped.

"Wait. How are you going to get me into America if Soto could not?"

"I'm going to bring you to your mother's island. Your sister sent a passport there."

"Oh," Mirabelle said. "Of course she did."

Doyle figured the Mormons were their best bet. They had built their ministry just off the road on the banks of the Sulaco. Fashioned from Honduran pine and quarried stone, trellised and arched and steepled, it was ridiculously ornate, a weird thing, an enchanter's castle magicked onto the bank of the sickly river. Down the road, up the road, across the river, the sun glinted off the tin roofs of the neighboring shanties. If anyone had a boat to spare or sell, it would be the Mormons.

They stood before the church, the immensity of it rising above the stand of gum and ceiba trees, the wild bananas and shade palms. Somewhere a dog began to yap.

"Look at that," Ethan said. "They've painted their fretwork white. They went to all that trouble and then painted it the same color as everything else."

"That's what bothers you here?" Doyle asked. "That's what really gets to you?"

"Hey," Ethan said. "My reach is vast. I can comprehend and comprehend and comprehend. There's no sorrow beyond my sounding."

Mirabelle appeared, by any measuring, a tad stricken. If she had fantasies of escape, they probably did not go like this. Ethan uncapped the half-drunk flask of guaro and emptied it onto the ground before the church.

"See, I consecrate the ground. I strengthen my will."

He wasn't sure if the impulse to discard the guaro was noble or simply aggressive. Hello, Elder Smith. Let me christen your doorstep, let me assuage your flock.

"Cut it out," Doyle said. "We come seeking favors."

The door opened before they knocked as if the man had been standing behind it all day waiting for the knock. He was dressed as they all were, everywhere. The pleated black pants, the white shirt ruined by heat, melting hair gel seeping like a film of wax down his face.

"Welcome to our church," he said. "Come in and have a Sprite."

When he spoke Ethan could tell that he was younger than he looked. His voice came high and tremulous, screechy almost. He sounded excitable, nothing like the friendly antifreeze diction of the missionaries who'd come to your door, all smiles and expectation.

"I'm sorry," Doyle said. "We're in a hurry. We have an emergency."

"Yeah," the missionary said. "An emergency, huh? That's no good."

"It's the girl, Mirabelle"—he nodded toward her—"from the town. Her sister is very sick. Dengue with complications, and we need to get to the coast."

The kid nodded and pursed his lips into a tight pout. They were thinner than lips should be, only a trace of lip, not red at all.

"That's not good," he said. "I got dengue. When I first came here. Dengue right off the bat. I thought, wow, is this a test?"

"And was it?" Ethan asked.

"Say what?"

Apparently it was a turn of phrase, not a question. Ethan wondered if he had known that all along. He had been aware for days now of his own growing anger. It started in Mexico and had been steadily rising. It was not tempered for long by despair or fear or alcohol. Despair

and fear were constant, but fluctuating and assuaged by rum or guaro.
The anger, though, did not tremble or modulate. It came and came, it
blossomed in his sleep, it was not slaked.

"You asked if it was a test. You asked if dengue, a fever carried by
mosquitoes in these heathenous climes, was a test. So I'm asking: was
it?"

"I don't know," the Mormon said. "Surely."

Ethan smiled, nodded.

"Perhaps it's the Indians who carry dengue. Not mosquitoes. I
don't remember now."

Doyle pushed forward, between them.

"Sorry," he said. "He's kind of ill. He's kind of in distress. I think
we all are. Can you help us?"

The Mormon stepped away from the door as if to invite them in.
Beyond him, the church looked blue with shade, unlit. The windows
were boarded closed, and from inside wafted the distinct smell of pine
and incense.

"You really should come in. If you want help, I need you to come
in."

They stepped inside, Mirabelle and Ethan and Doyle following,
stopping a moment and looking over his shoulder at the road behind
them, empty still.

The Mormon closed and locked the door. They entered a wide
foyer with high rafters and darkness broken only where a few slashes
of light came through the boarded windows. Dust whirled in the light
and a bird called from somewhere in the shadows. The incense hid the
smell of chicken feathers and mold, but not completely.

"John," the Mormon called, his voice even louder and screechier
inside. "John, we have visitors."

Outside something banged, a high metal report, a pot, perhaps,
being slammed against a cooking tin. John's footsteps were heavy and
slow, and when he opened the back door and flooded the church for
a moment with glaring light, Ethan heard him mumbling to himself.

He staggered as he walked, took long, wide strides, strides far too
long for his body, like a man clown-walking in oversized shoes. Even
in the dark Ethan could see that his clothes were in disrepair. His shirt,
torn and soiled with mud, clung too tightly to his body. He did not

wear the uniform black pants, but shorts instead. His shoes were black, unmatching Oxfords.

"Well, brother," he said. "You have guests, Andrew?"

"John," said the other Mormon, Andrew. "This girl is from the town. You've seen her before. Her sister has dengue."

"Dengue," John said, and began to scratch the right side of his face. "Well, it comes in these parts. It's kind of ubiquitous."

He smiled, though there was no reason for him to smile, and leaned his left arm against the wall. He continued to scratch his face and Ethan remembered the young policeman from the roadblock with the shifty feet and psychopath's grin. With John's entrance, the room had begun to thrum with the buzz of insects. Flies flitted through the rays of falling sun. The room stank—the hot rot of the river attended John. We have come to a crossways here, Ethan thought, where all are mad. The hermits in the forest, the questing knights, the maidens in the castle on the hill.

"They need help," Andrew said. "Don't you think we should help them?"

"Oh, definitely. They've come to the right place, haven't they? The three of them, come to grace us, I think. To try our ministry. Is that why you're here?"

"Sure," Doyle said.

"You've come to the right place. So what's it you need? Because there's no medicine for dengue. That's been revealed to me, brother. You have to ride that one out."

Mud streaked John's face from his scratching fingers. A fly lighted in his hair and did not move.

"We need a boat."

"What's that, Matthew?" John said. "Let the Brethren be the light of the world, a city on the mount?"

He pushed himself toward them.

"Well, I've seen some hills, brother, and I've seen some fire, and I'm all for giving boats away, but you have to tell me why."

"You don't need to give us the boat," Doyle said. "We'll rent it. We'll pay you right now."

John held his hand out and turned his head away from Doyle. He squinted like one listening for some distant noise, a girl's voice or a train's whistle sounding from realms still almost inaudible.

"No one's talking about money here," he said finally. "We're talking about the truth. Because dengue's no rush. I mean there's just nothing you can do. What I'm thinking, what I believe, is that this girl is pregnant, and in trouble, and you two are sort of on the run. And you're thinking, hey, there's no way I'm going to let my baby be born into this climate, among these folks. Because you want to save that baby. Am I right? Is there a baby to save?"

Once the Mormon church disappeared and the tin-roofed shacks and cratewood houses fell away farther into the hills, once the cleared muddy bank settled into full foliage and the shadowy mangroves gave way to open river framed by forest and looming mountains, Ethan said to Doyle, "Think we're in the clear?"

Doyle shrugged and looked behind them at their frothy wake, the green river snaking away in wide turns against the hanging jungle.

"Don't know," he said and turned back to steering. "This isn't really my expertise. Fleeing the police is different than fleeing a mercenary. The police probably stopped looking for me after a week. If Soto is as bad as Tireisias says, he's probably still coming. Anyway, we have a head start."

Doyle glanced to where Mirabelle sat in the front of the boat, watching the water break and curl away from their prow. She did not seem to be listening.

"Of course, there are other troubles on the water," he said.

"How's that?"

"Copal doesn't allow many unlicensed planes to overfly the interior near the coast. Supposedly, it's a way to mitigate revolution."

"Revolution from whom? Who has planes?"

"Right," Doyle said. "The real reason is probably to maintain a monopoly on coffee and emerald exports. Anyway, the roads, as you've seen, are not to be trusted. So most drug or gold or gunrunners move their wares up the river. There's a dirty fortune to be made between Qultepe and the coast."

He gestured toward the banks, the jungle there, the moss-strung tributaries and shallow coves.

"Welcome to pirate alley."

"Are you serious?" Ethan asked.

Doyle opened his bag and produced a bottle of Flor de Caña. He opened it, drank, and offered it to Mirabelle. She turned away from the prow and looked down to her feet, but accepted the rum. She drank and shuddered and drank some more. Doyle grinned.

"Shiver me timbers," he said.

JOHN WAS SITTING ON a cola crate and pulling cactus from the yard when Soto came down the road. He had planted the cactus around the periphery of the church when they built it, and now he sat and rent it barehanded in the afternoon heat. Soto stood before him and appraised his bloody hands.

"I did not know that Mormons paid penance," he said.

John stopped his work and looked up at Soto and licked his lips. He smiled his reasonless smile, made more crooked by the streaks of mud still on his face.

"I may do no penance," he said. "For I have toiled in the world. My life, brother, has been woe and pain."

He reached down again and grasped a cactus with both hands and began to pull. The sound, then, of skin shorn away as the cactus held to the earth.

"That's Sir Thomas Malory," he said. "The Sankgreal. The worldly knights, the sinners, the knights who have raped maidens and slain babies, they have toiled their lives in the world and the toil of the world is penance enough. To watch a baby die and then to wander again into day? Is there penance beyond that?"

"No," Soto said in his carnival lilt. "Definitely not. But there is always an accounting."

John pulled again and the cactus came free. "That's crap," he said. "That's the crappiest of crap."

"So, you have seen babies die?"

"Oh, like, jeez. I've seen it all, brother. In the Dakotas. The Indians and their SIDS. That's Sudden Infant Death. You should see it. The smell of it. The sheer fucking purpleness of the thing. It's hard to forgive. I mean, it's probably unforgivable. I was married, you know. The world turns and turns and we dizzy with its toil."

"Perhaps," Soto said, "you should spend your money on baby formula. Not books of Mormon and not"—he waved his hand toward the
church—"this palace."

"I know that tune. I've heard that song. But I wanted the city on
the hill. The city on the hill will always be in light, you follow?"

John stood like the tin man unwrenching himself after a day's rain:
one leg at a time, then his torso stiffly following. He wiped his bloody
hands on his white shirt.

"Say, brother, what can I do for you?"

"I'm looking for friends," Soto said. "I think you've seen them. A
local girl with whom I have an arrangement."

John turned and began loping down the machete path away from
the church.

"Come on then," he said. "I leant them a boat and I can lend you
one too. You'll catch up in no time. Zippo."

Soto followed behind down the long, poorly cleared path. Vines
hung and tangled about their faces. John, walking ahead, pushed
through them even as his skin, unaverted, cut and tore against the
flowering creepers. Behind him, Soto cleared brush with his machete.

"I never liked the Book of Mormon," John said. "Not really. It's got
no stuff, you know? No heft."

"This seems a strange way to the river," Soto said. "Why not keep
your boat by the near bank?"

"But I was born into the Mormons and they've got something going on. They're new enough for that. They've got some living history.
Not like here."

He stopped and turned to look at Soto.

"History's been dead here for a long time, brother. We're just
marching it out. A procession across the fields. Death and his pageant
in sorrowful aspect."

He began to walk again.

"It'll play out soon enough," he said. "You'll see."

The path turned and fell toward the river. The tangle of grass and
shrubbery diminished as the soil dried into sandy, shell-flecked earth.
They were approaching a brackish mangrove.

"How much farther?" Soto asked.

When they reached the water the path flattened and opened into the mangrove of twisted cypress and a green lagoon where the boat lay rotten and half submerged. White orchids flowered and twined about its sagging hull.

John said, "You're right about the baby formula and the Bibles. But I've done what I can. I had a wife once, you know."

Soto's face, now, a stilted posture of fury. Something carved into cathedral walls or illumined onto medieval texts by sorrowful monks. He shook his head and shook his head and looked at the ground and then back up to John. He closed his golden eyes and opened them again. When he spoke it was in his hollow, grotto voice.

"Why would you lie to me?"

"You know the writ. You, brethren, are not in darkness. You are sons of light and sons of day and not of the night and not of the darkness. But hey, brother, it doesn't take much to tell that you are not a child of light."

John put up his hand when Soto swung his machete, and the machete clove through it and settled in the bones of his nose. John fell amidst the scattering of his fingers as if he were reaching to retrieve them. Soto placed his boot on his face and tore the machete free. He raised and swung it twice more through the wet, rising sound, the echo of bird cries in its aftermath and Andrew calling John's name and running from the mission on the hill down the rough-cut path to the river.

THE GRINGOS WERE NOT looking too good.

With the day came the heat and the heat on the windless river was a torment. The sun fell directly in the open water where they made their passage, and the boat turned to a searing, glinting thing. The white fiberglass hull, the cream leather seat cushions, the chromed steel steering wheel all sharp with heat too hot to touch. The sun blazed and clouds of humidity rose off the water and did not break. Neither of the gringos had thought to buy hats and they'd taken off their shirts, dipped them overboard, and tied them around their heads. The water was tepid and silty and the shirts stank with the foul reek of mud and algae and diesel as they dried.

The river had long ago turned sick. Every restaurant and bar in Roycetown, the colonial pirate port on the Caribbean coast, poured their cooking oil and drained their waste into the river. Even deep in the interior, where the Sulaco cut through the cloud forest and rubbed up against the mountains, the Indians reported spearing strange, malformed fish. When the first wave of two-headed carp appeared in nets or stranded on the banks of de Caña, the fishermen came to the café and showed their catch to Mirabelle.

"A sign," one said, that first time. "This is clear."

What could she tell them? Nothing was clear to her. They could not seem to understand that she was not a mystic. Her vision was unattended by wisdom or understanding. It stank, rather, of inevitability and dread. The Mother had not appeared as Ixtab until it was quite clear that Rosa was going to die. Consequently, there was something nasty in Her appearance—unnecessary. She crawled about the floor, She yanked on Her black noose, She moaned and rolled Her wide, pulpy eyes. She denied Mirabelle any notion of hope. The river birthed strange fish and the mountains released clowns trailed by children.

When the Mother appeared She opened Her mouth but did not yet speak and Mirabelle felt certain that She would not do so until Her message was already obvious and beyond averting. Her appearance felt like a recrimination or a haunting. Mirabelle looked aft to where Ethan lay on his back in the baking sun. One could ask for little and expect less. There would be no light.

At times, when the water looked deep enough, Doyle steered the boat out of the open river and into the shade of the jungle canopy. It was dangerous there, Mirabelle could tell that: half-sunken logs jutted from shore, and the cypress roots that tangled about the mangroves extended from the banks like open, clawed hands beneath the surface. Centipedes dropped from the trees; warm, rank water fell from the cupped leaves; birds rustled and screamed above them, announced their presence to the forest. Ethan swore and slapped at insects. If they hit a root or ran aground, there would be no saving them. You couldn't drink the water, the forest was impenetrable—if they tried to float and swim downstream to Roycetown they would be simple prey to caiman and crocodiles and pirates. They decided after some time to endure the heat of the open water.

"Is this normal weather?" Ethan asked. "This heat seems a little unnecessary. A little post-colonial. A little indulgent."

Indulgent? Mirabelle thought. This heat? Take a look at yourself, man. Ethan lay on his back with his shirt off and his sunglasses on. The way he lay like that, with his stomach pulled down toward his spine, she could see his ribs and the first sharp jut of his hipbone. She turned away and looked back to the water sliding against their hull. So, he was not bad-looking. But he seemed wanton and lazy and angry. He had done nothing since they boarded the boat but lie there and slap at bugs and complain. He had behaved very poorly with the Mormons.

"Yeah," Doyle said. "The heat is strange. Very humid. I'd say that there's a storm coming, except that it's not storm season."

Ethan pulled his shirt from his face and sat up on his elbow. There was a tattoo on his right shoulder that she had not noticed. He smiled at her and at least his smile was not deranged.

"What do you say, Mirabelle?" he asked. "On a scale of one to ten, is this weather strange, or not strange?"

"I can't answer that. It is two different scales."

Ethan flopped down again onto his back.

"God, Doyle, why are the natives always inscrutable?"

Doyle grinned and shrugged and drove on. For some reason, he would not look at her. He trembled with weird energy. He was abrasive in the café, and ever since then, nearly silent. Ethan, anyway, to his credit, was friendly enough. He had reminded her several times to drink from the bottles of agua purificada they bought from the Mormons. He'd touch her shoulder and open the bottle, hold it out to her.

"Mirabelle," he said, "you need more water."

He averted his eyes when he said it, looked down and then past her, the muddy river breaking away in a yellow wake, the steam rising from the near banks, the jungle that led only to more jungle. He did this several times—every time, perhaps, that he grew thirsty, he offered her water, and his voice, when he did, came like an echo, a phrase repeated out of a dream in which it carried dire consequences. There was something in his tone she recognized but could not place.

After she drank he'd take the bottle from her, cap it.

The third time he did this she said, "Do you think that I cannot close my own water?"

He moved back and looked away. She could not see his eyes through his sunglasses.

"It's an old habit," he said. "From days with those who tremble."

The river turned and narrowed and the water darkened from orange to a muddy green under the hanging limbs. Birds called from branches overhead. Caimans followed in their wake. They came suddenly upon Indian settlements—smaller than villages, odd half-cleared banklands of cratewood shacks and cooking lean-tos—and just as suddenly passed them. At times dogs barked from the banks and once, as they approached a settlement, they heard an American evangelist calling from a radio in one of the distant shacks. *A great star fell from heaven burning like a torch,* the preacher cried. *And it fell on a third of the river and on the springs of water. A third of the water became wormwood, and many men died from the water because it was made bitter.* The signal broke into static as they came closer.

Doyle gulped from the rum and drove on. They were level with the settlement now and there was no sign of people. The signal wavered into sound again.

Outside are dogs and sorcerers and sexual deviants and murderers and idolaters and whoever loves and practices a lie.

"That's grim," Ethan said. "What is it, Revelations?"

".Yes, it is from Revelations," Mirabelle said. "Do you read the Bible?"

"No," Ethan said.

Mirabelle glanced to Doyle and he shrugged and offered her the bottle. She looked away toward the receding settlement, the shacks and abandoned mud huts broken and falling to ruin and weeds and then disappearing into the uninhabited jungle. Over the rot of the river and the warm gas of frogspawn and dead fish, the boat smelled like rum. She thought of Mr. Bernal, his wet, teary mustache, his hand on her face.

Once when she was lying on her back in the grass under the lime tree, she'd asked him, "How do you love me?"

He blew a cloud of cigar smoke into the air, up toward the thousand risen stars.

"I do not think there is any love left in the world," he said. "There may be some comfort. There is certainly obligation."

Now on the narrowing river, birds screamed and screamed as the day waned and Doyle checked their wake, whatever might follow them there, and then drove on under the sagging canopy. He slapped at a mosquito buzzing about his eyes and then at another on his arm. He turned again and looked behind them.

Thankfully, after hours on the river, though it had not gotten any cooler, the sun no longer blazed overhead. It was beginning to move against the mountains and Mirabelle knew that the dark and the cool would come quickly once it fell behind them. Doyle throttled back on the gas and killed the speed. They chugged slowly downriver and he steered the boat as far as he could into the canopied bankwaters, he turned again and again to look behind them. Whoever Soto really is, Mirabelle thought, these men are very frightened. It seemed ridiculous to her now that she had almost gone with him. She had known when she saw him first that he was wicked. But he had lured her, he had smiled and called her *darling* and presented her with charges more miserable than herself. Are you so lustful as that, she wondered, so much in need of love? Also, though, she had observed in him some vast sorrow that she took for compassion. And he had recognized her, he had called her by name as the Mother had prophesied—he had called her by name and so had Ethan.

She looked overboard, the horizon ahead streaked into a sunset the color of split papaya. An eerie, falling light. The jungle glowed as if with distant flame and a hundred thousand flies rose from the water. Bottle flies and mosquitoes and midges. Ethan and Doyle crawled with them. Her hands itched, she wore blue flying beetles like rings. The river turned and sludged, she heard it gurgling against their prow, she heard the first monkey howls of night, she heard behind her the click of the Mother's coral beads. Ethan was sitting up now, drinking Doyle's rum. He nodded and raised the bottle. The air sighed with the Mother's pitiful weeping. She did not turn around.

Later, as it grew darker, Ethan said, "We're not making any headway."

"Sure we are," Doyle said, and glanced back at their extra gas canisters. "But I'm conserving fuel. I don't know how much we'll be able to find between here and Roycetown. Anyway, we're with the current."

The night had not cooled considerably with the dark, but mist rose off the river and draped itself like a shroud from the overhanging Spanish moss. Ethan licked his finger, held it to the air.

"Christ, how can there be a current when there isn't any wind?"

He doesn't know anything, Mirabelle thought. Look at him flap about there. This is the man who is supposed to protect me? A man whom Yolanda would trust?

"We're heading downriver," she said. "Toward the sea. There is wind at sea. There are many currents."

"Sure," he said. "Right. Just another tributary."

She wanted to cross herself. Was each man more broken than the next? If Soto was as bad as they said, she was certain they would all die.

With full dark, Doyle steered the boat out of the open water and into one of the ancillary mangroves. He dropped anchor.

"Is this safe?" Ethan asked. "Shouldn't we keep driving through the night?"

"I don't know. We all need some sleep and we're pretty well hidden here."

"I think I saw some lights on the water."

"Maybe," Doyle said. "But we really don't want to meet anyone on this river tonight."

Ethan said, "I like Soto behind me. I like him where I can't see him."

"He needs to sleep too, Ethan."

"I don't think he does. I think he's still coming."

Ethan could feel him out there, moving toward them, gaining on them as he inevitably must.

"It's your choice. For the record I think that it's the wrong one, but there's no reason to break with tradition, I guess."

"No," Ethan said. "No reason at all."

Ethan steered as Doyle slept. Mirabelle sat on the aft bench near him and looked out over the dark water toward the darker jungle. She had not spoken for some time. She sat and stared and would not turn when he spoke to her. Fine, he didn't need the distractions anyway. The river was black and narrow, he didn't dare put on his lights, he had drunk, perhaps, too much rum.

"You awake there, Mirabelle?" he said.

She didn't answer, but she was sitting straight up and her right eye, he could see by the angle she sat, facing aft, was open. He had imagined that she would be something like Yolanda. Yolanda but younger, unsullied by a thousand brothel nights. He felt ashamed to admit it, but he had expected some kind of exotic village maiden. Someone whose face would not bleed out the world's damages. Younger than Yolanda, but beautiful too. A country girl who would thank him for his sacrifice, someone for whom it would be easy to make sacrifice. What are you, he thought, a fucking conquistador? The great white hope come to save the natives from themselves? You pitiful drunk asshole. Too bad for you, the Third World isn't all Club Med and mangoes. Too bad the Chiquita Banana Girl happens to be mad.

The river turned and he steered widely around the bend, arcing into the shallower bankwaters. A stupid move. At night, in the dark, he wouldn't have seen any logs or hidden roots. At the edge of the jungle something screamed and thrashed through the near foliage. There were jaguars here, and ocelots, the forest edge lit with fireflies. In the deeper reaches burned a thousand emerald eyes and the boat wake, when he checked it, frothed with phosphorescence. The mist had broken with full dark, but now rose again. His fever was growing worse and his hand trembled against the steering wheel as he pulled the boat through the turn, back into the deeper waters. He'd have to be more careful. This anger was just another form of self-indulgence, the flipside of self-pity. He remembered the guilt he'd felt at Yolanda's kitchen table, the certainty of his inevitable failure. Anger, despair, the impulse toward destruction. They masked fear and eluded responsibility. They felt more sophisticated than cowardice, but no better.

"Mirabelle," he said again, quietly so as not to wake Doyle, "I'm not feeling too well. I could use some conversation."

"Oh," she said. "But it's hard to hear. I didn't know that it was you who was speaking."

"I wasn't speaking. Not really."

"I didn't think it was you."

Perhaps silence was better, he thought. In this case he'd prefer not to know.

"What do you hear, then?" he asked anyway.

She started to turn toward him and then stopped as if suddenly stung. She shuddered.

"I don't know," she said. "There's the engine and the water and the howling monkeys, right?"

"Yes. That's right. I hear those things, too."

"It's the flies that bother me. The sound of their wings. It makes them sweat and I don't like to hear that. And the Mother—" she said, and paused and went on. "—you know I hear Her. I won't lie about that. Yolanda must have told you."

A mystic, he thought. Of course. Here where everything seeped with portent, who needed imagined mysteries? Still, look at her, this miserable girl. She almost left with Soto because—why? He knew her name? He promised her children to care for? How could she be sane? She had grown up alone in that wasted, heat-blighted town on the edge of this wicked river. One must accept something, and if the choice was between faith or poverty, reality or escape, who wouldn't choose faith and certainty and madness?

"Of course," he said. "Of course she told me."

"And it doesn't frighten you?"

He laughed and he was surprised by the sound of it, a reflex as sure as a gag. Doyle stirred and moaned but did not wake.

"Everything frightens me," Ethan said.

She turned with stony slowness, rigid neck, head not wanting to follow her body, hanging back and then snapping around as if she were turning toward something sure and dread. Her eyes glistened, as he'd known they would, with tears. She blinked twice and hard and looked over his shoulder, closed her eyes again, and then looked back at him. It was the same expression he'd seen in the café, the one he'd recognized as demented certainty, and he knew that she perceived someone else with them on the boat. The hair on his neck and arms raised, he felt it through his sweatshirt. He looked behind him once. Only the green amber trail of their wake, the river falling into mist and darkness.

"What do you see?" he asked.

For a time Mirabelle did not answer. Nameless shadows broke and moved on the river. Now there were no more monkey cries, the birds that called were far off and fading away. The jungle was silent but for frog croaks and the boat engine coughing over the water. They were a beacon for whatever was out there—Soto and pirates and the mad girl's specters dreamed into the world.

Finally she said, "I see Our Lady of Sorrow. She works Her beads and She weeps for us. She clashes Her beak."

Ethan decided not to ask about the beak. In the café the thought had come to him clearly: only the mad could be certain. He'd recognized her certainty for what it was: the twitching thing climbing from a rim of shadow, the presence on the road. But what of faith? Wasn't that what many would pronounce her sureness? And if she saw what she said she did—well, she had more reason for it than anyone. Also, there was his own certainty on the way to Plaza del Porros—*I have to. I don't know what want has to do with it.* Of course, probably, that was a lie. Every step so far he'd decided on somehow, or done nothing to stay. There was that moment at the table in the kitchen with Samantha. *I'm not saying it wasn't a mistake*, he had said. *I'm not saying it was out of my hands. But I was lonely.*

She had stood up, looked back once from the door. *No, Ethan*, she said. *You make choices and then you account for them. The rest is pretty much bullshit.*

Ethan nodded at Mirabelle, he tried to smile, he knew that at some point he should sleep.

"She's begun to speak again," Mirabelle said. "She knows the future."

"She does?"

"Yes, and She gloats. She's very gloating."

"What's she prophesy?" he asked

"I'd rather not say."

Mirabelle turned back to the water. Ethan checked the gas level and engine gauge but couldn't read them in the dark.

He was tapping his ring in the night when she woke, maybe, and said, "You're married, aren't you?"

"Sort of," he said. "Or, not anymore. I'm divorced. My wife is in a facility."

She mouthed the word. "A what?"

"A hospital. A home for rich people in despair."

"Like a nunnery?"

"No," he said. "Well, yes. Sort of like a nunnery."

"Do you visit her there?"

"No, I'm not allowed to."

"Do you write her letters?"

"I write her lawyer letters," he said. "I'm the executor of her estate."

Mirabelle seemed not to hear him; he was tapping his ring again.

"Is it expensive to write letters in America?"

"No," he said. "Of course not. It's nearly free."

"Then I don't know why Yolanda does not write to me anymore."

He didn't answer. If he did, it would have to be lie after lie. And anyway, if Yolanda could secret a passport to her mother's island, couldn't she send letters?

"Were you close to her?" he asked.

"Yes, she raised me. I never knew my mother."

"I believe that," Ethan said.

"Will I be able to live with Yolanda in Texas?"

The river straightened and opened before them in an undeviating line. Ethan thought for a moment of the highway he'd driven from San Antonio to Nuevo Laredo, the perfect straightness of it, the wide horizon rising copper and sere into dawn, the heat wavering and breaking from the road like a flock of birds, the flatbush and gnarled mesquite thickets whipping past, and the great wave of dust spreading in the gathering, inevitable distance. In retrospect it was a lure, the perfect straightness of it, the border drawing closer. There was no changing course, no place to turn, and if every path led straight to this, then this now, this river, led straight to what? Ahead, above and beyond the jungle's canopy of shadow, the sky glinted with the light of a hundred thousand stars. Southern stars he could not recognize. The girl was suddenly very talkative.

"You're not seeing the Mother right now, are you?"

"No, it's just you and me in this boat," she said, and smiled sadly, the mouth rising as the eyes clouded and looked away. Yolanda's smile.

Ethan nodded at Doyle.

"And him."

"Yes," Mirabelle said. "And him. He is a very angry man, isn't he?"

"Well, really, who isn't?" Ethan said.

"I don't know what any of you have to be angry about."

"Oh God," he said too loudly. "Don't start that shit, Mirabelle. Ask your Blessed Virgin if it's so confusing. Everything in the world can break your heart. It doesn't matter who you are."

For a moment she didn't answer, but looked down to his feet where the rum bottle rested against the aft hold. She reached for it, opened it, and drank.

"It's almost empty," she said.

"Discipline in all things, Mirabelle. Get used to it. It's the American way."

"You should not drink so much."

"It's a question of obligation," he said. "If a man sets out to drink a bottle of rum, that's what he should do. America was founded by such men. It's the very lifeblood of our history. Franklin drank a liter of rum and then invented the rocking chair. Doyle's people, Virginians, used to imbibe anti-fogmatics at dawn to stave off the treachery of the fog. Really—anti-fogmatics—that's what they were called. And look around, there's plenty of fog."

He was speaking too much. It was a stupid rant and there was nothing clever about it. On the river with Soto in their wake, with Mirabelle, this poor, abandoned girl, quivering before him, sarcasm evaporated into the thinnest of vapors. And he was not drunk, not really, not by the week's standard. It was the anger speaking again, talking through him. The Southern Cross wheeled overhead—that, at least, he could recognize. When he spoke again, his voice sounded far off and distinct from him. There was someone talking for him, out of him, chuckling with scorn as he drove on and on into the darkness.

"My wife," he was saying, "you should have seen her. Samantha— now she could drink."

Mirabelle watched him as he spoke and he wondered, in some place disassociated from the rambling voice, what she saw. How could she trust these sudden moods, this collapse of restraint? His face and arms itched with new sweat, his shirt stuck, drenched, to his middle back. He wiped something wet from his face.

"You think that you know someone. I mean, we married. Right? The premise should stand. But she was a riddle to me, even then. A riddle I wanted to uncover. That was the fun of it, I think. Here's the secret of signs, though, Mirabelle. Of omens. They are always masking something worse than themselves. Did you know that?"

"Yes, I knew that," the girl said quietly.

"Samantha was very cruel," Ethan said. "She was very cruel when she drank."

"That's why she's in a nunnery? Why you divorced?"

Ethan reached out to her for the bottle. Both behind and before them the mist was rising, thicker now, off the water, and the space between the two points collapsed, closed in on them. No tremors yet of dawn.

"No, that's not why," Ethan said.

What happened was Mallory stepped around the desk and said, "Would you like some mead?"

Ethan was shooting a brochure for the Cloisters Museum in New York and Mallory, a Chaucer scholar, was helping curate the exhibit while she finished her dissertation. Already, he was shutting off the lights and packing up his camera. It was well after hours.

"Mead?" he said. "Are you serious?"

"Sure. Become a medievalist and everyone gives you mead."

"Sounds like a predicament."

"Forsooth," she said. "It's like a joke, I guess, but it's not very funny."

He watched her as she pulled a bottle of Canterbury Mead out of the cabinet and started to open it. She looked like a medievalist, he thought, without really knowing what that meant. There was a certain bookishness about her: jet hair, Samantha's hair, pulled back tightly into a bob, glasses with black plastic rims forming harsh half-moons around her hazel eyes. Her lips, sharp with dark lipstick applied too severely to an already thin mouth. Lots of silver jewelry. Lots of laven-der hand lotion. A little more buxom, a little less clothing, and she'd be a librarian, he realized, out of his adolescent fantasies. She could not work the corkscrew.

"Here," he said, and walked around the counter where she stood leaning against a bookshelf. "Let me help."

She sighed and smiled, handed him the bottle.

"The lyf so short," she said. "The craft so long to lerne."

"That's familiar."

"It's Chaucer."

"That's right," he said as the cork came free. "I always liked Chaucer."

Mallory nodded.

"Of course. Everyone likes Chaucer. Chaucer's got it going on."

He looked at her, but she was not smiling. She produced two plas-tic water cups from under the desk. A galactic swirl of dust from the bookshelf clung to her blouse. He didn't like that he couldn't tell if she were mocking him.

"Why mead?" he said. "And why tonight?"

She smelled her mead and winced and when she did her glasses fell forward on her nose. She pushed them back and looked away, past him, at the tapestry he'd been photographing.

"I've been having illicit thoughts," she said. "All week. I'm trying to behave."

"And so you're drinking?"

"Drink wine and you will sleep well," she quoted. "Sleep well and you shall not sin. Avoid sin and you shall be saved. Ergo, drink wine and be saved."

Ethan sipped his mead, swallowed, and then realized that in the sway of the moment he had not tasted it. He could not feel the cup in his hand or the pull of the door behind him. Still one light illuminated the far wall: the unicorn there, with the maiden in its lap.

"You're a regular concordance," he said.

"It's what medievalists do. We read things, repeat them, and change their meaning."

"The oldest lines in the book."

She laughed and drank her mead in one gulp.

"Oh, golly. A pun," she said.

At home Samantha said, "Captain Jealousy's been out late. Can you show me your papers? Are they all stamped?"

At first, because the lights were off and he couldn't see her eyes, he thought she was being playful. But as he closed the door and smelled the bright reek of gin, as he waited for her laugh that did not come, he knew she was drunk and angry. Samantha was a cruel drunk or a tired drunk or a horny drunk, but never a nice one.

He turned on the lamp but it was unplugged or the bulb was blown. The neon glow of the hardware stores and billboards far below lit the room through the open blinds. Half of her face was blue and hard, coral under moonlight, and the other half wet with shadow. The false light sparkled on the array of open bottles strewn about the coffee table.

"What are you drinking, anyway?" he said.

"Martinis," Samantha drawled. "Half gin and half vodka."

"That's not a martini."

"I call it The Husband. Half fruit and half cold fish."

He found the power cord and plugged it in. When the light came on she covered her eyes.

"Half glass," Samantha said, "and half air. Half man and half neutered angel of self-righteous anger."

Ethan turned and stepped back into the kitchenette. He filled a tumbler with ice and the tumbler was shaking. Ice clinking up against the crystal. After a moment he reached into the cabinet and retrieved a bottle of rye—at least Samantha had left him that. He poured it and raised it to his lips. It tasted much better than mead. He turned out the light.

"I'm taking a shower," he said.

"Splish-splash," Samantha mumbled from the couch.

In the shower's scalding heat, with the steam rising like mist off a brackish river, with the drink puddling in his hand, in the shower he thought: she has a point, I have not honored my obligations. After her night with Rodney he had promised himself he would trust her, he would believe her story with all its demented logic. Suspicion, he told himself again and again, is a failure of compassion. But there was no staying it, suspicion and jealousy, a seething, growing panic. Samantha, he felt certain, was slipping from him.

When she'd work late, or go out for cocktails, or attend any of her firm's thousand functions, he'd find himself stalking the apartment or walking the streets or calling her on his phone, listening to it ring and ring into static and electric distance and a world of woeful possibility:

Rodney behind her, wrapping her black hair in his fist, Samantha laughing and bracing herself, putting one hand against the cold metal headboard. Sweat rising on her lower back.

Samantha dancing for Jack and Rodney, turning a weird belly dance, doing a wicked little striptease. Layer after layer falling away to their clapping, their roving, sweating eyes.

He would walk into the night, he would imagine following her to her bar and waiting in the rain, in the streetlamp's chemical glow, he would pull her to him when she returned and smell her, smell her neck and her hair and taste him, Rodney, as he tasted her.

He was not a jealous man. He believed this because he had never been jealous before. But now with Samantha, with the drinking and disappearing and the gathering coldness, he felt a narrowing, animal panic. As before, the banality of his fantasies shamed him—their irritating power dynamics, the whole pseudo-sadism of them. Who are you? he thought.

But now, after that night, her frank derision, her night with Rodney, he could not imagine her without trysts and he could not imagine her trysts any other way. Samantha would not go for the generic adulteries: quiet dinners, nights of candlelit passion, quick kisses in the lee of a darkened building, the taxi waiting in the street.

He knelt down in the shower, pulled his knees to his chest, and let the water break over his head and his back. He had made the decision already: if his choice was between loving or rejecting her, he would have to love her. But the rot of his fantasies frightened him—why could he not imagine Samantha in a romantic context?

When he got out of the shower she was sitting at her desk by their bed. The bottles in the living room were put away. She was working on the computer.

"These last few months I've been very jealous," he said.

"No shit?"

She didn't turn from the computer, but kept typing.

"I'm sorry for that," he said. "You deserve better than that."

He crossed the room and put his hand on her shoulder, reached up and touched her ear.

"It's been so hard, after that party and with all the drinking. I didn't know how I was supposed to respond."

She stared, still, at the computer.

"But it will be different now."

Samantha stood and touched his face and he closed his eyes and felt her lips come to his, felt her mouth and tongue against his and tasted the dry residue of her strange martini.

When he opened his eyes he saw that hers had never closed.

"Gosh, that's real sporting of you, fella," she said. "I just hope Rodney feels the same way."

He sets up his lights and camera after the last patron leaves the museum. Mallory stands at the carved gothic fireplace between two of the unicorn panels.

"He's a poor thing, the unicorn," she says. "Don't you think?"

"Sure. Entrapped. Lured by a virgin. Happens every time."

"In medieval iconography the unicorn represents both Christ and marriage," she says.

Ethan examines the maiden in the tapestry, her red dress, her slit-eyed, sideways glance. Mallory is in her after-work clothes. Torn jeans, a black frilly t-shirt, a large silver pendant around her neck, crystal bauble earrings. Ethan looks back to the tapestry. Her steps echo away, down the hall.

"We are entrapped in marriage by virgins?" he calls to her.

"You got it."

"That hasn't been my experience."

Later, she's looking through a portfolio he brought her. It's years old, from his first gallery days. He hears her close the folder, open another bottle of mead. He hears her cross the floor. But for his lights, it's dark in the gallery, vaulted and long-shadowed. She touches his hand and he turns away from the lights toward her where her hair is up but her strange long bangs hang down her face.

She says, "These are beautiful."

She says, "I'd like to imagine the impulse that created these. The prima causa."

She touches his face, she leaves her fingers there.

It's his turn now. He says, "Whatever else may make the too much loved earth more lovely."

"Sidney."

"Well, shit. Is there anything you do not know?"

She moves against him and he's looking away from her again, at the lit tapestry, the blue madness in the eyes of the men, the unicorn's vain pulse toward desire.

"You're trembling," she says.

When he speaks, his voice is louder than hers, too loud. It echoes in the stone cloister. A voice out of a well.

"It's that I don't see myself like this. I don't see myself as someone who would do this."

"Oh," she says, and he knows she's pouting because her lips are on his neck. "Love is lecherous and false and sure to entrap."

"That's not Sidney," he says, and turns again, away from the tapestry, to look at her. She smiles and pushes her bangs out of her face, her glasses back on her nose. Her bauble earrings catch and throw light. He closes his eyes, he opens them.

He thinks of her, as he does, as a photograph. Freeze this moment, take and store it. The rainbow of crystal-cast light splayed across her jaw, some of her hair. Her eyes widened in want, her lips pressed together and then opening toward paused speech. Take it and hold it, let it live in you and grant you what succor you may need. In a life suddenly short of sweetness, this is sweetness enough.

And then she's closing what small space remains between them and those thoughts prove forfeit in the echo of their breath in the room, their breath and the buzz of his lights and everything falling beyond the moment, its simple grace, into now and now—still lives—he hopes that will need no accounting.

And later, in her loft, she is not as assertive as Samantha is, she looks for him to take the lead, to take some kind of responsibility for what's happening, which he does not want to do, but does anyway. He pushes the stray strands of her hair away from her face and kisses the skin of her throat below her ear. He removes her glasses for her. She needs guidance, she needs encouragement, her earrings get in the way. There are the things he notices: the chips in the shitty plywood headboard, the book—*Pilgrim's Progress*—on her bedside table, the sound of the train rattling by. Out of habit he bites her collarbone as he does with Samantha, as Samantha makes him do, and she recoils under his teeth. She's watching him when she comes, staring down at him, trying to keep her eyes open, staring at him with clenched lips and a furrowed brow as if he's about to tell her something very important, something whispered, something she doesn't want to miss.

"Mallory," he says in the night, in the new night, their first, darkening, night. "Mallory, Mallory."

She rolls against him, he feels the heat of her, her warm hands. She kisses his throat, he thinks she is smiling in the dark

"Is that your real name?" he asks.

"Why wouldn't it be?"

"I don't know," he says. "I just thought…"

"That medievalists couldn't have a name like Mallory?"

"Sure," he says. "It's like something out of a dream, a perfect resonance."

He touches her face, traces the shadow of her shoulder with his fingertips. Ambulances pass in the street. For a moment the red throw of their flashes strobes the apartment, the futon on the floor, the tossed detritus of their clothes, the bony jut of her hip.

"Symmetry in all things," she says.

———

It's happening to him again, as it did over a year ago: he wakes in the night and when he wakes he does not know Samantha. He forgets her in the pitch dark that peels open to the shadowed room. Once, he shook to a crone's face, withered and shrunken, a husk of bark. He sat up and it was gone, not even her face at all, just the back of her head, her black hair, spread out and blurring against the dark pillow. He leans down to her, he pulls her to him and her body shifts against his in habit or dream. He smells her hair—something he often did in their first months together—and he does not recognize the smell. The last three nights she's showered before she's gone to bed, which is not like her. He thinks he knows what that means. He wraps his arms around her, he places his lips against the back of her neck. "We have time," he whispers. Holding her like this, he feels somehow obscene, like a man intruding upon a life in which he has no part. He kisses her again and wants to throttle her or shake her awake or weep. All our accounts, he thinks, are coming due. A man must make a choice while there's still a choice to make, but he has no idea what it might be.

After his last day at the Cloisters they're lying on Mallory's couch with the lights off watching *The Seventh Seal*.

"A Swedish knight plays chess against Death in an apocalyptic landscape," she tells him. "It'll be right up your alley."

"Am I that melancholy?"

"Nothing a good dose of leeches couldn't cure."

She reclines between his legs with her head on his collarbone. Her hair smells like cigarettes though she told him she quit smoking three years ago. He wonders whether she's started again or whether she never stopped. He likes that the answer doesn't matter to him. On screen, a pageant jester dances for a Swedish maiden. She smiles and turns away, but he takes her hand, he sings some more. She follows him into the forest. When Ethan finds himself rubbing the side of Mallory's face with his knuckles the way he used to caress Samantha's, he stops, he touches her lips and settles his hand at his side. There's some feeble, pulsing heat opening in his throat that he cannot ignore. Outside, a driver leans hard on his horn. The train rumbles by underground. Across town, Samantha will be arriving home soon, if tonight she's coming home at all.

"God," he says. "It's so Scandinavian."

The scene has shifted now. A retinue of flagellants invades the carnival. They moan and chant, they whip themselves. The smoke from rocking censers fills the screen. Ethan drums on her shoulder with his right hand, worries the woven blanket with his left.

"I mean it's terminal," he says. "We all know what's going to happen, don't we?"

She rocks her head back toward his chin but does not turn her eyes from the screen. "Why ruin it for yourself?" she says. "He's playing chess. He can still win."

"No," he says, "of course he can't."

The light from the television flickers and moves over her face. He sees her bite her bottom lip. As quickly as they came, the flagellants have disappeared.

She turns and sits up. She takes off her glasses and rubs her eyes.

"We can turn off the movie if you want," she says. "We can drink beers or make love or play Pick Up Stix. I don't care."

He raises his hands in a gesture meant maybe to communicate frustration or accommodation or confusion, but can't bring any of them off. He lowers his hands.

"The movie's fine. It's great and inevitable," he says.

She's fully facing him now with the television forming a halo about her head. Lights pass in the street. It's begun to rain and the rain against glass sounds closer than he'd like—just beyond the warmth of her body, the length of the couch and the space between the couch and the wall, the window and the rest of the world. Her voice when she speaks is so much different than Samantha's. He can hear her trying to keep control—a measured, logical Midwestern tone.

"Is there something I'm supposed to understand from this over-determined response?"

"I can't see how this continues without consequence," he says.

She nods at the screen, she says, "This world nys but a thurgfare of wo, and we been pilgrymes passynge to and fro. Deeth is an ende of every worldly soore."

"Let me be clear," he says. "I feel that I'm about to leave a pretty serious wake."

He watches as her expression changes, as she cocks her head to the side and opens her mouth ever so slightly, runs her tongue over her teeth. It's the same expression she has when she's bent over a book, working on her dissertation, coming to a conclusion.

"Right," she says. "Now you're worried about the damage you might cause. Look around you. You think it's not too late? You think you're not already covered in broken glass?"

"That's not what I meant."

"I see. You meant in your life, in your wife's life? I suppose what I want I was never going to have?"

He looks at her, the way she holds her composure, tilts her chin up at him, refuses to blink, does everything she can not to cry. He appreciates this. He could not stand up and leave if she were crying. At some place remote from himself he realizes that what he wants is to not be able to see that he's hurt her. He had felt beautiful to her, he had felt what he took for possibility. As if to be seen anew could make him so. How many times, he wonders, had he condemned Samantha for feeling much the same way, for failing to live, as she should, in the world she'd built? But he cannot ravage Samantha with his leaving. For someone he is married to, he knows very little about her, but knows that the world's touch on her has not been light. Mallory will be fine. He tells himself this. At some level she must feel that whatever price she haggled her heart down to was far too high. He stands and she's still there on the couch looking up at him.

"Is there no grace," she whispers, "is there no remedye?"

"Chaucer," Ethan says, and pulls her to him. He kisses the top of her head like someone boarding a train.

"That's right," she says from under his arms, a wet, muffled voice. "You nailed it."

Later he will retell it to himself a hundred times, a thousand. He will look for impulses and causes. He will say, this is why I did what I did.

He doesn't know where to start.

On Key West, maybe. That first sodden night. Samantha pulling him to her, working her hand into his underwear. Him saying *you won't feel anything*, and her moaning it off—*that doesn't matter*—and then moving hard against him, her body sluggish with drink, sweating rum, and her unclosing eyes so empty of attraction but full of need.

Or the night at the party, her night with Rodney, or his time at the Cloisters or right then sitting at the kitchen table that morning when she looked over her cereal and said, "What are you thinking?"

This is how it happened, then, when it did. He fell asleep on the couch waiting for her to come home. In the morning he stepped into their room where she was sleeping. He opened the window.

She called his name from the bed and then looked at him for the first time that morning and said it again, his name, like she was trying to fit it to what she saw and could not.

"It's the middle of December," she said.

He cleared the bedside table of the vodka and the vermouth. She must have continued drinking on her own after she came home.

"We needed some fresh air," he said, and meant it in every possible way. It was amazing, he realized in retrospect, how spiteful his voice sounded: some latent anger waking with him into morning. So maybe it was then, at that moment, that he decided to hurt her.

"You're a sanctimonious prick, Ethan," she said, and her voice was wet.

He closed the window but opened the shutters. Outside, the harsh glare of sun on passing windshields. Music playing in the street. A new fresh day out there beyond the boozy reek of the room.

"Coffee's ready," he said.

"Don't pour those out," Samantha said, and covered her wet eyes with the covers like a shroud.

When he heard the shower come on he began to sip his coffee; when he heard it turn off he poured two bowls of cereal and cut up some bananas. He stood at the balcony window. Outside, blue clouds drifted across the sun. Down in the street, fifteen floors below, the noodle vendor assembled his cart. What he wanted now was to meet her as she got out of the shower, to hold her and wander together out into morning. As if to step into a new life were as easy as her taking the day off and getting brunch together on the Lower East Side.

"It's going to snow," Ethan said to the closed door. "Don't forget your boots."

When she came out she was dressed for work and her hair was up and he could see the warm water from her hair slicking on her neck like sweat. He touched her arm.

"How are you feeling?" he said.

"Why were you sleeping on the couch last night?"

"I was waiting for you to get home. I was worried. Some women would find that a considerate gesture."

"Next time, I'll remember to punch in," she said.

They sat and ate and he stared at her across the table while cars revved and blew their horns and pigeons cooed and flushed and settled on the sill.

She looked up at him from her cereal. Already, even before breakfast, she was wearing lipstick.

"What?" she said. "What are you thinking now?"

He was thinking of how it used to be that she'd come out of the shower in the morning with her hair in a towel and glasses on because she hadn't put her contacts in yet; how he'd come up behind her, hand her her coffee and kiss her neck and her collarbone and her shoulders, how her damp skin would taste, how her hair where it escaped the towel in black strands would smell like lemon and mint. He was thinking that now she stepped out of a shower like that was all she needed to step out of. He was thinking that now her contacts were already in and she didn't smell like anything at all.

Somehow he'd become loathsome to her. He'd felt her loss for some months and now he felt it surely, without hope, a thing in distinct retrospect. Well then, he thought. If that's how it's going to be.

"I had an affair. It's over now," he said.

He had not expected her to drop her coffee. He had not expected her to start crying. The sound was horrible, childish and small. He wanted to take her in his arms, to unsay what he need never have said.

"How could you do that?"

"She was a medievalist," he said.

"Is that supposed to be some kind of answer?"

"I don't know how it happened."

"Oh, you don't?" she said. Her weeping had given way to anger. "Was it just some marvel? A strike of blue lightning? A chaste conjoining?"

"Do you think," he wondered, "that I never wanted anything? That I did not need love or understanding? Are you the only one afflicted?"

"This is starting to sound very much like an excuse," she said. "A rationalization."

"When you look into the mirror, you see a bottle."

"Of course," she said. "It all comes back to that. Forget your jealousy. Your fits and rages. It all comes back to your wanton, intemperate gash."

Her anger was something to behold. It was the first emotion he'd seen from her in months. He could move toward it like heat.

"I'm not saying it wasn't a mistake. I'm not saying it was out of my hands. But I was lonely. I don't know how it happened."

"No, Ethan," Samantha said, and picked up her bag, stepped to the door. "Take your own advice. You make choices, boy, and then you account for them. The rest is pretty much bullshit."

He raised his camera as the door closed and caught her shadow trembling on the threshold. That night when she did not come home, he called Mallory and went out into the odd red storm. The dwarf snarled in Spanish. Somewhere Samantha thrashed against whatever waited in the darkness. The phone rang and rang and Ethan did not know who could be calling.

IN THE NIGHT THERE was a sound on the river. One boat, maybe two, making for them. As suddenly as Ethan heard it, the wall of mist behind them began to glow, to radiate light from its center like a pearl: the boats had their bow lights on and were closing fast.

"Doyle," Ethan said, but Doyle was already up and on his knees and looking back at the light gaining on their wake.

"Fuck," he said. "You didn't hear them coming?"

"I hear what you hear. It was just Night Sounds of the Freaky Jungle, and then it was this."

Doyle looked back again as if staring at the mist would make it any more diffuse. The sound of boat engines and wave of lights still approached.

"They must have come out of one of the tributaries or hunting camps," he said.

Doyle swung around and took the wheel and throttle from Ethan. He pulled the throttle into full and the boat coughed and bounced and jumped forward. Ethan sat next to Mirabelle and watched the mist.

"I don't suppose the Blessed Virgin has any advice?" he asked.

"She gives commands," said Mirabelle. "She gloats. She doesn't offer advice."

Ethan found the rum bottle and opened it, raised it to his lips, even though he could feel by the weight that it was empty.

"Doyle, I have an observation to make," he said.

Doyle didn't turn. Again the river narrowed, the fronds from the bank hung down to the water like frail horses coming to drink. Without their lights the mist remained unbroken, thick and gliding toward them.

"We can't outrun them," Ethan said. "It's not going to happen."

Doyle turned and looked back. A white heat centering, brightening into nebulous form. The pulsing outline of four bowlights. Above the chug of engines, the sounds of men's voices. He killed the engine and pulled the boat toward the right bank, the alleys and mangroves there. He dropped anchor and it didn't fall far. The bankwaters were shallow with silt and tree roots, false bottoms.

"I think it's too shallow in the mangroves. Or at least too narrow," Ethan said.

Doyle watched their wake dissipate and roll on behind them.

"They might not have heard us," he said. "They might not know we're out here."

He opened his bag and pulled his wallet and passport from it.

"Get your valuables, both of you. We're going for a swim."

"I don't swim well," Mirabelle said.

"You grew up on a river."

Mirabelle looked over the side at the dark water curling around their hull, the bending eddies issuing from the mangroves, the ripples under the surface.

"We don't swim in this river," she said.

They swam as hard as they could into the tributaries bisecting the mangroves. Mirabelle splashed and floundered, her feet caught again and again in the tangle of silt and river weeds, her head dipped below the surface and she came up coughing.

"She can't do that," Doyle said. "She has to be quiet."

Ethan held out his right arm and let her latch onto it.

"Come on," he said. "I'll pull you. Hold your head out of the water and keep your feet moving."

As a boy he'd made a sport of fording rivers in flood, swimming or wading, letting the current pull him from boulder to boulder, boulder to far shore. Though the Sulaco was nothing like those cold, clear New England rivers, he knew what the dangers would be: if you let your feet rest in the silt of the river bottom they'd break through the thin false layer and grab in the settled marl. You'd be stuck before you realized it, you'd start to sink as you'd started to struggle. Then, of course, there was everything else he had no experience with: caimans and crocodiles, the filthy, tepid water.

They swam on into the dark inlets between the mangrove islands where the water ran loam-thick and warm, and weeds caught and tangled around their heels, snaked across their calves. They swam and the water luminesced about their feet and hands so that as they moved green auras arced out from their bodies in bursts and trailed behind them in slow, lessening flickers. They swam, the three of them, through the film of lagoon water where fish nudged their thighs and strands of half-rotten bog weeds washed up on their own moving current and slicked against their lips. They swam and Mirabelle coughed and river weeds slimed with algae brushed their faces and left warm green-gold light glimmering there with lingering, impossible luster, and because they glowed and the bow lights on the open river grew closer, imminent now, they continued on through the mist and underwater light into the farther dark.

Finally they stopped and turned and waited, treading water, as deep into the shadowed lee of the mangrove branches as they dared.

"Shouldn't we get under cover?" Ethan whispered. "We're still kind of in the open."

Doyle looked behind them into the cypress and jungle canopy.

"I think those banks are pretty well populated by caiman," he said.

"Mirabelle," Ethan said. "Lie on your back. Float that way. You're pulling too much on my arm."

He helped her roll over and placed one hand on her lower back to keep her afloat. Her skin was slick with silt. On the open river the boats broke through the curtain of mist. They appeared low and wide, spectral, as they cut their engines and pulled up astern of the abandoned Evinrude. The men on the boats called to each other in no language Ethan knew. They whistled and coughed and gestured through wavering silhouettes in nervous mimings. From the deck, they shone handheld lights into the boat and twirled them a few times through the near mangrove thickets. Two men cocked their automatic rifles and, lit by bow lights, boarded the empty boat.

"Will they take it?" Mirabelle said.

Ethan touched his finger to her lips and when he removed it her lips pulsed a wet neon. River weeds glowed in her hair and on her chin; her lips shone and dimmed again into darkness. The water ran warm and thick against Ethan's body. His fever, which had broken in the night, came again upon him in a wave of incandescence. Mirabelle glowed and floated and the weeds dimmed to brown mud-streaked tendons in her hair.

The men searched the boat, they tossed the bags and emptied them onto the deck. They shook their heads and played their hand lamps over the near mangroves one more time before leaping up into their own boats and roaring on again into the night.

After the men left, Mirabelle began to cough and would not stop. When they swam back to the boat and climbed inside and laid out their wet wallets and passports and found what dry clothes they had, Ethan held her against his chest and let her shiver and cough and look out into the last of night at whatever visions haunted her there. He used his sweatshirt as a towel and dried her and let her shudder against him and then pull away, still holding his sweatshirt, and lie down on the damp plastic cabin floor. Doyle drove and once Ethan looked up and caught his eye. Doyle shook his head and glanced away.

"Yes?"

"Hey, man, I'm just the driver," Doyle said.

Ethan followed his gaze, over and past the sleeping girl and the boat prow cutting the water, up and straight ahead beyond the breaking mist and the river unveiling into dawn, past the last blue stars revolving away into the low horizon and falling toward the ocean that pressed toward them, even now, at the wide, sick end of the river.

Dawn on the Sulaco. New mist rising and new bird cries and the drip of syrupy light coming through the trees. Ethan stood at the bow and pissed into the water. With the mist and the light came the heat, and he took off his shirt and put on his sunglasses and drank a bottle of agua purificada.

"Have some water, Mirabelle," he said.

"I don't want any water. If I need water, I will take it."

"You know, Mirabelle, if you need to go to the bathroom, we will turn away. We won't look."

"Leave her alone and get some sleep," Doyle said. "When was the last time you really slept?"

Two days, Ethan thought. At least. He drifted off several times in the back of the pickup on the way to Rio de Caña, but that was it. He should probably take Doyle's advice and shut up and go to sleep. Let Mirabelle fend for herself, let Doyle care for him. He had been wrong after all about boating through the night. It was because of him that

they had met the pirates or drug traffickers or whatever they were in the
dark. Certainly, they could all easily be dead by now. But of course they
weren't and these things did seem to have a momentum of their own.
At this point it was best not to question his impulses. No right choice
could have led him here, and still here he was in the boat on the river
that was widening again, heading toward Roycetown and the sea. His
hands shook around the water bottle. He braced it against the boat and
slowly turned the cap. Mirabelle watched him from the prow bench
where their belongings dried in the sun.

"Hey, Mirabelle," he said. "Did you know you had a passport?"

She looked away from him, down at the passports and wallets, pesos,
quets, lempiras and dollars laid out, drying and cracking in the heat.

"I don't know," she said. "My birth certificate was sent to me right
after Yolanda left."

"Yolanda sent it to you?"

"I guess so," she said.

Her nose was small and knobby in profile. Round and widening at
the base, like the stump of a felled tree. Not Yolanda's nose at all.

"Hey, Mirabelle," he said again. "Whose nose do you have? Your
father's or your mother's?"

She touched her face, the bridge of her nose, and jerked away from
him as if shocked. Again, some flowering menace in his tone that he
did not intend.

"I never knew either of my parents," Mirabelle said. "My father ran
off before I was born and my mother went to be with him."

"I thought your parents were dead?"

"Dead?" Mirabelle said. "I don't think so. That's not what Jose said.
I never knew my mother. But why would she leave us if my father were
dead?"

Doyle shook his head, wiped his face, and looked behind them
again at their empty wake.

"Raise your hand if you think we're being fucked," he said.

By midday they had passed beyond the river's realms of empty jungle.
They came upon abandoned villages and villages in the process of being
abandoned. They saw Indians packing up their homes, carrying what
possessions they could on their backs, loading them into motorboats

that idled on the river. Rainbow skins of leaking oil spread out behind the engines. There did not seem to be any children.

"It's the fish," Mirabelle said. "They're all poisonous and strange. They have several heads."

Now there were many boats on the river. On the banks, docks went to rot from weather and disuse, rows of stilt houses with tropically painted shutters and mansard roofs—once a whole river colony—decayed under the weight of uncleared foliage, sprawling vines of pulpy flowers, and rotten banana fronds. Iguanas basked on the sagging porches that leaned, as the stilts slowly sunk, into the sepia water.

They floated on and passed a series of crumbling, overgrown Mayan pyramids where a gangly ocelot slunk between fallen boulders. Someone fired a rifle at it from one of the boats and it darted into the jungle cover. Ethan watched as trails of dust rose from the bullet holes in the ruins.

He turned away and lay down. He did not like this ugly ocelot, the idea of fish with many heads. The feeling of communal madness he experienced at the Mormon mission had not abated. All the boats were headed the same way, downriver, toward the sea. It was as if they were all fleeing a certain pestilence. There was madness in the heart of the country, and it was not that he could not make any right choices, but that here there were no right choices to be made. Mosquitoes bit at his ankles; he should put on shoes. Dengue was always a fear, and on this river there was probably no shortage of malaria. Like everything else, the idea of malaria made him angry. He felt the anger winding in him, curling and curling—a spring waiting to be sprung. Unbidden, he saw Samantha in her pale, locked room. He had fled one madness for another. Look at this place, he thought. This was the problem with paradise. It was too extreme. Too textured and scented and rich with all the world's sweetnesses. Like a pantry of rotten fruit, when things that sweet go bad, they do it with gusto. He slapped at a mosquito and wiped some riversmell from his nose. There were men pursuing them on the river. He had agreed to an impossible responsibility. There was no more rum. This kind of thinking would not do. It was the fever talking, that was all.

He gestured out at the heat-seared world around them.

"This is the fever talking," he said.

As they neared the coast, the jungle changed from rainforest to tropical grove and the new landscape withered in a display of blight. The
brown, sickened forest curled about the high river banks where fish
bones and dead lizards, tin cans and nacho bags lay scattered before the
slopping water. They passed the ribcage of a mule, an overturned boat,
and a Pepsi-Cola sign. The smoke from scrub fires rose from the dry
interior. In the middle distance, day falling away and evening coming
on, they could hear the buzz of Roycetown, the last port between the
mainland and the Caribbean Sea. Everywhere chattering green birds
overflew the river in hectic, formationless chaos. Unreadable portents
or portents of winnowing possibility, void. A weird dog, hairless with
mange, howled from the near shore.

"The fuck is that?" Doyle said.

"Cerberus," Ethan said. "Welcoming us home."

They docked at one of the many makeshift marinas and went on into
Roycetown. Originally settled by the Garifuna from St. Vincent, in the
early nineteenth century the town fell to British pirates who, after finding that engaging in trade was more profitable than disrupting it, established Roycetown as a merchant port, from where they traded Copalan
sugarcane with the pirate ports in British Honduras to the north. For
some time the town flourished as a halfway point between the northern
lumber and southern cane routes, though after Copalan independence
many of the former pirates moved to British Honduras where, while
they paid only nominal taxes, they could still fly the King's flag, insult
the Spanish, and carry on speaking their own English.

What was left reverted over the centuries into some mean approximation of its colonial past. There were no roads into town—it could
only be accessed by sea or river—and Roycetown thrummed with the
lunacy peculiar to tropical ports outside of law or reason. As they walked
down Livingston Boulevard, the main street that ran along the banks of
the Sulaco and ended, as everything ended there, at the sea, they passed
rows of ornate wooden colonial pleasure-houses—once the homes of
British merchants, now hotels and bordellos—that seemed, with their
pastel-painted wooden doors, decorated fretwork and fancy patterned
iron latticing, like overblown gingerbread houses out of a madhouse bak-

ery. Beyond them there lay several blocks of rectangular cement cantinas and scuba shops and rundown discos. Afro-Caribbean men and women played punta and reggae on portable radios and sat in folding chairs on the street corners. The bars were filled with white expatriates.

"What's the plan?" Ethan asked.

They were still not far from the marina, only a hundred yards or so. Livingston Boulevard opened before them and stretched away in harlequin coloring for several blocks toward the sea.

"Let's walk the town," Doyle said. "Let's find a hotel and get the ferry schedule. Let's make sure that in the morning we'll be alive and ready to go. Then we can take care of everything else we might need."

Ethan watched his eyes as he spoke, watched how they dulled at the end of the sentence, glazed for a moment like a snake's. It was an expression not unlike the one he'd witnessed at the discothèque where Doyle danced his creepy dawn shuffle with the club girls and the dead chicken. Doyle was in one of his quickening phases, his staring phases; he seemed tense with what most people would take for anger. He glared at every woman they passed. The first time Ethan visited him, when he was still doing AIDS work, Doyle insisted on going out every night to the discos on the north shore, finding *new girlfriends*, dancing and grinding and flirting in Spanish. Ethan spent most of those nights sitting at Doyle's kitchen table drinking rum and electrolyte drinks while Doyle and his night's conquest moaned at each other in simpleton Spanish. Ethan couldn't comprehend Doyle's lusts—maybe it was loneliness or fear, or maybe it was just some new blossoming of whatever impulse drove him down here in the first place. Either way, the impulse was easily expressed but never satisfied. Doyle loved and loved and his love seemed no different than rage.

"How's that sound to you, Mirabelle?" Ethan asked. "Want to walk the town?"

She had never been this far from home before, and Roycetown, by anyone's measuring, was a wild sight to see. But her eyes were downcast, she worried her hair with her fingers and mumbled silently to herself. Like something governed by the physics of fairy tale, she turned strange with the sunset.

She stopped a moment and looked up, the carnival world opening around her, going on without her inspection.

"I do not feel well," she said. "Maybe you can drink yourselves to death without me?"

It was true, Ethan thought, she didn't look good. It was hot and they all were sweating, but her skin seemed wan and greasy, shellfish out of the shell. Besides, it would be best to get her in the room and out of sight. Soto might not be far behind them, and there was no reason to take unnecessary chances.

They were nearing the end of the way, the place where the boulevard and the city and the river and jungle around it ran up against the Caribbean. Roycetown finished in a sort of rounded peninsula, and at the end of the lane a grove of widely spaced coconut palms stood pressed in silhouette against the moving green sea. Before the palms there was the usual land's-end entertainment: a block of waterfront bars thatched and tied tiki-style from cut bamboo. Ethan smelled the air as they walked and hoped for the fresh salt and eucalyptus smell that accompanied so many of these ports. The scents he knew as those of paradise: flowers, St. Augustine grass, southern wind. But here there was just the rot of the stricken river sloshing up against the sea, sewer waste and fry oil piped out of the restaurants, and from everywhere the raw alcohol reek of guaro.

Ethan knew you could find many such ports littered about the Central American Caribbean. More than most, though, Roycetown did little to disguise its decaying grandeur. It was busy, vibrant, definitively sinister—it seemed to traffic in its own colorful despair. Like all of Copal, it was not home to tourists but instead a harbor for every manner of lost man. A pirate port where emeralds and cocaine and small arms were often currency enough and nationality was measured by your boat's registry.

They reached the end of the point, turned around and began to walk back the way they had come. Music rose like heat from the streets, where bloated white expatriates and bearded surfers who had pawned their surfboards for any number of immeasurable losses slumped outside the bamboo bars in the trembling play of dusking shadows and green electric light. It was not so different from Boystown. Soon, when the darkness had risen farther, come in with the current, those who could stand would stand and step inside, where the women waited at tables or behind bead curtains or out on thatched verandahs that faced the dark, beachless sea.

Later on, after they'd found Mirabelle a hotel room, Ethan sat at the bamboo counter at one of the awful waterfront bars and ate fish soup, even though he knew that the coconut-water base would probably hit his bowels pretty hard since he was already feeling a low, deepening, burn in his gut. He ordered a rum and a bottle of Coke and poured some of the rum into his soup. It wasn't bad that way, sweet and creamy, and the fish fell apart in his mouth, though he didn't know, really, what that meant.

Doyle stood by the jukebox in the far corner where the lounge opened onto a canopied sea deck. He leaned against one of the bamboo support stakes, drank Honduran beer, and flirted with an olive-skinned woman in khaki cargo pants and a wide-necked t-shirt with white and green horizontal stripes. Ethan watched them in the bar mirror. He didn't like horizontal stripes of any ilk, especially not in a town like this, where they seemed particularly out of place, somehow jaunty, performed—the sailor girl outfit for a yacht club gala. Around here, he thought, as he raised his hand for another rum, an outfit like that either meant you were a mark or someone too dangerous to touch. Either way, it didn't seem like the best company for Doyle to keep—but neither was he, and Doyle wasn't prone to keeping good company. She smiled and gestured widely, she looked Greek, she didn't appear, anyway, to be a prostitute.

The bartender poured Ethan another rum. It wasn't very good. Some thin and astringent homemade rotgut that tasted of burnt molasses and cheap grain alcohol. Already Ethan was feeling the heavy heat of it in his face. He turned his head from side to side and watched as his reflection blurred in the mirror. A bad sign. He ordered a Port Royal, the best of the rancid Honduran beers, to cut the weight of the rum. It would be best if he went back to the hotel now to sleep or watch over Mirabelle. She wasn't looking good, she could probably use some help, but he knew that Doyle would be out all night, and the idea of facing her weirdness alone was distressing. I've been there, he thought. I've been there and been there. The sea flings you from one ill shore to the next.

Or he could stay in the other room. When they checked in, they reserved two rooms, one that they put in the ledger—and left empty—and the other, next door, to stay in. It was a simple precaution, probably unnecessary. What was Soto going to do? Check every ledger in town? Break into every occupied room? Well, maybe. It occurred to Ethan that he had no idea what Soto might do.

In the mirror, Ethan watched Doyle and the woman walk outside and onto the verandah. Doyle was pointing to something on the water and Ethan could not imagine what it might be. The sea moved empty and black against a pitch horizon. The stars, so bright on the river, looked distant and small, flecks of broken glass, and Doyle didn't know stars, anyway. Outside there was a noise in the street, something drunken, laughing or yelling. A speedboat fired down the river thoroughfare to the sea. Ethan raised his hand for another rum.

The dim lights in the bar flickered and went out and when they came on again a moment later the bar was full of people. Ethan was surrounded by men: Copalan fishermen, Merchant Marines, a red-faced sailor with a Boston accent and a peach-colored shirt. Someone was laughing very loudly and saying, *no day to die*. Another voice answered, high-pitched, certain: *At least it's not Rio*. Ethan turned in his seat. *No day to die*. A gecko perched for a moment on his fingers, scrambled across his wedding ring. A woman touched his shoulder and he shrugged her away. "You want another rum, buddy?" the bartender said.

Ethan nodded. "You know," he said, "this wouldn't be such a bad bar if it weren't filled with degenerates."

He thought he saw the bartender smile as he turned away, but it was hard to tell through the curtain of his hanging dreadlocks. It might have been a grimace of rage.

Some trouble was brewing in the corner. There was a sailor sitting on a stool with a leashed mongoose curled at his feet. Not far from him, three stools over by the bar, stood a shirtless sailor with a green python wrapped around his neck.

"Don't you let him come over here!" he shouted. "I'll cut that mongoose's throat, no shit."

"I'd put my money on the mongoose," Ethan found himself saying to no one in particular.

"At least it's not Rio!"

The mongoose was up now, tail outstretched, baring teeth like the barman's smile.

Ethan finished his Port Royal.

"A mongoose is like a weasel with purpose," he added.

There was a hand, heavy, on his shoulder. A hand and the ripe stink of stale cologne and dried sweat. Ethan turned against the pressure. The man was wearing a white linen sports jacket over a yellow Hawaiian shirt. The wrinkles in the linen seemed as deep and permanent as scars. He had a broad, jowled face, thin blond hair, and a wide frog's nose. Gin blossoms radiated across his cheeks like fireworks.

"Hey, partner," the man said. "Haven't we met before? In Suez?"

What was this? Ethan thought. Some kind of code word? Some kind of gimpy come-on?

"Not me," he said. "Got the wrong contractor."

"Everybody's contracted something wrong around here," the man said.

It must have been a joke, because he was laughing. His accent was New England, Newport or Boston Brahmin. But it didn't fit the diction—*partner,* and all that. He was still laughing, he was reaching out and shaking Ethan's hand.

"Barry Cunningham," he said.

"Nice to meet you, Barry."

Doyle was nowhere to be seen. The tiki deck thronged with dancing people, though there didn't seem to be any music. A circle was beginning to form around the mongoose man. The snake was gone, but someone had produced a Mona iguana.

"Some sport, eh?" Cunningham said.

"Sure. A real clam bake."

"What?" Cunningham said. "You're not a betting man? Not a risk man?" He raised his hand to the bartender, and when he did Ethan saw an anchor tattooed on his forearm. "Dos rons," Cunningham said. "Dobles."

The sound of Cunningham speaking Spanish irritated Ethan—it was as out of place as the drawled *partner.* Now the old anger, flaming. Something bellowed.

"He speaks English," Ethan said.

"Hey, partner, I'm just making conversation here. I'm just making some small talk."

The evening, Ethan felt, was starting to take a sinister turn. The rums arrived. Cunningham smelled his like wine, he held it up to the indigo lights. He looked at it like it had somehow betrayed him.

"It's hard to find any first-rate conversation in these climes. You run into some real creeps," he said.

Ethan lifted his rum. "Sure. Creeps everywhere. Lurking. Creeping. As is their wont."

"Exactly." Cunningham drank and raised his hand for another. "It's a filthy sort you find here. Nasty little inditos looking for someone to blame. The cheapest putas. Foreign operators. Israelis, mostly. Hot dogs."

"Hot dogs?"

"Hebrew Nationals."

Where was Doyle? Ethan was not in the mood for rummy antisemitism, or anti-Zionism, or anything. He should get back to the room. It was time for that and that's what he would do.

"So why stay here?" he asked.

"One world is as bad as the next. Except some are worse than others," Cunningham said.

The bartender started to pour two more rums. Ethan covered his glass with his hand.

"I go where work takes me, and often it takes me here," Cunningham said. He stared at Ethan as he said it; he tried, Ethan could tell, to hold his gaze. His pupils lolled. Ethan looked over his shoulder. On the boardwalk in the street, a couple kissed under the lanterns.

"And what's work?"

"Post-colonialism. Trade. Seething and burgeoning. All sorts of things, really, but mostly American post-partum depression."

Cunningham sputtered as he spoke. His words were all a little too wet, and the accent, the faux–New England, was falling away into something else, some sloppy parody of itself as fancy and soiled as his jacket. Cunningham had turned in his stool so that he was facing Ethan directly. He propped himself on the bar with his left arm and his knuckles were whitening around the glass. His hair stuck to his head with sweat.

"We've given birth to this place," he said. "It's our child and we feel pretty bad about it. We have certain tendencies. We lean toward self-pity and self-indulgence. We lean toward despair."

In the corner, the crowd began to hoot and wave money. Something yelped and Cunningham leaned closer, shouted over the fray.

"But what are you going to do? Are you going to let it rot? Grow up a fledgling? Fall into the hands of nasty foster parents?"

"God, I thought Communism was dead," Ethan said.

"I have to tell you," Cunningham said. "I don't like that kind of cynicism. I don't find it very appealing. Not from an American. Not from a fellow who should know better."

Ethan lifted his empty glass to his mouth and took some comfort, anyway, in the action. He knew he should not have another drink, he knew he should be back with Mirabelle in the hotel room, but he didn't feel this was a conversation that he could get up and walk away from, and he didn't want Cunningham following him into the street.

"How am I the cynical one here?" Ethan said. "Didn't we legitimate El Lobo?"

"Precisely. So it's a question of obligation. Don't you think that the son should take after the mother? Otherwise, it could go the other way."

Ethan wished he had accepted the rum. It seemed from the shouts and the scuffle of claws on wood that the iguana, improbably, was winning.

"Consider," Cunningham said, "a world where our spastic children are allowed out to play with the others. Consider Copal an idiot savant. Great particular merits coupled with general retardation. Infinite beauty and total rot. Imagine America like this. Imagine"—his eyes narrowed as much as they could, he reached out and touched Ethan's hand—"folks meddling in affairs of state."

The fight was over. The iguana won and a lot of people had lost money. Now the bar had settled into drunken quiet. Something was happening in the street but Ethan could not see what it was, and Cunningham, he was certain, was threatening him. He had one hand wrapped around his glass and the other on Ethan's shoulder.

"Imagine it," he was saying. "Folks meddling in affairs of state. Of kings and dukes and generals. Folks who don't know their place. Who were waiting to die. You've got to admit—it's pretty goddamn silly."

Ethan did consider the situation. He was less drunk than Cunningham and so maybe he had the drop on him. Probably not. If it wasn't clear already, if it hadn't been clear from the first impossible moment in Boystown, it was clear now. He had been lied to.

"I think there's been some sort of misunderstanding here," Ethan said. "I'm sure you hear this all the time, but you've got the wrong guy."

"Oh, come off it. I saw you ride in. I saw you get off a boat with Camillo Campo's daughter. Let's say that those are verified facts."

Whatever was happening in the street was over. The party, it seemed, had moved downriver, away from the sea. Outside, the Japanese lanterns and hung lights rocked and swayed and cast shadows over the empty road, the river beyond it.

"I'm very tired," Ethan said. "In fact, I may even be drunk. I'm afraid this has all gone a bit over my head."

"Well, that's obvious, partner," Cunningham said. "I'm not asking anything from you. I don't really care why you're doing what you're doing. It's a foolish thing to do, but that's not my problem. That's not to say that other people won't care, but I just go where I'm asked to. Where the zephyrs blow me."

Once, on a spring day sitting in the garden outside the Cloisters, Mallory kissed Ethan's jawbone and whispered the opening of the *Canterbury Tales* into his ear. He heard her voice now, rising out of fear or fever or both. *When Zephyrus eek with his swete brethe...*

"What I would like you to do," Cunningham continued, "and this is certainly for your own good, is to tell me where you're taking her."

Ethan considered the distance to the door, if he could make it at a half-drunken run. He thought so, but Cunningham still had his hand on his shoulder.

"I'm sorry," Ethan said, "but there's been some mistake. This girl is mentally ill. All I'm doing is escorting her to her family."

Cunningham pursed his thick red lips as if to spit. Slowly, he exhaled a spray of rummy air. He began to nod his head.

"Right. Of course. Her family. I forgot about them. A lovely bunch. Do you have any idea how many people her daddy killed when he was with FARC?"

Ethan signaled the bartender for another rum.

"No one said anything about FARC."

Cunningham's heavy face seemed to collapse in on itself in a mess of red wrinkles. He cast the same look of disgust on Ethan as he had on his rum.

"You lefties are all the same. Who do you think you're helping? I mean, look around—is anyone being helped?"

He gestured at the mellow despair of the bar: the drunk couples on the tiki deck, the mongoose man, dead mongoose at his feet, slumped in drink over his table.

"What good are Campo's guerrillas doing here? Who do you think arms them? Campo lets the cartels massacre whole villages of Indians along their muling routes in the cloud forest. He kidnaps oil prospectors. He bombs markets. He undermines commerce and order. Now chaos is the rule, and the rule of chaos is that it spreads. Guatemala, Mexico, and points north. That, comrade, is not philosophy—it's science. And science requires an absolute perspective. I hate to say it, but there is no law but the law imposed by men like me."

He banged his fist down on the bar and rum splashed from his glass onto his hand. He licked it from his skin. His shoulders slouched under his terrible jacket. He pointed at Ethan.

"You don't know it, but you're peering at the end of your world here. At deviants and dogs and murderers. It'll be a war on your borders soon enough. Arizona, Texas, California. There'll be plague on your streets and in your hospitals. Consider the refugees into Mexico. Consider the trade problems. I suppose you think you could live without bananas?"

Ethan felt that he had staggered into someone else's malarial dream. He stood and Cunningham let him.

"Whatever you think about me is wrong," he said. "I'm just escorting the girl to her sister."

"Look," Cunningham said. "Maybe you're carrying a torch for this girl? Maybe you want to fuck her a little bit? Hey, that's no problem here. Nobody cares. That's Anglo life in the Central American Carib, partner. Get on with it."

"We're going to Tlaxcultepec," Ethan said. "We're meeting her at the Hotel Guadelupe. Is that what you want?"

Ethan felt his weight shifting unsteadily from foot to foot, his hand shaking against the barstool. Hopefully, by the time they passed through the capital on their way to the States, Cunningham would be gone, or thrown off the trail, staking out an empty hotel for a woman who wouldn't show. The lies seemed good enough, supposing that Cunningham couldn't spot a lie. Tlax would make sense and so would the Guadelupe. It was Doyle's favorite hotel in the capital, the one they'd always stayed at while traveling, which meant it was cheap and seedy and in a bad part of town. Glue junkies prowled the entrance for travelers they could bum or steal a few pesos off of. From the roof deck you could watch the lights fail with regularity in the city. You could sometimes see the flash of gunfire. Cunningham would dig it.

"I'm leaving now," Ethan said. "Do you know anything about this man following me? Soto?"

Cunningham whistled through his teeth.

"We all have the same agenda, just different employers. He's with the generals. El Lobo and the boys with epaulets."

Cunningham peered into his empty glass and frowned.

"He's a moral spasm, not a man. Be glad that I found you first," Cunningham said. "I'm much more genteel. I can occasionally forgive a fellow his flaws."

He mopped his brow with his linen sleeve that was yellowed from similar wipings. So no one was immune to that here.

"You know, if you wanted I could take her off your hands, the girl. Save you the trouble of meeting Soto."

It was all too tempting to imagine. He could be gone, he could leave with Doyle. It's not like he was without cause. He had been lied to, he had no interest in aiding guerrillas or FARC or anyone else. Of course there was still a chance, however slim, that Yolanda had saved his life, and Mirabelle was clearly incapable of guile. In the end one must be able to explain one's actions to oneself.

Ethan turned away and walked to the door, the night's final watches beyond it.

"No worries, partner," Cunningham said. "I'll get the tab."

Ethan heard him pick up the empty soup bowl, drop it on the bar.

"I wouldn't have eaten that," he called. "Have you seen those fish? Get ready for some weird dreams tonight."

Ethan stumbled as he walked down the boulevard to his hotel. He was going too quickly. A man doesn't run in the tropics unless he's being chased, and he didn't need to draw attention to himself. It was late. The freaky bird cries that attended the first hours before dawn were just commencing in the jungle. Music still rose from the boat decks, but the bars were mostly quiet. What patrons Ethan saw as he walked sat slumped over their tables, alone or in small, melancholy groups. Three times he passed drunk Indians singing Bon Jovi karaoke to empty bars. At least it wasn't the Eagles. The coasts, they always said, were different.

He slowed as he neared his hotel and scanned the street. The hotel was a white Victorian river house with two levels of covered, wraparound porches. Electric lanterns hung between the gables and the light swayed and cast long shadows in the warm wind. Here the street was empty, and from where he was standing the low, vine-tangled power lines latticed the heavy blue sky. He looked behind him toward the sound of music but in the night he could not see the river.

The lights were off in the lobby and he climbed the stairs in the hot, pine-smelling dark. They would have to be up to catch the ferry by first light. That would leave two hours of sleep, maybe fewer, and now, after days without, there was nothing in the world for him but sleep. A cat shied from his feet as he made the landing. He went down the hall in the dark to his door.

Things were not going well in the room. Mirabelle lay half out of the bed and tangled in her sheets like something that had died as it broke through the shell of its chrysalis. The air smelled of sweat and bile and maybe even faintly of feces. Next door, in the room that they were supposed to have left empty, the dummy room, Doyle was clearly entertaining the woman from the bar. She laughed hysterically.

"You're crazy," Ethan heard her call. "Tu loco, baby."

He banged on the wall and opened the window. Outside, there was still no glow of dawn but the grackles called and called in the ceiba trees. He saw a flock of them flush at some noise, black and swarming against the sky. At a distance they seemed small, insect-like, somehow ominous. He breathed deeply of the open air, the river gas and fry oil and sea salt. It was much better than the room.

"Why is it so cold in here," Mirabelle mumbled from the bed.

"It's not cold," Ethan said. "I opened a window."

She tried to pull herself back into the bed.

"I feel very cold," she said.

Ethan turned from the window to look at her, but glanced away quickly.

"We need some fresh air," he said. "Are you sick?"

"Maybe that's what She means," Mirabelle said. "She thinks I'm ill."

Ethan waited a moment. Somewhere far off a light flashed on the water.

"The Virgin Mary?" he said. "She tells you that you're sick?"

"Maybe," Mirabelle said. "It's hard to say what She means."

Ethan banged on the door of the dummy room. He heard them suddenly go quiet and start whispering. A pointless precaution.

"Doyle, it's me. Open the door."

The woman was buttoning her shirt by the window. She smiled and waved and her shirt fell open. Doyle was wearing a sailor's cap and Ethan's sunglasses.

"Ethan, you've caught me *in medias res*."

The woman had turned away to put up her hair. She checked her makeup in the window glass.

"You shouldn't have the light on," Ethan said. "You shouldn't be in here at all."

"Fine," Doyle said. He flipped the switch and the woman sat down on the bed. Outside, the light flashed again on the water. Doyle took off Ethan's sunglasses and handed them back to him.

"It's best not to ask," he said.

By first light on the water Ethan nodded in and out of sleep as the ferry bounced and rocked toward Santa Maria. Gulls rose from the waves, wheeled overhead.

They had checked out of the hotel just before dawn and made their way down to the ferry launch.

"Just bang on the door of the boathouse," the hotel proprietor had told them. "Bang and don't stop banging until Roberto answers. He'll be asleep or drunk. Or maybe he'll be both. Either way, he'll take you where you want to go."

Roberto was drunk, but not yet asleep. His gray hair was pulled into a stringy ponytail. He wore khaki boat shorts and nothing else. His prodigious belly hung heavily over his belt like some enormous, overripe fruit sagging from the bough. He stood at the boathouse door, rubbed his red eyes, and stared hard at the three of them. The sun had not yet risen over the water.

"Is it night yet?" he asked.

"No," Doyle said. "It's morning, man. It's a new day."

"Okay, good," the captain said. "Because I do not ferry at night."

Morning came on the Caribbean. Gulls broke from the water. The sun rose quickly—it crested the far gray horizon and then it was over-head—with the sea opening in layers of aqueous shades to its light: aqua to periwinkle to azure, all lined, intermittently, with the purple shadow of risen reefs where the sea caught and foamed.

And then they were past all that as the ocean floor dropped out to the empty depths of the sea, where the pretty sun-sluiced green and light blues gave way to the deep-dark of the open water, a sky at dusk, the impossible fathoms of vanishing light.

In the far distance islands rose, lush and hazy, from the sea. Ethan closed his eyes and let the boat rock him back into shallow sleep. A tilting, rocking sleep. The sleep of doldrums, horse latitudes. When he opened them again the islands were gone. There was just the sound of the engine and the water spreading out before him.

In his dream there is a scorpion in the boat. It scrabbles about in the dirty bilge water.

"That's Soto," Mirabelle says. "He's going to take me with him."

Ethan looks about, but Doyle and Roberto are gone. It's just the three of them in the boat. The rank-smelling sea all around.

"He found us pretty quickly," he says.

"No," Mirabelle answers. "He was here the whole time."

Ethan looks down and his feet are bare. He cannot step on the scorpion in bare feet. It skitters about in the bilge water. Mirabelle starts to cry.

When he woke, Mirabelle was in the downstairs cabin shitting noisily.

"The girl's sick," Doyle said. "Like big-time."

Ethan rubbed his eyes and put on his sunglasses. A cormorant followed them overhead. The sounds from the galley were not diminishing. As in his dream, she had begun to cry.

"Goddamn," he said.

The cormorant was gone. Another string of islands wavered in the distant haze.

"How much farther?" he asked Roberto.

"Thirty minutes," the captain said. "If that girl doesn't keep adding weight to my bow."

Roberto laughed and swigged from a bottle of clear Nicaraguan rum. He offered it to Ethan and somehow Ethan declined. He had not told Doyle about Cunningham yet and he didn't want to. The conversation would not go well. Doyle, again, had been right. Doyle who killed police officers and opened bars and slept with every woman who passed his way—Doyle who seemed the poster boy for bad decisions—was right again, as always. If he's as bad as I think he is, thought Ethan, then I must be worse.

The water lightened. They were nearing the island shallows where it was cooler. Flocks of birds cast shadows over the cabin and there were other boats tugging their way between the fishing reefs. Mirabelle did not sound any better. He wondered if Cunningham had known that he was lying, if he was out there behind them somewhere, or if Soto was—one of the boats in the distance, gaining on them.

Cunningham bothered Ethan in that he demanded a moral perspective and Ethan had always tried to avoid such arguments about Copal. With its total lack of balance or subtlety, Copal undermined the intricacies of moral reasoning. One could make any argument and not be wrong. One could support any position—righteous or pragmatic— but every perspective was ultimately rendered null by the acuteness of poverty, climate, and despair. One saw terrible things: children sleeping in rusted-out ovens, beggars without arms wailing by the side of the road, sixteen-year-old girls sleeping with foreign contractors for bean money. There seemed a palpable lack of nuance.

Cunningham was right: the guerrillas were no good. Since there was no longer any Soviet funding, they relied on the drug trade and robbery and kidnappings to finance a movement increasingly devoid of ideology. Copal was not El Salvador. The guerrillas had no interest in hanging up their bandoliers and joining the government. Besides, there was no government for them to join. But Cunningham had been wrong about Ethan. FARC? Guerrillas? He had no stake in those things. If forced to have an opinion, he'd come out against them every time. But he'd also come out against El Lobo, his military cronies and their psychotic death squads. He'd come out against the gangs and the cartels and the people who seemed content to let them hack the country into despair. He'd come out against the corrupt domination of the poor by the vastly wealthy, the corporations that undermined any attempts to establish a middle class, the U.S. fruit companies and Japanese mining firms and local sugar plantations that lined El Lobo's coffers. Here, Ethan would come out against everything. It was like Doyle said at Tireisias's cabin: things are what they are, or they're worse. Ethan knew that this kind of moral relativism was useless, cowardly even. He had to make a choice about Mirabelle and to do so was also to take a stand.

Below decks the crazy girl wept with shame. The waters before them opened into tranquil aquamarine reef shallows and the west winds carried the smell of tropical earth out to the boat: tamarind and sea grapes and the wet heat of flowering jasmine.

———————

Yolanda's directions had been perfectly clear, and they found the house easily enough. Luckily, Doyle had packed a box of electrolyte rehydration packets, and they bought two bottles of sweet Cuban rum and a case of purified water at a bodega on the dock and then followed the road through town and along the shore. The island was as Yolanda described it: pink and yellow and aqua-painted houses lined the road, fishing boats rocked in shallow moorings, children played soccer in the road and women hung laundry on the lines strung up between the coconut palms as boom boxes blared static and music into the fragrant air.

Clearly the blight that scourged the mainland had not yet reached Santa Maria. Jacaranda and Indian almond and tamarind trees canopied the street, the shore was lined with wild roses and sea grapes, untended banana groves bordered the lane leading to Yolanda's house. Ethan cracked the first bottle of ron dulce and took a swig and passed it to Doyle. Wind out of the mountains carried the smell of cooking oil and plantains down the hill from the Spanish plaza. A flaking white picket fence overgrown with vines circled the house and the roof sagged under the damp of the tree shade. They stood before the small house as Ethan fumbled through the bag for Yolanda's key.

"What do you think, Mirabelle?" he asked. "This is your mother's island. Not bad, eh?"

Mirabelle's sweaty face had accrued a pallid hue like cheese left out under lights.

"Please hurry and find the key," she said. "I need to use the bathroom."

Under the sea chest by the back window Ethan found the packet of identification papers, a passport, and—*For Emergency*—a phone number.

Mirabelle lay on the concrete floor in the bathroom and refused to come out.

"There's no point," she said. "I'll just have to crawl back."

Ethan left a pillow and a thermos of electrolyte water outside the door and followed Doyle outside where they sat on the stoop and drank sweet rum mixed with water and watched the tide ripple through the trees.

"We have a problem," Ethan said.

Doyle nodded and added more rum to his water. "I think that girl has cholera."

"Then we have two problems," Ethan said.

He told Doyle about the night before, about Cunningham and Camillo and FARC. Doyle didn't say anything as he spoke, but refilled his glass almost to the rim with rum, sipped it and then put it down, far away from him, far enough so that he'd really have to stretch to reach it. When he was finished speaking, Doyle stood up and went inside. Ethan heard him open a bottle of water in the kitchen and shake another electrolyte packet, heard him talking to Mirabelle through the door. When he came back outside he didn't look at Ethan, but down and away, toward the green, metallic sea.

"This is what we need to do," he said. "We need to make her a sickbed."

"There's a bed in the house," Ethan said. "There's two."

Doyle started to reach for his rum but stopped. He turned and looked down the canopied lane: the children playing soccer there, the empty paths beyond them.

"Pretty soon she won't be able to get out of bed. She'll be too weak for that. We have to cut a hole in the bed. We'll need a bucket. Maybe two."

"Shouldn't we find a doctor?"

Doyle shook his head and reached for his rum. Drank it this time.

"There's nothing a doctor can do now but spread fear of contamination in the village. We just have to keep her hydrated. It'll run its course."

The poor girl, thought Ethan. Relegated, before him, to a wasted, shitting thing. To shit into a bucket she would not have the strength to move. The shame of it. He would have to sit by her bed and mop her brow. He would have to keep her hydrated. He would open and close the windows. He felt a sudden affection for her that he didn't wish to consider.

"Come help me make up these rehydration packets," Doyle said.

Ethan followed him into the kitchen, where two thermoses of electrolyte water already stood on the counter. Doyle began opening packages and pouring the powder into water bottles.

"Why are we making the rest of these now?" Ethan asked.

"It's the least we can do, don't you think?"

Ethan knew, then, where this was going. He tried to keep his voice level. He turned to look out the window as he spoke.

"What do you mean by that, Brendan?"

"She's going to be bedridden for days. Two or three at the very least."

"So?"

"So this is the end of the line. You can't move her, and by the time you can it'll be too late."

Ethan stepped back outside and Doyle followed him. They closed the door. The sun was high over the sea and there were no boats coming from the mainland.

"You're saying that we just leave her?"

"What would you do, Ethan? Sit here with her and wait for Soto? You think he's not coming? You think that maybe you outfoxed him?"

"Of course he's coming," Ethan said.

"So that's it. He'll come and he'll kill you and it won't mean a thing. That's if that spook from Roycetown doesn't get here first. Not that it matters. However you shake it, it ends the same way."

For once, take his advice, thought Ethan. He's been right every time.

"You have no obligation to these people," Doyle said. "You've been had. You've been played. You're the oldest joke in the book of gringo jokes."

Ethan imagined Yolanda's wry scorn. How sheepish and ashamed and drunk he had felt at her kitchen table. How she put him—a sloppy, indulgent, privileged American—in his place: *I bought you your life*, and then offered him grace as if it were hers to bestow. He remembered the streets of whores, the ruin of the Mexican city. His guilt had compounded itself. A woman who lived in the clockless darkness of colonial rot had risked her life for his. He had felt ashamed of his own sadness. Compared to her, he had not earned his despair. It was a low trick to have played, and not one that he needed to die for.

Still, no boats on the horizon. The wind through the trees brought a smell of jasmine. He imagined tending to the girl inside. Mopping her sweating brow, sleeping on the couch. What did he walk toward, if he walked away from this?

"I can't leave her alone, Doyle."

Doyle turned on his heel like a soldier drilling in the yard.

"I know you're in pain," he said. "I feel some sympathy for that. But you don't belong here. This isn't as complicated as you want to make it. You've been lied to. It happens. Now you can leave with me or you can stay here and die. Those are the only options, because Ethan, get hip to this: as much as I love you, I am not going to sit here and wait for these people to find me."

He was slipping into his punchy expat jargon. North coast talk. He didn't wait for Ethan to respond before turning and looking over his shoulder: empty water, empty road. So he's afraid, thought Ethan, and he's abandoning me and he can't do it without playing Panama Jack. Fine. I'm hip to it.

"I need to stay with the girl, Doyle. I can't imagine abandoning her."

Doyle didn't turn around. When he spoke, he spoke to the sea, the ways beyond it, the whole world that, like Ethan, disappointed him with its folly.

"What you should try to imagine is getting a life. Getting a grip."

"This is advice? This is advice coming from you?"

"No, it's a fucking warning," Doyle said. "It's your run-of-the-mill caveat. Perhaps, Ethan, you do not approve of my life? But get this, because this is important: the past is in the past. Irredeemably, irrevocably. You make a choice. Say, for example, to kill a police officer. That's it. It's over and done with. You make one choice and then you make another."

He turned, finally, to look at Ethan. He seemed as certain now as he had fourteen years earlier when he insisted on only drinking Tullamore Dew. It was a beautiful thing almost, that certainty, that total lack of ambivalence: Doyle, standing there against the palm-break shore, certain of the way clarity would reveal itself to a man who walked an undeviating line.

"So you ruined your marriage? Your wife was raped? No arrangement of idiotic behavior will undo that." He nodded toward the house, the girl inside. "Leave redemption to the pious and shitting peasants."

Ethan leaned against the front door and slid slowly down to the stoop. Doyle swigged the rest of the ron dulce from his glass. It was overly sweet, cloying, and Ethan watched his throat chug like a piston to get it down. His eyes had begun to hood as they had in the bar in Roycetown. He was chewing on the inside of his cheek, and when he spoke again there was blood on his teeth.

"You know, this isn't a country for the living," he said. "It's one of the great advantages we have over them that we may spend so many of our years alive, while they, from birth, struggle to stave off death. It creates a sort of moral whimsy, an attitude of longing. Those policía would have killed me for another fucking drink. Women who are already dead cling to life with their thighs. We want to disdain them, to remain apart, but it's impossible. They have so much it's so easy to take."

"That's not what's happening here," Ethan said.

"I've glutted myself in the slums," Doyle said. "And then I've passed out pesos like Indulgences. This is no different."

Blood rouged his lips and stained his teeth. He looked like a child who'd gone a round with a candy apple. In her last night at home Samantha had bit her tongue and spat blood in Ethan's face. She bit and spat and bit again and he'd had to grab her by the hair and force his hand into her mouth, between her teeth, and pull her toward him, against his chest. They'd spent their last night like that—him kissing the top of her head, kissing and kissing it, whispering into dawn with his hand like a gag in her mouth.

"What do you think will happen when Soto finds her?" Ethan asked.

"Hey, I'm all for nobility," Doyle said. "But there's nothing noble about this. You're not going to make any difference at all. Whatever's going to happen to her is still going to happen."

"You called it. Things are what they are or they're worse."

"Fine," Doyle said, as he turned and walked back into the house. "I wish you'd told me you came down here to die. We could have gone about it with a bit more gusto."

"Help me make up the cholera bed," Ethan said. "Before you go."

Butterflies light on Mirabelle's face. She can feel their sticky feet tracking across her skin, their wings when they flap leaving a down of dusty scales. She wipes them off and wipes them off and the fan overhead turns and wobbles and she feels that too, a turning in her gut, and she is shitting again, through the cut hole in the table that she's using as a bed, into the bucket.

The butterflies are gone, but when she wipes her face her hands come away wet. Has someone been crying? She turns her head to the side but there's just the curtained window, the trees hanging down beyond the curtains, the sea darkening beyond the trees. She listens and smells; she does not sense the Mother.

She kicks her feet. Flies scramble between her toes. "Rosa," she says, "was it this bad for you? Or was it worse?"

"Ay, Mirabelle," Rosa says. "You are very filthy. I think that is why the men have left."

Mirabelle drinks from the thermos of electrolytes and almost retches. The infused water is tepid; it tastes salty and viscous and she drinks it down, swallowing hard against the urge to retch, until the thermos is empty. She feels, immediately, a new throb in her bowels and she is at it again.

She wipes her forehead and cold sweat pimples her skin. Oyster sweat. She trembles, she says "Mother of God" and then laughs. "Mother of God Mother of God Mother of God."

Outside the palms whisper in the low, soughing sea breeze.

She looks out through the window and Rosa is sitting in the tree, way up in its high canopy, cracking coconuts with her teeth.

"You need to drink electrolytes, Rosa," Mirabelle says. "I told you that. I told you that's what you needed."

Rosa opens the coconut and drains it into her mouth. The milk is brown and thick.

"I like these more," she says. "They will grow my breasts."

"It will make you sick," Mirabelle says, and then closes her eyes and keeps them closed, because she wants to tell Rosa that her breasts will never develop now that she's dead. When she opens her eyes Rosa is hunched up in the corner, dry heaving.

"Maybe that man was telling true," Rosa says. "Maybe I am nothing."

"Telling the truth," Mirabelle says. "Not telling true."

She doesn't know why she still bothers to correct Rosa's English. Against the wall the girl continues to heave.

———

Ethan waited till she slept, till he heard her mumbling cease and her breathing settle, before stepping in off the stoop and sitting by her bed. He didn't want her to see him while she was awake. She must have her pride. He stood and approached her bed, he pulled her sheet up over her shoulders. She lay on her back—the way they'd fashioned the cholera bed, with a hole just big enough for her to fit her bottom through, it was the only way possible.

He sat and watched her sleep. He watched her sweat and moan and worry her covers about her throat. He listened to her teeth chatter. First it was just a light sound, tooth grazing tooth, but then as she fell deeper into sleep or dream or fever it grew louder: molar on molar and jawbone suddenly tense, standing out. Finally he did what he'd known he'd do: he reached out—a gesture from long ago, a movement of the hand beginning over a year ago and completing, or beginning again, in this moment, here—he reached out and touched her brow. He touched her brow and said, "Easy, Mirabelle. You're grinding your teeth again." And when the sound didn't stop, when she ground them louder, gnashed them so hard he thought they'd break, he ran his fingers down her face to her jaw, her throat, he lay his lips as slowly and surely as he could on her forehead.

When she settled but stayed sleeping, he stood and went to the window. He opened the curtains and wiped some dust from the sill. There was wind now on the water. He thought of the flagellants in *The Seventh Seal*. In a life devoid of redemption, judgment might be grace enough. He looked back once at the girl on the bed and then out again to the empty lane that led to the sea, the sea where a new breeze came on the turning tide. He was waiting for Soto.

He wakes on the stoop with the ron dulce in his lap and knows that some time has passed. The tide is in—it slicks up against the sea wall at the end of the lane—and the light has changed. The whitewashed house, the palms and mangoes in the yard—everything glows pink in the low light of a tropic dusk. Beyond the leafline of hanging sea grapes and buttonwood trees, the beach is gone and there is just the evening sea moving out against the darkening sky in layers of amethyst and slate. Tree frogs croak. The night birds begin to call. He stands from the stoop and leaves the rum there; he steps inside and starts to close the door but can't, with the smell. Inside, he changes the waste bucket as quietly as he can and hopes she doesn't awaken. He walks the bucket outside and empties it into the pit Doyle dug behind the house. Inside again, he replaces the bucket and washes his hands and turns to the open door as the back window streaks with reflected green flashes of distant heat lightning.

MIRABELLE WAKES AND SEES the Mother sitting by her bed,

"Where have you been?" she asks. "I thought you would come sooner."

The Mother nods and rocks and Her headdress of feathers shivers and molts at the motion. She opens Her eyes wide in pity or sorrow and then closes them. Her eyelids are wrinkled and slate-colored, damp like the cold walls of a well seen from the inside.

"I'm sick," Mirabelle says. "I think I have cholera. That's why I'm drinking all these waters."

She opens the thermos and holds it up to the Mother.

"Would you like one? They are very disgusting."

The Mother shakes Her head and does not open Her eyes. Mirabelle turns away and looks out through the window where there is little light left on the water. In the coming darkness the room settles into a smoky blue and she cannot see far beyond the Mother's hunched shoulders, the outline of the kitchen door.

"Are the men gone?" she asks.

The Mother opens Her eyes, clacks Her golden beak. Sometimes She has lips, sometimes a beak, always a blue parrot's tongue. She does not answer the question. Mirabelle has not seen the men in hours. Maybe they left her. Isn't that what Rosa said? It could have been a dream, but she thinks she remembers Ethan once by her bed; she remembers hearing somebody walking around, outside, on the porch. Then comes the pain, the sudden heat and wrenching movement in her intestines that's followed by a spasming in her bowels. She's shitting again into the bucket. The Mother ruffles Her feathers and clacks Her beak and Mirabelle hopes that Ethan has not abandoned her.

When she is finished, another cold sweat comes over her. She wipes the perspiration from her brow, she closes her eyes, and when she opens them again the room blurs with new dark. She sees only the Mother's trembling outline kneeling just beyond her bed. By the sound of clacking beads she knows the Mother has begun to finger Her coral rosary.

There was a time, once, when the Mother's appearances did not command such melancholy, when the Mother would come and sing to her or tell stories of Her days in the jungle among the Indians and the Romans, when She'd reach out and almost touch Mirabelle, when Her shirt would moisten with breast milk. That was before Yolanda left and Jose died and Rosa died and Mr. Bernal took her in and did what he did.

Someone moves around outside on the porch in the dark. The room flashes once with green heat lightning and Rosa says, "Did you know that once I let Jose touch me?"

"No, you did not."

"Es la verdad," Rosa says. "He was very mean on me."

The Mother shakes and ruffles Her feathers, looks up at Mirabelle through Her veil of tears and feathers and Her sagging skin. She opens Her beak and moves Her black tongue.

"Ill," She says, and it's the same thing She said on the boat and in the hotel room in Roycetown.

"Yes, I know I'm ill. I have cholera. I told you that already."

She says it again—*ill*—and Her voice is soft and sweet. Clear and sharp as wind on the open sea. Nothing like a parrot's voice.

"Please tell me more," Mirabelle says. "Speak to me. Do not stop speaking to me."

"All will be ill," the Mother says.

Mirabelle wipes her head and drinks from the thermos until it is empty. She begins to shit again. She turns her eyes away from the Mother. What is it when the world has come to this, when you have come to this? The world broke you down until you were nothing. It surrounded you with trembling men and dead children and cafés filled with rotten fruit and goddesses who did nothing but proclaim the obvious. On the shores of the river, idiot inditos without shoes tried to spear the worst fish anyone had ever seen. Her father had abandoned her and her mother had abandoned her and Yolanda, always so full of wisdom and wit and knowledge of the ways of the world, she had abandoned her too.

"I am not even an insect," Mirabelle says.

There is wind in the trees and bird screams and the manic clatter-ing of the Mother's rosary, and Her voice rising as sweet and melodious as a lullaby.

"All will be ill and all will be ill and all will be ill."

Mirabelle turns as far from her as she can. There is no one who will love her without rubbing her face in the world's trash.

"Shut up," she says. "Even if you are real, I don't believe in you anymore."

ETHAN WOKE ON THE porch in the night and knew that Soto was coming. He poured the last of the rum into his glass, filled it almost half full, and lit the paraffin lamp that hung from the rafters. Mosquitoes sparked through its wavering corona and moths, ghostly and elongate as orchids, drifted in swarms out of the forest.

He waited. By now Doyle was probably back in Roycetown with his Greek sailor girl. He would not have traveled at night.

In his dream there had been a hound with a child in its mouth. It came through the stands of wild palms on the shore and loped up the lane to the house. Now, he looked down the road and waited. In the west, a red cloudbank scudded out toward sea where the stars still turned in cold blue symmetries. He had seen the hound's teeth and its breath misting into the air and then had seen that it wasn't vapor but smoke, for the hound held a cigar, along with the child, in his mouth.

Ethan sipped his rum and listened to the flap of ghost moths about the lamp's golden light. Insects trilled in all the trees and the moving cloudbank now hung uniform and solid as a sarcophagal lid. Over the water the stars disappeared and the world beyond the porch fell to darkness and insect cries, the whisper of the sea against the shore and the tremulous keen of wind through stands of dry palms. Ethan held out his carving knife to the lamp's glintings and stuck it in the soft stoopwood. He could not imagine what use it would really be to him. He sat on the lit porch, a beacon for whatever moved toward him through the dark. A light that he too had followed, choice by choice, to this spot. He drank his rum. When he saw the man, lit only by the pale cherry of a burning cigar, coming down the lane toward the house, he picked up the knife, dropped it again, closed the front door, and stood waiting on the stoop.

———

When Soto crossed into the lamplight he swept off his hat, put one foot on the steps, and wiped his face with a handkerchief as if, in some other world, he were asking a girl out for malts. Somewhere along the way, Roycetown maybe, he had showered and shaved, and his beard was trimmed and neat. He wore a white linen sports coat and like Cunningham's it was wrinkled with heat or wear. Underneath it, his blue shirt was halfway open and a gold necklace shone against his skin; he folded his handkerchief and stuffed it sloppily into his breast pocket; he held his machete unsheathed in his right hand; he dropped his cigar and ground it into the stoop. He looked up at Ethan and spread his arms.

"Well," he said, "where is she?"

Ethan did not like his voice. It was too deep and theatrical. He stepped back against the door. There was no way to appear unafraid.

"She's inside."

"Is she sleeping?"

"She has cholera."

"Is that so?" Soto lifted his nose, sniffed the air twice like a dog, and made an elaborate face of disgust. He wiped his nose with his hand, put his Panama back on and dipped his face into shadow.

"I hate cholera," he said. "Once when I was a boy I saw it infect a whole Mayan village. Rows and rows of people, the whole town really, shitting into buckets in an outdoor infirmary. It was something to behold. It was disgusting. You cannot imagine the sound or the smell."

A stiletto opened out of nowhere, it seemed, into his hand. He rested his machete against his leg. He smiled and shook his head and trimmed a new cigar.

"It was instructive to see. I watched full-bodied men and women shrink to nothing. They shat and shat and they withered like dried fruit. They shat and they were nothing without their shit. I carried their buckets of waste, I burned their blankets. I realized that these Indians were less than their own excrement."

He lit his cigar and tossed the match away.

"It made quite an impression on me," he said. "Obviously. But the Mayans deserve what they get, don't you think?"

He was mad. His voice was preposterous, his perfect English lilted with rising Spanish intonations. Why had he not asked to see

Mirabelle? Why had he not killed Ethan? At the moment Ethan had no feelings about the Mayans and he was sure that his answer to this question did not matter.

"When I came here, I did not understand the situation," Ethan said.

Soto blew smoke and waved it away from his face as if he found it unpleasant. He drew his foot from the step, wiped it on the ground, and then replaced it again.

"Originally, the Mayans did not engage in human sacrifice," he said. "They were a peaceful people of great culture and learning. Of all the people on all the shores of the earth, in those days none were as wise as the Mayans."

He gestured as he spoke toward the lightless sky.

"They were astrologers who could read the fabric of the heavens beyond any of today's astronomers. They trafficked in portents and solstices. They were good augers. And then a people came among them, a warlike race who knew only the way of bones and bloodletting. These people did not learn wisdom or peace or agriculture from the Mayans, but instead taught them human sacrifices. And that was the end of the Mayans. They reveled, then, in bones and false slayings, the ways of their colonizers. How can so knowledgeable a people fall for such cruel and obvious practices? That is why they are punished now. That is why their crops rot and their people are forced to sell trinkets to Anglos."

Soto paused. He raised the brim of his hat slightly so that Ethan could see his eyes, golden and beautiful and dull in the paraffin halo. He spat onto the stoop. Behind him, thunder rumbled over the sea. He spoke again and as he did his shadow-lengthened features contorted through a series of freakish postures. He was not like the killers in the bars or the bandits on the road. His performance did not move toward any clear effect—it served no purpose beyond its own weirdness.

"I'm telling you all this because you claimed you did not understand the situation. And that is a poor excuse. It is unacceptable to me. Everyone should know and claim their actions. They should know their cause, they should accept their effect."

Ethan reached down and lifted his glass of rum. He drank from it, long and hard, until he had to wince and close his eyes, and when he opened them again Soto was still there, eyebrows raised in some question. More lightning pulsed behind the clouds, over the sea.

"I met a woman in a bar in Mexico," Ethan said. "She saved my life, or so I thought. I felt that I owed her. I felt some obligation."

"Did you know that a Mormon gave his life and the life of his companion for you? You did not? They died in the marsh and in the heat and in the stink of their own waste. I left them in the open for the spider monkeys and the vultures."

"Monkeys do not eat people," Ethan said.

Soto shook his head. He stamped his foot, he snarled. For a moment he seemed simply ridiculous, a character out of a fairy tale. Rumpelstiltskin with a machete.

"You don't know anything," he said.

"No, it's a fact. Spider monkeys eat fruit and shrubs, not Mormons. There's absolutely no precedent for it."

Ethan finished the rum and pushed himself up against the door, barring Soto from the girl. The knife still stuck in the porch wood and the glass in his hand felt light and useless; he could barely hold it for his trembling. He did not know why he was antagonizing Soto, but the sudden anger felt better than fear.

Soto did not react to his statement. Perhaps he had not heard it.

"You do not know anything," he said again. "And that is a problem. Tell me, did you know Mirabelle Campo's friend, the café owner's daughter, died of cholera?"

Ethan shook his head. The thunder had moved closer inland. Rain fell in sudden sheets on the ocean.

"This is my point," Soto said. "You've been missing it all along, and now I want you to pay attention. It is foolish and selfish and short-sighted of you to believe that you are here for no reason. The world is composed of symmetries. Of signs and wonders. And one is always an agent of those wonders, a product of cause. So why are you here? This you can tell me. Your cause is known. It is written and done. It is your effect that is yet to be determined."

For months Ethan had felt the urge to confess, to kneel before Samantha in her white room and explain himself. For months he spoke to her as he walked the streets; he woke, when he slept at all, with her name like a rough-cut stone on his lips. If he could not take back his words, that moment at the kitchen table, then at least he could explain them. There is a reason for everything, he had thought, and if he could only explain it to her, if he could only bear his hurt before her so she could see that his damage approached her own, that they had damaged each other together, then somehow they could find some grace, could step back, word by word, into a world bereft of madness. He could hold her to him, he could rock her, like a child, into morning.

Of course, this was delusion, vanity, fever. Their lives would not be cobbled into what they had never been and Samantha would grant no absolution. And neither, he knew, would Soto.

"I don't owe you an explanation," he said.

"Maybe not," said Soto. "You are American, after all. If your destiny is manifest you need never explain yourself to anybody. But perhaps you should offer it as a gift, because it is the only thing preventing me from killing you here on this porch and delivering that girl into the hands of men who slaver for her."

The rain came, as it did in the tropics, in moving sheets. Ethan heard it make landfall over the beach, then sweep into the palmbreak before the road. It sounded in the lane and on the street dust and in the mangoes before it hit the cane roof overhead. Soto stepped fully onto the porch and shook the water from the brim of his hat. There was less than four feet between them now, and the world beyond Soto was invisible beneath the haze and steam of sudden rain.

"As I told you," Ethan said, "I was not aware of the situation when I arrived here. But from what I know now, I promise you—that girl is useless. She's deranged. No one will ransom her."

"Wrong again. Already two Mormons ransomed their lives for her. They were eaten by spider monkeys."

Soto stood too close. Ethan could smell the cigar smoke on his jacket, and all around the ripe heat of the earth steaming into the air. Above them, something stirred in the cane.

"For Christ's sake, have some mercy," Ethan said. "It's as easy as not having it."

"I asked you to explain your motives, not mine. I am always merciful, but I don't think you could begin to comprehend the nature or consequences of mercy."

"I understand the consequences of not getting macheted. I understand those very clearly."

"There's no evidence of that," Soto said. "Everything you've done, every single choice you've made since you arrived in Copal, since before that even, all point toward you getting chopped into monkey food on this porch. It would seem that it was your singular goal."

"Why would I do that?"

"That's what I'm asking you. Explain the situation to me. Let me see what other symmetries are in place. Why are you here?"

Wind rose now with the rain and the water came in torrents. It whipped under the porch awning on gusts and leaked through the roof. Whatever lived in the cane continued to scramble.

"I was married," Ethan said over the sound of the wind. "I lived in New York with my wife. She drank too much and I think she cheated on me. I was very jealous."

"And did she? Did she cheat on you?"

"I don't know. Probably. It hardly matters. You have to understand I was angry. I mean, I was hurt. You can imagine."

"No, I cannot," Soto said.

"I had an affair. For a while. My wife refused to get help. She let our lives fall apart and I thought she was reveling in the loss. She demeaned me. She ruined every beautiful thing."

Ethan did not like the tone of his voice. In the hundred nights where he whispered his confession to the empty dark, to Samantha asleep or spectral, it did not ever go like this.

"So I told her about the affair. I had already ended it. I had recommitted. There was no reason to tell her."

"No, there is always a reason," Soto said.

Ethan had stood at the window in the room that reeked of gin and sweat. *It's the middle of December*, Samantha had said. Outside, the world moved on in shards of broken light.

"I chose to hurt her," Ethan said, and raised the empty glass to his lips. When he brought it away he looked up to the cane ceiling. "She went out that night. She went to a bar. A bar she frequented. She met a man there and something terrible happened to her."

"She was seeking vengeance?"

"I don't know what she was thinking. Does it matter? Something terrible happened to her. Something she could not recover from. I tried to help her. You cannot know what it is like to hold a woman you love through that. Through the nights where she wakes clawing at your face. Through the shaking in the night and the fever. Through the nights that will not end. Through the cough syrup and the vomiting and the police. Finally she committed herself. I think I was relieved. I left New York. I traveled here on her money."

Soto turned and looked behind him, out to the rain and the invisible sea. He followed Ethan's gaze into the scrambling rafters. Water dripped and pooled on the porch. He waved toward him with elaborate flourish—a fool announcing a king.

"So here you are?"

"I told you that I did not understand the situation," Ethan said. "I have no interest in politics or revolution. I knew only that there was nothing I could do to remedy what happened to Samantha."

"Samantha," Soto said. He drawled the syllables, drew them out over the sound of the rain. Ethan did not like her name on his tongue.

"That girl in there is sick. She's unstable."

"Yes, well, are you hydrating her?"

Ethan nodded, his voice now rank and soiled, impossible beneath the rain.

"Then she will live," Soto said. "Keep her hydrated. Watch her fever. Give her carbohydrates."

Soto tapped the machete against the porch. As if Ethan were not already aware of it. It thunked and thunked into the soft porchwood and it was the only sound in the world but the rain.

"You are self-indulgent," Soto said. "And you deserve to die. About this I am serious. In a world without mercy you do not deserve to live. You say to me that I cannot imagine the pain of some raped puta? Or not even that. You did not ask me to imagine that. You said I could not comprehend your pain, your pain at her violation."

He spat onto the porch and his saliva strung in his sheared beard.

"Do you know what I have seen in the jungles? On the islands? The dead children under the banana trees after a Sandinista raid? You walk through a glade and the glade is buzzing. There are mounds covered in flies, mounds so thick with flies and spiders and moving insects that you cannot tell what is under them but for the smell. You approach one and you kick it and the world riots with flies and insects like you are the Lord of Hosts, and then you look down and it is a child, a boy with a rotten face and no eyes and beetles where his eyes should be and his tongue pulled through a slit in his throat and maggots chewing on his tongue. You can hear them, everywhere in the glade—you can hear them chewing the tongues like gypsy moths in pine woods."

A scorpion fell out of the cane and Soto crushed it with his boot. He scraped the blue skeletal husk on the step as another landed on the brim of his hat. He shook off the hat and kicked the scorpion into the weeds. With his hat off and the paraffin light flickering on his face, his mouth drooped into an elongated frown.

"Once I was in a jungle drinking coffee and a woman fell out of the sky. She splattered before me. I was sitting in a makeshift infirmary and there was a woman in a crater at my feet. Do you know where she came from?"

Ethan nodded. He knew about the Indians thrown from planes.

Soto said, "That too made quite an impression on me. That too was instructive. Because she was pregnant, see? And her fetus burst into the flowers and the vines and I wrapped it in a blanket and I held it to my chest and I ate a banana flecked with blood. I do not think there are any more children.

"But there is mercy. There are symmetries and causes and the wills of men who have held the world's last children to their chests. You can be an agent of that. You can be an agent of something other than fuck-up."

Another scorpion fell to the porch. He crushed it, he waved inside.

"You have a way to contact Yolanda Campo?"

Ethan nodded.

"Then you will do so after the girl recovers. You will ask her to meet you in Tlaxcultepec. You will tell her that her sister needs her, that she is ill and has a message to deliver. An important package to deliver. Then you will bring Yolanda Campo to the Jesus of the Poor statue outside of Barrio Gómez. Do you know this statue?"

The statue perched on the rocky hillside overlooking the western barrios. At night it was illuminated by green lights and Ethan had seen it many times from the roof deck of the Hotel Guadelupe.

"What will happen to her?" he said.

"The same thing that was going to happen anyway. Her destiny is set. The difference is that maybe this way you and the girl survive."

"What if she doesn't come?"

Soto shrugged. "I doubt she is as far away as you think."

More scorpions fell now as the rain flushed them from the cane. They dropped to the ground and skittered and snapped, they caught on the walls and the windowsill, one perched on the brim of Soto's Panama.

"Do you think that Campo cares for the people of this country?" Soto said. "For any people? He is not a Copalan and he does not ponder symmetry or mercy. He lives with his guerrillas in the jungles with the Indians, and he is destroying them, the Indians, village by village. The younger ones growing up in his midst do not follow the ways of their elders. They do not listen to the chiefs. They go off with Campo. They want the pretty and golden things. And do you think he loves these Indians? He steals their children. He burns their crops. He burns their fields and closes the mines so that the corporations cannot do business in the interior. When the traficantes want to pass through their villages, he does not protect them. Does that help anybody?"

He held out his hands, he skewed his head, he seemed to wait for an answer as scorpions fell around them.

"Did you know," he said, "that Sandino believed his battlefield would be attended by demons and angels? Such men think their actions beyond the judgments of the world, and I promise that Camillo Campo will not escape my hounding."

And then the scorpions were upon them. Fifty, a hundred, flushing at the storm, falling from the ceiling, landing on the porch and on the ground and on the men. The scorpions hissed and scrambled across the floorboards and Soto danced and hooted and pounded them down in a freakish hopping two-step, in the paraffin light, as the storm came, kept beat, raged, and passed on.

"Ill," says the Mother by her bed in the night.

Mirabelle trembles and turns her head away, but the Mother has moved—She sits now by Mirabelle's feet.

"Ill," She sings. "All will be ill and all will be ill and all manner of things will be ill."

Mirabelle wipes her face and reaches for her thermos. She drinks and gags and drinks again. She will not die, she thinks, the way Rosa did.

She sleeps and wakes as a storm breaks over the water. She watches the lightning striking wide and diffuse behind the clouds. The men's voices burr and tremble from the porch.

Yolanda wipes her brow and touches her throat and kisses her forehead. Yolanda changes her bucket.

"I'm sorry," Mirabelle says.

Yolanda waves the words away as she does. She laughs and pulls her hair back.

"This is nonsense," she says. "It's not so bad as when you tried to eat that lizard."

She's walking then with Yolanda through the dry red roads of Rio de Caña. It's dawn but the streets remain empty. No one lurches toward the fields. Ahead of them, a dog crosses the boulevard. Vultures sleep and flutter on the roof of Mr. Bernal's café.

"Look over there," Yolanda says.

The sky beyond the pine mountains swells into a ripe purple. Mirabelle thinks of coral jewelry, the Mother's rosary, which she hears clicking not far behind her.

"Do you know what that means?" Yolanda asks.

Because Mirabelle suddenly stands only to Yolanda's hip, she nestles her face into the fabric of her skirt. She kisses her leg and she reaches up toward where Yolanda's hand must be. The skirt feels wet, warm, and she thinks that maybe she is crying. She reaches again for Yolanda's hand and finds that it is in her hair. She does not want to look back at the sky, but does. It darkens as with smoke.

Mirabelle shakes her head as the dog lumbers back into the street and trots toward them. There is a dead horse in the road. She will hold Yolanda, and this time she will not let her go.

"Mirabelle, you're gnashing your teeth again," Yolanda says.

Mirabelle woke to light and fresh sea wind through the open window, a figure sitting by the bed. She closed and opened her eyes as the room and the figure unsmoked from the blur of fevered sleep. It was not the Mother or Yolanda but Ethan who sat there wiping her brow with a wet rag.

"You were gnashing your teeth again," he said. "I was afraid you would break them."

His face hung slack and pale, unshaven. His eyes were bright, sober maybe, but bloodshot and tired. Tear tracks stained his skin and his fingers trembled as he withdrew them from her brow.

"Really," he said. "You have to be careful. Your teeth can crack. I've seen it happen."

Where, she thought, does someone see that? Outside, a pelican screeched as it flushed from the shore. Thankfully, the sound of the demented grackles that haunted the room was gone and the scent of bougainvillea drifted on the moving breeze. There was no smell, anywhere, of the Mother.

"How long have I been like this?" she asked.

"Three days."

He reached out and dabbed her brow again with the rag. An instinctual motion, she thought—he didn't even realize he was doing it. She had become like that with Rosa by the end. He handed her a plain tortilla.

"Eat this," he said. "And drink another thermos."

"Did Soto come?"

Ethan nodded and withdrew his hand from her brow. She followed his gaze out the window, where the palms were black against the purple sky. It was a strange color for the sky and she wondered for a moment if she were still dreaming.

"And he left?" she said. "He did not hurt you?"

"It was fine. He took one look at you and your cholera and bolted. I think you grossed him out."

"Really?"

"He's a slave trader. You were damaged goods. Best bit of cholera you've ever had."

It hurt to laugh. Her abdominal muscles were still spasming. Under the sheet, she touched her stomach and the skin felt dry and thin, like parchment.

"I'm better now, I think."

"You will be. We'll have to get you packed up in a day or so."

"Where are we going?"

"Tlax," he said. "The capital. You'll love it."

IN THE CAR, ON the mainland, Ethan imagined that he had not made the phone call. He had dialed the number he found in the drawer and at first there had been nothing but electric sound. Doors opening and closing and then a man's voice over the static.

"Halo?" the man said. "Si?"

"I have a message for Yolanda," Ethan said. "Is this the right number?"

"What is the message? Speak very quickly, please."

Ethan said Mirabelle was sick, he said she had a package for Yolanda, he said they needed to meet before he could cross the border. He gave a date, a time, he named one of the few places where he might seem innocuous. "The T.G.I. Friday's on Avenue Ua Xac, just off Boulevard Suyapa," he said.

Then the man was gone and there was nothing but static, a dial tone, a valve clicking on the empty line.

"It's fine if she can't make it," Ethan said.

Now, as he drove the shore road away from the marina where he'd bought the car, he thought maybe she did not get the message. There had been a confusion. An error in translation. Perhaps she wouldn't come.

He drove and the girl, sleeping in the seat beside him, looked almost like an old woman. Her flesh clung to her bones like date skin. He drove too fast, he wanted to make it to Tlax by night and the chances didn't look good—the streets thronged with wanderers. In the towns, women hawking bags of sweet water, bottles of Coke, and roasted peanuts ran behind the car, banged on the windows with their hawking poles, and in the country lines of families wandered the open road. People with their possessions on their backs, with donkeys and carriages, old men on bicycles. Everyone, it seemed fled on some exodus or pilgrimage.

"Mirabelle," he said, "what is this? Is there some kind of festival? Another Holy Week? A saint's day?"

The girl stirred and opened her eyes. He thought she'd want to see her country, a land she'd never known, but she turned from the window and closed her eyes again.

"No," she said. "There is nothing."

He drove on. Swerved to avoid a dead horse lying in the middle of the road. People sang as they walked, and once he thought he saw a retinue of penitents crawling on their knees, but as they passed he saw that it was simply a traveling troop of the legless. They swung themselves forward along the highway on their arms, and their flabby hanging torso flesh left winding trails in the dust. There were no children.

Smoke rose in the distance. Maybe there were roadblocks. Certainly, fires burned on the road to the capital.

An hour later they passed heapings of flaming tires and truck cabins, but the barricade had been abandoned and left unfinished, never strewn fully across the road, as if its makers had taken sudden flight. Two white goats scavenged the street edge under the seep and billow of black rubber smoke.

Twenty miles outside the city limits, the road turned, as roads did there, totally insane. The coast route and the Pan-American Highway converged into the capital motorway, where the truck traffic out of the south intersected the eastern bus routes and four lanes of speeding, lawless, brakeless traffic joined into a pitted, half-paved highway. Ethan had never driven in the capital before, he had always taken buses, and he held the wheel now with both hands and drove as fast as he could since he knew that to slow down was to allow the truck and bus drivers the chance to run you off the shoulder and into the jagged barrancas that fell away through valleys of scrub pine, cactus, and dust. The yellow roadside signs read PELIGRO LOMO and pointed in a crooked, aimless scribble toward the unrailed shoulder. "No shit," Ethan said, and Mirabelle stirred and looked up.

"Do you want me to drive?" she asked as she yawned.

Tlaxcultepec was built in a valley and, like most Central American cities, its outer neighborhoods sprawled up the mountainsides, where they hung impossibly in ranging, cluttered barrios. Ahead, in the distance, the tin roofs of the western settlements glinted like a hill of broken glass in the setting sun.

"Is that the city?" Mirabelle said.

"Just the outskirts. The tip of the iceberg."

"The what?"

Ethan knew Tlax well enough. The western reaches sat beneath a range of logged mountains and one ugly, bare volcano. The locals called the volcano El Hueso—The Bone—and apparently El Lobo mandated a national holiday in its honor in which the local Indians, whose celebratory rites did not concern it, were supposed to dance and sell textiles at a trinket pavilion erected at its base. But El Hueso commanded little appeal. It was taller than the other mountains, and in its complete chalky bareness it seemed a place forlorn and sinister. Travelers passing beneath its shadow did not ever look up.

Though Tlax lay in a valley, the city sloped gradually west to east down the coastal plateau until it ran up against the sea. Whenever it rained, the eastern barrios flooded—a situation that considerably shortened any imagined tourist season, since most of the established luxury hotels, the ones erected when United Fruit and Axel Diamonds still had interests in the city, were constructed as seaside resorts.

By now, Ethan thought, the sun should have set. It hung low and seething over the volcano. In the smog of exhaust that rose from the city, its light wavered and pulsed, something static and molten. It did not seem to be dropping. Ethan shielded his eyes and lowered the visor, but it didn't help. They were driving west and all around them the traffic slowed and chugged against the sun's sudden glare, and as they crested the valley wall the whole city lay below them, vast and tinny and sun-twanged, a city of fire. The Spanish stone architecture bled crimson, neighborhoods stretched out in rows of red clay roofs, the tin and iron shantytowns glinted painfully up from the shore where the sea, now that Ethan saw it through the lit smog, seemed a sheet of just-forged steel. Illuminated clouds of starlings jerked and turned and overflew the city like bellowed embers.

"Ay," Mirabelle said as the road descended. "It is very beautiful."

"You won't think that for long," Ethan said.

———

It took Ethan an hour, after checking Mirabelle into the hotel, to find the T.G.I. Friday's. The restaurant was several miles west of the docks, near the Hotel Guadelupe, and since Ethan felt sure Cunningham would be there, at the Guadelupe, he had decided to stay at the Cabaña Azul, a hotel on the water. He chose the Azul because it faced the ocean and the large glass doors to its lobby were security locked—you had to give your name and room number to the desk manager before he buzzed you in. The docks were strangely empty, no boats flecked the bay, and the coconut stands, palm cafés, and reggaeton kiosks were all abandoned. It was a welcome change from the glue junkies who lurked outside the Guadelupe.

"We only have a penthouse free," the manager said. "Top floor, fantastic view. Very beautiful."

Ethan looked at the green flood-stained carpet, the mold line on the marble desk, and down the hall to the deserted hotel bar. Clearly, the hotel was empty.

"Okay, we'll take it," he said.

The penthouse was beautiful—about that the manager had not lied. The eastern wall of the main room consisted of enormous glass window-doors that opened out onto a railinged deck. Ethan saw Samantha sitting on the balcony in Key West with the sun going red in her black hair and the dew of shower water still beading on her throat. He turned away from the window. The deck canted dangerously to the left and the impossible light still spread over the sea.

"You should rest," he said to Mirabelle.

"I've been sleeping all day."

He opened the door to the bedroom. The bed stood huge and canopied. Mirrors paneled two of the walls. An enormous potted palm drooped in the corner. For a moment he imagined Yolanda in a room like this, naked and sweating, her eyes closed as in pain, her face pressed against the headboard, the image refracting and refracting. He needed to remember to get more rum.

"I'm going out to meet your sister," he said. "Don't open the door. There's no reason for anyone to knock. I may be a few hours."

Mirabelle frowned, and when she did so, her face still parched, drew back against her cheekbones, something grimacing and skeletal.

"Yolanda is coming with you, yes?"

"Yes," Ethan said. "Of course she is."

———

Later, as he walked, the city was not as he remembered it. People all seemed to be hurrying, here where people did not hurry. Beggars and junkies did not accost him, no children peddled flowers or cabbages and women did not whistle from the porches. Hand radios played through open windows and there were rumors on the wires. The signal was weak and cut by static and he could not follow all the Spanish, but he heard reports of guerrillas in the hills, an off-season storm moving up the coast. He had to admit, as he wandered the labyrinthine streets that were laid, in their day, to resemble the great curling cities of Spain, that he was lost.

Ethan had always prided himself on his sense of direction, but he could not find his way in the city. The lanes turned in winding routes he did not remember, the sun hung and hung, it would not fall behind the volcano and the horizon, as he walked, trembled in a haze of lit smog. He found himself on strange boulevards, he passed empty clubs and shanty villages, a zoo where animals bellowed from their cages. He came through an abandoned Indian market and found himself running, once, with a group of squawking chickens. Behind them skulked three dogs, and he wondered if the chickens ran from the dogs or if they all, together, fled the same pestilence. It was hard to ignore that the sky, as it did sometimes, had filled with volcanic ash.

And then he came upon it, Friday's, standing in a former two-story diplomatic mansion near the Suyapa boulevard. He wiped his face, he checked the empty street and the purple, roiling horizon. He went inside.

The Friday's in Tlaxcultepec was an institution without American precedent. The restaurant proper lay in the old diplomatic banquet hall. Waiters wore tuxedos but the menu, the same as every other Friday's, was in English only. Ethan followed the brass-banistered spiral staircase upstairs to the dark bar, where a cluster of gaunt American youths sat and watched football on the satellite feed. It was a comfortable area—a consular lounge with plush leather chairs, mahogany cigar humidors, and green-glass shaded banker's lamps. But the group of Americans shouted drunkenly at the screen and Ethan didn't want any expatriate companionship.

He took a table on the empty outdoor patio that overlooked the street several stories below. The waiter approached with a towel over

his arm as if he were about to pour a bottle of wine, and Ethan realized that here, where nobody drank wine, he must have mimicked the
gesture without knowing its purpose. Pictures of local political candi-
dates—Ethan recognized their names from the graffiti spray-painted in
the road—were pinned to his lapel.

Ethan ordered a margarita and waited for Yolanda. Perhaps, he
thought again, she would not come. The electric lights had gone on in
the city, and they blinked and wavered as generators failed and restart-
ed and failed again. Still the sun hung over the volcano and the rising
exhaust merged with the ash and the whole city settled into a murky
red glow, like a model viewed under a darkroom safety light.

The margarita came and it was terrible. Here, in the citrus capital
of the world, they made margaritas from mix. Still, it was probably
better not to eat the blighted fruit. Driving the mountain roads to
the city, he had seen grove after grove of brown, bulbous bananas and
withered black limes. An old man had slept under a rotting United
Fruit billboard.

The Americans in the bar turned every so often to look at him.
They did not appear friendly. They pointed and glared and shook their
heads. They drank, he saw with relative envy, from a bottle of Cutty
Sark. Down in the street, two men passed carrying a carved wooden
Jesus over their heads. Beyond that, the road was empty. It was almost
impossible to drink the margarita. He sipped and winced and sipped
it again. The liquid was thick and warm and unctuous and the glass
was rimmed with sugar instead of salt. He did not know how long he
should wait for Yolanda.

One of the gangly Americans stood before him at the table. His
hair was matted to his head with sweat and his eyes were splayed with
veins like a glue-sniffer's.

"Hey, guy," he said. "You're from stateside, right? You're from the
mother country. Tierra madre?"

"Sure," Ethan said. He wished he hadn't ordered the margarita with
its electric Jell-O color and enormous stemmed glass. It was a ridiculous drink. It made it hard to appear disdainful. He lifted it to his lips.

"A little advice from an old hand," the kid said. "You don't sit on
outdoor decks. Not if you're an Anglo. Not in Tlax."

"Thanks for the advice."

"You better come watch some football with us. You like football, don't you?" He frowned as if he thought Ethan might answer in the negative. He did not blink his bloodshot eyes. "We're not your run-of-the-mill creepazoids. We're not the federales. We're PCVs. We're drinking Scotch."

"I thought Peace Corps pulled out of Copal?"

"Well, sure, officially. But we didn't want to be reassigned. This is where the groove is. They wanted to send us to The Goose but we did not want to go to The Goose. No way."

"The Goose?"

"Tegucigalpa, Honduras. The Goose."

Ethan had been to Tegus with Doyle and Paolo.

"No one calls it that," he said. "Never."

"Well, sure," the kid said, turning to leave, maybe forgetting why he was there in the first place. "Not yet they don't. Not in The Goose."

"You shouldn't appear on balconies," Yolanda said as she sat.

How long had it been since he left Mexico? About two weeks. Now her hair was down and shorter than when he last saw her, just past her shoulders. Her skin was darker than he remembered it, darker than Mirabelle's, suntanned. The skin of someone spending her time outside.

Ethan looked down to the boulevard, a twisting cobbled river empty and silent on the night's current.

"There's no one here," he said. "We're alone."

"No," said Yolanda. "The whole world is watching us. They just don't know it yet."

More than anything, Ethan wanted to sleep. A bed somewhere beyond all this, someplace empty. He envied Samantha her corridors closed to the maddening world.

"I don't suppose you're going to tell me the truth about anything?"

She looked suddenly impatient. She raised her hands from the table like he was a child asking an annoying question. *Are we there yet?*

"And what difference would it make?" she asked. "Enough truth will force inaction out of anyone, while those who don't care about it continue to destroy the world. Do you think Los Patrióticos cared about truth when they ravaged San Salvador?"

"You know," he said, "I think I'm sick of being lectured. Of being told what I need to know and what I don't. You're all so righteous? Look at this place. It's a petting zoo for psychopaths."

She started to speak and he stopped her. When he held his hand up they both saw that it was trembling.

"And don't start with the whole fruit and free trade spiel. I'm sick of that shtick as well. I'm sick of death squads."

Yolanda, he saw, looked frightened. Twice more she started to speak and then stopped. She wanted him to be the crass American, the gringo patsy? Well, here he was. The waiter had not yet come to the table.

A howling, like that of a coyote, rose from some near street. Ethan watched Yolanda raise a hand slowly to her lips. She seemed for a moment like her sister, suddenly divorced from herself, a blind person tracing her own face into form. Ethan did not trust his own anger. It was the sham that masked what everything else masked.

"Look, I'm sorry," he said. "It's just that I feel guilty enough. For everything."

A memory appeared like a shipwreck breaching on the tide.

"When I was about twelve my mother bought a knitting machine," Ethan said. "Now my mother, it should be noted, did not knit. Or sow, or cook, or buy me books for school. What my mother did was play the piano. Sometimes for days at a time, nonstop. She'd fall asleep at the piano, she'd wake there. You should have seen her fingers. They were really awful."

Yolanda looked down at her own hands, rough and larger than seemed proportional, hands chapped and callused by jungle living and nothing like his mother's, which were skeletal and grotesque, an interweaving of bone and blue veins, fingertips spackled by blood blisters.

He told her the rest of it, then, raising and setting his revolting drink as he spoke, looking past her, over her left shoulder into the darkening city. His mother saw an ad in the paper. Some woman in Revere was selling a knitting machine. At first he could not imagine why his mother would want it—she didn't have hobbies, and who had ever heard of a knitting machine anyway? Then he saw the sketch in the paper, hand-drawn, of a smiling woman sitting at the contraption which looked, of course, just like a giant keyboard. His mother became excited and hugged him, and said *let's go get it, let's just go buy it, eh?* He remembers this specifically, her hand on his shoulder, her sudden energy that he took for pleasure.

They bought the machine and brought it home in its enormous cardboard box and spent all day assembling it, putting in screws and tightening bolts—his mother was good with her hands, far better than he was—and when they were done it stood on a tripod and was about the length of a keyboard but instead of keys it was fitted with a wild metal needle bed.

The next day they drove to Amherst to buy wool where his mother dragged him through the store and let him pick whatever colors he wanted. She handed him skeins of cobalt and copper and green, all the while telling him what she was going to make for him when they got home—a sweater, linked mittens, a striped scarf. And it was beautiful, because although he didn't really want those things, he was too old for linked mittens or Christmas sweaters, it was lovely to see the way his mother loved him when she was happy.

That afternoon, at home, she spread all the yarn about her on the floor and arranged her packages of patterns on a music stand that she set beside the machine. Ethan watched her as she went through them one by one, lifting each pattern, not even opening it but running her fingers over the faces of the women and children on the covers, brushing across them over and over, her smile giving way to something else as she began to realize that there was no way she could key her obsession into the world and make it look like love. So the yarn lay there unused about her, until finally she picked a pattern and threaded the machine and then sat there, uncertain of what to do next, with her hands poised above the needles. That night when he heard the piano from the living room, he covered his ears with a pillow and knew that it wouldn't help.

Yolanda clearly did not know what to say. She looked at Ethan the way Doyle had at the bullfight. He could see that she wanted to say *and?*—she wanted to tell him about dead children and poisoned wells and El Lobo's death squads unleashed again onto the cities of the poor. He did not want to hear it.

"Ethan," she said finally, "we are running out of time."

He raised his hands in something like apology.

"I didn't think you'd make it. I didn't think you could get here so quickly."

Yolanda cocked her head as she did.

"You said it was an emergency."

"Well, yeah, it was. Your sister had cholera. She was very sick. We couldn't travel and I wasn't sure she'd live."

Yolanda reached up and fingered her scar. She traced from her ear to her collarbone. She watched him.

"Anyway, people are dying from less every day," he said.

She said nothing. She signaled the waiter for a drink.

"Also she has a package for you," he said. "She said it was Jose's. It's important and I can't travel with it. We can't talk about it here."

The waiter did not come. Ethan looked over her shoulder. The PCVs in the bar were gone and the waiter would not look up from the television. Ethan raised his hand and waved. He felt her staring at him.

"I can trust you, can't I?" she said.

Ethan finished the margarita. He wanted to be out of here, out of here and driving toward the Statue of the Poor and then on a plane and away from Copal and the mad girl and everything else he knew would strip whatever he had left from him. No, he thought. Not by a long shot.

"I never told you that you could," he said.

"But I have," she said. "And now I'm sitting here in Copal. I could get up and leave. I think that maybe I should. What do you want me to do?"

The moment, he told himself, does not present a choice. The choice has been made already. And not by me.

"If you thought you should leave, you wouldn't have come," he said.

She opened her eyes wide and ran her hand through her shorter hair. She was not as he remembered her, she did not seem confident or cold or certain. She bit her lower lip and brought her fingers again to her scar. When she spoke it was almost in a whisper.

"I want to know that my sister will be safe."

"Come on then," he said and stood. "I'm repaying a debt. It has nothing to do with trust."

They waited in the street for a taxi. Yolanda stood behind Ethan, away from the road, against the concrete of an abandoned storefront. She was wearing a black tank top, and the silhouettes of barbed wire tattooed her bare right shoulder under the glow of the store's perimeter lights.

"I thought you bought a car?" she said.

"I don't know how to drive in this city and I figured it would make me too easy to follow."

It was pretty much the truth, and Yolanda didn't seem to be listening to his answer anyway. He did not know what he'd do if she questioned him.

"Let's walk," she said. "We'll find a cab as we go."

They turned and walked the deserted streets. Normally, he would never wander unarmed through the city at night. It was the first lesson you learned in Copal, the first thing Doyle ever told him about the country. Central America 101: Avoid the boulevards by dark. But they were heading, he knew, toward a greater danger, and the idea of being accosted by gangs felt almost welcoming, an escape beyond his control. Besides, it seemed fitting that he was walking again with Yolanda under empty palisades and columned colonial buildings tendriled with mold and shadows. He heard distant sirens, the repeated thump and hiss of the ocean on some seawall. Besides those things, though, they were alone together, moving into a new night ill lit by a freak sun and flickering hurricane lamps.

"Look," Yolanda said. "Here comes a cab."

In the taxi heading west toward the Statue of the Poor, Yolanda said, "Why did you not stay at a hotel?"

"The hotels aren't safe. Soto might check them."

As he said it, he thought it was probably true.

"That's smart," she said, and touched his knee. "See, Ethan, you're better at this than you thought you'd be."

He could hold her hand and move toward her touch. He wanted to confess the truth to her and let her grant some forgiveness, to cradle him through the world's betrayals—the two of them confounded together. Outside, people cheered and held signs that he couldn't read. The sun still cast a sliver of light, a ray of annunciation or spectacle, over the mountains.

"Was any of this ever real?" he asked. "Were you ever really a pros-titute?"

She turned away, toward the window and the sun.

"Such a silly question. We all sell ourselves a hundred times a day."

"That's not an answer. That's not even an ideology."

She looked back at him, and for a moment she was as he wanted her to be: she forked her hair out of her face with two splayed fingers, she cocked her head. She winced and he didn't know if it was in pain or anger.

"What do you want, Ethan? I found you lurking in a brothel and feeling very bad for yourself. I gave you a chance to do something significant. To see the world in action. To be something other than another wandering gringo. You wanted to save a woman? I gave you a woman to save. You wanted to die? I gave you something to die for."

"So that guy in the bar, Javier, was just a setup? How many other losers did you run that on?"

For the first time, Yolanda laughed.

"Well, it's hard to find the right balance of despair and nobility. You weren't supposed to hit him with that bottle. That wasn't the plan."

No, thought Ethan. I could have told you, Yolanda, that things don't play out as you'd expect. Even the best plans fail. And this was far from the best plan.

"But when you did hit him," Yolanda said, "when you got back up on your feet and fought a man with a knife, I knew that you were the one I was looking for. I knew that you were a man a woman could trust."

Ethan looked away from her, out the window. He did not recog-nize the person she described. Before he left New York he'd watched and then erased a video that he and Samantha had made together in bed. *Give it to me, baby,* she crooned. *Give it to me.* Divorced from the moment, her voice sounded desperate. Like she knew that whatever she begged for he would not be able to provide. Watching it was like watching a stranger's porn. Their voices sounded hollow and only faint-ly familiar, like running into an old friend in a dream whom you never knew in life. Even now, he had to believe that he was being played.

Beggars chased the car as they passed through the shanty villages leading to the Statue of the Poor. Chickens hustled from the dirt road before them in noisy disarray, a woman wailed from the shadowed lee of a tin shack. Someone fired a pistol in the air. You have to remember, thought Ethan, that it will get worse than this.

They exited the shantytown, attended for a while by a pack of snapping dogs, and turned up the rocky road toward the illuminated statue. The road rose over the bare hills, houses fell away, the dogs disappeared, yowling into the distance, and the taxi continued on, quietly now, up the hill and into the green neon light.

They stopped thirty yards before the statue of whitewashed cement—Jesus weeping and holding his huge arms open in flickering neon benediction. Behind it, a grove of low scrub tangled over the remains of Coca-Cola and United Fruit billboards. The hills beyond crested toward the base of the volcano where the sun refused to set. A road led away from the statue and down a worn path past an abandoned car and on toward a series of squatters' cabins.

"Look at this," Yolanda said as they stepped out of the cab. "I bet my sister loves it here. It's as crazy as she is."

Ethan paid the driver and the driver spat through the open window into the dirt.

"You are wrong. This is the best country in the world," he called to Yolanda as he drove off, bumping and rocking over the cratered road.

Yolanda turned to inspect the statue, and in its light her face appeared young and smooth, untouched by time or the heat of roads or jungles.

"Well, what now?" she said.

Ethan scanned the hill for any sign of Soto: the barren rock, the thin line of scrub. He shrugged and she frowned and started to paw wildly with her hands like a cat falling out of a tree. She reached for him and then, as she turned and staggered, she clawed at the air and fell moaning like a dreamer tormented in sleep.

He saw it then: the black dart sticking from her thigh and Soto rising from the tree scrub with the crossbow already slung across his back and his Panama hat pulled low over his eyes. He lit a cigar as he walked, and under the light his long shadow fell toward them like a pool of spreading ink.

"Help me carry her," he said, and hooked her feet under his arm. Ethan lifted her arms and began to walk. Her pulse throbbed weakly in her wrist.

"I should have let you take her feet," Soto said as they walked. "Her boots are making me dirty."

They stopped, as Ethan realized they would, at the car. Soto dropped her feet.

"Put her in," he said.

Ethan wrapped one of her arms around his neck and lifted her into the passenger seat. *Why are there so many stairs?* Samantha had asked as he carried her in Key West. Yolanda's head rocked against his face as he straightened her in the seat. He could smell vanilla in her hair. He fastened the safety belt, closed the door, and turned to face Soto.

"What's going to happen to her?"

Soto puffed some smoke into the green air, tossed the cigar to the ground, and stamped it out like a living thing. He reached into his pocket and removed his handkerchief, wiped his forehead. Ethan could not see his eyes beneath the hat's brindled shadow but his mouth tumbled in crooked, muddy contortions.

"They will torture her until she gives up her father," he said. "And then, if she is still alive, they will drop her out of a plane or shoot her or rape her or machete her. She is dead but for time. As are we all, I suppose."

He lifted his hat a little to gauge, maybe, Ethan's reaction.

"Did you want a sweeter tale? A colonial fairy story? There are no more children and we should not dishonor them with such stories."

He moved toward the car and reached for the door.

"I thought you would kill me," Ethan said.

Soto twisted around toward Ethan. His mouth pitched into a wild sneer.

"I suppose you would have liked that? Well, I considered it. But that would suggest that nothing had changed. That you had no effect. And you did."

He pulled a dart from his bandolier and held it to the air.

"You realize now, I hope, that you are an arrow. You choose your direction and your direction matters. You do not come down here to play out your little drama and then go home. That girl is your charge now."

Ethan gestured to the empty hill, the shacks and pine scrub leading down to the shantytown.

"What now? I'll never make it back to her."

Soto reached into his coat and tossed Ethan his stiletto.

"You're an American," he said. "Go conquer."

Soto tipped the brim of his hat toward the volcano and closed the door. He turned on the car and drove away and Yolanda's head rocked and bobbed beneath the green illumination of the Statue of the Poor.

DOWN THE HILL AWAY from the statue and into the darkness of the shantytown where the generators failed. The street twined its cluttered way between the shacks of tin and corrugated iron, old signs, and taped cardboard. The road's trash banked upon the sidewalks in mounds of razor wire and scrapwood, and between the shacks lay the bulldozed rubble of the previous shanties. A lean dog sat and appraised a man lying in his own open doorway. Trash fires burned in the road. Ethan ran through the streets bearing Soto's knife before him like a lantern.

He rested a moment at the base of the hill where the shantytown ended. Before him was the Zelaya Boulevard, a wide street empty of cars and lined with shabby eateries, junk heaps, and abandoned discos. A windbreak of blighted flamboyana trees separated the boulevard from the city barrios and through its leaves the lights of the city winked and failed and came on again. Ethan looked up for a moment at the clouds of red ash moving out over the city and the sea. Behind him, in the bare hills above the shantytown, there were a few lights of cars or trucks moving across the darkness. Yolanda was in one of those cars with Soto, drugged or maybe awake now, heading into her last morning. Ethan crossed the empty boulevard and jogged under the trees and back into the city.

Somewhere in his descent into the winding avenues of the old city, two men stepped out of a bodega and into the street before him. He continued toward them, he did not stop walking, he recognized them easily as mareros. They stood in the middle of the road. Their heads were shaved and their faces vined with a webbing of green tattoos. The one to Ethan's right wore a white work shirt buttoned at the collar and the wrists, and he appeared oddly staid, almost reverential—but the one to his left was shirtless and the inkings spread down his neck, sleeved his arms, and continued across his chest in a design which charted, for a gringo walking alone through the streets at night, a very specific topography of nightmare. In the poor light the tattoos seemed simply dark, a hemorrhage blossoming beneath skin, but as Ethan grew closer he saw what he knew he would: strangely etched imprints of two outstretched hands, a black cross, the unmistakable MS-13 lettered across the chest. Also, he could not miss as he drew closer, that both men carried machetes.

He kept walking; he could not think what else to do. As he neared the curve in the road where they stood, he reached down and picked up a rock and went on that way, walking toward them. He began to laugh. First the broken bottleneck in Boystown, and now a switchblade and a rock. It seemed he spent an undue amount of time brandishing paltry weapons through deserted slums. When he reached them he nodded and said, "Buenas," and the marero wearing the shirt raised his machete and set it casually over his shoulder. He smiled then at Ethan and the tattooed teardrops under his eyes bunched on his creased skin like freckles. He seemed in that moment jolly and clownlike, not at all threatening.

"Where are you going?" he asked in English.

The English was somehow comforting. Perhaps, if he needed to, Ethan could make himself understood. Still, he did not know what to say. Beyond the mareros, in the farther descents of the capital, the frail red sun burned on the windows of distant buildings. Soon it would recede, as it long should have, into darkness. This was the way the night had arranged itself for him. He was at the point in dream where, without choices or possibilities, he usually woke up.

Ethan pushed passed the mareros and began to walk away into the city.

"Where you going, man?" the marero said again, and Ethan looked back at them. He held his knife and his rock out before him. They appeared confused—certainly no one had responded to them this way before. Their shock, he was certain, would not last long. He began to walk again and they let him go. He turned back once. There were noises behind him. He did not know if he was being followed.

FOUR BLOCKS FROM HIS hotel and moving through the dark, Ethan rounded a corner toward the sea and Cunningham was there, reaching out and touching his arm and saying, "Hey, partner, let's take a stroll."

Ethan stopped walking and turned to face Cunningham, who had one hand on his arm and the other in the pocket of his linen jacket. It seemed that no one had a change of clothes in the tropics.

"No, don't stop walking," Cunningham said. "Never stop walking. We're two fellows taking in the rotten sea. Gentlemen of leisure on an evening constitutional along the balmy boardwalks."

How they looked, Ethan thought as he glanced at their reflections in the darkened windows of abandoned empanada shops, was perverted. Cunningham's jacket had gathered some vast new webbing of wrinkles. His shirt collar was soiled and his blond hair lay, like something hit by a car, across his brow. Ethan had avoided his own reflection, but he knew it would not be good.

"You're too late," he said. "Soto's got Yolanda. Don't you all communicate?"

The streetlights on the boulevard flickered off, and the road was dark but for light cast from the windows of the empty hotels. It was well past midnight—Ethan had heard the cathedral toll the hour as he walked—but still some sun tinted the far-off water.

"That's fine," Cunningham said. "That's well and good. We've all got the same interests, though I'm a bit more chivalrous than the boys with epaulets. They'll give her a rough time."

A mangy dog with a low, hanging snout skulked toward them along the dock. Cunningham dropped to his knees as if reaching for a rock and the dog yelped and scampered off.

"There's not a pisshole in the world where that doesn't work," Cunningham said. "I think that might be the definitive difference between the First and Third Worlds. We don't beat our dogs."

They walked for a few moments in silence. Ethan watched the light hang on the far water. There were no stars and the clouds of purple ash drifted out over the city, toward the sea. An explosion sounded in a distant barrio. Ethan heard it echo off the mountains.

"They've been bombing the markets all week," Cunningham said. "God knows why."

"Do you have a sense," Ethan asked, "that everyone is disturbed? That something is happening here?"

"Forget it. Think not upon it. I just have a few questions I want to ask you."

"Oh, good. A debriefing."

Ethan could not hide his scorn, though since Soto drove away with Yolanda, his anger had begun to subside.

"Watch your tone. We could call it a debriefing or a cocktail. Whichever you'd prefer."

Ethan wondered if Cunningham really had a gun in his pocket. He could have been holding a banana, there certainly was no shortage of them. It probably didn't matter.

"Where are we going?" Ethan said.

"To your hotel. Your hotel bar, say. See the nightlife. The local color."

It occurred to Ethan that Cunningham might not actually know which hotel he was staying in. He didn't think he had been followed. Three hotels before his, at the Palmas de la Mar, he said, "Here we are," and Cunningham made no move to stop him.

The Palmas was fancier than the Azul, but no less deserted. The bar was vintage Panama chic: wide green fans turned slowly from the low ceilings and the floors gleamed with black and white checkered marble. Tall potted palms stood along the walls. The tables were made of glass, the chairs woven from wicker. In the corner, a spotlight illuminated a bare stage. Ethan and Cunningham sat at the mahogany and brass bar and drank rum. Cunningham held his empty glass out to Ethan as if it illustrated a specific point.

"Can't say I appreciated the lie there in Roycetown. I was in my cups and off my game. Bad form to take advantage of a fellow like that. Especially when he's trying to do you a good turn."

Ethan raised his hand for another rum.

"Why don't you leave the bottle?" Cunningham said to the bartender. "And some more ice, yeah?"

"I don't trust the ice here," Ethan said.

Cunningham filled his glass with ice and poured a rum to the brim.

"You just have to give up on solid stools. There's no one to judge you here and man is the most adaptable of creatures."

In the back, a woman wearing a sequined black dress stepped onto the stage and began to sing "As Time Goes By." There was no accompanying music and this time the song was in English. Her voice was low and throaty, a smoker's voice, and from her intonation it was clear that she had no idea what the words meant. She could have been singing anything. Gibberish. It recalled that night in the bar in New York. The bellowing dwarf, the off-season storm, and Ethan's phone ringing in a new future. He could still see the dwarf's face: frantic, snarling, dripping tears. A portent of some nascent panic. That moment did not seem so long ago now. A moment he could reach back and touch. He poured another drink.

"I'm very tired," he said to Cunningham. "I've done things today I never thought I'd do."

Another explosion, this time a little closer. The lights flickered but came back on. Cunningham raised his glass.

"Cheers to that. Life in le tropiques."

A kiss is just a kiss, the woman sang with listless Spanish intonation, *a sigh is just a sigh*.

"She doesn't know what she's saying," Ethan said. "It doesn't mean anything."

"Latin America isn't what it used to be," Cunningham said. "It's all democracy and free trade. For the right people there's plenty of coffee and plenty of cocoa. Everybody who wants a boat has a boat."

"I want a boat," Ethan said.

"But if Copal, our seething little Banana Republic—if Copal should have a revolution, well, there'd be a number of problems. There'd be refugees into Mexico, and Mexico does not want any more refugees. They're jam-packed, it seems, with gang warfare, Copal's primary export. You know how it is. Bombs in the markets, lepers on the road. Women disappearing in the night. There'll be more death squads. There'll be trade implications."

"I never liked this song," Ethan said. "Do you realize, Barry, that at this point I really don't give a fuck?"

"Hey, now. No reason to take that tone. No reason at all. We're just gentlemen on the verandah here. We're having drinks."

"This is flagellants at the carnival. Not a verandah."

Cunningham poured another rum.

"Consider the situation from the humanitarian perspective. Where would these people be without the banana trade to the U.S.? Without a little imposed order? They'd be shitting in the street, that's where."

One of the thousand clocks in the city struck the hour.

"Do you realize," Ethan said again, "that it's one in the morning and the sun has not set?"

"What we need," Cunningham said, "is that girl. Mirabelle Campo. For her own good. Her safety."

Through the lobby glass Ethan saw that the mareros from the road were outside in the street, drinking guaro. So he had been followed.

"I thought that if I gave up Yolanda, you guys left Mirabelle alone. I mean, that's what Soto promised."

"Ah," Cunningham crooned over the rising song, "that was your deal with Soto. Not with me. I gave you a chance to play pass the cookie and you told me to go fuck myself. You sent me to a rotten hotel. Besides, as I said, it's for her own good. Her own safety."

"That's hard to believe," Ethan said. "In fact, it's unbelievable."

"I suppose at a certain point, if you're not a man of belief already, if you don't have an ideology to fall back on, you believe what you have to. That's what I like about this work. It forces certain choices into stark relief. In such a situation, I find it comforting that you must act with absolute honesty. So now, be honest. Take in the smell. You're lost and dying slow. Right now you're like the mariners of old. You're in the doldrums and there are no winds that can save you. In such situations, in such climes, with the sea becalmed and water running out, they'd toss their horses overboard. Take stock. It's time to abandon what you can live without."

Here, thought Ethan, in the clockless hours, in the shadow of the volcano where the sun will not set, another chance to renounce grace. Whatever Cunningham would do with Mirabelle would not be good. Mystic or mad girl, or frail, sick, cholerous child, whatever these people wanted could not fail to ruin her. The woman continued to sing, she did not realize, clearly, that the song must end. There was Mallory in his arms, staring up: *is there no grace, is there no remedye*, and Samantha, that first night back from the hospital, and all the nights disappearing beyond it. The mareros were in the lobby. The security guard had disappeared. There was some comfort, now, in clarity. He stood.

"Come on, then," he said. "It's late, Barry. Let's go get her."

They took the steps, not the elevator. "Wouldn't trust those things," Cunningham said. "Not here." He stumbled and sweated and panted as they went. Once they came to the seventh floor, Ethan stopped and turned toward the hall.

"This way," he said.

Halfway down the corridor he began to look for his key. He reached in his pockets, he untied his sweatshirt from his waist and shook it out over the floor. They reached the last door. Beside them, at the end of the hall, a Plexiglas picture window looked out at the moving, half-lit sea.

"I've lost the fucking key," Ethan said. "Somewhere along the way."

"Better knock, then. I'm not doing those stairs again."

"Won't work," Ethan said. "I told her not to open the door. Not for anyone."

They stood for a moment, the two of them, at the end of the hall by the window. Cunningham with his hands on his knees, still wheezing.

"Can't you jimmy this thing?" Ethan said. "Don't they teach that in spook academy?"

Cunningham straightened. His red face splayed a wide, rubbery smile.

"What they teach you is not to drink a gimlet in Mumbai. It's not often that a fellow gets to apply his craft abroad."

He produced, as if he'd had them at the ready, a set of lock picks. He knelt before the door.

"Could you step out of my light, please?"

Ethan moved away from the window and walked around Cunningham.

In his dreams of vengeance he finds the man who raped Samantha. He finds him in a bar or an alley, or sometimes in his apartment with

Samantha there, looking on, and he beats him very slowly to death. He kicks him to the ground, he jams his foot between his teeth, he listens as his mouth, rent open, tears back through his cheeks. When he presses harder, he registers the last tension before the jaw cracks with a sound like twigs snapped over a knee and slaps, slack and askew, against the man's shoulder. Then Ethan climbs down, astride him, and pounds his face into the ground. As he beats him he can smell the sudden copper of the man's blood and the rank vegetable rot of his breath, which he tastes in his own mouth as he retches and punches until the man's face gives way. He sees it the same way every time: the fine architecture of the man's long nose twists and then pancakes into the concave hollow between his collapsing cheekbones as they soften into a ragged, bearded mush. When Ethan wakes, he wakes sweating, muscles flexed and adrenaline spiking through him. The feeling of the phantom skull under his fists is real and pleasurable, and now he thinks if nothing can avenge the way he abandoned Samantha to the world she always knew was waiting for her—the way he abandoned Samantha and then Yolanda—there is no turning away from this. Seven floors below, the song still came. There were footsteps on the stairs. It was *Annie and the Wolves* all over again, and he wouldn't leave Mirabelle to them. He slid Soto's stiletto from his belt. Outside, the volcano puffed smoke over the sea where the storm clouds gathered in layers of moving dark.

"Looks like something's coming," he said.

Cunningham stopped and turned and looked to the window, away from Ethan, for a moment. He wiped his brow.

"That's how it is down here, compadre. Always another storm."

The knife flicked open with a sound meant to impress and terrify and Cunningham moved at the sound. In one motion, he turned and grabbed Ethan's wrist and slammed his knee into his groin as he stood. Ethan fell forward and Cunningham wrenched his wrist behind his back and had him up against the wall with the muzzle of his pistol pressed below his ear. So the pistol, anyway, was real.

"Oh, come off it. What was that?" Cunningham said.

His labored and rummy breath moistened the back of Ethan's neck like a wet blanket. The drink, clearly, had not slowed him much.

"Thought you had the drop on me?" asked Cunningham. "Thought I'd fall for some cheap assassin's trick? Is that really what you thought?"

Not far below there were footsteps on the stairs. Doors being closed and opened. This was what the world had fractured into: sounds on the stairs, the cold metal of the pistol, the smell of mildew against Ethan's face. Somewhere farther off, he heard what sounded like a boat horn signaling through the fog. The song had ended.

"Did you think you could stab me? There is probably no harder way to kill a fellow than that. The sheer guts it takes. The sickening sensation. Most Navy Seals can't even do it."

Cunningham stepped back and let Ethan off the wall. When Ethan turned to face him, Cunningham slouched against the window and wielded the pistol like a woman holding a cigarette: his elbow was bent, his arm was hardly extended, and his wrist hung limply.

"Now, if you don't mind me asking again, where is the fucking girl?"

"I don't think I'm going to tell you," Ethan said.

Cunningham shrugged his shoulders in a huge display of exhaustion. Under the hanging sunlight his sweaty face glistened like something lacquered.

"Oh God, are you serious? Yes, you will. You absolutely will tell me."

He pushed himself off the window, walked over to Ethan, and threw his left arm around him. The sound of boots echoing on the stairs drew closer. Cunningham seemed not to notice.

"Why expose yourself to this pain?" he asked. "Why try to stab a man in the back? One shouldn't approach violence with such little discipline."

He brought the butt of the pistol up and into Ethan's solar plexus and then whipped the barrel across his face. Ethan fell against the wall beside the stairwell door.

"There are violences of human nature and violences of history. Make sure you know which you're approaching. I myself am a man of history. An agent of it, if you will."

When the mareros came through the door Ethan was still sitting against the wall. The door opened into his face, and when it closed they had already stepped onto the landing and into the hall. They stood facing Cunningham and Ethan was behind them, unnoticed, on the floor.

Cunningham gestured at the men with his pistol.

"This is exactly what I mean," he said. "This is the sort of trash with which Copal wants to grace the shores of the future."

He reached into his pocket and threw a wad of pesos at the shirtless marero.

"Now fuck off, Queequeg."

The shirtless marero stepped forward and Cunningham shot him in the face. He turned toward the second one and took the brunt of the machete blow to his forehead. The first marero fell headless at Ethan's feet and Cunningham slumped to his knees with the machete still centered in his half-cleaved skull. Ethan tried to stand and slipped on the new slick of brainy blood. He scrambled for a moment on the floor in cartoonish urgency and pulled himself up by the door handle. The second marero spun around, saw him for the first time, and shook his head. In the clear light of the hallway, Ethan saw that he was maybe twenty years old. He no longer looked amused, as he had in the street, but there was also no sign of rage. "Cállate," he said, and brought his finger to his lips. Then he unbuttoned his sleeves, rolled them up, and turned back toward Cunningham, who was sitting now with the weight of the machete handle pulling his head toward the floor between his feet. The marero stepped up to him and wrenched it free. Ethan opened the door to the stairwell and took the stairs two or three at a time. Falling and standing and falling again as he went. On the second floor landing he stopped for a moment and listened. There was a speck of brain, small and round like a grape nut, stuck to his pants. He flicked it off and listened some more. No one followed.

When he opened the door to their penthouse suite, Mirabelle rose from the window where she was watching the clouds gather over the water in the dark. He turned on the lights and the window became a black pane. A frail line of light moved over the water.

"Where have you been?" she said. "Where is my sister?"

Ethan saw that her hands were balled into fists. He crossed the room and put his palms, as slowly as he could, on her shoulders. He realized now as he touched her that he wanted to see her expression as he said this, he wanted to feel her shudder against his touch. As if, as he had thought in Boystown, to hold this damage up to his own. She was young and virtuous. There were fires of madness or faith or certainty smoldering in her and he knew that as he spoke he would watch those things fall away. He would like to see what they left in their wake.

"Yolanda's dead," he said.

She jerked, as he'd known she would, and tried to fly from him, but he reached out and pulled her close and held her as she wept. The sound of it, of her crying in his arms in a room by the sea, was not as awful as he had expected. A keen. A seabird. A lover waking from dream. He held her. He felt some slow, settling comfort.

He knew how it was. We all must abandon our charmed lives. Everyone does it: Doyle fleeing not away, but into, his own tropical prison; Paolo sitting beneath the shadow of a crazy wife, sitting and waiting and writing travel pieces about places he'd never seen—a thousand imaginary worlds. And Samantha. Samantha waking in the morning. Samantha whose hair smelled of raspberries and sleep. Samantha nestling against him in the park and saying *I could drink you like wine.* Samantha at the table in the morning looking up from her cereal as the world prepared to unbuckle into ruptured sound, as windows readied to blow from their sills, car alarms sirening out into wind: *what are you thinking?*

And then there was the first night after it all when she approached him on the couch and said, *come here, come to bed, I can't sleep alone.* And he did that too, laid so as not to touch her, to keep space so that she could hear him breathe, know that he was there.

Then he felt her hand on his hip, his stomach.

Her fingers were cold and he focused on that. Imagined them like metal or stone or anything but flesh.

"Don't you think it's a little soon?" he said. "Don't you think we need more time?"

She rolled over, placed her head on his chest as she used to.

"I need to know it can be good, Ethan. I need to know it can be safe."

His eyes were closed when he took her in his arms, rocked her and kissed her, and, though he tried not to, imagined her there in the bar with booze sheen sweating on her skin and her hair glinting under the chemical light. Her hair that he held now in his hands, his frail hands like it, the frail light, holding her and watching her taking a drink and smiling and now, here, she's crying into his shoulder, his neck, whispering something in his ear that even if he listened to he would never understand at all.

The girl still sobbed against his shoulder. He held her, he kissed her forehead. Slowly, he pushed her from him. He touched her hair and the wet rim of her lips. He wiped tears from her face with his hands. She might not recover, he thought. She might fall into a fever from which only I can shake her.

"How did she die?" the girl whispered.

"I'm sorry," he said. "There was nothing I could do."

He put her to bed. He pulled the covers about her and said, "We'll leave in the morning for America." He tried to shower but the water was off. It didn't matter. He closed the door to the bedroom and went out onto the balcony to watch the sun, that had never set, begin to rise. The radio came on without him touching it and he did not know how to turn it off. There were more rumors on the wires: explosions in the market, fires on the road. The airport was smoked in. No flights could leave the capital. They said an eruption was imminent, they said El Lobo disappeared in the night, they said a storm was coming.

He lowered the volume and stood on the crooked balcony facing the sea. Hundreds of feet below, the smell of fish rot rose from the empty malecón. Flocks of large black birds passed through the new morning of the turning world and he saw some glinting white wreckage breaching on the tide. The sea hurled itself at the dawn. There was fire on the wind. The girl who slept in the other room continued to breathe. His comfort began to dissipate, but it was not gone yet. He stood at the balcony, he smelled the fires, he felt something still in his chest. He spoke her name out loud and then said it again and listened to the girl who sighed and mumbled through dream and turned in her sleep like the sea.

Morris Collins's fiction and poetry has recently appeared in *Pleiades, Gulf Coast, The Chattahoochee Review, Michigan Quarterly Review, Passages North, Neon Literary Journal, Tampa Review, Iron Horse Review, Saranac Review*, and *Nimrod*, among others. He received his MFA in fiction from The Pennsylvania State University in 2008. He lives in Boston and teaches at The College of the Holy Cross and Clark University.